2015 YOUNG EXPLORER'S ADVENTURE GUIDE

dreaming robot press

quality middle grade and young adult science fiction and fantasy
· Las Vegas, New Mexico ·

The 2015 Young Explorer's Adventure Guide
Edited by Sean and Corie Weaver
Copyright c. 2015 by Corie J. Weaver. All Rights Reserved
First Print Edition: January 2015

ISBN: 978-1-940924-06-9

Published by Dreaming Robot Press
1214 San Francisco Avenue
Las Vegas, NM 87701
www.dreamingrobotpress.com

Contents

Acknowledgements

The Young Explorer's Adventure Guide began as a casual conversation which ended with "wouldn't it be cool if...."

Obviously, we couldn't have made it this far without an amazing amount of support, patience and help from family, friends, beta readers, Kickstarter supporters and even the friends of friends who were pulled into this crazy plan.

Our thanks go to Helen Jacobs, Kim Klimek, Martina Holguin, William Ewers, Mieka Kramer, Dani QL, Madison Spillard, Kenneth Hargis, Sarah Goshman as well as Ronald Gardner and Maggie Allen of Silence in the Library and a host of other friends and well-wishers.

And of course, all of our amazing authors, who saw our vision of what this anthology could be.

Permissions

This way, this way!

In this volume we are pleased to present 24 tales of adventure. Stories of alien ships and human ingenuity, of faraway skies and maybe-just-around-the-corner Earth.

Of exploration, survival, kindness and friendship.

In these stories you'll encounter robot dogs, baffling aliens, space pirates, airships, the recipe for the best cheesecake in the Universe and much more.

And we hope you'll also find friends who you'll want to revisit through the years.

Nothing is quite like the first time you read a story, and we envy the adventure you're about to embark on.

Have a great trip, and write us when you get back!

Sean and Corie Weaver
Dreaming Robot Press
books@dreamingrobotpress.com

Why I Hate earth

Nancy Kress

Nancy Kress is the author of thirty-three books, including twenty-six novels, four collections of short stories, and three books on writing. Her work has won five Nebulas, two Hugos, a Sturgeon, and the John W. Campbell Memorial Award. Most recent works are After The Fall, Before The Fall, During The Fall *(Tachyon, 2012), a novel of apocalypse, and* Yesterday's Kin, *about genetic inheritance (Tachyon, 2014). In addition to writing, Kress often teaches at various venues around the country and abroad; in 2008 she was the Picador visiting lecturer at the University of Leipzig. Kress lives in Seattle with her husband, writer Jack Skillingstead, and Cosette, the world's most spoiled toy poodle. Visit her website at www.sff.net/people/nankress/.*

My name is Nia. I'm nine and three-quarters. I live on Earth. And I hate it.

Before you tell me how beautiful Earth is, let me tell you that I don't care. Everybody tells me how beautiful Earth is. Everybody tells me and tells me. And I tell everybody: You haven't seen the moon.

I grew up on Moon Colony Alpha. It was all wonderful. The warm, cozy underground habitats, where Dad and Mom and I had our apartment. The tunnels where we played, clean and smooth-floored and well lighted. You didn't trip over rocks or roots; you didn't get too cold or too hot; you weren't surrounded by strangers who might or might not be dangerous. There were no strangers; we were only one hundred fifty people. And on the moon, you feel light and can run faster and jump higher. Gravity doesn't pull at you like some sort of tentacled monster, the way it does on Earth. Basketball, which my friends and I played all the time, was awesome.

And on the moon, when we went up to the surface for a picnic under the dome, you could see a gazillion stars in the clear black sky. The Earth hung above like a blue-and-white ball, the way it was supposed to. The view just took your breath away.

I loved living in Alpha Colony.

Then we moved to Chicago.

....

"I won't go," I said, for about the hundredth time.

"Nia, we have to go," Dad said patiently. He is always patient. Mom—not so much, which is why I was talking to Dad.

"But I don't even remember Earth!"

"I know." He patted my arm. "But we're already over the five-year limit. And your mother's been reposted."

People aren't supposed to stay on the moon longer than five years. Human muscles don't grow strong enough without Earth gravity. We moved here when I was four.

"Dad, I do the exercise machines every day! Sometimes twice a day!" Well, one time I did them twice. But *once* is *sometimes*, isn't it?

"That helps, Nia, but it's not enough. Eat your dinner, honey. Mom said to make sure you eat your broccoli."

"I hate broccoli. And where is Mom, anyway?"

"Packing up the plant samples for the trip down. She'll be home soon."

Mom is an important scientist, a geneticist who creates plants that will grow well in our underground farms. You'd think she would grow something better than broccoli. Dad is a scientist, too, but not as important as Mom, except to me. But nobody listens to me because if they did, we wouldn't be moving to stupid Earth, where they probably eat broccoli for breakfast, lunch, and dinner.

"Nia," Dad said, trying another argument, "you'll make new friends, have new experiences. You can even have a real dog."

"I don't need a real dog! I have Luna!"

Luna, who was sitting under the table, barked when she heard her name. I programmed her to do that. I did a lot of her programming myself, and she's the best robo-dog ever.

Dad said, "Well, *I* need a real dog. I miss dogs."

I didn't say anything because Dad looked unhappy, and I hate that. Although I'm the one who should look unhappy. I have to leave my friends, Jillian and Ben and Katie and Jack and Rosa. I have to leave my bedroom, all safely sealed into smooth rock where nothing bad could get me. And all I could do to show how unfair this was, was leave all my uneaten broccoli on my plate. So I did.

Dad said nothing about it.

....

Earth was awful even before we got there. The shuttle from the moon entered the atmosphere, and gravity slammed out of the ceiling and pushed me so hard into my seat that I thought my bones would be crushed. It was the most horrible thing I'd ever experienced, but at least I knew that it would only last a few minutes. The shuttle screamed and everything shook and then we were down—*only the gravity didn't go away.* It kept pressing on me so that when Mom unstrapped me and pulled me to my feet, immediately I fell over.

"Take it slow, Nia," she said. "You'll get used to it."

Stones on my shoulders. Stones on my feet. Stones at the end of my arms and a big heavy stone on the top of my head. That's what it felt like. Dad and Mom wobbled, too, but they both had that look on their face that said *I can do this.* So I had to do it, too. But there were tears behind my eyes. I would never jump for a basketball again, never run as fast as Luna, never even bounce on a bed. Not in this gravity!

But I could walk. After a few lurching steps, I did get a little used to it. At least I was upright.

Dad said, "You're doing great, Nia!" Even Mom looked proud of me, and that was enough to keep me going down the aisle of the shuttle and out the door.

Where I started screaming.

There was *nothing*. No walls, no roof, not even a clear dome. The shuttle sat on a huge expanse of white stone with empty land around it and nothing above it, just a lot of empty hot blue. Nothing to hold you in place, nothing to keep you bounded and safe, just a whole lot of dangerous open space....

I tried to claw my way back into the shuttle, but the door had already closed. Still screaming, I dropped to the ground and curled into as tight a ball as I could. Anything to keep out the nothingness, keep out the vast emptiness large enough that I would just fly apart in it, swallowed up by the huge vacant blankness.

"Nia!"

"No," I cried over the pounding on my heart, "no no no no...."

....

Agoraphobia.

An ugly word for a perfectly reasonable condition. I had agoraphobia, which meant I was afraid of open spaces. Well, who wouldn't be? *Anything* could be out there, and "anything" was only a little bit better than nothing was. That was Earth: anything dangerous, with no walls and stone roofs to keep it out, or nothing, with empty space to swallow you so that your molecules spread out all through it, and you didn't exist anymore.

Some choice.

"Nia," Dad said, yet again, "you have to get used to it bit by bit. Just come stand in the doorway with me. That's all—we won't actually go outside. We'll just stand in the doorway together."

"No," I said. "I can't."

"Nia, sweetheart—"

"I *can't*."

That was the truth. Every time I tried to leave our new house, my heart sped up and I sweated hard and the space behind my eyes burned. Then I got dizzy. Then I ran back into my bedroom, where Dad had nailed boards over the two windows. The rest of the house had curtains but at least my room was properly closed up. In here I felt safe. Gravity could still get me, but I was getting used to the gravity. I would never get used to the empty, swallow-you-up outside.

Besides, it was dirty and hot. Dust blew in the hot wind—"Well, it's August in the Midwest," Mom said, like that excused anything—and the sun burned down. On the moon, the dust stayed where it belonged, up under the surface dome and not where people lived. The temperature was always the same, and the sun kept its proper distance. We didn't need weather. Plants grew with irrigation and grow-lights. It was civilized. Weather is not civilized, as I found out when the "heat wave broke" and there was a huge "thunderstorm" with terrifying rain and sound and electricity just loose in the air! And then the power went out. The Midwest did not have a back-up generator.

So I stayed in my room and played with Luna and used up my allowance on radio messages to my friends on the moon. Which are not cheap.

"Just come out into the woods with me," Dad said. "You know we're not in the city anymore; we're way out in the country and it's cool in the woods, and it smells wonderful."

"No, thanks," I said. Woods were just a lot of trees, and trees were just really tall plants. Why did they need to get so tall? What was the *point*? I just didn't see why trees were necessary. We didn't have them on Alpha.

Mom was gone a lot, mostly doing science things with the government. Dad worked at home on his computer so that he could be with me. Two grandparents and three aunts came for a visit, and I had to come out of my room, but they were a lot of strangers, and I didn't know what to say to them. The visit wasn't fun at all. Nothing was fun.

After her family left, Mom looked grim. "You could have made more of an effort, Nia."

I looked at the floor.

Her voice got softer. "I know you miss Alpha, honey. And your friends. But things will be better when school starts next week. You'll meet kids your own age."

I took a long breath. This was as good a time as any to tell her. "I'm not going to school."

"Of course you're going to school."

A long pause. I risked a peek away from staring at my shoes. Mom wasn't looking at me but at Dad. She said, "Wayne—you knew."

"I knew that Nia doesn't want to go to school."

I said, "Not just don't want to—I'm *not* going."

Dad and Mom gave each other That Look. They do that a lot. That Look can mean different things but in this case, I knew exactly what it meant. Dad was going to be on Mom's side, not mine.

I ran into my room and slammed the door. Luna sat on my bed. I turned her on and she licked my face with her cool metal tongue and crawled into my lap. She does that whenever I cry.

I couldn't run away—there's no way to run away to the moon. I couldn't stay in my room, because Mom would drag me out and Dad would look really unhappy. I would have to go to school.

I said a bad word and hugged Luna.

....

The very next day, Dad brought home the puppy.

"I don't want that! I told you!" I said.

Dad said, "It's not for you, it's for me. I told you I miss dogs."

Nothing I could say to that—I had Luna so it was only fair that Dad have a dog, too. The puppy was smaller than Luna and had hair all over it, like on a person's head. Its head was too big for its body. It sat in the middle of the kitchen floor and blinked, then it rushed at me and started licking my toes. I jumped on a chair.

"Eewww! Make it stop! Its tongue is all wet!"

Dad laughed. "So is your tongue, Nia."

"I don't *lick* people!"

Luna, who was still turned on, poked her head out of my bedroom. Then she walked over to the puppy. She put her head down and stuck her butt up in the air, which is what she does when I give her the *Play!* command.

I said, "I didn't tell her to do that!"

Dad said, "I think robo-dogs are factory-set to play when they see another dog."

The puppy gave a little squeak and stuck its butt in the air, too. They circled around each other, barking and yipping. Then they chased each other and cuffed each other and rolled around together while I watched from on top of the chair. It was pretty funny.

Dad was laughing his head off. Finally, I got down off the chair and said, "Does that dog have a name?"

"Bandit."

Bandit's fur was really, really soft.

. . . .

School was even worse than I feared.

Dad took me there in his new car, and I kept my eyes closed the whole way. He stopped right by a back door and led me inside after school had already started, so I didn't have to see any outside at all, although I felt the awful heat until we were in the school. At least it had AC like civilized places such as, for instance, the moon.

I said, "Does the teacher know I have agoraphobia?"

"Yes, but the kids don't. You won't have to go outside, Nia—I explained all that. Your class will be told that you have allergies."

Well, that was true anyway. I was allergic to Earth.

"Class," the teacher said, "this is our new student, from Alpha Colony on the moon, Nia Phillips. I hope you'll all make her feel welcome. Nia, that's your desk right here."

So many kids! And all the same age! On Alpha, there were only seventeen kids and two teachers, and my group had little Ben, six years old, and Jillian, twelve. This class was too big. They all stared at me, and a few girls smiled. I didn't smile back. I wanted to be on the moon with Jillian and Kate and Ben and Jack and Rosa. Or in my bedroom with Luna and Bandit. I didn't belong here.

But at least the window blinds were down.

Everybody was doing math. The teacher, Ms. Bukowski, told me the URL, and I got it on my tablet. It was fractions—dead easy. But next came history. Ms. Bukowski said, "Who can name the group that makes laws for our whole country?"

"I can!"

"You have to raise your hand, Nia. But go ahead."

I felt my face get warm. Nobody in my old class had to raise their hand; the nine of us just talked normally with Leila, our teacher. But Ms. Bukowski looked encouraging, so I said, "The NASA-Moon Council!"

A girl across from me snickered. Then a boy in the back of the room laughed. Then they were all laughing and giggling, and I felt so stupid I wanted to die. It wasn't the NASA-Moon Council; it was something called "the United States Congress." Dumb name!

I didn't say anything to anybody until we all pushed our desks into groups of four for science. There were a bunch of rocks to identify by dripping acid on them and looking at pieces through a microscope and other stuff that might have been interesting except that the other three girls in my group all kept staring at me. Finally one said, "I'm Ellen."

"Nia," I said.

"We know," Ellen said, and started giggling. Why? I hadn't said anything funny.

Another girl, who had gorgeous black hair that looked shiny and hard, said, "What's it like on the moon?"

I could have told her. I could have described the caverns and tunnels and domes and farms. I could have talked about our school. I could have shown them on my tablet pictures of my friends or the spaceport or the ship that brought me here. If I had done that, maybe things would have been different.

But Ellen was the girl who'd snickered when I answered wrong before. And the other two girls sat way closer to her than to me, and they stared like I was some sort of exhibit in the Alpha Pioneers Museum. And anyway, that other girl's hair was way too shiny. What did she put on it, machine oil?

So I said, "What's the moon like? It's way better than here."

"I suppose you think you're so special," Ellen said.

"Yes," I said. "And you're not."

After that, nobody talked to me except to sneer. Nobody wanted my help during peer tutoring time. Nobody sat with me at lunch. And lunch included broccoli.

....

So that was my life now. I stayed in our house and played with the dogs or messaged my friends on Alpha or watched TV. I went to school where everyone hated me. I didn't let Dad or Mom talk to me about anything important because I had enough misery at school. So Dad and I played video games, and Mom and I baked cookies. Every night I went to bed with Luna on one side of me and Bandit on the other, and I didn't even care when Bandit, who was almost house-broken but not all the way, peed in a corner of my room in the middle of the night.

"Nia," Dad said to me after I just slammed him on the fourth level of Planet Doom, "next week I have to go to Dallas for a Council conference."

I didn't know where Dallas was, and I didn't care, but Mom was away in Washington, talking to *Congress* (take that, Ellen!) I said, "Where will I be?" On the moon, I would have just stayed with Kate's family.

"A babysitter is going to—"

"I'm not a baby!"

Dad ran his hand through his hair like he does when he's worried. I think that's why his hair is getting thin. "No, of course you're not, that's just the Earth word. Anyway, she's a very nice woman, and she'll stay here while I'm gone and take you to school and everything. Her name is Mrs. Allen. You'll like her."

No, I won't, I thought. But Mrs. Allen wasn't too bad. She was old—white hair and a little limp—and she didn't try to be friends or anything. She mostly left me alone except for meals and a reminder it was bedtime and did I do my homework yet? And when Bandit had an accident in the living room, she didn't get upset.

Still, I didn't tell her when Bandit bit me. I didn't want her to freak out, and it wasn't Bandit's fault. I dropped a cookie on the floor of my room and he rushed over to eat it. I tried to get there first, we reached the cookie at the same time, and his little teeth sank into my finger. It *hurt*.

"Bandit!" I cried, and immediately he got all whimpery, crawling around at my feet. Luna never did any of this because she never ate, so I was just as much shocked as hurt. But after I bandaged my finger, I went online and read that you're never supposed to take food from a dog, and that you're supposed to teach them to "leave it." So it wasn't Bandit's fault.

"It's okay," I told him. "We'll work on 'leave it.' You'll learn."

He cuddled up next to me on my bed and licked my hand, right near the bandaged finger.

....

There was a new girl at school, so I didn't have to be the only one who didn't know how stuff was done here. But unlike me, she was popular from the first day. Her name was Alice Hunter. She was really pretty, and she walked on crutches because of a "skiing accident." Skiing is when you strap boards on your feet and slide down a mountain, and how dumb did *that* sound? Alice had run her skis into a tree—I knew that trees were trouble!—and broke her leg in three places. It would heal, but for now she had a cast on her leg and all the girls signed it, oohing and ahhing over Alice's clothes and hair and stories about skiing someplace called Europe. But at least they weren't putting their attention on me.

Except for Ellen.

When I sat down at my desk, something ugly and slimy fell off the edge of it and onto my lap. I screamed and jumped away, and the thing fell to the floor. Everybody rushed over to look, and then they all roared with laughter.

"It's just a worm, you moron!" one of the boys said. "You afraid of a worm?"

Ms. Bukowski sent the kids back to their desks and Ellen to the principal's office and the worm out the window. She tried to explain to me that worms were not dangerous but were good, burrowing around in the soil and getting air into it. I didn't care.

On Alpha, robots get air into the soil, and robots aren't slimy. Or on my desk. And now everybody here not only hated me but thought I was a Fraidy Freddie.

In English we had to write an essay, and I wrote mine on "Why I Hate earth." And I wouldn't capitalize "earth," either, not even in the essay's title, although I know you're supposed to. I made a small "e;" my tablet corrected it to a capital "E;" I put it back to a small one. This planet doesn't deserve a capital letter.

It was that essay that started all the trouble.

....

"Mom! Why are you home?"

Mom stood in the doorway to my room, holding a little red suitcase I'd never seen before. She wasn't supposed to be home until Wednesday. She did not look happy.

"I flew home to see you," Mom said. "I'm going back early tomorrow morning."

"You flew home just for one night? Is that a new suitcase?"

"Yes. Nia—"

"Did you buy a new suitcase just for this trip? Because it's smaller, and you don't need so much stuff for overnight?"

"Forget the suitcase! I'm here because your teacher called me."

Mrs. Allen passed behind Mom in the hallway, and I heard the door to her room close. She was giving us privacy. The only reason I didn't try to close my own door is that Mom didn't look angry, she looked really sad. Usually it's Dad that looks sad when I don't behave. Somehow it was much worse to see Mom like that. It meant I couldn't yell back.

She came into my room and sat on the edge of my bed. Bandit raised his head from his basket, blinked, and went back to sleep. Luna was turned off.

Mom said gently, "I know you miss Alpha, Nia. The moon is your home and it's natural to miss your home. We'll go back there when my posting changes and—"

"*If* it changes," I said, but I didn't say it mean. She looked so tired.

"—and when you're older, you can make the decision for yourself where you want to live. But for now, you aren't being fair. Not to me and your father, because Earth is where our work needs to be now. And you're not fair to Earth, either. You made up your mind to hate it before you even saw it. You pre-judged, which is where the word 'prejudice' comes from. You wouldn't be prejudiced about a person, so why are you about a planet?"

All I could think of to say was, "I don't like it." That sounded pretty lame.

"Isn't there anything you like about it?"

Suddenly I wanted to say something that would please her. She was being so soft to me like Dad usually was. Mom and I fight a lot, but I didn't want to fight right now. I said, "I like Bandit."

She gave a tiny smile. "Well, I suppose that's something."

"Yes! Bandit is something!"

We both stared at Bandit in his basket, because Mom and I didn't ever talk like this, and we were both embarrassed. Bandit yawned, showing all the inside of his little pink mouth.

When I woke for school the next morning, Mom and her small red suitcase had already gone back to Washington.

....

David, one of the boys at school, started calling me "Moony." The first time I heard it, I kind of liked it, but then I saw how nasty the boys with him were smiling, and one of them said, "Hey, Moony—moon us! Drop your pants!"

It wasn't a good thing to be called.

I hated them all.

....

The weather stopped being so hot—I knew this from the quick two feet of open air I had to cross to get from the car to the school's back door—so the gym teacher took everybody outside for soccer. Until now, we'd had gym inside, which wasn't too bad except that we didn't play basketball. "That's a winter sport," the gym teacher explained, which seemed dumb. The ball and net don't care about seasons. On Alpha we played basketball all the time.

I didn't have to go outside for soccer, because of my agoraphobia. Neither did Alice, because of her broken leg. We stayed with Ms. Bukowski in our classroom, both of us reading, me with my back to the windows. Then Mrs. Bukowski said, "Girls—I'm going to just duck down to the faculty room for a cup of coffee. Will you two be all right here?"

Well, of course we would—what did she think? On Alpha kids were left without adults most of the time. Everything was safe, and we weren't babies.

As soon as the teacher left, Alice's crutches thumped on the floor. I heard the window blinds swish. After risking a peek behind me, I turned around. She'd closed all the blinds all the way to the bottom.

"Hey," I said, before I knew I was going to, "why did you do that?"

"I don't like the view," she said. "It's too crowded."

Too crowded? I blurted, "It's too empty!"

We stared at each other a moment and then Alice laughed. "Not to me. I come from Wyoming."

I didn't know where that was, but if it was even emptier than the Midwest, it must be really awful. I probably would have ended the conversation right there but Alice said, "I miss Wyoming. Here there are so many buildings and cars and everything, and so many lights you can hardly see the stars at night. Do you miss the moon?"

"Yes," I said. I wasn't going to say any more because what if she was trying to trick me into saying something she could make fun of? But Alice kept talking.

"On summer mornings in Wyoming, really early, I go outside to the barn to the horses and the sky is so wide and everything smells…so…so great." She didn't have words. She smiled at me instead. "What's the moon like?"

And I found myself telling her. Not much, because there wasn't time. But more than I'd told anybody else, until Ms. Bukowski came back with her coffee. Just as she pushed open the classroom door, Alice said quickly, "Some of us girls think that David and his group are being awful to you. Ellen, too. Just ignore them. They're jerks."

"Girls," Ms. Bukowski said, "why are the blinds closed?'

Alice smiled at me again.

....

After dinner I sat on my bed, thinking. But I didn't get to think very long because Mrs. Allen suddenly screamed.

I ran out into the kitchen. Mrs. Allen lay sprawled on the floor, face down, and Bandit cowered in a corner, barking.

"I tripped over him," she gasped. "Nia, help me up."

I did. She leaned on me, shaky, with one foot off the floor. I said, "I can call 911." Dad taught me that.

"No, no….just help me to the sofa."

I did, and I got her ice for her ankle. She wouldn't call a doctor. Instead, I brought her a bottle of pills from her purse and a glass of water. "Mild painkillers," she said after she swallowed them. "I'll be fine."

"I still think I should call 911."

"No, this has happened before. I just have weak ankles. I'll be fine."

We turned on the television and watched for a while, me shooting little glances at her to make sure she didn't die or anything. She went to sleep, and I went to find Bandit. I'd checked him right after Mrs. Allen fell, and he'd seemed okay. But probably he was still scared, hiding under my bed or something.

He wasn't under my bed.

He wasn't anywhere in my parents' bedroom, or Mrs. Allen's.

He wasn't anywhere in the house, and the kitchen door was part way open.

My heart froze. A little clump of fresh herbs sat on the countertop. Had Mrs. Allen picked them in the little garden that Dad said was out there, put them on the counter, then tripped over Bandit when she went to close the door? When she'd screamed, I'd been too worried about her to even notice the door.

It was only open a little bit.

I edged toward it, closed my eyes, and leaned out. "Bandit!"

Nothing.

Eyes still closed, I groped my way out the door.

The smells hit me first: strange sweet odors that I'd never smelled on Alpha. Some came from the herb garden. Air moved against my face, cool and whispery. Next came sounds: *whooo whooo*, very low and soft. Rustles, like Mom's party dress swishing. And a puppy's cries.

"Bandit!" I opened my eyes and clutched the door frame to hold myself up. Dizziness flooded me. Bandit's cries got louder.

The cries came from the "woods," a bunch of trees across a big open space of grass. That open space looked as huge as a whole spaceport. I could never cross it, never never never I couldn't it was too empty....

Bandit barked, and it sounded like he was hurt.

I couldn't close my eyes—I would trip and fall and then both Mrs. Allen *and* I would both be useless. So I half-closed my eyes, squinting just enough to see the trees, and ran like I was running down the basketball court like I was chasing Kate or Jack or Rosa through the corridors of Alpha, like I was being chased by my worst nightmare. I made it to the trees and crashed through them. It was darker here, but there was enough silvery light to see, and Bandit was only a little way into the woods. His front left leg was caught under a root of the tree that came up from the ground and then went back down again. He whimpered.

I got him out and held him to me like I might never let him go. His warm little body squirmed in my arms and he licked my face. We sat on a pile of dead leaves, while I got up my courage to run back across the grass.

Only...halfway to the house, it happened.

From the corner of my eye, I caught sight of something big and bright, and before I knew it, I was standing completely still, eyes fully open, staring at the sky.

The bright thing was the moon. It shone full and round in the dark blue sky, and around it were stars. They weren't small and steady like they looked from the Alpha dome. They twinkled and glowed, and together the moon and the stars made that silvery light I'd seen through the trees. The trees waved at me in the breeze, and their almost bare branches made lacy patterns against the sky. The air smelled of leaves and dirt and, somewhere, smoke.

It was all beautiful.

I stared up at the moon until my neck hurt. Kate and Jillian and Jack were up there. My life was up there. But this all around me was life, too. Mom and Dad were making a different life here on Earth. Alice was making a different life away from Wyoming. Mom said I'd "pre-judged" Earth, hadn't given it a chance. Alice said some of the kids at school thought David and Ellen were jerks.

Maybe some parts of Earth were different from others, were actually okay. Maybe some parts of school could be okay, too, if I "gave it a chance," like Mom said. Maybe Alice and I could be friends.

Bandit squirmed in my arms. It was colder now. I had to go inside. My face was wet from tears, looking up at the moon, but I didn't feel dizzy or anything. I felt okay. And I could wipe away the tears inside.

....

It's a month later. Alice and Sarah and I are going to the movies with Sarah's mother. I have on a cool red hoodie that Alice loaned me. Bandit is all house-broken. Dad took the boards off my bedroom windows.

But I'm never, ever going to like broccoli.

Standing Up
Anne E. Johnson

Anne E. Johnson lives in Brooklyn. Dozens of her short stories for young readers can be found in publications such as Spaceports & Spidersilk, Jack & Jill, Red Squirrel, *and* Rainbow Rumpus. *Her middle-grade paranormal novel,* Ebenezer's Locker, *was published by MuseItUp. Candlemark & Gleam is publishing her series of humorous science fiction novels,* The Webrid Chronicles, *and they will also release her YA adventure novel,* Space Surfers, *in 2015. Learn more about Anne at her website, AnneEJohnson.com.*

"You won't believe how strong these legs are," Dr. Wend said to Leli. "You'll be able to kick down a building."

"Please don't do that," begged her mom.

Leli didn't want to kick down any buildings. She didn't even want legs. She'd lost hers as a baby back on Earth in the same explosion that killed her dad. Walking on her hands served her just fine for the past twelve years. But now there was new technology developed on the planet Orfo by Humans and the native species, the Dofras. Leli's mom decided Leli *had* to have a pair of intelligent legs.

"You'll learn to control them with your thoughts, even if you're not wearing them," Dr. Wend said.

"Even if you're not wearing them," her mom sighed dreamily. "That's a wonder!"

"In fact, they'll eventually do everything you tell them, down to the last detail. You might even win a dance contest!" Dr. Wend had a nice laugh. He was a good guy. He meant well. "Why don't you try taking a few steps?"

Sighing, Leli gazed at her two robotic legs covered in shiny silver mesh.

"Just think about standing up," her mom coached.

"Okay," Leli huffed. "I can do it myself." Not knowing how the experiment would turn out, she slid off the exam table and slowly put weight on the legs. She imagined the right one moving forward a few inches. It moved. Then the left leg. It was scary and wobbly up there. When Leli put out her hands, Dr. Wend took them to steady her.

"Well?" her mom almost squealed. "How does it feel to walk, sweetie?"

Leli could think of a whole list of words to describe how it felt: awkward, dorky, fake, shaky. But the tears of hope in her mom's eyes made her careful not to complain. "I feel really tall."

But, deep down, she even meant that as a complaint. Although Leli was one hundred percent Human, she thought of herself as mostly Dofra. They had wide tentacles instead of legs, keeping them close to the ground. Just like Leli. She made friends with Dofras more easily than with Humans, and she was proud to identify as one.

"You're not tall," Dr. Wend explained. "We had these legs made so you'd be the average height for your age. You'll get a bigger pair when you grow."

"Just think, sweetie," Mom gushed, helping Leli to sit down, "you're going to be just like everyone else now. Isn't that wonderful?"

Nothing could have sounded worse to Leli. "Can I please take them off?" She tried to keep her lip from quivering. Grabbing the weirdly spongy surface of the left leg with both hands, she yanked it off. She was surprised when the right leg seemed to loosen its grip on her, making it easy to remove. "I guess I'll get used to them," she said, not meaning it.

....

Sitting next to Leli on the HoverTram, Mom held the new legs in a black plastic case across her lap. "I've dreamed of this day ever since we left Earth almost twelve years ago. They told us the Dofras had medicine more advanced than ours. That's one of the reasons I gave up our home among Humans to come here."

"We're still among Humans," Leli said bitterly, turning her head away to wipe her cheek.

Her mom knew her too well. "What's wrong, lovely Leli?"

Sniffing, Leli pointed to the leg case. "Do I *have* to wear those?"

Mom leaned over and kissed her forehead. "I know it's strange, but you'll adjust. You're smart, and you're strong. You can adapt to anything. Just give them a chance."

Leli nodded sadly. She gazed out the window of the HoverTram at the glittery orange and purple rocks of the Frabba Canyon below them. Out of the corner of her eye, she noticed something on the other end of the car. A Dofra baby dropped a small green toy out of its slippery tentacles. Being fond of little kids, Leli didn't hesitate to hoist herself off her seat to go help. She walked on her hands, like she usually did. With no problem she jumped over people's feet and bags on the tram floor.

"Your kid dropped this, sir," she said, balancing on one arm and holding the toy out toward the baby's father. He was short and wide, like all grown-up Dofras, so his face was down at the level of Leli's head when she was on her hands. They smiled at each other.

"Thanks, miss." He wrapped the end of a squishy tentacle around the toy. "He'd cry all night if we lost this silly thing."

In just a few arm-steps, Leli was back at her mom's side. Looking around her, she saw the usual reactions. The Humans on the tram were leaning their heads together, staring at her and whispering. The Dofras were minding their own business. *I really am one of them*, she said to herself. It was a comforting thought.

....

"Show me how you put them on," her mom challenged Leli after dinner. Over their meal of stewed zeptin grasses, they'd talked of nothing but those new legs. Leli was so sick of them, she was ready to toss them into the Frabba Canyon the next time the HoverTram floated over it.

"I'll try them on tomorrow, Mom," she grumbled.

"But don't you want to practice with them before you wear them to school?"

Leli felt the blood drain from her face. "I have to wear them to *school?*"

With a sympathetic smile, her mom pointed to the two metal limbs lying in the corner. "You'll only get used to them if you *try.*"

A long, defeated sigh poured out of Leli's lungs.

"Please just concentrate," Mom instructed.

Leli furrowed her brow and stared at the legs. They shuddered to life, standing up and balancing on their silver feet.

"Good, sweetie. Now call them to you."

The moment Leli pictured them walking, the legs pranced toward her. "Stop!" she shouted right before they crashed into her chair.

"Remember, you can just think the commands," Mom reminded her. "No need to say them aloud."

"I *know*. I'll *get* it."

"Of course you will, sweetie. Do you need help putting them on?"

But Leli had already fitted the limbs to her upper thighs. She pictured herself standing up, and the legs pulled her off her chair. "Whoa!" She teetered and grabbed the wall.

"Think up a balance image, like the physical therapist said."

The physical therapist was a Dofra, Leli thought. *Lucky guy gets to stay down on the ground and not worry about balance.*

"You'll be a pro in no time."

"If you say so, Mom." Even her own mother looked different from this new angle, like she was someone else's parent. Feeling suddenly lost, Leli pulled off her legs and scrambled up the stairs on her hands. She buried her face in her pillow and cried. She knew she'd been doing that a lot the last couple of days, but she couldn't help it. Things were changing too fast.

....

Going to school with legs was a weird experience. All at once, Leli, who'd been able to do everything on her own, needed help doing anything. She toppled over bending to reach her storage cubby, which was near the floor with those for the Dofra children. She got trapped when her legs and her desk's legs got twisted together. Most embarrassing of all, two kids were assigned to keep her upright while she walked down the hall.

"This was the longest day of my life," she moaned to her best friend, Volkie, after classes were over.

Volkie blew air out her side vents. "I don't understand why legs are so important to your mom."

"That's because you're Dofra," Leli grumbled enviously. "It's a Human thing." She pulled off her legs. It was a huge relief to pad over to the HoverTram stop on her hands. Her legs followed obediently.

"You should have a circus act with those," Volkie giggled as she squished along, trying to keep up. Usually Volkie and Leli found all the same things funny. Today, however, Leli couldn't see a thing to laugh about.

The two girls took different HoverTrams home. As she was about to say good-bye, Leli noticed Volkie looking at her oddly. "What?" she demanded.

Volkie rubbed her head thoughtfully with a tentacle. "You need cheering up. You should come to my Soarers Club meeting tomorrow. Everyone's really nice."

Leli had heard of Soarers Club. It was a science group mainly for older kids. Volkie was the youngest member. There was only one thing Leli wanted to know: "Will I have to wear my legs?"

"Definitely not," Volkie laughed, "considering you'll be the only Human!"

"Oh, I can't *wait*." Leli gave her friend a hug. "Even hugging you would be tough with those dumb things on."

"Don't worry about it," Volkie advised. "Tomorrow you'll see the sled we're working on, and you'll forget all about legs and start thinking about wings!"

....

The moment school ended the next day, Leli removed her legs and eagerly waited by the side door. Volkie hurried toward her, tentacles flopping in all directions. "Our ride's already here," she panted. "Don't want to be late."

"I'll stay out of the way," Leli promised, concerned she wouldn't fit in.

"I'm sure they'll love you," Volkie said with a smile.

On the transitway just outside the school, a black and silver flyboat was in temporary docking. Volkie's brother, Migo, paced in front of it. He was older than Volkie with darker, shinier skin. "Wow!" he exclaimed, raising two tentacles as the girls approached.

For one horrible second, Leli thought he was freaked out by the way she walked on her hands. But the boy squished right past her. He stopped next to her legs, gushing like he wanted to ask them on a date. "Aw, you're gorgeous. Look at you, covered in burnished gentak steel mesh."

"This is so embarrassing," groaned Volkie, climbing up the flyboat's ladder. "Come on in, Leli."

With three pulls of her muscular arms, Leli made it up the ladder and vaulted into a seat. "Comfy!" she declared, patting the leather.

"What are we going to do with these beauties?" Migo asked, holding up one leg. "My flyboat's built for Dofras, so I'm not sure they'll fit."

Leli shrugged. "Just put them down. They'll follow me."

Migo's rubbery mouth plopped open so wide, he could have swallowed one of the legs. "They're psychically controlled?" he squealed. "Oh, *wow!*" Lowering the legs to the ground, he bounded up into the flyboat's driving hutch.

Before Leli could warn him that she didn't have much practice with her legs, the flyboat took off. They sped along the transitway, snaking around the slower vehicles. Balling her fists and squeezing her eyes shut, Leli pictured her legs sprinting after the vehicle through heavy traffic.

"Volkie?" she whispered, "can you please check if my legs are following us? Because my mom'll *kill* me if I lose them." She pried one eye open just enough to watch Volkie turn and pull herself up the back seat with two tentacles.

"There they are!" she assured Leli. "They're catching up to us."

"Woo-hoo!" crowed Migo from the front. "I want legs like that!" With the yank of a lever, he turned sharply off the main transitway. Leli dared to peek at her legs. They skillfully jumped out of the way of a honking hovercar and turned onto the side road behind them.

"There they are!" shouted Migo, who never seemed to say things at a normal volume.

Peering over Migo's shoulder, Leli saw a group of kids in an open field, standing around a large white disc. Migo drove over to them, cheering, "We're gonna make it fly today!"

"What *is* that thing?" Leli asked as they climbed to the ground.

"We're calling it an Air Sled," Volkie explained. "It's got this new type of motor we invented that's thin as a piece of foil."

"Does it work?"

An older Dofra girl answered. "It works once it's in the air. It's launching that's the problem."

"Not anymore!" Migo declared loudly. He pointed one tentacle at Leli and another at her robotic legs. "Meet Leli and her legs, our new launching system."

"Psychically powered?" another boy swooned. "That's so awesome!" He slopped clumsily over to Leli. "If you let us use those legs to launch the sled, you can be the first one to ride it."

"Um, oookay." Leli hand-walked closer to the sled. It was just a thin plastic disc with four handles, presumably to keep the rider from sliding off. "Is it safe?" she asked in a small voice, not quite loud enough to drown out the voice inside her head. That one sounded just like her mom, screaming, "That is *not* safe, young lady!"

But all the nice, smart kids, down near the ground like her, were smiling and nodding their heads, shouting out encouraging things.

"Sure, it's safe."

"We'll keep you very low."

"Our remote control is totally reliable."

Volkie and another Dofra girl had already lifted the disc and balanced it on top of Leli's legs. "Come on," said Volkie in a tone that made it seem like a good idea. "We'll help you get up there."

Leli felt herself heaved upward. At least the sled seemed sturdier under her than she'd expected.

"The handles were made to fit Dofra limbs," a particularly pudgy Dofra boy said. "Sorry about that."

"Just hang on super-tight," Migo advised. "You get your legs running, and we'll launch the sled once there's enough speed."

Leli's knuckles went white as she grasped two of the handles. She didn't want to let on how terrified she was, worried that these interesting kids wouldn't like her anymore. Yet she really just wanted to go home. "Okay, I guess I'm ready," she said in a cracking voice.

She pictured the legs walking forward. Almost immediately the sled started to move. Leli could feel the steps the legs took as they carried her. But the ride was smoother than she'd feared, as if the legs were stepping carefully to protect her. She imagined going faster.

The wind against her face told her they were really rolling now. "You're up to speed!" called one of the kids. "Make your legs stop!"

She did, and was rewarded with a violent jolt. Feeling the disc shift off the robotic legs, Leli hung on for dear life. The sled caught the air and stayed level. The paper-thin engine buzzed under her.

"You look great, Leli!" she heard Volkie shout. "You're flying!"

That prompted Leli to make a huge mistake: leaning to one side, she looked down. Suddenly, the ground came rushing toward her. Before she knew what was happening, the edge of the sled was skidding through the dirt and Leli did a painful somersault.

She would have flipped over a second time, but something held her still. At first she thought it was some of the kids, but they were far away, running toward her. Then she realized she was grasping metal mesh. "My legs! They helped me!" Her robotic limbs bent at the knee so she could pull them on. For the first time, she felt affection for them.

"I'm fine," she lied to the kids who reached her first. She wasn't hurt, but she was deeply shaken. The idea of how close she'd come to breaking her neck made her shudder.

Volkie hurried to her, breathless. Too low to the ground to hug Leli in the normal way, she wrapped her tentacles around the robotic legs. "I'm so sorry about this!" she said, looking upward. "Come, on, Leli. I'll walk you to the HoverTram."

"No, thanks," Leli snapped. She wondered how someone she thought was her friend could get her into such a dangerous mess. "I'll go by myself."

After one last look at the half-buried sled, Leli pictured herself stepping up the front walk to her house. Her legs sprang into action. Although she wobbled a bit, Leli found her balance quickly as the legs caught a rhythm. With huge, powerful strides, she loped along the side of the HoverTram expressway. She even caught up with the tram she normally rode home.

A bunch of little Human kids waved at her as she passed. Waving back, she thought defiantly, *Having legs isn't so bad. Who wants to be down on the ground like a bunch of dumb Dofras?*

In a few minutes, she was home, winded and bursting with all kinds of crazy, conflicting thoughts.

"Sweetie? What's wrong?" her mom asked as she clomped through the kitchen.

Leli hadn't even realized she was crying. She plopped down on the sofa and yanked her legs off. She'd have thrown them across the room, but they scuttled into the corner on their own as if they sensed danger.

"What is it, honey?"

"Volkie's a stupid jerk with stupid, jerky friends!" Leli blurted out. Too sad and angry to say anything else, she curled up in a ball. She felt her mom's comforting hands stroke her head.

"Was Volkie mean to you?"

Wishing she could answer "Yes," Leli knew it would be a lie. Volkie had tried to be nice. She'd invited Leli to join her special club. And everyone in the club had like her so much that they let her ride the sled.

No! she thought miserably. *They liked my legs, not me.* "Mommy?

Does wearing legs make me a better person?"

"Oh, Leli!" Her mom leaned over and wrapped her in a big, warm hug. "You'd be the same wonderful person no matter how many limbs you had."

Leli wanted to believe that. "What if I had three arms?" she sniffed.

"Then I'd get extra-tight hugs," replied her mom, nuzzling Leli's neck.

"What if I had no ears or nose?" Leli sat up. "Or what if, like, my eyeballs fell out?"

"Leli!"

The gruesome game was doing her good. "No, wait! What if all that was left of me was one single eyeball?" She started laughing.

Her mom laughed, too, shaking her head. "Then you'd be the most wonderful, beautiful eyeball in the universe." She stood. "And you *will* get used to those legs, in whatever way is right for you. Dinner in an hour, sweetie."

....

All the next day, Leli avoided Volkie. She also kept her legs on most of the day, as a message to the Dofra kids. She wanted them to remember that she was Human and therefore should be tall. She even started up a conversation with a cute Human boy when she caught him staring at her legs. He really was only interested in the psychic technology, but it was thrilling to get any attention from a boy.

Leli was filling her backpack after her last class when she heard a commotion outside. She let her legs follow the sounds. Outrunning all the students and staff, she soon found herself at the edge of Frabba Canyon, just off the school grounds. A fence kept kids from getting into danger. However, the fence wasn't high enough to stop a flying disc.

"Volkie!" Leli screamed, seeing her friend totter perilously over the steep rocks.

Mogi ran up behind her. "She felt so bad about what happened to you yesterday," he sobbed. "She wanted to prove the sled was safe. That girl's too clever for her own good. She launched by climbing the fence and belly flopping off! We can't control the sled for some reason." He punched frantically at the remote control box.

"Hang on, Volkie!" Leli called. But it was hopeless. The disc went sideways, dumping Volkie between two jutting rock formations. She shrieked, and the growing crowd around Leli shrieked, too.

"She's stuck!" someone shouted.

Police flew in, lowering a rescue team to help the terrified girl. Leli could see how hard Volkie was crying. She thought her heart would break. All her anger was forgotten, drowned by the love she felt for her best friend.

"You'll be out soon, Volkie!" Leli promised.

The police didn't look so hopeful. One of them spoke through a megaphone. "We have to wait for equipment that can break this rock. Then it will be a slow process, so we don't hurt the child as we free her."

Mogi flailed his tentacles. "Where are they going to get equipment that's powerful and careful at the same time?"

Something about the phrase sparked Leli's memory. She recalled her doctor's description of her legs: strong enough to kick down a building, but could do anything detailed, even win a dance contest.

"I've got this!" Leli announced, pulling off her legs. Using her hands, she hauled herself halfway up the fence so she could see exactly what was happening below. And she pictured what she wanted her legs to do.

The crowd gasped as her legs jumped over the fence and started to pick their way down the rugged canyon wall. "Help is coming, Volkie!" Leli called over and over. Soon the others joined her. The canyon echoed with the comforting words, "Help is coming, Volkie!"

The legs made it to the rock formation where Volkie was stuck. When the police backed away in confusion, the legs obeyed Leli's thoughts. With fast, careful kicks, they cracked the stone around Volkie until it crumbled away. Within minutes the rescue team was able to pull the girl out safely and send her up to a flying ambulance.

The crowd's cheers were deafening as the legs climbed back to their proud owner. Leli didn't get a chance to put them on, though, because dozens of joyful people, Humans and Dofras alike, smothered her in hugs and lifted her up. Now the canyon rang with a different chant: "Hurray for Leli's legs!"

A friendly police officer gave Leli a ride home. She let her legs jog behind the flying cruiser, which made the crowd cheer even louder.

....

Leli slept for fifteen hours. By the time she dragged herself into the school, the morning bell had already rung. She expected the hall monitor robot to issue her a detention ticket. Something very different was waiting for her when she entered the school.

Hundreds of students and faculty packed the foyer. Many of the Dofras had draped their floppy bodies over stepladders. A few were standing on stilts. The Humans sat on the floor or on skateboards, which they paddled around on using their hands. Spanning the hallway was a huge banner lettered with a message in a rainbow of colors:

WE LOVE YOU, LELI,
SHORT OR TALL!

Leli realized that she loved them back. All of them. Short *and* tall. She pictured a happy little dance step, and everyone clapped when the legs did it perfectly.

Goliath vs. Robodog

Ron Collins

Ron Collins' work has appeared in numerous magazines and anthologies, including Analog, Asimov's *and* Nature. *This winter saw the initial publication of stories that comprise the* Saga of the God-Touched Mage, *an eight-part serial of novella length stories that have been listed in Amazon's top ten dark fantasies in both the US and the UK. Of* Goliath vs. Robodog, *he writes: "It's interesting to imagine everything robots will be able to do in the not-so-distant future, but sometimes it's too easy to overlook things that really matter." Find out more about Ron at www.typosphere.com*

It was 3:17 on a Friday afternoon in early May. Kids chattered in the hallway, and the sounds of slamming SUV doors filled the parking lot.

Kevin Robbins was thirteen and finishing 8th grade. Kevin was also standing under the elm tree at the back of the school, trying to get past Trevor Johnson and his band of merry men so he could walk home.

"You think you're something special," Trevor said, towering over him and enjoying the intimidating edge thirty pounds gives. "But you ain't so hot now, are you, Robbins? You ain't nothing but a freaking snotball hanging at the end of my nose. Everything about me is better than you. I'm taller than you. I play ball better than you. Hell, my robodog's even better than that mangy mutt of yours."

"Come on, Trevor," he said, praying no one else heard the waver in his voice. "Let me through."

"Ya scared?" Trevor pushed Kevin hard enough that his algebra book landed in a fluttering heap at Jimmie May's feet.

Jimmie May snapped his gum and stared at him.

Kevin brushed thin bangs from his eyes and knelt to gather his book, cheeks burning with humiliation. He realized beyond doubt that he should never have opened his big, humongously fat mouth in Ms. Thompson's class.

Kevin muttered to himself.

"What did you say?" Trevor asked.

"I said Goliath is better than any old robot."

"Didja hear that?" Trevor called to his growing audience. "Kevy here thinks his mutt is a match for Robodog."

"That's because he is!" a female voice said. Meredith Michaels, book bag slung over one shoulder, marched into the area.

Kevin's stomach dropped. Meredith was his neighbor and a good friend. A thick patch of freckles covered her nose, and her blonde hair was cut short in a way that usually made her look playful. Today, though, her cheeks were crimson with anger.

"Goliath can take your dog any old day of the week," she said.

"Look, everyone," Trevor called. "Kevin Robbins needs his girlfriend to take up for him."

"She's *not* my girlfriend."

"Ohhhooohhhhoooo," Trevor mooned back. "Thou protesteth too hard."

"That's supposed to be 'doth protest too much,' jerk," Meredith said.

"Whatever."

"Come on, Meredith," Kevin said. "Let's go."

Meredith wasn't done, though.

"You think Robodog is so hot," she said. "Why don't you prove it?"

Trevor stuck his jaw out. "Name it."

"Fetch match. Here at the school in half an hour."

Trevor gave Kevin a carnivorous smile. "What do you think, Robbins? Loser's underwear goes on Mr. Calhoun's desk

Monday morning?"

Kevin squirmed. His mom expected him to be home when she and dad got back, but the ring of kids around them loomed with expectant leers. "Chicken," he could hear them whispering.

"You're on," Kevin said before he could stop himself.

"All right, then. See you in a half hour, loser."

....

"Come on, Goliath," Kevin said.

Goliath was a Belgian shepherd, eight years old, with dark black eyes and velvety tan fur. He was happy to see Kevin, and even happier when Kevin opened the fence and picked up his throwing stick. Kevin scratched Goliath behind the ears, right where he knew Goliath liked it best. Kevin glanced to the kitchen window to be sure it was still dark.

It had been another bad week. Mom took dad to the hospital for another round of tests this afternoon. If Kevin didn't have his homework done before they returned, Mom would go off on him again. Dad was always tired, so he wouldn't be any help. It would add up to an uncomfortable dinner and another evening alone.

They weren't due home until five, though, and with luck, he and Goliath could be back before then.

"Let's go, boy" he said.

Kevin lived in a suburb of small brick houses lined up in perfect little rows. Each house had a concrete driveway, and each driveway had a car parked out front.

As they walked, Goliath sniffed bushes and clumps of grass growing from cracks in the sidewalk. Kevin held Goliath's throwing stick in one hand. It was over two feet long and maybe twice as thick as a broom handle.

Goliath ran up past the Carter place.

"Get back here," Kevin snapped.

The dog jogged back, his big black eyes wide as if to apologize.

"Don't get too far ahead, all right? We don't want Mr. Carter to come out and shoot you or anything, you know?"

Goliath gave a half-bark, half-whimper, then went to an

evergreen in front of the Carter's place and lifted his leg.

Kevin groaned as he waited for Goliath to finish, thinking he should just go back home and face the barbs that being a no-show would bring. Why did he let Meredith goad him into this?

A door opened from across the street. Meredith came out. She was a 7th grader, but taller than Kevin. She had changed to jean shorts and a T-shirt top. They had lived on the same street for as long as Kevin could remember. Kevin's father worked for Meredith's, and they had gone to all the same summer programs for years. He thought of her more as a sister than a friend.

"Jill called, and word's out," Meredith said. "Everyone wants to see Trevor's robodog. I wouldn't be surprised if half the school shows up."

Kevin looked at the ground. Goliath barked, having run farther up the street. "Why me?" he groaned. "I'm just gonna to go home."

"It'll be worse if you don't show up."

He sighed. "It can't get any worse."

"Why do you say that?"

"Goliath will never beat Robodog."

"Well, then," Meredith said, "maybe you should have thought about that while you were making fun of Robodog in Ms. Thompson's class."

"I know." He kicked concrete that had broken loose from the sidewalk. "I just couldn't take it anymore. That stupid Robodog is all Trevor ever talks about – *Robodog gets the paper. Robodog watches TV with me. Robodog's favorite show is 'Fallout Shelter,' just like mine.*"

Meredith laughed. "You do a good Trevor."

"Just what I needed to hear."

"For what it's worth," she said. "It really was funny when you asked if Robodog drank from the toilet, just like Trevor."

Kevin grinned.

The class laughed, and Trevor's face had gone red as Ms. Thompson's nails.

"Yeah, I suppose it was. But I've been dreading this ever since I said it."

They walked toward the schoolyard.

"How's your dad?" she asked.

He shrugged. "They're not due home until five."

"You worried?"

Kevin nodded. His dad dropped forty pounds in three months, and now spent all day in front of the TV. He didn't golf. He didn't play catch. He didn't do much of anything else except read and sleep.

"They don't talk like they used to," Kevin said. "Mom and Dad, I mean. They used to get into arguments and stuff before, but it was always over quick, and things were ... I don't know. Now nobody talks at all."

"Why are parents like that?" Meredith said. "They tell us to deal with things, then can't handle it themselves."

"Yeah," Kevin said.

Something didn't feel right about that. He thought of the way Dad watched him now. He would stare so deeply while Kevin ate, or would watch Kevin while he did his homework or played ball in the front yard. It was a little creepy sometimes, but... Then there was Mom, who worked at the law office three or four times a week. She was always busy. But he would catch her staring at Dad with her lips tight and lines spreading over her face.

Kevin didn't know what was wrong, and he didn't know what to do to make things better. Worse, he had come to understand that neither of his parents knew any more than he did.

"I think they're just scared," he said.

"I'm sorry," Meredith replied.

"Nothing to be sorry for."

"I shouldn't have gotten you into this robodog thing."

Goliath turned the corner and ran off into the open field.

"Maybe Goliath will win," she said. "Maybe he could beat Robodog."

"Ha!"

"Why not?"

"Well, dummy," Kevin said, "in the first place Goliath's no puppy. He'll get tired in a flash, and that'll be it. Then there's the fact that robodogs use special alloys and composite bindings to keep them light. And they have computers that control balance and muscle movements. They can turn corners in the blink of an eye."

"Sounds like you know a lot about 'em."

"Yeah," he said. "I've read a bit."

Truth was, Kevin had wanted a robodog himself. He even asked for one for Christmas a few months back, but Mom and Dad said they didn't have the money. Besides, what would Goliath do with a fake dog around? But Kevin knew that robodogs were sleek and cool and came in hundreds of breeds. You didn't have to feed them like a real dog or deal with dung bombs when you wanted to play ball in the yard. Keeping a robodog going was just a matter of charging the batteries at night. It even took care of itself if you told it to.

Robodogs didn't even slobber.

And you could program them to do tricks.

Once, when Kevin was eight or nine, he had tried to teach Goliath to roll over. He had gotten down on his hands and knees and shouted, "roll over," while pushing the dog. Goliath just pranced around and licked his face with that rubbery tongue of his.

He smiled, despite himself. Those had been good days.

"Pif," Meredith said.

"What?" Kevin replied.

"Do you believe everything you read?"

"Well, no."

"And we've never actually seen a robodog, have we?"

"No. Not in person, anyway."

"Well, then," she said. "I've got faith in Goliath. I bet he'll beat Robodog."

Kevin straightened up. Meredith could be right. Maybe he was giving Robodog too much credence. Goliath was a good dog, and he had been penned in his yard all day. He was obviously excited about being outside. He looked ready to run.

Kevin felt better.

"Thanks," he said.

"No problem, dummy."

They turned the corner. There must have been fifty kids around the schoolyard. Goliath was squatting down in the grass, quite obviously taking a dump.

Meredith laughed.

Kevin's face flushed.

This, he realized, was going to be bad.

....

Kevin stood in the middle of the field with his back to Trevor, their dogs each at their heels.

Robodog was a black lab, the young adult model. Its coat shone in the sun and its tongue hung in a fake pant that gave its cooling system access to the air. Goliath sat still, also panting. His own pink tongue lolled out the side of his mouth, a long sliver of dog saliva dripping molasses-like toward the ground.

The schoolyard was an open field with empty soccer goals at each end, some swings, and a few sparse trees here and there. The grass had worn patches where the team practiced.

Goliath whined. His gaze was focused with intense longing on the throwing stick.

"Twenty-five tosses, right Robbins?" Trevor asked.

"Yeah," Kevin replied, "You have to throw the stick at least past Mr. Kennedy's ginko trees for the toss to count. I have to make it past the line that runs across the swings."

Trevor nodded acceptance. "We need someone to count down."

"I'll do it," Meredith said, stepping forward.

Trevor glared at her for a moment, then smiled.

"On three," she said, raising her hand.

The crowd grew silent.

"One."

Kevin twisted to get leverage for his own toss.

"Two."

Trevor cocked his arm.

"Three!"

Kevin threw the stick, and Goliath took off, his collar jangling with each stride.

Voices from the crowd rose.

The first toss was farther than Kevin wanted. Goliath chased it down, grabbed it, and lumbered home. "Good boy," Kevin said as he winged the stick back into the schoolyard.

It was a good start. He took a backward glance at Robodog, who was just returning his stick. Great! Maybe Goliath could beat this machine. The mob's voices receded into the distance as the game wore on. Kevin cheered for Goliath with each throw, and the dog barked for the pure joy of chasing the stick. By the eighth toss, though, Goliath was slowing, and by the twelfth he was nearly sauntering after the stick.

"Come on, boy," Kevin yelled. "You can do it!"

"Twenty-five!" Trevor called.

"What?"

Kevin looked at Meredith, who nodded morosely.

"But Goliath was ahead after the first toss," Kevin complained.

Trevor cackled. "Hear that? He thinks his fleabag was ahead."

"I saw it. Robodog was just returning when…"

"Robodog was on his second stick when you looked back, Kev," Meredith said quietly.

"Can't wait to see the look on Calhoun's face when he sees your underwear spread out all over his desk," Trevor said. "I expect it'll be there first thing Monday morning, right Robbins?"

The kids laughed and gathered around Robodog, asking a barrage of questions.

Kevin hung his head. Goliath gave a plaintive whine and stepped up beside Kevin. Goliath's wet nose nuzzled his hand.

He pulled it back.

"I'm sorry, Kev." Meredith put her hand on Kevin's shoulder. "At least Goliath is a better friend than Robodog will ever be."

"Don't take that to the bank," Trevor said.

Robodog sat at his heel.

"Shake hands!" Trevor said. Robodog raised a paw. "Roll over." Robodog did a crisp barrel-roll in the grass.

Kevin's face burned.

"Come on, boy," Kevin said to Goliath. "We've got to get home."

....

Kevin trudged home. Goliath ambled beside him, his tags rattling, looking as defeated as Kevin felt. The spryness of their step was long gone. The muscles in Kevin's jaw clenched, and he made fists so tight his nails bit into the meat of his palms. All he wanted to do right now was scream. He punched the air. Right, left. Right, left. He kicked the fire hydrant at the corner of the street.

What good was a real dog anyway?

What good was school or friends? Or, when it got down to it, what good was he? Maybe Mom and Dad should just go out and get a roboboy and be done with it. At least then they would have someone who finished his homework, and cleaned up, and didn't get pushed around in school.

Kevin turned the corner and froze when he saw his mother's white car parked in the driveway. He was late.

There went dinner.

Kevin hung his head and bit back tears. Might as well get it over with.

"Come on, boy."

He tugged on the dog's collar.

Goliath, who had taken advantage of the pause to sit down, came along without a whimper. Kevin let Goliath into the yard, and ran him some water from the hose.

....

Music was playing as he stepped through the door. Old stuff, the stuff his parents listened to when they were kids. Was it Cold Play? Who could tell?

"Mom?" he called.

"We're in the living room," she yelled, her voice muffled.

He walked through the house. They were dancing, if you want

to call it that, pressed together arm-in-arm and swaying to the music. Mom's head was buried in Dad's shoulder. Dad's eyes were closed. He looked tired, but he held her tightly to him.

"What's going on?" he asked.

Mom turned her head, leaving a damp spot on Dad's shirt. Her eyes were soggy.

"It's cancer," Dad said, swaying a little further.

Kevin was stunned. He sat down on the couch.

"So ... why are you dancing?"

They stopped, and Dad gave a half shrug and a thin smile. "Because I feel better just knowing."

"What?"

His mother put her arm around his father's waist.

"It's in his kidney," she said. "And it's in the early stages. It's good news because there's an approach that should get rid of it."

Kevin sat, listening, trying to hear it all.

"The treatment is fairly new," Dad said. "They remove a bit of the tissue, and take proteins from it."

His mother followed, "Then they tailor a drug to hunt out the cancer cells."

They were talking like they did in the old days, Kevin noticed, bouncing sentences back and forth. It was kind of like watching a ping pong match. Was that good? Was it not good?

"The doctor was optimistic," his dad said.

"They already took the baseline tissue," his mother added.

"I'll get the procedure in two days."

"Sunday?" Kevin finally said something.

"Yes," Mom replied.

"That's quick."

"They want to move fast."

Dad took a visible breath. "It's going to be a tough few weeks, though."

"Pish," Mom said, patting his chest and pressing her lips into a hard line. "Now is not the time to be Debbie Downer."

The song ended, and the three of them stood there, Kevin

more than a bit dumbstruck.

"I better get dinner ready," Mom said, looking at Dad. "You lie down and get some rest."

Dad nodded and sagged into the recliner, kicked the leg support, and laid back.

He *did* look tired. In fact, Kevin thought, he looked like a balloon deflating before his very eyes.

"And you, young man," Mom said, "can feed the dog."

She went to the kitchen to put something together. Kevin looked at his father.

"You heard your mother," Dad said.

Kevin nodded, suddenly afraid. He wanted to ask Dad how he really felt. Was he as tired as he looked? Did it hurt? Was he as afraid as Kevin was?

Instead, he put his head down, went to the mud room to fill Goliath's bowl, and stepped into the back yard to feed him. He put the bowl down on the concrete slab that served as their patio, and sat on the bottom of the four steps that led back to the house. The breeze was cool against the late afternoon sun. He smelled clover from the yard. A car rolled down the street across the back way. Tears welled in his eyes. *Why,* he thought. *Why now? Why me?* He hadn't cried about anything for a long time, but now he had just listened to his mom and dad talk as if everything was so promising. He saw the way they had been holding each other so close, as if it could be the very last time that might ever happen. And now he cried.

He didn't understand.

Or maybe he did understand, and it was all just too much.

He wiped his eyes on his shirt sleeves, and drew a cleansing breath.

Looking down, he saw Goliath sitting quietly next to him, his tail twitching every so often. Goliath had to be hungry after their earlier adventures, but his bowl was untouched.

Kevin scratched Goliath behind his ears.

The dog gave a gentle whine and rested against Kevin's knee.

"You're a good boy," Kevin said. "But I've got to go in." He stood up, and pointed to the bowl. "And you've got to eat."

Goliath waited, staring back as Kevin climbed the stairs. Kevin watched him from inside. Once the dog was certain he had left, he gave a grumbling growl, then went to his bowl.

Kevin smiled despite himself.

It wasn't until he was falling asleep that night that he realized his mother hadn't said a word about him getting home late.

....

Saturday was an endless process of waiting while Kevin's dad underwent a barrage of tests.

Kevin read a book in one waiting room. He walked up and down the halls at another. He watched television. For a while, he looked at other patients being wheeled around, but it felt like he was prying, and he didn't like that. His mom and dad chatted briefly at times and read. Mom brought her crochet but didn't spend much time with it.

Hospitals made Kevin anxious. They seemed so cold and so stark. Everyone talked in big words and with such practiced professionalism. It created a distance that made Kevin feel alone. The doctors and nurses strode with purpose. You could hear their voices, but their rubber-soled shoes muffled their footsteps and made it seem like they weren't really there.

It was dark by the time they got home. Mom was cranky, and Dad was so tired he conked out within seconds of hitting the recliner.

....

They had to be back at the hospital at 8:00 on a Sunday morning, which flat-out sucked.

Meredith offered to look in on Goliath through the day, so Kevin fed him early.

Doctor Schivitz came into the waiting room after a few hours to let them know the procedure had gone "just beautifully."

He took a seat across from them and explained.

"We placed a half-dollar-sized wafer alongside his kidney," he said, making his thumb and finger into a round shape to indicate the size. "It will dissolve over the next week and release the counter-drug directly into the cancer."

They planned to get Dad up and moving today, and he would be released tomorrow if all went well.

"Any other questions?" the doctor asked.

The words came out of Kevin's mouth before he could stop them. "When will we know if he's getting better or not?"

"Kevin!" his mother said.

"That's all right, Mrs. Robbins," Dr. Schivitz said. "It's a darn good question."

He leaned over and looked at Kevin straight on.

"Your dad's a trouper. We think he'll do fine."

"But you don't know, right? I mean. It's not certain."

"You're right," Dr. Schivitz said. "Nothing is ever certain. But we're doing everything we can, and the procedure has been successful in other cases."

Kevin chewed his lip, and the doctor sat back.

"You've got a dog, right?" the doctor said.

"Yeah."

"You might be interested to know that one of the very first patients they tried this on was a dog. A Belgian shepherd, I believe. Lived a good long life in Hawaii."

"A Belgian?" Kevin said. "That's what Goliath is."

"Well," Dr. Schivitz replied with a grin that was more honest than the one he had pasted on earlier. "What do you know about that? Maybe that's a sign, then, eh? We'll just hope for the best, and see what happens, all right?"

"Yeah," Kevin said.

Then they were alone in the waiting room, and Kevin actually did feel better.

"Thank goodness for dogs, eh?" his mother asked.

Kevin nodded. "Yeah, thank goodness for dogs."

They had an early lunch, then went up to see Dad.

Dad looked awful. He was drugged out, and, for a long time, could barely raise his hand. Dad lay on his side to keep pressure off the incision, which was wrapped in enough gauze to bandage the entire Civil War. The beep of a heart monitor pinged every second or so.

Later that night, Dad was able to get up and walk and eat his mashed potatoes and his meat-something-or-other. It seemed to help. By the end of visiting hours, there was color in his face, and he was laughing at the television. It was enough to make Kevin think there was real hope.

Goliath was hungry when they got home, and pranced around the yard when they arrived. He nuzzled Kevin's leg as he put the bowl down.

It was dark out, and Kevin was tired enough for bed, but he watched from the window as the dog ate, lapping chunks of food, and huffing breaths between bites in his rapid-fire dog way of eating. There was something about Goliath at that moment, something about this dog with his slobber and his dog-breath and his fur all tufted up ... he thought about Goliath running against Robodog, and he choked down a breath.

Goliath paused to scratch himself just like he had been doing since about as far back as Kevin could remember. Actually, Kevin couldn't actually remember a time without Goliath, just like he couldn't really imagine a future without the mangy beast, just like he couldn't imagine...

He had been such a dweeb, the darkest, dumbest, lowest form of dweeb that could ever exist.

How could he ever think Robodog was better than Goliath?

....

Trevor Johnson pressed Kevin up against his locker.

"So, Robbins, where's the underwear?"

With everything going on, he had truly forgotten the bet until he saw Trevor coming down the hallway. For an instant he hoped Trevor would give it a pass, that the humiliation of losing would have been enough. But that was silly. Trevor wasn't going to let up.

Kevin wasn't going to give him anything here, though. He wasn't going to break down. He wasn't going to cry. For a flickering instant, he imagined himself punching Trevor in the face, his fist connecting and Trevor flying skyward like Superman had launched him.

Instead, Trevor bellied up to him, and Jimmie May and Kal McDaniels stood to either side, blocking his escape. Jimmie May cracked his gum.

Kevin glanced up the hallway.

"What's the matter?" Trevor said. "Looking for your girlfriend?"

"No," Kevin said. "I just..."

"You just chickened out is what you did."

"No, I didn't," Kevin said, using the wall to help him stand a little taller. "I just forgot. I'll do it tomorrow. I promise."

"He forgot!" Trevor said, his voice rising. "You hear that, girls? Kevy Robbins just forgot that his sorry-assed dog got his sorry-assed butt whipped by Robodog."

"I said I'll do it tomorrow," Kevin said from between clenched teeth.

The one-minute bell buzzed its warning, and kids scurried for class. Trevor leaned in so close Kevin could smell the sour odor of Trevor's breath.

"You better, if you know what's good for you."

....

They released Dad around noon, and he was on the couch when Kevin got home. There were flowers on the side stand and a row of cards open on the coffee table, arranged around a potted plant with another card from Meredith's family.

"How you doing, Champ?" Dad asked as Kevin sat on a patch of couch.

"Aren't I supposed to be the one to say that?"

Dad chuckled. "Yeah, maybe so."

"So?"

"I'm sick and tired of lying on my side, I can tell you that much."

"How long do you have to do it?"

"Nurse said three days."

"Are you getting better?" He said it straight out this time. No beating around the bush. "I mean, really better? That's what I really want to know."

Dad shrugged. "You and me both, kid. I'm sure it's too early. But I'm thinking good thoughts, you know? And I'm trying hard to fight it. I think about it all the time – taking my meds and telling my body to focus."

Dad moved a bit, taking pressure off his back. "No idea if all that 'think good thoughts' crap works, but if I don't get better you can bet your behind it won't be because I'm not doing everything I can."

Kevin nodded.

"That's all you can really ask for, right?" Dad asked.

"Maybe you can't ask for more," Kevin said. "But I can ask for you to be all-the-way better."

Dad laughed and gave him a gentle punch on the arm.

"I love you, Kevin. You're a good kid."

"Thanks," he said.

Kevin looked at Dad.

"Would it be okay if Goliath sleeps in my room again?"

They had stopped that a year or so ago because dog hair got all over the place and both Kevin and Goliath had grown a few sizes since they were a kid and a puppy.

"Fine by me," Dad replied. "And if you do your sheets, I don't see that your mother would mind."

Kevin smiled.

"Thanks."

....

There was no getting around it, Kevin realized. There was business he had to take care of, so he got up extra early and rode his bike to make sure he got to school before most everyone else.

It was strange to be there with the hallways so empty and silent. His footsteps echoed forever as he passed rows of lockers. It wouldn't take long, but he was nervous enough he had to wipe sweat from his palms three times before he got to Trevor's locker. He hoped he wouldn't get caught.

He put his book bag on the floor, and pulled out a glue stick and the pack of pictures he printed last night. One-by-one, he put them in place. The first showed Goliath when he was a puppy and Kevin was five. They were playing with the garden hose in the front yard, and both of them were drenched to the bone. The next showed Kevin at eight. He had just had his tonsils out, and Goliath was sprawled at the foot of his bed as Kevin ate ice cream. In all he pasted up twelve photos. When that was done Kevin took a marker and wrote a sprawling string of text that snaked all around the locker, "What Robodog would dream ... if he could."

He stepped back. It was good. Perfect. He snapped a picture, and sent it to Meredith because he knew she would get a kick out of it.

There would be a price, of course. Trevor would hunt Kevin down, and Jimmie May would crack his gum. But that was okay. He was going to have to deal with Trevor Johnson sometime, and Goliath was worth it – every day of the week and twice on Sundays, as Dad would say. In a strange way, Kevin even looked forward to the confrontation. It didn't matter about any stupid fetch match, or whether robodogs could do a hundred roll-overs at a time. Goliath was the best dog in the entire world, and more. If no one else saw that, well, that wasn't his problem.

Kevin pocketed his phone and shouldered his book bag.

He glanced once more at Trevor's locker, then he stood up straight and walked down the hallway toward his home room.

Unsealed

Jeanne Kramer-Smyth

Jeanne Kramer-Smyth has been writing since she first got her hands on a typewriter at age nine. Since then she has worked as a software developer, traveled the world, and written poetry. She is currently an archivist by day and a writer, glass artist and fan of board games by night. She has studied fiction writing with both Judith Tarr and Mary Robinette Kowal. She especially enjoys fantasy, science-fiction, YA, and historical fiction. She lives in Maryland with her husband, son, sister-in-law, and cat. You can find her online at www.jeannekramersmyth.com.

"Today we say good-bye to Dr. Alice, Engineer Felicia and our own Cheese Craftsman Joseph. Please join me in this moment of silence as we wish them well on their journey into whatever the horizon holds for them beyond this life." The radio voice was replaced by a crackling silence.

Ida stopped turning the radio's crank, resting her aching right arm. Did those people have children? Her eyes filled with tears. She reached for the chain around her neck and touched the memorial disks for her own parents. Her mother's disk was worn smooth with time. Ida had worn it for three years—since she was nine.

Father's disk, only six weeks old, was still hard edged and crisp. Since he had spent less time outdoors, he had lasted longer.

Ida stared through her tears at the door to the bedroom where her five-year-old brother Maurice now slept. Maurice had cried himself to sleep every night for weeks after Father died, clutching the new disk made from Father's ashes. Mother's disk had always been there, a matching decoration to Ida's, but Maurice had no memory of their mother.

Ida wiped her eyes on her sleeve and picked up the radio. It had been almost a week since the last time she had caught the signal.

"...happier news." The young woman's voice returned against the whirring of the turning crank. "We have three open immigration slots for the West City Dome. Those able to pass full skin and lung exams will be given top priority."

Ida let go of the crank, and silence fell over the apartment again. She tipped her head back to lean against the wall, staring up through the window at the stars over the city. They were twelve stories up. Her mother used to reminisce about wide-open windows and fresh breezes. The big window had been sealed shut for as long as Ida could remember.

The apartment was stuffy. The air cycled only once an hour. They had barely anything left to barter for food. The water filter was so old she wasn't sure it was actually safe to drink anything it claimed to purify. At least the apartment door still locked, and the toilet flushed. And they still had the bed where Maurice now slept.

Ida set the radio aside. She stood up and turned to look out the big window, stretching her sore arms over her head. When Ida was little, the night sky had been full of brightly lit buildings. Tonight the lights were scattered, looking more like fallen stars decorating the lonely silhouette of urban skyline. She pressed her face against the glass and could just make out the brightly lit mouth of the subway entrance, twelve stories down and three blocks away.

She turned back to the room and picked up their tiny electric candle, then opened the door to what had been their parents' bedroom as quietly as she could. Maurice lay curled around his stuffed pig. Barely pink and barely furry, it was Maurice's one precious comfort; his link to a time when Father took them to the roof to stare at the stars through the telescope. That was before Father got sick. Before his skin rashes kept him in bed. Before he could barely speak because of the cough.

Ida crawled into bed with her little brother, and he snuggled close. They had no other family left. The few friends they had made in the building over the years had migrated, usually disappearing with no word as to their destination.

Tomorrow it was their turn.

....

The next morning, Ida and Maurice ate the last of the food and packed their one bag. Two ragged toothbrushes. What remained of their clothing. A dozen mini-drives she hoped they might find a way to read someday, containing photos and family documents. Father's telescope. The radio and the electric candle.

Putting on their air-skins was always a struggle. They were a snug fit. The opaque surface of Ida's was glossy and decorated with multicolored swirls like marbled paint. It covered her body, leaving only her face and hands bare until those were hidden by matching gloves and her air-mask. She pulled on a long navy skirt and black tunic before turning to help Maurice with his air-skin. His was covered in vertical blue stripes in shades from indigo to aquamarine.

"Ida, it's too tight." Maurice tried to twist away from her as she pulled it onto his shoulders. "It hurts." He danced from foot to foot, his eyes welling up.

"I know." Ida ran her hands down the sides of the skin, smoothing it and trying to stretch it, "but we can't go outside without it."

"Where are we even going?" Maurice whined then added, "Pig wants to know."

"Tell Pig, we are going to the West Dome. They have space." Ida touched Maurice's face, his skin soft and unscarred against her palm. "And you and I can pass any health check they want to put us through." Maurice didn't look convinced, but he let her tuck his ash-blond curls under the hood and fit his mask over his face. He helped her pull on his loose pale blue tunic and trousers. Father had always admired the sunny domes that sprang up on the outskirts of their city. The only way in was through the old subway system, taken over and maintained by the groups who colonized the train cars and inhabited the stations. The Dome immigration checkpoints were very strict; Father could never have passed the health checks.

Ida stood in the doorway, trying to memorize the stark space until Maurice's wiggly gloved fingers pulled her toward the stairwell.

Inside the underground station entry, Ida and Maurice waited for the air to finish cycling. The scrubbed air from the whirring fans pushed against Ida's air-skin, giving her goose bumps. Maurice laughed, the sound muffled by his mask, as a gust almost pushed him off his feet. Abruptly, the fans shut off, leaving an echoing silence. Maurice yanked Ida forward before the doors even began to move.

As they passed beyond the airlock door sensors, the glass panels slid shut behind them. With a whoosh and a pop, the seal re-established. Just inside the station, two guards stood still and aloof. One man and one woman – both tall, their hair short and clipped, their skin pale. The uniforms looked hot and itchy, grey jumpsuits the color of a thundercloud made of some rough looking fabric.

Ida walked slowly, her fierce grip on Maurice's small hand forcing him to match her pace. She felt the eyes of the guards on them as they walked, two children in the station alone.

When they reached the entry-level atrium, Ida paused near a bench and pulled off her mask. She relished the cool slightly sweet air. It was a relief to breathe the well-filtered air in a wide-open space.

Maurice tugged at his mask. It caught on the air-skin hood, made bumpy by his curly hair underneath. Before she could stop him, he pulled hard and the mask popped off, ripping a hole in the hood of the air-skin and breaking the mask's buckle at the same time. Ida couldn't hold back her gasp of dismay.

"Sorry, Ida." Maurice mumbled. He stood very still, holding his mask in one hand, Pig in the other.

Ida swallowed a sigh of frustration. "Don't worry about it,

Maurice." She helped him pull the hood down, tousling his curls as they sprang free. "Where we're going, we don't need air-masks anymore."

"We don't?"

"Nope. The air inside the dome is clean."

Maurice smiled as Ida pushed back her own hood. She tucked their masks and gloves into the backpack. She unfastened her hair, letting the long dark curls hang free down her back. Rubbing her scalp with her fingers, she watched Maurice, now scrambling up on a bench. Ida pulled her clothing straight. The blouse had been her mother's. It was much too big, hanging loose on her small frame. She would probably never be as tall as Mother had been. Father had always told her she took after his mother, small-framed and under five feet in height.

"I'm taller than you."

"Get down, Maurice."

"I'm hungry," he grumbled, as he scrambled off the bench.

Father had taken them here to see acrobats soar through the air and flip across the red-tiled floor. Today, the adults bustling through were not there for a performance, and the tall woman high up on the ladder they passed was not an acrobat. Dressed in station grey, her short-cropped hair was fiery red, and she wore a tool belt slung across her hips.

Ida and Maurice hurried down the steps to the lower level, urged on by the shrieking brakes of an oncoming train. Finally on the platform, Ida felt the press of air ahead of the train against the backs of her legs, making the thin fabric of her long skirt shift back and forth like water against her air-skin. Maurice stopped, pulling on her arm and turning to put his face into the breeze.

Near a tall concrete column, Ida and Maurice stepped out of the stream of people. The train was barreling into the station, painted with the bold red flowers and fresh vegetables of the Harvest Crew. Most importantly, this train was headed the right direction – end of the line, the West City Dome.

The car that stopped directly in front of her was well lit. Bright flowers filled all the windows on display. When the door opened, frosty cool air billowed out, blowing Ida's hair away from her face and filling the air with the scents of lilacs and lilies. People jostled in and out of the cars. The train pulled forward every few minutes, the tunnel swallowing up the lead car at one end and revealing a new car at the rear.

Ida began to run toward the end of the platform.

"Are we getting flowers?" Maurice called from behind her, tugging back on her arm as his legs couldn't keep pace.

"Flowers? No." Ida looked over her shoulder and slowed down a little. "We need the passenger car."

As they reached the mouth of the tunnel, a car emerged with no food or flowers. It had a few rows of seats, mostly full, and an official man seated behind a battered counter. Ida hurried Maurice through the door.

"Two tickets to West City Dome please." Ida felt a little dizzy and out of breath. She was hungry and exhausted, but they could rest once they had their tickets.

"What can you offer, young lady?" The man looked over the counter at Maurice. "We don't give discounts for children."

Ida pulled off her pack and proudly dug out the hand-crank radio. "The batteries don't hold a charge, but the radio works if you keep the crank turning."

"What do we need a radio for? No radio reception down here."

"Oh." Ida's heart raced and her face flushed with embarrassment. She should have thought of that. The train lurched forward for a few moments before stopping again.

"Anything else?"

She pulled out Father's telescope, watching Maurice's eyes grow wide as she placed it on the counter.

"What is it?" The man picked it up and turned it over.

"It is a compact telescope, for looking at stars."

"Do you see any sky here, young lady?" The man set it on the counter and pushed it back towards Ida. "How about your air-skins?"

"Our air-skins?" Ida was tempted to just say yes, but until they made it through the West Dome immigration point she couldn't risk it. "I'm sorry, we can't."

"Well, we generally look for seeds or tools for working our greenhouses. Anything like that?"

Ida shook her head. "No, sir."

"Find something we want, and we'll be happy to take you out to the dome. Good day to you." He turned toward the adults who had lined up behind her.

"Good day." Ida mumbled. She shoved everything back in their bag and led Maurice off the train just as it stopped shifting forward again. Ida set their pack down and sat on the hexagonal tiles a few feet from the platform's edge, pulling Maurice into her lap. Ida rested her chin on Maurice's head, his curls tickling her nose. She cried silently, breathing evenly to keep Maurice from noticing.

How was she going to get them to West City Dome before the two spots they needed were already claimed?

She watched children race along the platform before they jumped back onto the train. They seemed happy and had the energy to run. Their clothing was mismatched but seemed tidy. There were enough children on that train that she and Maurice might blend in.

Ida got them up and walked Maurice back down to the end of the platform. She spotted a likely car, one with dark windows, maybe meant for storage? The car in front of it was bright and busy. Yanking Maurice in behind her, shivering a bit at the cold air within the refrigerated car, Ida walked confidently towards the door at the far end. They walked between overflowing displays of fresh corn. Just being near them made Ida feel even hungrier. The handle at the far end was covered in a thin film of frost. Her fingers chilled as she grabbed it and tried to pull it sideways.

It didn't budge. She tried again, pushing down with all her weight. Still it didn't move. Suddenly, one of the Harvest Crew was shouting. Ida had just enough time to get them back off the train before the crewman reached them. He leaned out of the car, eyes on them until just before his car was swallowed up by the tunnel.

Only a few moments later, the dairy train pulled onto the other side of the platform, covered with portraits of cows large and small. Ida was so hungry she could barely think. She put her arm around Maurice.

"What color cheese do you want?"

"Cheese?" Maurice's blue eyes lit up, "Orange!" he replied without hesitation. His answer never changed, but Ida always asked. "Do we have enough?"

"I'm not sure." Ida replied honestly. "I have some clothes that should get us something. You pick the car!"

This time, Maurice pulled Ida down the platform, evaluating the cars and finding each lacking. Finally, he stopped solemnly in front of a dim car whose overhead lights cast only a hint of warm glow on the space within.

Inside, the pungent smell of cheese enveloped them. A wide cold case featured blocks in every shade of beige, yellow and orange.

"Which one do you want?"

"That one!" Maurice pointed through the glass at the biggest orange-colored cheese. The man accepted one of Ida's last shirts in exchange for a nice large chunk.

They sat with their cheese on a concrete bench. Ida broke it into small chunks on the unfolded waxed paper. Then she scooped about a third of the chunks into her hand and left the rest for Maurice.

"Eat them slow," Ida whispered before she slipped the first chunk into her mouth. She hummed in pleasure. The flavor was so strong and bright. She hadn't had any food since they ate the last of their rice that morning.

The crowds on the platform were thinning out for the day. They wouldn't let them spend the night on this bench.

"Maurice, turn around." Maurice turned without protest, still focused on licking his fingers. Ida pulled at his air-skin hood. The tear was definitely going to let in enough air to burn his exposed scalp, but she had no way to fix it. Maybe his hair would cover it enough that the West Dome exam wouldn't catch it? "Let's go back to the apartment Maurice. We'll find a train tomorrow." They could only trade away clothing for food for so long, but for now she saw no other options.

"What about my hood?" He trusted her.

"It'll be fine," she lied, "It's a short walk. I'll cover it with my hand. You'll have to hold the mask on, okay?" He nodded, standing up and holding out his hands for his gloves.

As they reached the stationmaster's kiosk on the same level as the air lock, a loud shrill blaring broke the general quiet of the station. Three sharp alarm blasts were followed by a short silence, then three more sharp blasts. A set of flashing amber lights came on all along the ceiling.

"What's it mean, Ida?" Maurice shouted, his hands covering his ears.

"Air seal leak." Ida shouted back. Ida pulled out her brother's mask. "Hold this on." Ida wrenched her own mask in place and was wrestling to get her hair tucked back into her hood as a group of station guards convened at the kiosk.

"So fix the seal!" The stationmaster growled over his shoulder, stomping out of the kiosk door a few feet from them. He was a heavyset man, his hair white and his skin dark brown. Ida had never seen him leave the kiosk.

"If I could get in there I would," replied the same red-haired tall woman Ida had seen up the ladder in the atrium, stepping out right behind him. "The alarms show a leak inside a duct. None of us will fit. Even then, we probably can't suit up fast enough and get in there before the air balance tips. The front entry air chamber already can't be used until we fix it."

"So, evacuation isn't an option? Give me some other choice. What about your robot? I thought this was what it was for!"

"In the tunnels. Under the tracks. Not for up ladders and down ducts."

The stationmaster threw up his hands and turned to stalk back past Ida and Maurice.

Before she lost her nerve, Ida stepped in his path. "I'm small."

He looked down at Ida, then back at the engineer. "What about this kid? Would she fit?"

"Sure," the engineer admitted, "She would fit, but then what?"

"I'm sure I could do it." Ida volunteered. "And I have my full air-skin on already."

The engineer stepped around the stationmaster to look Ida up and down.

"You can tell her over the radio what to do." The stationmaster decided. "Let's get her in there. We can't wait any longer, or we're going to have to beg trains to come in for a full evac. It'll take all night to clean the air. No train is going to want to stop here while our alarms are coded like this." He stalked away to talk to the group of security guards, calling back over his shoulder. "Just fix it. I'll send someone back with the smallest mask with a radio we can find." He turned away from them yelling, "Someone turn off the siren." A few moments later, the alarm fell silent, but the amber lights still flashed.

"What about my brother?" Ida gestured to Maurice huddled by the base of the kiosk and holding his mask in place. His hood still flopped on his back, his ash blond curls wild on his head. Ida stepped closer to the woman, speaking under her breath so Maurice wouldn't hear and get even more scared. "His hood has a tear."

"Then I guess we better work fast. As long as the warning lights don't shift to red, he'll be fine." Up close, the engineer was even taller than Ida had realized. "I'm Rayna." She offered Ida her hand. "What's your name?"

"Ida." She shook Rayna's hand.

Rayna spotted her necklace, pulling her own out of the neck of her uniform. Hers also had two disks.

"You two on your own?" she jingled her necklace and gestured with her chin at Ida's.

"Yes. Mom three years ago. Dad last month." Ida looked back at Maurice who started at her with his big blue eyes wide with fear. "We're alone."

When Ida looked back at her, Rayna was watching Maurice.

"Not now you aren't." She shook her head and turned back to Ida. "We need you. I am going to give you the world's fastest lesson on how to use this air-seal tool." She pulled a strange cylinder from her equipment belt. It looked like a cross between a flashlight and a small hand drill. "Then you need to go up the ladder and into that duct."

Ida stared up at where Rayna was pointing. Could she back out of this? Maurice would be alone. What if she couldn't do it? What if she fell?

"The biggest challenge to fixing a breach like this," Rayna's voice pulled her attention back, "is the flexibility of the material. You need to fuse the edges of the tear or patch it if the tear is too big. Everything must be tight, no gaps."

Ida nodded.

"The tool works through a combination of heat and chemical reaction. You have to keep it away from your own air-skin or it will make a new hole where you don't want one." Rayna looked back at Maurice. "Get his hood up. It will still help some. One of the staff can keep an eye on him."

Ida helped Maurice with his hood and told him she would be back soon. A woman sat with Maurice, whispering something that made him smile, still clutching his mask to his face as he held Pig close.

Ida practiced on some air-skin scraps, Rayna hovering over her shoulder giving tips. It was harder than it looked. The sealer felt strange and awkward in her hand, but by the time the radio-mask appeared, Ida felt like she was getting the hang of it.

Rayna had Ida take off her loose clothing, leaving her standing exposed in just the tight protective skin. Rayna dumped everything out of her equipment belt and onto the floor with a huge clatter. She wrapped the belt around Ida's slim hips, showing her how to stash the tool and the patches.

Ida swapped her mask for the new one. The air in this mask was crisper than in her mask. Maybe drier? She let her thoughts on the texture of the air distract her as they moved to the bottom of the ladder. Rayna held it steady as Ida climbed. Ida heard a train rush through the station without stopping, felt the metal vibrate as it passed somewhere far below.

Ida didn't look down, just up at the next step on the ladder. The new mask had a headlamp that lit her way as she clambered over the ledge and crawled into the narrow dark channel. It quickly got too small to crawl, forcing her to lie flat and pull herself forward with her elbows. Around the first tight turn, the equipment belt got hooked on something. She had to shimmy backwards and roll over to get herself free, before rolling back onto her belly to continue inching forward.

She almost fell over the edge at the far end of the shaft, surprised by the empty space suddenly gaping ahead. Her gasp had Rayna calling through the radio.

"Ida?"

"I found the end of the duct."

"There will be a ladder leading down from that end too."

"I've got it." Ida found the first rung with her right hand. "Wait. How am I going to turn around?" There was a long pause. Ida stared at the ladder leading down into murky shadows. The headlamp made little impact on the inky blackness. No way she was going down head first. "Should I come back and go in feet first?"

"No." Rayna finally replied. "No. I have an idea. Can you lie on your back and reach up? There should be a ladder leading up, too. You can grab a rung above and pull yourself up enough to get your feet on the ladder going down."

Ida turned over and looked up. The bottom step of another ladder glinted in the beam of her headlamp, leading upwards into more darkness.

"Yes. I see it. Let me try." She rested her head against the bottom of the tunnel and reached. It was too far away. Ida carefully shifted further forward until her head was no longer supported. She reached up and her hand came close, but not close enough to wrap her fingers around the rung. "I still can't reach. How did anyone ever do this?"

"They didn't," Rayna replied. "Before the underground was sealed, there were easier ways to get to that section from the outside.

They were never meant to be accessed from inside the station."

"Couldn't I go through the old doors from outside? I have my air-skin." Ida tipped her head back, letting her headlamp rove the far reaches of the cavernous space. She would have had better luck with her father's telescope.

"No." Rayna sighed. "Great idea, only that would contaminate the whole station."

"Oh."

"Can you brace your legs and push out further?"

"Umm..." Ida experimented with her legs, trying to figure out a way to keep herself from sliding all the way out of the duct and into the gloom below. "Maybe?"

"Keep trying," she said in a whisper.

She rolled back onto her stomach to look down the ladder. She could grab the first rung and flip herself over, but she could picture all too easily her back smacking against the ladder, her grip slipping, and falling who knew how far down. She rolled onto her back once more, this time finding some indentations into which she wedged her feet on the sides of the duct.

And then, without thinking about all the ways it could go wrong, Ida pushed herself back and over the edge until her entire torso was out over the emptiness. She quickly sat up and reached as far as she could.

She caught the lowest rung above her with her left hand. For a moment Ida just hung there, breathing. Finally she pulled herself up high enough to grab on with her right hand as well and pulled her legs out of the duct to put them on the rung below.

"Okay. I'm on the ladder."

"What?" Rayna barked with a laugh. "How?"

"If I live through this," Ida laughed back, "I promise I'll explain. Now what?"

"Down the ladder, across the bottom of the air shaft and then back up the ladder to the right."

Before Rayna even finished, Ida was moving down the ladder, looking down to shine the headlamp at her feet. She had to jump down to the floor at the bottom. Across the open space she found the ladder on the opposite side easily enough.

"Rayna, the ladder is too high; I can't reach." Ida waited. "Rayna?" The radio remained silent. She pointed her headlamp carefully at the floor around her. The space stretched far beyond the beam of light. Ida tried not to think about getting stuck down here with no food or water as everyone else was forced to evacuate the station. She couldn't think about Maurice alone, angry red burns branching down from his hairline and across his forehead.

Ida put her hand on the wall and began to walk along the edge of the space. She almost tripped on something. It was a broken wooden crate that looked like it had been dropped down the shaft.

It was huge and heavy and awkward as she dragged it into place. Finally, she was able to clamber up its side and get onto the ladder.

Halfway to the top, Ida finally heard Rayna's voice again.

"Ida?" Rayna sounded panicked.

"I'm here." Ida replied, out of breath from the climb.

"Are you okay?"

"Yes. The bottom of the ladder was too high. I had to find something to climb on." She paused to catch her breath. "Where am I going?"

"At the top of the ladder near the ceiling, you should find a small door." Rayna's voice hitched, like maybe she had been crying. "Given the distribution of air degradation reported from this shaft's sensors, the breach has to be in there somewhere."

Getting the door unlatched was easy. Leaning back far enough to pull it open was hard. Then she was half inside a weird little box and looking for the breach.

It was obvious once she saw it. The panel covering one of the air exchanges with the outside was damaged. The left edge had torn free, the translucent material flapping as air rushed in.

Ida pulled out the tool. It felt cold and heavy in her hand. She had a moment of panic that she would fumble and the tool would fall all the way back to the floor far below, but then she got it turned around and pointed in the right direction.

"Remember, let each inch of re-fused material set for at least ninety seconds. That way it won't pull out as you go."

"Okay." Ida fused the first inch. "Can you keep time for me? I just finished the first inch."

"Started."

She took a breath, and after a few beats of silence, "Orion. Cassiopeia. Pegasus."

"Ida?"

"Sorry. My father and I used to look at constellations together on the roof of our building. He taught me to name as many as I can remember when I needed to stay calm."

"I haven't seen the stars in a long time."

"It was the only time I liked putting on my air-skin." Ida closed her eyes, remembering. "As more city lights went out, we just could see more and more stars."

"It sounds beautiful."

"It was." Ida squeezed her eyes, trying to hold the tears in. "It still is."

"Time's up. You can do the next inch."

"Thanks," she choked out, opening her eyes to a blur of tears. They trailed down her cheeks where she couldn't reach to wipe them away. They were salty and warm when they reached her tongue. She blinked her eyes clear and fused the next inch. "Restart timer please. Ursa Minor. Ursa Major. Draco. Cygnus..."

When she finished the last inch, the air pressure dropped and Ida slumped against the side of the chamber. She closed her eyes.

"It's done," she whispered.

"Good job!" Rayna's cheerful voice was followed by a flood of shouts. They hurt her ears, but she didn't care. She did it. She hadn't died. Maurice was safe, and the station was fixed. Her father would have been so proud.

Getting back out was easier once she wrangled the broken box across the floor to the first ladder. She took the opportunity at the end of the duct to show Rayna how she had gotten onto the ladder at the other end.

Down on the floor, Rayna pulled her into a quick hug. Then she took her by the shoulders and looked her in the eyes.

"Well done." She had a huge grin on her face.

"Looks like you might have found someone to train," said a voice over the radio; Ida thought it might have been the stationmaster.

"We are planning to relocate," Ida confessed, "if we can just find a train that will take us out to the West City Dome."

"I see." Rayna was interrupted by a long low tone broadcast over the speakers. The amber warning lights went out. She looked up. "That's the all clear. you don't need this anymore." She reached over, pulled off Ida's mask and handed it back to her.

"Ida!" The next thing Ida knew, Maurice was throwing himself into her arms, and she was kissing his smiling face.

After Maurice and Pig peppered Ida with questions about her adventure for a few minutes, Rayna interrupted, a serious tone in her voice. "I understand you have your eyes on the West City Dome, but I would like to propose something different."

"Okay." Ida moved to stand beside Maurice, watching Rayna's face as she held him close.

"I need an assistant. I can pay you with a combination of station scrip and food."

"I'm hungry." Maurice volunteered. Rayna and Ida both laughed.

"Someone bring this young man a sandwich." Rayna called out, to a chorus of more laughter. "Scrip will work at any station and on most trains. If you want to move on in a few months, won't be anything I can do to stop you."

"I understand." Ida nodded. An adult in station gray brought Maurice a sandwich. As he devoured it, Ida swore she could see him grow. "But Maurice needs a new air-skin. We barely got this on him this morning, even before the hood got torn."

"We can take care of that." Rayna waited patiently.

"Maurice?" Ida asked, watching him eat. "Should we stay?"

"This sandwich is good," he replied around a mouthful of food. "Pig likes it here."

"In that case," Ida turned back to Rayna, "our answer is yes."

"One final condition," replied Rayna. "You owe me some star gazing."

"Good thing we kept the telescope."

Someone handed Ida a sandwich. It tasted amazing.

The Doom of Wonder Bread

Sonja Thomas

Sonja Thomas, a recovering CPA, writes for children of all ages, from humorous middle grade to young adult fantasy to adult horror. Raised in Central Florida (the wonderful world of Disney, humidity and hurricanes) and transplanted to DC for eleven years (go Nats!), she's now 'keeping it weird' in Portland, OR. To stay sane she dances, doodles and plays with furry, four-legged friends. You may even hear her belt out an awesome Xena yodel. Visit her at www. bysonjathomas.com or follow her on twitter @bysonjathomas.

As it did every morning, Mom's wide backside bounced in rhythm to the "*Uh-oh, uh-oh, uh-oh, oh-no-no*" thumping in the kitchen. The R&B bootylicious beat, passed down from her great-great-grandmother, was the secret ingredient to drool-worthy chick'n and waffles. That and kimchi—way premium than tired old hot sauce.

Luna poured a thick stream of sans-maple syrup into each mock-waffle square, careful not to let any overflow onto her plate and contaminate her chick'n. Her lip curled at her older brother, Sting, drowning his waffle-chick'n tower in synthetic syrup.

Technically, everything on his plate was fake, so comingling food groups shouldn't matter. Chickens, along with all livestock, went extinct eons ago. With all the droughts and ozone pollution, flour had been artificially produced for even longer. Thank greatness for genetically faux foods. Without GFOs, mankind would have been fossil dust like the dinosaurs.

"Heard on the news about another dreamscape case," Mom

said, pouring coffee into Dad's cup.

Dad snorted. "Reliving the same day over and over and over? That mess isn't real."

Luna nodded in agreement. Her best friend Ashley constantly droned on about the supposed do-over opportunities. And Luna always tuned Ashley out. She had as much confidence in dreamscapes as she did Nessie the Loch Ness Monster and Bigfoot.

"My bio teacher says the brain is able to do much more than we think," Sting said.

"For those of us that have a brain." Luna snickered. Sting pulled Luna's face towards his by her afro puffs, dropped open his jaw and exposed chewed-up waffle and chick'n guts.

"Ewww!" Luna jerked her head free.

"Enough." Mom's tone shut down Sting's mush-mouth display. Luna grinned, fluffing her fros back to health.

Mom settled into the chair next to Dad, her crossed leg bouncing. "Real or not," she continued, "something's going on. This is the third person in Florida that's slipped into a coma for no reason. Man, woman, black, white…don't matter. On the up, it sure would be jazz to revise history."

"I would so reverse global warming extinction," Sting said. "Always wondered what real chicken tasted like."

"Like chick'n." Luna shrugged.

Dad shook his head. "There's no such thing as second chances. What's—

"Done is done," Luna finished.

"Exactly." Dad nodded. Luna beamed.

"Suck up," Sting hissed under his breath.

Resisting the urge to flab jab her brother with her fork, Luna instead dug into the backpack resting at her feet and pulled out a wrinkled sheet of paper.

"Guess what, Dad." She slapped the paper on the table top, her finger tapping the A+. "I ripped my algebra exam."

Sting rolled his eyes.

"Looks like we have two math whizzes in the family," Mom

said. Luna puffed out her chest, glancing at her father.

He offered her a half smile and clamped a hand on Sting's shoulder. "Ready for the big game this weekend, champ?"

Luna deflated in her chair. Why did everything revolve around Sting?

Sure, he was good at throwing a prolate spheroid shaped ball and could burp half the alphabet without taking a breath, but Sting didn't give two ribbits about anything besides himself. Luna had been spending one weekend a month for a year removing litter along the new Atlantic Coast twenty minutes from their Maitland home. Sting only volunteered because it was a graduation requirement. Luna couldn't help that she sucked at sports. Curse her stupid horrendous eye-hand coordination.

A shrill "cuc-koo, cuc-koo" blasted overhead from Mom's archaic heirloom clock, announcing that it was 6:30. Luna watched the tiny mechanical bird bounce with each call, but on the last note, instead of retreating back inside its wooden home carved with oversized leaves and squirrels, the cuckoo made a weird popping noise. Luna gasped. Everyone looked up. The bird dangled on the edge of its plank. It finally had enough.

Mom jumped from her chair—"No, no, no,"—and caressed the wooden bird.

Luna remained slumped, arms folded in stubborn self-pity. She never liked that stupid bird, chirping every half hour for as long as she could remember. There was no reason for Mom to freak. Like Dad always said, what's done was done.

....

At the ungreatly lunch hour of 10 a.m., Luna and Ashley weaved through the Maitland Middle School cafeteria and snagged an empty spot tucked between the jockoids and headbangers. "Can you believe the latest dreamscape happened in Orlando? That's like around the corner," Ashley gushed.

Luna's tray, piled high with chick'n fingers and faux-fries, clattered against the table. "Dreamscapes aren't real."

"Then explain all the weird comas."

Luna dunked a chick'n finger into BBQ sauce. "I can't." She shrugged. "But neither can you."

"Scientists found fifty similar cases throughout the country," Ashley said. "Every single one saying they had to live the same day over and over."

"They're all a bunch of looney tunes." Luna tore into the crispy nugget, sick of the same conversation.

"Every one? All of them perfect strangers."

"Yup."

"Then explain how all fifty said they woke up by changing the past."

"Nothing to explain." Luna licked the tangy sauce sliding down her thumb. "My dad says it's not real."

Ashley's cheeks blazed a deep red. "Your father's opinion is as wack as a Jackson 5 reunion on the Dead & Kicking hologram tour."

Luna chucked her half-chewed chick'n finger at Ashley. The BBQ smothered finger tumbled through the air. Unfortunately, her not-so-hot aim sent it sailing past Ashley and smacking Tony Perkins on his pimpled forehead.

Tony leapt to his feet, growling some not-so-nice words, and slung a fist full of fries in Luna's direction. She ducked and a second later heard someone behind her shriek. Next thing, the entire cafeteria exploded into a BBQ dripping, finger-licking food fight. Chairs skidded across the floor. Tables were flipped onto their sides for cover. Luna even witnessed one of the kitchen ladies toss a spoonful of mock potatoes into the crowd. Unfortunately, that juicy bit of intel couldn't save her with Principal Belcher.

"I've seen your face too many times this year, Miss Luna Rey," Mrs. Belcher said, her hands folded on top of a thick file on her otherwise spotless desktop. "There was the altercation last month with a fellow student about good hair."

"But natural is good," Luna whined.

"What about holding the science lab's frogs hostage when you found out they were going to be dissected."

"Do you really want to contribute to the torture and extinction of innocent amphibians?"

"I appreciate your passion," Mrs. Belcher said, "but your actions have consequences. Since warnings and detentions have no effect, how about three days suspension."

"But—

"Would you rather face charges of vandalism and disorderly conduct?"

Luna sank in her chair. Her father always said she had a bite like an African bullfrog when provoked. But that defense sure wasn't going to stop Mom from burning her backside a new shade of black.

....

Who would have thought that eight hours later Principal Belcher's suspension would be the least of her problems? Luna huddled with her mother and brother on wooden benches, front and center, in the Orange County Courthouse. Being prime time on a school night, Luna wasn't surprised they were the only ones seated in the gallery. What didn't make sense was why her father was facing an old white dude in a black robe. Her father had never been in trouble before. Not even a speeding ticket. All her mother had said on the ride over was that Dad needed their prayers and support.

"Do you have anything to say about the charges set forth against you today?" The judge's gruff voice echoed in the enormous hall decked out in marble floors, massive bronze doors and stained-glass domes.

Dad nodded hesitantly. "I, uh…"

"Speak up then," the judge said, waving his gavel. "I don't have all night."

"I admit, Your Honor, that I am guilty as charged. And although I'm not one to make excuses, after the day I've had, it kind of just…well…happened."

"Explain yourself."

Dad cleared his throat and, with a deep breath, confessed

everything. That for fifteen years he'd loyally served as second in command of everything money at the nonprofit Save Amphibians from Extinction, or SAFE. How after lunch he'd uncovered that someone was smuggling hundreds of thousands from the Macaya Breast-Spot Frog De-extinction Fund. And as he drove home, he'd dipped into his Wonder Bread stash—his oldest and most burdensome addiction—hoping for a moment of pause to make sense of it all. But things just kept getting worse: creeping traffic, his daughter's suspension, a busted A/C in ninety-degree weather. His stress elevated to a severe meltdown.

Luna shook her head, confused. If someone was stealing from SAFE, then why was her father the one facing the judge?

"Your Honor," Dad concluded, "my emotions got the best of me. I threw chunks of bread out my car window. I didn't even realize I was doing it until the cop pulled me over. It's like I was under some kind of spell."

Luna gasped, the reality of the situation sinking in.

The judge released a stern harrumph. "Mr. Rey, as an employee of SAFE, you should know better. Hasn't our planet suffered enough? Despite any alleged wrong doing at your place of work, I find your performance absolutely incomprehensible."

Luna whimpered as her mother's grip tightened around her limp shoulders.

"For that reason, I have no choice, but to serve you with the maximum penalty for defiling our Mother Earth. I sentence you, Mr. Charles Rey, to ten years at the Ocala Work Camp where you will sift through mounds of garbage every day for any recyclables our generation has tossed aside."

Ten years? Luna would be twenty-two and done with college. Luna's head throbbed harder than the time her brother had accidentally whacked it with his skateboard. Except for a high-pitched ringing in both ears, she was swallowed in silence.

Luna came to as Mom pulled her in tight, smothering her in sour apple perfume. Her eyes met with Dad's, hopelessness overshadowing his usually confident glow. She wanted to shout,

"Dirty bully!" and punch the crusty old judge in his wrinkled face. She wanted to save the day with a "Take me instead" or scream, "Don't leave me!" and hug her father one more time.

But before Luna could do anything, the bailiff led her dad out of the courtroom and out of her life.

....

The next morning, Luna dragged herself out of bed and down the dim hall. She'd barely slept, just tossing and turning, unable to breathe, the judge's crabby, old voice haunting her thoughts. *I, Mr. Honorable Crotchety Pants, sentence you, Mr. 'never did a bad thing in his life' Rey, to stinky garbage picking and a lifetime without your daughter.*

She inched her way to the kitchen and froze in the doorway. Her eyes widened. Sitting next to Sting, chowing down on chick'n and waffles was her father. Luna zipped over and tackled him with a hug.

"Morning to you too." Dad laughed.

"What are you doing here?" Luna cried. "The cops must be looking for you. We've got to get you out of here…get you somewhere safe."

Dad's forehead wrinkled. "Cops?"

Mom's apple-bottom stopped swinging to the "uh-oh" breakfast theme song as she turned from the stove. "What has gotten into you?"

Luna pulled away and eyed her father. He was clean shaven, dressed in his usual blue suit and paisley tie. Except for the baffled stare, he appeared as normal as any other morning. She looked from her mother to her brother and back to her father. "But we were all there in the courtroom last night when the judge sentenced you to forever at a work camp."

"For what?" Sting laughed. "Forgetting to carry the one at work?"

"Quit playing, Luna, and sit your behind down," Mom commanded. Luna did as she was told. Shaking her head, Mom poured coffee into Dad's cup. "Heard on the news about another dreamscape case."

Dad snorted. "Reliving the same day over and over and over? That mess isn't real."

The hair on Luna's arms stood at attention.

"My bio teacher says the brain is able to do much more than we think," Sting said.

Luna sucked in her breath.

"Real or not," Mom continued, "something's going on…"

Luna squeezed her hands into fists, digging her nails into her palms. Maybe the pain would wake her up from this…this…déjà vu nightmare.

As Dad moved the conversation to Sting and his upcoming game, the mechanical bird burst from its cuckoo heirloom home. Luna's stomach somersaulted with each shrill "cuc-koo." She watched as the tiny bird made its final popping sound and, for the second time, dangled over the edge.

Mom jumped from her chair, just like yesterday, to coddle the dead bird.

Luna hugged her belly. "I'm stuck in a dreamscape."

"What, Luna-tic?" Sting cocked his brow.

Mom and Dad stared at Luna as if they were contemplating whether or not to commit her to a juvie ward for the mischievous and deranged.

"Enough with the nonsense, Luna Del Ray," Mom snapped.

Luna picked at her breakfast. She wanted to crawl back under the covers and start over again, tomorrow. *Start over again.* Luna sat up. If dreamscapes were real, then maybe the other stuff was true too. She could change history. She could save her father.

Since littering was what got them into this funk, the solution must be to keep her father from tossing bread out the car window. Luna considered her options.

She knew her dad turned to popping slices whenever stressed out. If she made sure he never uncovered the fraud at SAFE in the first place, ergo no stressor. Luna shoved a forkful of syrup-soaked waffle in her mouth. Short of a natural disaster, Luna's father would not even slightly consider missing work. The last time he'd taken a personal day was over three years ago. Luna's chewing grinded to a halt. Even if she could convince her father to stay home for just one day, what if he uncovered the fraud all over again tomorrow?

Luna ripped off chunks from her crispy chick'n. What if she could figure out who was stealing at SAFE and turn in the perpetrator? If her father got ten years for littering, imagine what the judge would serve up for embezzlement. She squished the torn chick'n bits between her fingers. No, that wouldn't work. Although Luna had an ego only a few shades lighter than Sherlock Holmes, she wasn't into playing detective. Plus she refused to smush her afro puffs under some ridiculous hat like the pipe-toting sleuth.

Luna's final option was to keep the loaf out of her father's reach at all costs. She knew keeping bread from her dad when he's stressed would be hard, but thank greatness her father was only half right. What's done was done, except maybe, just maybe, this day could be fixed. And Luna would wake up for real tomorrow.

....

After fibbing to her mom that she was headed to the park with Ashley, Luna hiked a mile after school to catch the 4:15 bus and rode for over an hour to beat Dad to his car. With every ticking second, her nerves tangled into knots. Luna paced by his Mercedes Biome, her heavy steps echoing through the parking garage.

Within minutes, her dad approached. "What are you doing here?"

Luna flashed a nervous grin. "We…um…learned about the awful side effects of, uh, diabetes today," she flubbed, "like how Ashley's uncle had his foot chopped off. And our teacher said that too much sugar is a huge factor in causing the disease. And with your bread addiction and all I…" Luna's speech drifted into silence under Dad's narrowed eyes.

Without a word, they climbed into the car, and Dad rolled down the windows. Luna countered with, "My hair," and the windows rolled back up. Grumbling, Dad drove out of the garage.

"Dad?"

"Not another word until we get home."

Luna relaxed her jagged breath. She could handle this. Just thirty minutes, and then this rewind-and-repeat would all be over.

Dad hit a triangular-shaped button on the center console. *You have two voicemail messages*, a monotonous female voice spat. *First message…*

"This is Gladys, SAFE's CEO executive assistant, again—

Dad smashed the button. *Next message*, the computer announced.

"Mr. Rey, SAFE's board chair here."

Dad's hands tightened around the steering wheel.

"In addition to my earlier requests, please send over—

Dad opened his window and swallowed in the fresh, humid air.

"Is everything okay?" Luna asked.

He nodded, his face pale. "Just work stuff."

His fingers tapped repeatedly as traffic slowed, his eyes lingering on the glove box. Luna held her breath. Dad's gaze bounced between the rear-view mirror and his window. He jumped the car into the middle lane. The car picked up speed at a sparrow's pace.

Luna fiddled with the radio. Maybe some soft jazz would ease his mind.

Rush hour slow jams, brought to you by wheat-slims. The synthetic low-cal carb substitute. It's yummerrific!

Dad dove for the glove box.

"Dad!" Luna snatched away the half-eaten loaf.

"Luna Del Rey, give it to me. Right. Now." Dad lunged, grabbing at the red, yellow and blue balloon logo. The silver Biome swerved.

"No. It's a matter of life without your daughter."

He managed to grasp at a corner of plastic wrapping, and the two indulged in a hostile game of tug-o-war.

"Let go, Luna."

"No way."

Luna pulled. Dad dipped forward. The car jerked. Dad tugged back. Luna tightened her grip. And yanked. A neighboring car honked. The loaf slipped from Dad's fingertips. The plastic ripped. Bread flew—slices on the floor, Luna's lap, and the windshield. The Biome barrelled, headed for a stopped car. Luna shrieked. Brakes squealed, burning rubber.

The car stopped in time. Luna exhaled.

"Dad, are you—

BOOM. Luna's head lurched forward. Someone smacked the Biome's bumper. Thank greatness, no one was hurt. Dings, dents and Dad's jacked up stress was not the outcome Luna had planned, but she'd changed the past. She had stopped Dad from littering.

. . . .

Luna and Ashley snaked through the school cafeteria, Luna huffing in disgust. Turns out, she hadn't done what she was supposed to, whatever that was. She was stuck eating the same food, listening to the same "blah-blah-blah" and watching Mom's cuckoo walk the plank all over again. Wonder Bread, one. Luna, zero.

They snagged an empty spot between the jockoids and headbangers. "Can you believe the latest dreamscape happened in Orlando? That's like around the corner," Ashley gushed.

For once, Luna looked at her friend with interest.

"How do they know it's a dreamscape?" She asked. "I mean, what makes all these cases the same?"

Ashley's honey-mustard-covered chick'n finger froze inches from her open mouth.

"What's the sudden interest?"

Luna shrugged. Maybe if she understood all there was to know about dreamscapes, she could figure a way out of this mess.

"Since you're asking," Ashley leaned in, "they share three things in common. First, someone slips into a coma for no reason. One day they're fine, the next they don't wake up. They relive their last waking day, over and over, until finally, the coma ends within three days."

"Three days?" Luna popped a fry in her mouth. She could ride that out, no problem.

"After making a significant change." Ashley nodded. "But

scientists believe there are some people who *never* wake up."

Luna's fry caught in her throat.

"They think it's because the coma person didn't change the right moment within three days."

A three-day limit? The right moment?

Luna's jaw clenched. What if she never woke up? Trapped in the same day…*forever*. Keeping bread from her father's grip hadn't worked. Maybe stopping him from discovering the fraud would be significant enough. She had two chances left to get it right. Otherwise, this dreamscape would become her only waking nightmare.

....

Luna slipped out of school after lunch, quickly gathered supplies from the corner store, and trekked the long mile to the city bus stop. Clutching her overstuffed backpack, her pits swelled in sweat as the bus wormed through heavy traffic.

Sixty minutes later, she paced in front of the SunTrust Center in downtown Orlando, the beige and green skyscraper her father worked in. She ran her plan through her head, hoping she'd devised a fail-proof strategy to make sure her father never uncovered fraud at SAFE. Not today, tomorrow or ever.

A security guard with a handlebar mustache swaggered in Luna's direction. "What's your business here, Miss?"

"Excuse me?" Luna challenged, hands on hips.

He leaned in close. Luna cringed under his sardine-coffee breath. "If you got no reason to be here, then roll out."

"My *dad* works here. He's the finance director at SAFE." Luna thumbed at the building. "Just waiting to meet him for lunch."

The wanna-be law enforcer cocked a brow. "Shouldn't you be in school, quarter pint?"

"Teacher in-service day." She shifted her heavy backpack.

He fingered a walkie-talkie clipped at his hip, his narrowed eyes flickering with distrust. Near the building's entrance, wheels swooshed on the sidewalk, followed by a loud crash. The guard rushed off, his sights on a gang of skaters.

Luna glanced at her watch. 12:40. In approximately five minutes, her father would dine on a pseudo-turkey sandwich and faux-fries. He'd made a foofaraw over this fact during 'take your daughter to work day' two years ago.

At exactly 12:45, her father strolled from the building. Luna hunkered down behind yellowish-brown hedges. As soon as he turned the corner, Luna dashed past the nosy security guard harassing the skateboard-clutching teens.

"Oh my greatness, look at you Miss Luna," Mrs. Oakly exclaimed when Luna arrived at the front desk on the seventh floor. "You've shot up like a tree frog over the last two years."

Mrs. Oakly had grown too. She now resembled a hippo—in both size and color—wearing a platinum blond wig and swimming in a garlic scent. Luna decided not to mention this.

"Unfortunately," Mrs. Oakly said, "you just missed your dad. You know, 12:45 lunch." She tapped her naked wrist. "He didn't mention you were blessing us with your presence today."

"It's a surprise. I can just wait in his office."

Mrs. Oakly ushered Luna into a 10x10 room, stuffed with a metal desk, three chairs, a four-drawer file cabinet and credenza. She waved for Luna to sit at one of the stiff chairs facing her father's desk. "Mr. Rey was just praising you and your gifted math skills. Something about an A+." She winked.

"Really?"

"Oh yes. He never stops bragging about you. He always says he never has to worry about his baby Luna. So smart and dependable and trustworthy. Sting, on the other hand…" Mrs. Oakly shook her head, clicking her tongue.

Whoa. Her dad had more faith in her than Sting. Luna squirmed in her chair as thoughts about what she was about to do nagged on her nerves.

"Alright, Miss Luna, I'll leave you be."

As soon as Mrs. Oakly closed the door, Luna got to work.

She pulled out two gallon jugs, a hooded raincoat, and a lighter from her backpack. She opened each drawer in the file cabinet, credenza and desk, drowning its contents with water. With hesitation, Luna held the second jug over her dad's computer. Knowing now that her father trusted her, it tore her insides to think how disappointed he'd be at her for trashing his office. Even if meant saving him from ten years of garbage picking.

But Luna had to get out of this time warp. She'd go cuckoo if she had to endure this same day yet again. And this plan would only work if she destroyed everything.

Luna shut her eyes and emptied the jug. The laptop sizzled and popped in protest. She stuffed the empty jugs back in her bag and glanced at the wall clock. 1:05. Plenty of time to wrap this up and leave the scene.

Luna slipped on the raincoat and slowly climbed onto her father's swivel chair, arms outstretched to steady herself, and then carefully placed one foot, followed by the other, onto the desk. After pulling the hood tight over her precious afro puffs, she held the lighter underneath the fire sprinkler and flicked the spark wheel to ignite the flame.

The four-inch blaze rippled and snaked for what felt like forever. Finally, the sprinkler kicked into action. The cap seal burst and water streamed out, spraying Luna in the face.

She slid off the desk, grabbed her backpack and rushed out the office. Zooming past a confused Mrs. Oakly, she continued on into the hall and into the stairwell. The fire alarm blared. She bounded down the stairs, reaching the fifth floor before it swarmed with evacuees. Smushed within a single-file line, Luna plodded down the steps. With each descended floor, her nerves slightly lessened.

Sunlight streamed into the dim stairwell once they reached the ground floor. Outside in the humid heat, Luna snaked through the milling crowd, a skip in her step. She'd done it!

A hand clutched the hood of Luna's raincoat and spun her around. "Just as I thought," the security guard said, stroking his 'stache. "Up to no good."

....

Luna sat on the edge of her brother's bed, the last place in the world she wanted to be. Today was 'Day Three' and her very last chance. If she didn't get it right, she'd be stuck in this revolving door nightmare for eternity.

She swatted a pillow at her brother's snoring head.

Sting bolted upright. "Get. Out."

"What if I told you that right now, I was reliving the same day over and over in a dreamscape?"

Sting stared blankly at Luna, all eyes, no neck and lanky limbs like a brown tree frog. Without warning, he erupted into a fit of laughter. "You…dreamscape…yeah….right," he managed between snorts.

"I bet you twenty bucks I can predict the future." Luna held out her hand.

Sting took hold and shook. "Loser."

Luna proceeded to share with Sting the upcoming highlights of today's breakfast: the menu; Mom saying she heard on the news about another dreamscape; Dad's adamant stance that they weren't real; and the death of Mom's prized cuckoo clock at exactly 6:30.

Together they walked down the hallway, Sting humming, "Mo money," and into the kitchen. Luna pointed at Sting's plate of chick'n and waffles as he sat down. He mouthed the words, "Lucky guess."

Mom wiggled her rump to the "uh-oh" breakfast tune while pouring coffee into Dad's cup. "Heard on the news about another dreamscape case."

Sting's fork paused in mid-air, syrup bleeding from his stabbed waffle and chick'n combo.

Dad snorted. "Reliving the same day over and over and over? That mess isn't real."

Luna wiggled her brows at her brother's scowl.

Dad moved the conversation from dueling opinions on dreamscapes to Sting's big weekend game just before the cuckoo bird announced the 6:30 half hour. Luna watched her brother's jaw drop, followed by his fork, as the poor bird dangled over the edge.

Sting grabbed Luna's wrist and yanked her into the living room. "What the...? How did...?"

For the first time during this instant replay nightmare, Luna was actually enjoying herself. Unfortunately, the savory moment came to a bitter end.

"Like I said before, I'm stuck in a dreamscape. I have to change the right moment or I'll never get out." Luna paused, not wanting to say the words. "Sting, I need your help."

She explained how later today their father would uncover fraud at work, and with no trial or jury get sentenced to ten years at a work camp for mindlessly chucking Wonder Bread bits out the car window. Finally, reluctantly, she detailed her first two disastrous attempts to change history.

"Today is my last chance," Luna said. "Not only to save Dad, but myself."

"Figures that this day would all be your fault," Sting said.

Luna's temper raged. How was all this her fault? SAFE's thief, her father's addiction and the stupid judge, their combined actions caused this nightmare. It was because of them she was stuck in this rewind-and-repeat. Maybe even forever. Frustration dug under skin. Luna just wanted to move on. Back to a normal day at school, hanging with Ashley, eating chick'n fingers and...

Oh my greatness. Was it really her fault? She replayed the scene at the courthouse, the words her father had told the judge floating through her head: someone smuggling money at SAFE, creeping traffic, the broken A/C *and his daughter's suspension*. Could that be what put her father over the edge? But how could something so trivial, so stupid cause so much trouble?

....

Luna and Ashley navigated through the bustling cafeteria before squeezing into an empty space between the jockoids and headbangers. "Can you believe the latest dreamscape happened in Orlando? That's like around the corner," Ashley gushed.

Luna slowly nodded, staring straight ahead. Her soft gaze

registered nothing. Not even Tony Perkins digging deep into his ears and sniffing the golden wax on his fingertips could hold her attention. Luna's mind was fixed somewhere else.

If Luna was right, all she had to do to escape a lifetime sentence in this dreamscape was to avoid Mrs. Belcher at all costs. How hard could it be to not argue with Ashley? Especially now that Luna was a firm believer in second chances.

"Earth to Luna," Ashley said. A series of pokes struck Luna in the face. She turned her attention onto Ashley, who was about to toss another wadded-up piece of napkin. "Where are you?"

"What were you saying?"

"Dreamscapes," Ashley said. "What would you do-over if given the chance?"

Luna grinned. The moment had passed. She and her dad were safe! "Anything that put me in Mrs. Belcher's office. You?"

A freckle-faced boy wearing a Panthers basketball jersey leaned over Ashley and said, "Only losers believe in dreamscapes."

"Says the loser." Luna smirked, dunking her nugget in BBQ sauce.

"They are too real," Ashley said.

"My cousin's best friend's sister's dentist swore he did a root canal on the last victim," a kid next to Luna chimed in, running a hand through his dirty blond hair.

"Keep out of this, greasy-locks," freckle-faced spat.

"Dude, harsh." Greasy-locks pouted. "Anyway, I agree with you. Dreamscapes are bogus."

"And you're an expert because?" Luna said, waving her chick'n finger.

"Can't we all, anti- and pro-, get along?" Greasy-locks reached out his hand onto Luna's shoulder, right on top of her afro-puff. Luna shrieked. Her hand jerked. The BBQ dripping chick'n finger shot from her grasp. Even though futile, Luna lunged forward with stretched fingertips, reaching for the somersaulting nugget. It sailed past Ashley's wide eyes and smacked Tony Perkins square in the forehead.

Luna scrambled over the table towards Tony, crying "It was an accident!"

Tony leapt to his feet, sauce sliding down his blushing cheeks. No words could remove the hate in his eyes. Once again, Tony slung a fist full of fries and thanks to stupid self-preservation reflexes, Luna ducked.

She watched in horror as the scene played out the same: projectile chick'n; chairs skidding; flipped tables; the kitchen lady tossing mock potatoes; and Luna in Principal Belcher's office.

Mrs. Belcher's hands lay folded on top of a thick file on her desk. "I've seen—

"I know what you're going to say, Principal Belcher," Luna cut in. "That you've seen my face too many times this year, from the 'good hair' incident to holding the dissection frogs hostage."

Mrs. Belcher tightened her lips.

"And I get that actions have consequences. More than you'll ever know," Luna took a deep breath, "but this wasn't my fault. Ask Ashley, or the guys sitting next to us. It was an accident. I swear. I tried to tell Tony that, but he wouldn't listen. Please, please, please don't suspend me."

Mrs. Belcher leaned back in her chair, tapping her fingers together. Sweat beaded on Ashley's forehead. There was nothing left to say. Nothing more she could do. Her fate was in the principal's hands.

The silence stretched into eternity. It was impossible to read Belcher's blank face. She wore the same look whether offering a congratulations or doling out a suspension.

"Do you know what I'm about to say now?" Mrs. Belcher asked.

Luna slowly shook her head.

"Your accurate assessment of the situation appears genuine." Principal Belcher smirked. "I couldn't have said it better myself."

....

5:30 p.m. Sting kicked and jabbed, grunted and dodged across the living room, wearing a full-face 3D helmet (promising all five sensory sensations) as he played the latest version of 'Avatar Mindbender, Kung Fu Yo! Style.'

Luna paced the knotted carpet, every few seconds peeking through the blinds, hoping, praying their father was on his way home with no…issues.

Sting sailed in front of Luna with a perfectly pointed toe hi-yah. She snuck another glance out the window. Sting yanked off his mask and cried, "Would you *please* quit with the peep patrol?"

A key jingled in the front door. Luna pounced on her father before he could cross the threshold.

Dad chuckled. "Good to see you, too."

Arms still wrapped around his waist, Luna asked, "How was work?"

Dad's face flickered with worry, but then quickly recovered. "Eventful."

"Let the man breathe, Luna-tic." Sting peeled his sister off their father.

"Any cuckoo like incidents after work?" Luna followed her father into the kitchen, Sting in tow.

Mom was busy conducting a finger-licking taste test, adjusting heat levels with her secret weapon, kimchi, and doing da-butt to the roaring dinner music. "*Whoa-oh-oh, oh-oh-oh, oh-oh, oh, oh-oh-oh….*"

"Cuckoo?" Dad pointed at the empty space above the dining table. "Like your mother's bird?"

Mom's bottom bounced off beat, but she continued to stir her cheese-whiz sauce.

Luna shook her head. "More like airborne bread out the car window."

"What has gotten into you, Luna Del Rey?"

"Just ignore her, Dad," Sting said. "She forgot her meds."

All throughout dinner, Luna's nerves yo-yoed between hopeful satisfaction and twisted anxiety. She shoveled a forkful of mock lasagna into her mouth, relieved that there had been no suspension, no car crashes, and no security guard. Yet she squirmed in her seat, not fully convinced she was in the clear. And as the minutes kept on ticking into the late-night hour, with no "cuc-koo" acknowledgement of the time, she rocked in bed staring into the pitch-black nothingness.

What if she hadn't changed the right moment? Just because her dad had arrived home with no police sirens and no crusty judge verdicts, Luna didn't trust what tomorrow morning would bring.

. . . .

Luna woke to the smell of rubbing alcohol and a repetitive beep…beep…beep.

"My baby's back!" Mom cried, smothering Luna in moist kisses.

"Where am I?" Luna croaked. She pushed herself up into a sitting position in an unfamiliar bed, her body cocooned in starched white sheets. Colorful bouquets, cards and balloons decorated a side table. A green line of mountain peaks and valleys ran across a heart monitor screen, next to an IV bag hooked into Luna's arm.

"Welcome back, Luna-tic." Light streaming through the blinds danced across Sting's grinning face.

Dad rose from his chair and shuffled over to the hospital bed. He grabbed Luna's hand. "You were in a coma."

"How long?" Luna asked, even though she already had a clue.

"Three days," Dad whispered. "I was so afraid…"

"What's done is done." Luna squeezed his hand. "All that matters is what we do today."

He squeezed her hand back. "Thank greatness for second chances."

Luna grinned. "You have no idea."

Lobstersaurus

Eric James Stone

A Nebula Award winner and Hugo nominee, Eric James Stone has been published in Year's Best SF, Analog, *and elsewhere. His first novel,* Unforgettable, *is forthcoming from Baen Books. Eric is a Writers of the Future winner, graduate of Orson Scott Card's writing workshop, and assistant editor at* Intergalactic Medicine Show. *Eric lives in Utah. His website is www.ericjamesstone.com.*

The only predator that poses a significant danger for colonists is Species C-3506, a well-armored hexapod ranging up to five meters in height and up to nine meters in length and massing up to twelve metric tons. The pincers on its two arms are strong enough to crack the shells of most smaller species, after which the sharp-toothed, beak-like mouth is capable of shredding the flesh into chunks it can swallow.

—Pre-colonization survey report

....

The dead lobstersaurus, sprawled in the remains of the tomato patch, blocked the sunlight that usually streamed into the kitchen through the diamondglass wall in the mornings. Over the rim of her glass of orange juice, eight-year-old Esperanza Vega peered at the giant creature her father killed during the night. A cluster of black eyes on the side of its head seemed to stare unblinkingly back at her. The lower part of its head was gone, but its top beak still displayed a row of jagged green teeth.

"Stop looking at it, Espe," Mamá said.

Esperanza jerked her eyes away.

Mamá frowned at Papá. "I want that thing moved before lunch today. It makes me lose my appetite."

Papá reached his fork over to Mamá's plate, speared a pancake, and plopped it onto his own plate. "More for me, I guess."

"Rico, I mean it," Mamá said.

"Jack Sanders said he'd fly his tractor over this afternoon to help haul it away," Papá said.

Out of the corner of her eye, Esperanza thought she saw something moving outside. She looked back at the lobstersaurus. A tiny piece of sun had risen over the top of its shell.

Papá continued, "I suppose if I sliced it in two, our tractor could handle it. But if I had anything that could cut through that shell, I—"

One of the lobstersaurus's legs wiggled, and Esperanza shrieked and dropped her glass. Orange juice spilled across the white tablecloth.

"Espe!" Mamá scolded.

"It's still alive," Esperanza said. "It's moving."

Her parents turned their heads to follow her gaze.

For a few seconds, the lobstersaurus lay still. Then the same leg wiggled again.

"Postmortem reflex," Papá said. "Sometimes nerve signals still go to the muscles after something's dead."

The leg started shaking.

"You're sure it's dead?" Mamá said.

"A pound of blastique blew up in its mouth," Papá said. "It wasn't easy to kill, but it's dead."

Espe remembered something she had read in her science studies. "Some dinosaurs on Earth had nerve clusters near their tails. Maybe lobstersauruses have an extra brain not in their heads."

Papá smiled. "A good theory, mija. But it is not true. The survey robots took scans of the lobstersauruses long ago. They have only one brain – larger than most dinosaurs', but only one, in the head."

The armored segment of leg that connected to the lobstersaurus's shell seemed to get longer, then a black line appeared at the joint.

"Is the leg coming off?" Esperanza asked. "Can it go off on its own like a starfish arm and grow another lobstersaurus?"

The leg popped off the body and thudded to the ground, leaving a dark hole in the smooth yellow shell of the body. The leg lay still.

"No," Papá said, but his voice was unsure.

Something moved at the hole. Three small segmented legs, only about twenty centimeters long, stretched out.

"It's like the Hydra," Esperanza said, "but growing legs instead of heads."

A small head appeared, and she realized it was a baby lobstersaurus. The baby pulled itself out of the hole and then, limbs flailing, fell two meters to the ground.

"That can't be how they normally give birth," Mamá said, voice tinged with horror. As a botanist, Mamá had extensively studied the native plants, but she didn't know much about the animals.

The baby tried to stand up but fell over.

"No." Papá pushed back from the table and stood. "Normally, kind of a hatch in the shell would open up in the belly, but – well …."

After a moment's thought, Esperanza understood. "Since the mom is lying dead on its belly, the baby couldn't get out. It had to find another way. Oh, the poor thing could have died!" She stared at the baby lobstersaurus as it wobbled into a standing position, reminding her of the vid she had seen of a baby horse back on earth. It was about a half meter tall. As if trying to see the whole world with its multiple black eyes, it waved its head about. It gaped its toothless yellow beak and wagged its tiny pincer arms.

It was the cutest thing Esperanza had ever seen in real life.

"Most likely it would die anyway even if I don't kill it," Papá said. "Without its mother to catch food for –"

"I could," Esperanza said.

Papá blinked at her. "What?"

"I could catch food for it," Esperanza said. "Please? Can I keep it? You can't kill it, it's just a baby."

"Keep it?" Mamá said. "It's a monster."

"It could be my pet," Esperanza said. "I could train it." She searched her memory desperately for what she had learned about lobstersauruses in her science studies. "They're territorial animals. If I can get it to mark our farm as its territory, we won't have to worry about other lobstersauruses coming through."

"Mija," said Papá, "It's small now, but it will grow quickly, and it's a dangerous animal."

"Please," she begged. "Before dogs became pets, weren't they dangerous animals? It could be like … like a science experiment. If I can't train it, then you can kill it."

"I don't know," Papá said. Esperanza had a moment of hope because he hadn't said no.

"Rico," Mamá said, "it's too dangerous."

"But Mamá," Esperanza said, "it could be my friend. Please. A friend."

That was the one thing she thought might persuade Mamá. Esperanza heard her parents talking at night when they thought she was asleep, so she knew that they worried about her not having friends. She had been born six years before the colony ship arrived in the Kallisto system. Even at ten times the speed of light, it had taken over twelve years for the ship to travel from Earth, and the five thousand colonists had made the trip in cryo – except that Mamá's tube had malfunctioned after five years, so the ship had revived her. She had woken Papá to keep her company, and Esperanza had been born a year later due to a malfunctioning birth control implant.

For the two years since landing on Arcas, Esperanza had been the lone child in a society of adults. With the colony now firmly established, many of the women had turned off their birth control implants and were pregnant. But even after the babies were born, she would still be alone: twelve years younger than the closest adult, nine years older than the closest child.

Looking out the window at the baby lobstersaurus, Mamá sighed. "You will not bring it in the house. You will feed it and clean up after it, not me."

"Yes, Mamá. Thank you, Mamá." Filled with excitement, Esperanza rushed toward the door.

"Wait," said Papá, and her heart fell.

She turned to face him.

"When it grows teeth in that beak, you will have to file them down so they are not sharp," he said. "And we may need to do something about those pincers."

"Yes, Papá."

He picked up his work pack and walked over to her. "And I will come with you now. It may be small, but we do not know how it will react to you. It may not want to be your pet; it may not be possible to train it." Taking her hand, he led her out the door.

The baby lobstersaurus wobbled on six legs in the shadow of its mother. A trilling cry came from its beak.

When Esperanza and Papá got within two meters, it suddenly dropped on its belly. Esperanza's grip tightened on Papá's hand. The baby withdrew its head, legs, and pincer arms inside its shell, and sealed the holes.

"Oh, the poor baby's scared of us," Esperanza said.

"That's good," Papá said. "If it had attacked us, I probably would have had to kill it." He slipped some object Esperanza had not noticed him carrying into his pack.

"Did you know it could hide like a turtle?" she asked.

Papá shrugged. "Can't remember if that was in the survey robots' reports. Probably was, because they're very thorough. But I've never seen an adult do that, so maybe just babies can."

"But how can I tame it if it hides in its shell?"

"It will get hungry," he said. "Come." He led her over to the Arcasian scrap heap, where non-Earth biological material was placed for eventual protein conversion. Papá pulled out a dead crabbit about ten centimeters long. He whacked it a couple of times against the metal edge of the container until its shell cracked.

"Pull out the meat. If you feed it," he said, "it may think you're its mother."

With Papá standing guard, Esperanza waited in front of the baby lobstersaurus until finally the shell's head-hole opened. She remained very still.

The lobstersaurus's head slowly came out. It opened its beak and chirped.

Ever so slowly, Esperanza held out her hand holding a piece of crabbit meat. She put it down on the ground just a few centimeters from its beak, then withdrew her hand.

In a quick motion, the lobstersaurus snapped the meat up in its beak. With a slurping sound, it swallowed the meat whole.

After a few more trips to the scrap heap, Esperanza had fed the baby until it refused more food, and it followed her around with a wobbling six-legged gait.

"What will you name it?" Papá asked.

Ezperanza thought about it for a moment, and the answer came to her in the form of a traditional Argentine folk song her parents often sang to her because it contained her name: 'Zamba de mi esperanza.' "Zamba," she said. "Its name is Zamba."

....

Since they keep their reproductive organs inside their shells except during mating, the only visible difference between the sexes is that the female has an armored flap on her underside through which live offspring emerge.

—Pre-colonization survey report

....

Zamba grew more quickly than Esperanza expected. On her ninth birthday, less than six Earth months after she had adopted him, he was over a meter tall, a meter wide, and two meters long. She was still a good twenty centimeters taller than him, but that would not last long.

As a treat for her birthday, Papá had diverted water from the river, which ran along the eastern edge of their property, into a hole four meters wide he'd had the farmbots dig. "Someday we'll build a real swimming pool," he said as she splashed about in the waist-deep, muddy water. "But this will do for now."

Zamba tentatively dipped the tip of his left foreleg into the water, but stayed on the bank.

"Come on, Zamba," Esperanza said. "You can do it. See, it's fun." She splashed some water on his shell.

"I don't think he wants to, mija." Papá also stood on the bank. "He's not sure he can find his footing in there, and he can't float."

Esperanza frowned. "But I read that lobstersauruses have an aquatic origin. He should like being in water."

"Even if they evolved from aquatic creatures, it's been a long, long time. If you go back far enough, humans evolved from monkeys. That doesn't mean we have to like swinging from tree branches."

"But I like swinging from tree branches," Esperanza said.

Papá gazed at her for a moment. "Hmm. I can see the monkey resemblance. I think I shall call you monita, my little monkey."

She replied to that by sending a big splash of water his way. Papá leapt nimbly backward to dodge it, but some of the force of his leap caused a meter-long section of dirt to collapse into the water, sending little waves across. Esperanza giggled.

One of the farmbots that had dug the pool jolted into motion toward the collapsed rim, shovel arm extended.

Zamba sprang sideways, away from the pool, then jumped more than double his length to crash into the farmbot.

Esperanza shrieked. "Zamba! Stop!"

Zamba grabbed the farmbot's neck in one pincer and its shovel arm in the other. Metal twisted and groaned. Zamba let out a roar Esperanza had never heard before as the arm tore from the farmbot's frame.

Then Zamba dropped the farmbot and its arm and stepped back. The farmbot's shoulder sparked erratically.

Esperanza stood completely still, staring at the scene.

From somewhere across the river, wild territory still untouched by humans, came a deeper answering roar.

"Out of the pool, away from Zamba." Papá's voice was quiet but firm. "Now." Facing Zamba, he moved slowly toward his work pack, which lay on the ground a few meters away.

Panic rose inside Esperanza. Papá was going to do something to Zamba, maybe even kill him. She couldn't let that happen. So she moved forward, climbing out on the edge closest to Zamba.

"Espe!" Papá said. He froze in place.

"Bad Zamba," Esperanza said, staring at Zamba's black eyes and putting all the anger she could into her voice. "Don't break things. Bad Zamba."

Papá moved toward her, away from his pack.

Zamba's head drooped. He turned to face her then backed up a step and sank onto his belly.

Esperanza ran forward and gave Zamba's beak a light slap. Then she made her voice friendly. "You're a good boy, Zamba. But you can't break things just because you're big and strong."

"Get away from him, mija."

"No, Papá." She stroked Zamba's head and he made cheeping sounds like he used to when he was a baby. "See, he hasn't gone wild. He must have thought the farmbot was attacking or something."

"You can't really know what he's thinking. He's a wild creature. He may act tame sometimes, but he's not like a dog or cat or horse, that has evolved to live with humans." Papá sighed. "Now that he's grown so big, maybe it's time to let him go live in the wild."

"No, Papá. Please." Tears welled in her eyes. "He's a good boy. He'll behave."

Papá was silent for a minute. "Okay. But remember how I said we might need to do something about his pincers? It's necessary. I can't stand the thought of . . . It's necessary."

That night, while Esperanza held Zamba's head and sang to him, Papá banded Zamba's pincers with a nanofiber strip, slightly elastic to allow room for a few weeks' growth.

....

There are no venomous animals on the main continent, probably because all its animal species have shells, making venom delivery impossible. Thus, small species may present a minor problem as pests, but are not dangerous. High-tensile fencing is capable of keeping out larger species, except for C-3506. Not even electrified fencing will work for C-3506, due to its protective shell, which also renders it virtually invulnerable to standard-grade projectile and energy weapons. Military-grade weapons or high explosives will be needed to kill C-3506, so the colony should be supplied with such.

—Pre-colonization survey report

....

At two Earth-years old — about 2.05 Arcasian years — Zamba was almost three meters tall, more than double Esperanza's height and about the size of an adult African elephant on Earth. And he was not nearly full grown. Since his pincers were banded, she had to crack the shells of the dead pest animals brought in by the farmbots so that Zamba could eat them. That and collecting Zamba's scat to put in the scrap heap for protein conversion were her main chores associated with keeping Zamba. The farmbots could have done both jobs for her, but her parents insisted that she do the work herself because Zamba was her responsibility.

"Espe? Where are you?" Mamá called from inside the house.

"Fixing supper for Zamba," Esperanza replied. She smashed the sledgehammer onto a blue crabbit and its shell crunched.

"The power's gone out." Mamá came to the back door, her belly eight months pregnant with a baby sister for Esperanza. "I can't raise your father on the comm, so you'll have to fetch him to look at the generator."

Esperanza smashed a red crabbit then put down the hammer. "Zamba and I will find him." She picked up the two cracked crabbits by their tails and tossed them to Zamba, who gulped them down with a satisfied grunt.

A stinging sensation near her left ankle made Esperanza look down. A two-centimeter-long, six-legged creature was biting her. She kicked it off with her right foot. A trickle of blood ran down from the bite. She stomped on the thing and twisted her foot until she heard the shell crack. She saw a couple more of the same species crawling along the ground and stomped them for good measure. If the stupid animals on this planet would just learn that Earth-based life didn't provide them with any real nutrition . . .

From far to the east, a lobstersaurus bellowed. Esperanza instinctively covered her ears, having learned from past experience that Zamba's response could be annoyingly loud.

She didn't hear a bellow, but did hear a muffled scream. Puzzled, Esperanza turned toward her mother, who was running toward her, pregnant belly bouncing.

Something grabbed Esperanza's torso and twisted her up into the air. Pinpricks of pain spread across her back as she was bounced around. Wind whipped her hair.

Esperanza looked at what was holding her. It was Zamba's beak. "Zamba! Bad boy! Put me down. Put me down, now!"

Zamba kept running across their crop fields, trampling the pest fences without slowing down.

She made eye contact and repeated her command, but there was a wildness in Zamba's eyes she had never seen before.

"Papá!" she screamed. "Papá, help!"

They were headed east, toward the river and the wild country beyond. She tried to think what had triggered this attack. Was the bellow she had heard some sort of mating call? She had read about species on Earth for which the male offered food to the female before mating. Was that what she was, a food offering?

At least she was alive, so far. And Zamba's teeth had been filed so they weren't very sharp, although they still felt like they were tearing into her skin a bit. But if Zamba was taking her to a wild lobstersaurus . . . A memory of Zamba using his pincers to rip the arm off the farmbot involuntarily came to her mind.

"Zamba, please," she said, trying to make her voice calm. "Be a good boy and put me down."

Zamba swerved, shuddered as there was a cracking sound, then started falling forward. His mouth opened and Esperanza tumbled to the ground, the cornstalks partially breaking her fall.

She pulled herself to her feet and looked back to make sense of what had happened. Zamba screeched in pain – his front two legs were shattered. Papá's tractor lay crumpled a few meters away.

"Papá!" she called and began stumbling toward the tractor.

He appeared out of the cornstalks nearby, running toward her. "Mija, are you all right?"

"Yes," she said as he enveloped her in a hug. "I don't know what got into –"

"Later," Papá said. "Back to the house, quick as we can."

Zamba cheeped at her, but she turned her back and began to run alongside Papá through the crops toward home.

"It's my fault," she said.

"No," Papá said.

"I should have let you take him to the wild."

"Do you think you could have stopped me if I had decided to do it? I am the one to blame, for being too soft-hearted. I never wanted you to get hurt, mija. I knew losing Zamba would hurt you. But sometimes you must hurt those you love to save them from a greater pain."

They met Mamá coming the other way when they were a half-kilometer from the house. She wept with joy when she saw Esperanza. "You're alive," she kept repeating as they continued toward home.

·····························

The seeds of all plant species on the main continent are covered in a highly mineralized shell that is resistant to the digestive systems of the local fauna. This probably evolved as a method of spreading the seeds via herbivore scat. The mineral compound in the shells is durable enough that it may have industrial uses.

—Pre-colonization survey report

·····························

Because the power was still out, Papá had to use a flashlight so he could see the lock on his office safe where he kept the blastique.

"Do you have to do that now?" Mamá asked.

Papá sighed. "Zamba was a good pet the past two years. No matter what happened today, I should end his suffering. He deserves that much mercy."

Esperanza couldn't hold back tears, but she kept herself from sobbing.

"Can you at least try to get the generator back on before you go?" Mamá said. "It's getting dark."

Papá took three bricks of blastique out of the safe then closed it. He nodded. "Mija, come with me to hold the flashlight while I try to fix the generator."

As Esperanza and Papá stepped out the kitchen door, he suddenly grabbed her arm.

"What?" she said, then she heard the cheeping.

In the twilight, Zamba staggered toward them on his middle and back legs. His front legs dangled uselessly.

"Back inside," Papá said. They stepped back into the house. Papá bolted the door. "Maria!"

Mamá entered the kitchen. "What is it?"

Zamba came close to the diamondglass wall and banged against it with his pincers.

Mamá gasped.

Esperanza couldn't believe this was happening. Zamba was still cheeping at her like he did when he was sorry for something, yet here he was attacking the house. "Go away," she yelled. "I hate you!"

"I need something sticky," Papá said to Mamá. "So I can stick the explosives to it."

"I'll find something," Mamá said. "Give me the flashlight." In a moment, she was gone.

Zamba lifted his left pincer to his beak and bit at the nanofiber band. It resisted at first, but then tore and the pincer was free. He then did the same to the other.

Esperanza watched in horror as he used his pincers to tear off his front legs. The holes in his shell where the legs had come out sealed up.

With his pincers, Zamba reached up to the roof, grabbed ahold, and began to pull. Above them, something creaked and then snapped.

"Into the living room," Papá said.

They hurried in the dark, almost slipping and falling in their rush. Mamá and the flashlight joined them in huddling behind the couch, right after a huge crashing noise from the kitchen.

"Superglue," she said, handing a tube to Papá.

"That'll do," he replied. He began working on the explosives while Mamá held the flashlight for him.

Something stung Esperanza's ankle. She reached down and felt the shell of a small creature. She brushed it away.

"Ow," said Mamá. The flashlight wavered, and for a moment Esperanza thought she saw the floor moving. Was Zamba somehow digging under them? That couldn't be possible, could it?

"Mamá," she said, "shine the light on the floor."

"Why?"

"Please."

Mamá turned the flashlight down.

The floor was a seething mass of tiny creatures like the one that had bitten Esperanza just before Zamba went crazy.

"What are those? Where did they come from?" Mamá asked.

Papá stayed focused on the explosives.

Esperanza could see some of the creatures crawling up Mamá's legs. She reached down and swatted at them, knocking most of them off. One grabbed onto her hand and bit her finger. She could feel more bites on her legs.

With a tremendous crash, Zamba tore through the kitchen wall and into the living room. The ceiling collapsed behind him. He cheeped at them.

Papá stood up, a brick of blastique in his right hand.

"Wait!" Esperanza shouted. "He was trying to save me. From the swarm."

Papá hesitated. "What swarm?"

"Look down," Mamá said.

Papá looked down then began stomping with his boots.

Esperanza came out from behind the couch. "I'm so sorry, Zamba," she said. "I didn't understand."

"What are you doing?" Papá said. He still held a brick of blastique.

Esperanza knew she was right. She had to be. She rushed toward Zamba, who reached out with his pincer and grabbed her by the waist.

"Espe!" Mamá cried.

Zamba lifted Esperanza up and onto his back.

"See?" Esperanza said. "He couldn't use his pincers, so his mouth was the only way he could carry me."

Zamba reached out his pincers toward Mamá and Papá. After a brief hesitation, they came around the couch and Zamba lifted them onto his back.

Zamba turned and lumbered out of the house, heading east.

Everywhere Mamá shone the flashlight on the ground, the swarm writhed. "Our crops," she said. "We are losing everything."

"Not everything." Papá hugged the two of them close. "Not the most important things."

Once Zamba reached the river, he waded out a couple of meters and then stopped.

"Of course," Esperanza said. "The swarm would be swept away if it came into the river. That's why he was bringing me here."

The three of them stayed on Zamba's back all night, huddled together for warmth. Esperanza didn't get much sleep, as crashing sounds in the wild country across the river kept startling her awake.

As the sun rose the next morning, they could see the result of the swarms – for there must have been another swarm across the river. Not a tree was left standing, and the surface of the land glittered with tiny moving shells. Various larger animals, including some lobstersauruses, roamed about, feeding off the tiny creatures.

As for their farm, blanketed by the swarm, none of the crops remained. Parts of their house still stood, though, diamondglass and metal glinting in the sun.

"What I can't understand is why the survey robots never reported on these swarms," Papá said. "They were here twenty years before we arrived, and they never saw these things."

Esperanza remembered something she'd read in her science studies. "Maybe they're like cicadas, and only come out after many years underground."

"The seeds!" said Mamá. "This is why all the native seeds have such tough shells. If every few decades a swarm eats all the plants, then the seeds still survive."

"Not just seeds," Papá said. "All the land animals have shells. Of course – hardly anything without a shell would survive."

"We don't have shells," Esperanza said. "Without Zamba, we might be dead." She rubbed her hand over Zamba's shell, and he made a low, almost purring sound. "But what do we do now? We can't stay on Zamba's back forever."

"With the food exhausted," said Papá, "my guess is the swarm will mate, dig down to wherever they lay their eggs then die. And the cycle will be over for however many years until the eggs hatch. We'll have to bring down more seeds from the ship and start over."

"And this time we'll have to figure out what to do before they come back," Esperanza said.

"Someone will figure something out." Papá winked at her. "Maybe even you."

....

Because Earth species provide no real nutritional value to Arcasian animals, the swarmers that fed on colonist crops mostly failed to reproduce after burrowing. Thirty-seven years from now, the eggs that do hatch under areas that were already cultivated during the swarm fifteen years ago will be reduced by over ninety-five percent. This suggests that strategy of mass cultivation of Earth crops in the year before each swarm might be highly effective in reducing future swarms in that area.

—Esperanza Vega, master's thesis in biology

The Journey of a Thousand Miles

C.J. Daring

C.J. Daring, alter-ego of the evil William R.D. Wood, lives in Virginia's Shenandoah Valley in an old farmhouse turned backwards to the road. C.J Daring pens works of mystery and adventure for readers of all ages. Some are set in the far reaches of space. Some in the murkiest depths of time. And sometimes, when you're not looking, maybe even your own back yard! Check in and see what coming next at www.williamRDwood.com.

David held the testing center door as his older classmates exited. The air in the courtyard always smelled fresher, even though it was the same air everywhere on the ship. A couple of students glanced down at him as they passed; one of the girls even gave him a smile. Not a single one said thanks. Mom said they treated him that way because David was as smart as them, but four years their junior, and no kid liked having a blipsqueak in their class. He didn't care. All that mattered was that in a few years he'd be an engineer just like his parents.

"You're welcome," he said to their backs.

The courtyard was crowded today. A projection of the captain played on the sky. He was talking about his visit to one of the primary schools this morning.

"…our young people today are carrying on in the best traditions of our forefathers," the captain said. "Obeying the rules. Offering a helping hand. And never being afraid to do the right thing. We're teaching the generation who are going to stand in gravity, folks. Let's get it right. The journey of a thousand miles…"

The captain let the words hang as the projection faded into drifting clouds, knowing everyone was finishing the phrase in their heads. The overhead sunlights were turned up to mid-afternoon, and the temperature was regulating to the warmest summer level they'd enjoyed this year. David took a deep breath. A few kids his age were throwing a ball on the far side of the light fountain. David smiled. Today he was going to ask if he could join them.

A shrill voice pierced the serenity. A little girl's voice.

"No," said David. "Please, no."

But the voice was unmistakable. Mom was right about the older kids. He knew just how they felt sometimes. With a final glance at the kids across the courtyard, David jogged around the corner toward the commotion.

Abby, his little sister, squared off against a monster of a kid named Elliot. Fists at her side and head thrown back, Abby glared up at him. Elliot towered over her and had her by thirty kilos easy, but his little sister didn't understand those sorts of things.

"*Am not!*" Abby shouted.

The scene was comical, and David was tempted to let it play out. But he had responsibilities.

"Yelling isn't going to make it so, runt," said Elliot.

Abby kicked Elliot in the shin. Elliot yelped, drawing back an arm. David pushed between them just in time to throw Elliot off balance and stop his swing. With his own arm, David moved Abby behind him.

"Better keep her outa my face." Elliot bumped his chest into David's face.

"Or what?" said David pushing back. "You afraid she's gonna kick your butt? Then everyone'll know you got beat up by a five year old."

"Yeah." Abby giggled. David had to sidestep to keep her from coming back around.

Elliot balled his fists, his face flushing red.

A shadow moved over their trio and a familiar voice asked, "What seems to be the trouble, citizens?"

"C-captain," Elliot sputtered as he stumbled back. "N-no trouble, sir. No trouble."

"Is that true?" asked the captain, looking directly at Abby.

Abby pointed an accusing finger at Elliot. "He said—"

"Everything is fine, sir," David interrupted. "Just headed to our quarters. Chores and studying to do."

The captain looked down at them; one corner of his mouth turned up. His uniform was clean, but a pair of dirty work gloves hung from his belt. Dad said he did this for public relations, to show he didn't mind getting dirty.

"You were the little girl from the assembly this morning," the captain said to Abby. "The one with all of the questions."

"She's always like that, Captain," Elliot blurted. "Too many, if you ask me."

The captain pulled a glass wedge, his phone, from a pocket and quickly scrolled until he found what he was looking for. "Ah, yes. Abigail Salvadore. Phillip and Kiyomi's youngest."

Abby nodded.

"Your parents are two of the best engineers we have. So good they've earned a permit for a third. You children knew already? I hope I didn't let the air out of the lock." His smile was infectious.

David nodded but Abby just looked on, her mind somewhere else. Probably working out how to kick Elliot again.

The captain knelt before them. "You should be proud of them. They're doing important work out on spar one-eleven for the next couple of days. We'll be at Gliese in your lifetimes, you know. We have to make sure the ship is ready."

The kids all nodded.

"They follow the rules set down by our forefathers because those rules have gotten us ninety percent of the way across the Big Gulf. They'll take us the next fifty years too, but we have to follow them, don't we?"

"Yes, sir," said Elliot. "I follow the rules. Mrs. McNamara always says—"

"Abigail," said the captain. "You're going to follow the rules better, aren't you?"

Abby's focused on him, brow furrowed. David bumped her shoulder lightly. "Yes, sir."

"You promise?"

David bumped her again. "I promise."

"Me, too, Captain," said Elliot.

The captain's phone chimed, and he turned to listen to it as Abby and Elliot sneered at one another. David sighed, ready to get back to their quarters and out of the sunlights.

"Just initialize the peripheral hybridizers," the captain was saying into his phone, his voice hushed enough the crowd couldn't hear, but not enough the three of them couldn't. "Yes, I know it's not protocol...look, I'll call you right back. You children have a great day. Remember, the journey of a thousand miles..."

"Begins with a single step," said David and Elliot in unison and the captain walked briskly toward the nearest lift.

"It ends with a single step, too," said Abby.

The captain paused in the lift doors long enough to give Abby a wink. Then he was gone.

....

David leaned over the ship's schematic displayed on the dinner table in their quarters. Engineering commentary looped quietly from the speakers as sections illuminated. The ship was kilometers long, home to fifty thousand people, and the details were lost at this scale. He just needed to know the basics for the test on Friday. Drive sections, power plants, habitation rings—which parts rotated. And the major cargo pods. Some had been repurposed, their contents used up along the journey, but most were empty and left to their own devices.

His stomach rumbled. He glanced up at the clock.

19:49.

Had he really been absorbed in the schematic that long? Abby must be starving. If she told Mom and Dad he hadn't fed her or he'd ignored her, they'd never leave him in charge again. They might even decide David wasn't old enough for his own phone and sign it back into Stores.

"Abby?"

Abby didn't answer. David heard quiet sobbing from down the hallway.

Great. He could kiss his phone goodbye.

Muting the tabletop, David moved to Abby's bedroom. The room was dark except for the soft red spokes from the baseboard safety lights. Abby lay on the bed, face buried in her pillow.

"You hungry, Abby? I could heat up some piggen." If anything would get him out of reclamatory with her, it was piggen nuggets.

She shook her head.

He had been a lousy brother, so focused on reviewing for the test, he hadn't even noticed when she'd stopped brooding on the couch and went to her room. Worse, he hadn't talked to her on the way to their quarters. He wasn't mad. He just had to score as high as the bigger kids or they would make fun of him and tell him he should go back with kids his own age.

"Come on and let me make some for you."

The crying stopped, replaced by sniffles. Abby rolled over. "You're not scared, are you?" She was using her baby voice, like the time she asked Dad for reassurance the air wasn't going to run out. She'd learned about the ship's reclamatory systems in kindergarten that day.

"No, Abigail. I'm not scared."

"Don't you want to know what of?" Abby's voice was stronger now, a little less hard on his older, more mature nerves. He'd overheard Mom speculating to Dad that nature had given human offspring squeaky voices so their parents couldn't ignore them. It was the only way the race survived to expand to the stars on generation ships like theirs.

Must work on big brothers too.

"Sure. What?"

Abby sat up and whispered, ""The Bogeyman."

David stifled a laugh. "Is that what you and Elliot were arguing about?"

"He said I was scared. But I'm not."

"Well, you don't need to be. He's just glitching with you. There's no reason to be scared of something that doesn't exist."

"He said the Bogeyman lives in Repo One, and he's gonna come and get us little kids and use us *for parts*."

David enjoyed tormenting the younger kids as much as the next guy, but the Bogeyman? Really? "Abby, that's just stupid."

"Is not."

"He's just telling you a bunch of dumb stories about Repo One." Repository One was the largest of the cargo storage pods and had been the first depleted. Crews had repurposed it early on as an oxygen farm and arboretum, but that had been abandoned – except by the automated systems – for over two hundred years.

"He's thirteen."

She said Elliot's age as if it were a decree from the captain. The journey of a thousand miles would not be possible without Elliot Higginsbotham. His every word is truer than truest truth!

The truth was that Elliot was a jerk. "You can't believe someone just because they're older."

"You can't?"

"No. Being older makes you smarter, not honester—more honest. And, honestly, even smart people lie sometimes."

She paused. "Do Mom and Dad lie?"

That went aft fast. She was good at piecing things together, that was for sure. "No. At least not to us."

The room was silent except for a rhythmic squeak from a ceiling ventilator. "Would you ever lie to me, Davie?"

Maybe it was because they were alone in their quarters with both parents kilometers away, but that moment seemed as big as the whole ship. "I never would."

She sniffled, noisily wiping her nose. "Okay."

"Let me get you those nuggets."

"What did the captain mean when he said Mom and Dad had a permit for a third?"

David sighed, not sure how comfortable he was with the idea himself. Leading her from the room he tried not to gag at the thought. "Well, Mom and Dad are pretty smart, and they've shown they don't mind working hard, so the Council has decided that Mom and Dad can have another baby."

David was sure her squeal of delight could be heard all the way across the Big Gulf back to Earth.

....

David knew he was dreaming since there was never an extra ration of chocolyte.

"Davie?" The voice was familiar and very squeaky. Was she still scared of the Bogeyman? Maybe the squeak was just the ceiling ventilator again. Nothing a little squirt of oil wouldn't solve. He'd fix it in the morning. Dad liked it when he took responsibility for repairs in their quarters.

"Do you think I'm gonna make a good big sister?" asked Abby.

David squinted at the clock.

02:42

"Let's go." Abby bounced up and crossed to the door. She was fully clothed—but not in sleepwear or even daywear. She wore her expeditionary clothes, the ones intended for jaunts into the less rigidly climate-controlled and comfortable areas of the ship.

His expeditionaries were laid out on the foot of his bed with his boots. Alongside them was his phone, one end pulsing softly with newly received data. He gritted his teeth. He hated when she messed with his phone. It was one of the ancient hinged models and very fragile. "It's three in the morning."

"That's why we gotta hurry."

He shook his head. What on the ship had possessed him to convince Mom and Dad to leave him in charge? Did Abby do this all the time?

"Come on. You promised," she said.

"Promised what? Hurry where?"

She smacked the latch release and the door slid aside. The corridor outside was lit in dim, night-cycle red. Abby turned to him, a gleam in her eye. "Repo One."

....

He looked back along the length of the spar access tube. The tangle of pipe, conduit and equipment diminished to a single shadowy point a half kilometer away. No one had been this way for years.

Abby was so going to get it when David caught up to her.

How had Abby gotten through the door, anyway? She was smart, sure. She scared him sometimes—other kids too—the way she'd hang back, studying. Worst of all was when she would blurt out questions that made the kids laugh until they realized all the adults had stopped to look at her.

David keyed in the code he'd just spent a month's chocolyte rations on. The older kid from his class had promised the string of symbols was an old universal access key used by the staff officers in their own phones, but he'd refused to swear it was still valid. He'd also been smiling when he cut the connection.

A whole month's chocolyte. David felt sick.

Suppose the code had expired. It *was* ancient. What if alarms were blaring all over the ship right now? Command would contact his parents out on spar one-eleven and they'd have to come back. They'd probably lose their permit and, if that happened, they'd take his phone for sure. David wished the wobble in his stomach was only because of the zero-gee.

Maybe he keyed in the wrong sequence. It was a really long one. He hadn't wanted to use his phone directly so no one could trace it back to him, but he didn't have a choice now. Seating the phone in the lock's interface slot, he called up the code.

The transparent glass of the phone flickered neutral white, connecting to the door.

INNER DOOR BREACH appeared along the phone's edge. Below that, BYPASS and CANCEL.

These doors were actual locks, like those on the outer skin of the ship. The systems were designed to prevent accidentally exposing crew members to dangerous pressure changes. A quick peek through the dirty observation port showed a shifting shipscape beyond the other lock door, already rolled aside. Green lights shone along its edge.

No danger, he thought. David tapped the analog pressure gauge above the interface slot. The needle on the gauges quivered like his stomach, so it wasn't stuck. Pressure was good on both sides.

He held his breath and pressed BYPASS.

The circular door rumbled aside, a dozen tiny cylinders discharging with a hiss. David pushed away as the geared edge rolled into the wall.

How had Abby gotten through this door on her own? He pulled the phone from the interface and keyed up tracking links, still set for the beacon clipped to Abby's expedition jacket. She'd figured out months ago how to disable the shipnet's automated child alerts, but he knew to look specifically for her, and that feature couldn't be blocked. David followed the map Abby left on his phone, leading straight to this very door. David found her floating beacon where it must have snagged and come off as she passed through.

How had Abby done it if he barely had the resources to pull it off? She was brilliant, all right; a brilliant pain in his—

Movement flashed to one side, a flimsy aluminum panel dislodging from the wall. Swatting the panel away, David caught the look of grim determination on Abby's face as she launched herself from the tiny hiding place. She rebounded from the door frame and sailed through the airlock into the openness beyond.

....

"*Abby, no!*"

David whipped himself across the threshold, seeing clearly for the first time beyond the inner lock and into the endless air. His heart thundered in his chest, and he thrust arms and legs outward, desperately trying to stop his forward momentum. David hooked a bracket with a single index finger and yelped in pain as inertia attempted to pull the digit out by the root.

"There is no down no down no down," he chanted between gasps. In zero gee, Dad always preached, there is no bottom except wherever you are. Everywhere else is up. Swallowing hard, David scanned the interior for Abby. She was somewhere in Repo One.

One minute she was bawling about the Bogeyman, and the next she was rocketing into the bottomless unknown. David did not get it. And Mom and Dad were going to have another one.

Everywhere David looked, he could only see greenery intermixed with pipework and equipment. The arboretum, left alone all these years, was a jungle. And in zero-gee, it was as random of a mess as anyone could imagine. The far side was hundreds of meters away, major sections lost in swaths of gloom from disabled lighting. Structure peeked through in places, but it wasn't always easy to find. There was order. You just had to look passed the trees.

Abby's trajectory should have taken her through the gap in the foliage across from the massive plenum of intersecting ducts. A web of guy wires and flexible conduits held it in place.

A glint of light from the vicinity of the plenum caught his eye, and he saw Abby's tiny body diving through a wall of leaves and webbing. Just before passing through the far side, Abby caught one of the heavier flex conduits. Sparks erupted from one side as the conduit pulled free, uncoiling as Abby held on for dear life, a tiny popper on the end of an electric whip.

The conduit snapped taut around a thick branch. Abby maintained her grip and the recoil sent her drifting back toward the plenum. At least circuit breakers had tripped, ending the shower of sparks from conduit and the plenum.

"*I'm coming!*"

....

David swung out, his stomach lurching in protest. Nothing to fear. A few meters along the inner wall were two alcoves, each containing a U-shaped MMU—the same manned maneuvering units still used for zero-gee repairs and inspections. They were mostly automated, although crew members could ride along in their saddles if needed. All David needed was in the storage box beneath them.

Pulling open a panel, David removed two bulky orange belts. The belts were canvas with a box in the center and two small, open-ended cylinders attached by short, jointed arms to each side. Red and yellow LEDs flickered on one belt. Low battery, but still functional. The other was all green.

Cinching the fully charged belt around his waist, he pulled the control pendant from the box and pushed off from the wall. With a whine of tiny servos, the belt's fans spun to life, propelling David slowly and steadily on a course to retrieve the ship's most troublesome girl.

They were going to blame him, he knew. Why hadn't he kept a better eye on her, they'd ask? Why hadn't he been a better big brother?

"Davie." Abby's voice was a barely perceptible squeak among the rustling of leaves and the echoing clunks and clanks of Repo One.

Abby shimmied along the damaged cable, anchoring herself to the intake cowl of a one of the smaller ducts, this one only about three meters in diameter.

Was she waving at him now?

No. Pointing.

David craned his neck to look over his shoulder. Air washed over him as two MMUs flashed by, banking left and right. Buffeted by the turbulence, he had to fight to keep control of the belt's tiny fans. Chest heaving, he managed to keep his eyes locked onto Abby. Can't panic now.

The MMUs were alongside one another again, their gas jets— far superior to the belt's tiny fans—powering them straight toward Abby.

....

They were probably activated because of the damaged cable. The sleds were pretty stupid, designed to repair machinery and electronic systems, not enforce curfews or patrol abandoned cargo modules for intruders.

Fans at maximum, David sped across the gap, guiding around

the larger tree trunks. The junction loomed larger than he expected. He'd done the math in his head, but things often seemed small until you got close to them. Dad called it perspective.

Abby seemed to be getting smaller as the MMUs bore down on her. She pulled herself along a set of personnel rungs until she disappeared into the clamshell-shaped cowling of the duct. She must be terrified.

"They're just going to fix the cable," David shouted, his voice swallowed up by the ambient roar.

As the MMU approached the interface where the cable had torn free, stowed arms unfolded into a half-dozen articulated appendages and ball-jointed tentacles, each sporting a set of specialized tools. The second sled maneuvered through a tangle of branches and conduits. A magnetic clamp on a wire rope deployed, snatching the free end of the cable from the air. Reeling in its prize, tiny metal fingers went to work amidst a buzzing of grinders and laser flashes.

David reversed the fans to brake then shut them off, his momentum carrying him forward until he grabbed the edge of the cowling and flipped himself inside.

Two meters inside the shadowy recess, Abby hung, hands and feet tucked into the louvers of a safety grill that prevented foreign objects from being sucked inside. The grill was loose, rattling as Abby moved.

David glared at Abby. "We're going back right now. What in the ship were you thinking?"

Abby drifted over to him. Outside the two MMUs were reattaching the cable in a flurry of multi-jointed limbs, like two spiders fighting over the same piece of food. "I just had to know, Davie."

"Know what?"

Seconds passed and she didn't answer. He scowled and turned away. She was probably about to start crying again. With a sudden burst of anger, David pulled himself around to face her, lips parting in preparation for a Dad-level tirade. But she was looking out into the jungle of trees and pipes.

A third MMU was jetting their way. This one had a passenger wearing an environment suit, his helmet emblazoned with the blue and green emblem of engineering.

"This is your fault," David whispered, but he knew that didn't matter. He was the big brother. He was responsible.

Mom and Dad were never going to trust him again.

....

"S-sir, I can ex-explain," David stammered. For captain's sake, he sounded like Elliot. "You see, my little sister—I mean, we were just—it's just this jerk told her..."

A small panel on the engineer's MMU popped open. An arm extended and bathed the inside of the cowling with red laser light. David closed his eyes and used his free hand to cover Abby's as the light played across their faces.

"We can be out of here in a flash, and I'll make sure she never does anything like this ever again."

The gold-encrusted engineer's visor showed only their own distorted reflections. Funny he should be wearing full EVA gear in Repo One. There was plenty of oxygen in here, and this was the good stuff before it was circulated.

White light flashed from behind the safety grate. The smell of ozone filled David's nostrils, and Abby coughed. Sterilizing blast to keep stray biologicals from getting into the ductwork.

"Sir?"

The engineer didn't answer. He hadn't spoken at all. Had he moved? David scanned the environment suit. The glove joint was cracked, and rubber fingertips were crumbling.

The engineer's scanner withdrew and several manipulators extended, a set of stubby pincers grabbing the spare maneuvering belt from the clip at David's waist.

For the first time, David noticed a couple of working tethers snaking up slowly against the engineer's back. They must have been trailing him as he approached and now coiled up against his back from their own inertia. With an audible clack, the end of one tether glanced off the engineer's helmet. One of its two clips was broken and burned.

"Sir?" David waved his hand in front of the visor.

A tug from behind, and Abby drifted away from him, pushing herself gently toward the engineer. David tried to grab her but it was too late. She cleared the busy sled's moving arms, hooking her toe on one side of the MMU's passenger saddle. Eyes wide and unblinking, Abby's face hung centimeters from the visor. Still the engineer remained silent and still.

Abby glanced back at David, and he shook his head sharply. Maybe the engineer was sleeping after a long, hard duty shift.

Abby grabbed the bottom edge of the visor and snapped it upward.

Her scream pierced David's eardrums. She kicked off and, before David could get a look at the engineer, Abby slammed into him, twisting and spinning as she squirmed away amongst the clusters of control modules and cabinets surrounding the cowling.

"Abby." In vain, he tried to grab her before she vanished into the tangle of equipment and foliage outside. The engineer's MMU, jets firing to correct the transfer of inertia, rotated, bringing the engineer's face around.

A skull stared out of the visor. David's heart hammered and he couldn't make himself breathe.

The engineer was suddenly moving away. No, not the engineer. David instinctively pushed himself backwards, deeper into the duct. He flailed wildly, seeking a handhold. Slamming into the safety guard, it dislodged and he was completely inside before he regained control and snatched a corner of the grate.

With a screech of metal, the grate sprang back, rusty latches snapping home.

Keep it together. Keep it together.

The engineer was long dead. Taking several quick breaths, David forced himself to look beyond the busy spiderlike limbs of the MMU, still hard at work on the belt, and into the visor.

Behind the glass wasn't a skull. Just a shriveled, chalky face. The eye sockets were shadowy holes, and the lips cracked and pulled back from large white teeth. He'd been dead a long, long time, the MMU continuing its program in automatic.

David grabbed the latch and tugged. It didn't budge. Bracing himself with his feet, he took the small handle in both hands and pulled. For a second, he thought the rusted rods were moving, but they were only bending.

"Abby!" He pressed his face against the grate trying to spot her. "He can't hurt us."

No answer.

"Can you hear me?" He watched as the MMU inserted a new fuel cell from a storage box and began to reassemble the belt.

Pushing away from the grating, David planted his feet on the back of the cowling trying to ignore the mouth-like duct shooting off beneath his feet like the gullet of a giant worm. With all his strength, he launched himself at the grating, impacting the metal grill with a groan of metal and a cry of his own.

David shook the grate. If anything, he'd wedged it in even tighter. "*Abby, come back.*"

Outside the sleds whined and whirred as they worked, but there wasn't a squeak from Abby. The duct shuddered, and air began to pour through the grate from outside. Tiny glass beads, scattered like glitter along the inside of the duct, twinkled. Another sterilizing sweep was building and the tug of a huge air handler deep in the duct was growing stronger.

David stretched the fingers of both hands through the louvers to stabilize himself. If he stayed here he'd be flashed with sterilizing radiation. It might not be enough to hurt him but the fan pulling air from the old oxygen farm for the rest of the ship was definitely enough to ruin his whole day.

The dead engineer's sled continued fiddling with the maneuvering belt oblivious to everything but its program.

He had no choice. Pulling his phone from his pocket, he keyed it on. Maybe they could shut down the duct from Command. He'd just have to take his punishment. Along the edge of the phone flashed four words.

NO NETWORK. PROXIMITY ONLY.

Droplets formed in front of his face, sucked instantly down the duct. David realized for the first time since he was Abby's age, he could still cry. "Abby, please, I need you."

A tiny hand clasped his fingers where they poked through the grate. Abby floated outside, her expression unreadable as her eyes darted back and forth between the engineer and him.

"Hey, you stupid Bogeyman," she said. "This thing's broken. Fix it."

David watched as she smacked the mangled latch again and again with her open palm, sending a metallic warble echoing down the duct. The sled's played its scanning laser in their direction, its other arms continuing their task.

David couldn't fight back the sob that erupted from deep in his throat. He'd failed his parents. He'd failed himself. Worst of all, he'd failed to take care of his little sister.

Abby smacked the grating, startling him. "Give me your phone." Her eyes were more intense than he'd ever seen.

"There's no time," David snapped. "The sterili—"

"*Give me your phone, Davie.*"

David shoved the device through the louvers. "Bogeyman." Abby waved the phone in front of the engineer's visor, then the sensing arm. The arm unfolded and the red light winked on then off, sensing no problems.

"It's no use," said David.

A soft crack came from the phone, and David realized Abby had opened the phone too far, snapping its ancient hinge. Small pieces of plastic clinked through the louvers, sucked away as she thrust the phone at the sensing arm again.

The red light snapped on. Three clawed arms released the maneuvering belt and reached for the damaged phone. Retreating into the cowling, Abby coaxed them in. The body of the sled struck the edges of the cowl, jets firing to hold its position as its arms stretched for the phone, new segments unfolding from the MMU's casings to increase its range. One set of claws snatched the phone from her tiny fingers and she followed, scrambling along the walls of the cowling toward the MMU. Taking both of the engineer's drifting tethers in hand, she pushed off from the sled, rolled and landed on the grating a half second later.

"What are you doing?"

She only smiled back, her face illuminated by bands of brightening white light stabbing out from behind him. The main sterilizing pulse must be only seconds away.

Abby clipped the good tether to the grating's latch and shoved the other one through the louvers for David. Arms tight against her sides, tiny legs springing taut, she dove at the MMU. In the instant she flashed by the sled, she pulled the phone from the clawed grip of the repair arms and flew headfirst down the bottomless chamber beyond.

The grating groaned, shifting outward in his grip.

Abby...you're a genius.

David looped the second tether in and out of the louvers near the latch as the MMU pursued Abby. Gas jets fired and the cables unspooled as it receded. David did the math in his head. The sled was going to catch her in seconds. Probably before the working tethers ran out.

He coughed, fumes from his smoldering clothes reaching his nose.

She was so far away. So small. Something orange moved against the dark brown of her jumpsuit, and suddenly she was diminishing even faster, no more than a pinpoint against the shipscape.

Vapor trails formed behind the MMU as it switched to maximum. The light behind him throbbed brighter. With a screech of tearing metal, the tethers straightened and the grate whipped away, pulling David into the sky.

....

David manually closed the lock. Tiny blisters dotted his skin. Every twitch brought little stabs of pain.

"I'm sorry, Davie." Abby wiped her nose on a sleeve. "He scared me so much. Then, then you said you weren't scared—not even a little. I just had to know if he was real."

"Didn't you think even once about all the rules you were breaking? Everything that could go wrong?"

"'Course, I did." She pinned him with her eyes. "But people shouldn't be scared of stuff unless it's real. Not even the real stuff if they can figure out what to do."

David smiled. Who was this kid?

"Next time Elliot says the Bogeyman is going to get me or one of my friends, I'm gonna call him a big, ugly liar."

"Oh?"

"And a jerk."

David's smile faded as he saw three people at the end of the spar. Drifting just inside the door leading to the habitation modules were Mom and Dad. And to one side, the captain.

Dad looked furious. David's heart hurt at the sight, almost as much as when he looked at Mom's red, swollen eyes.

The captain's expression made no sense. How many times had he reminded them—reminded everyone—of the rules? The rules were meant to be followed. People who didn't follow the rules were a hazard to everyone. His head was cocked to one side as if he were sizing them up, especially Abby. And he was grinning.

David remembered the call the captain had received in the courtyard and how he'd seemed annoyed with whoever he was talking to. Maybe there were jobs for people who could think outside of the ship, too.

"Abby, I never answered your question." David reached out and took Abby's hand. "I don't think you're going to be a good big sister."

Abby's eyes welled with tears, and she looked away.

Taking her chin in his hand, David turned her eyes to meet his. "You're going to be amazing."

She took a second to process before she squealed, arms clamping around him, squeezing the fire out of every little blister.

And together they drifted toward home.

The Mystery of the Missing Clockwork Birds

Deanna Baran

Deanna Baran lives in Texas and is a librarian and former museum curator. She writes in between cups of tea, playing Go, and trading postcards with people around the world.

"These sandwiches are way better than black bread and fishpickles," I told the waiter, who was a boy about my age. "Can I have some more?"

He seemed amused as he said, "Yes, sir." I felt a little embarrassed. The people who usually took tea in an Auraen airship were rich, important people, like ambassadors and nobility and industrialists. They wouldn't have to eat black bread and fishpickles unless they wanted to and would think that taking more than one or two sandwiches would be greedy. But I was hungry. And these sandwiches were amazing.

The waiter came back with six more sandwiches on a silver salver, and I said, "Thanks!" Instead of hurrying away to the other tables, whose occupants were mostly done eating and were now reading or conversing quietly, he lingered around mine for a bit.

"Is this your first time in an airship?" the waiter kindly asked me.

"We've flown Paris to London a few times," I said. "And Dresden to Munich. And Frankfurt to Dusseldorf. But never this long of a journey. Rome, Athens, *and* Constantinople!" I felt self-conscious again. "But, um, I'm sure you've made the trip so many times."

"My father's the elevator of the *Nephele*," the waiter told me, proud to share that information. "When I'm older, I'll get to join the crew, too. But for now, I get to wait tables."

"The elevator?" I asked blankly.

"Well, actually, there's two," said the boy. "There's two of everything for these long trips, because there are two twelve-hour shifts. Two captains, two elevators, two navigators, two coxswains. That sort of thing."

"The elevator?" I repeated.

"Oh. The elevator is the pilot who controls the altitude of an airship. The steersman is the pilot who steers the lateral direction. It takes a very strong man to be the elevator!" Now it was my waiter's turn to feel self-conscious. "I don't usually see boys my age traveling first class on these trips."

And my turn for boasting. "I'm traveling with Professor Zoltán. He's only the greatest automaton engineer in Europe. We're delivering some of his automata, in person, to a client of his. I'm only his apprentice, but someday, I'll master all his secrets."

We grinned at each other. We traded names – he was William; I was Kázmér – and he soon disappeared back into the kitchen with a plate full of crumbs.

Those sandwiches were amazing.

....

The Professor didn't bother to answer my knock, so I had to search my pockets for my key before I could slide the bolt that secured our cabin. Professor Zoltán was sitting on his rumpled berth in our room, a magnifier loupe over his eye as he carefully manipulated tiny gears and clockwork spread out on his lap desk. Sheets and blankets were shoved haphazardly to the foot of his bed, but his workspace was neat and tidy. A cool breeze came through the open sliding windows. I stayed by the doorway, even though I knew there was no danger of the airship rolling and tipping me out the window. I loved watching us pass through clouds, but it always unnerved me to see our shadow slipping across the ground beneath us. Far, far, beneath us.

"They've finished putting the lunch things out of the way,

Professor," I said. "Wouldn't the light be better on the observation deck?" What I wanted to say was, "If we're not doing anything, I'd like to take a nap, so go work somewhere else," but of course, I couldn't.

The Professor nudged the locked case under his berth with his heel, as though to reassure himself it was still there. "I refuse to leave my little pets unattended. I will not feel safe until we have delivered them. They must not fall into the wrong hands." He shifted his focus back to the tiny inner workings strewn in front of him.

I understood. They were some of the Professor's cleverest work yet. There were some larger automata safely stowed away in the cargo area, but this small case stayed with him at all times. In it were four beautiful, jeweled clockwork birds. They could sing five different songs separately or in harmony. While they were spiffy little knickknacks by themselves, they also concealed a listening device of the most recent innovation. While the Ottoman Empire had discarded the practice of "survival of the fittest" long ago, there was plenty enough intrigue amongst the upper ranks of the nobility that made such devices far more valuable than the worth of their gold and jewels. Many people would do much to eavesdrop on their enemies.

"I guess I'll go back to the observation deck," I said. "We should land in Athens in about two hours."

The Professor nodded, his eyes still fixed on his work. "Amuse yourself for now. I will ask you to resume work on your clockwork hedgehog after the *Nephele* has departed Athens."

I escaped. Working on the small bits and pieces of my clockwork hedgehog made my eyes cross and my fingers clumsy. It hurt just thinking about it.

I found myself on the first-class observation deck where I had dined earlier. There were maybe a dozen first-class passengers on this trip, including the Professor and me. Most people traveled in third class, crammed together in closely grouped chairs, but in first class we had the options of drifting between comfortable private cabins or the roomy observation deck. For short trips, it didn't matter so much; for longer trips, it made all the difference. I knew it was reflected in the price difference, but Professor Zoltán's clients seemed incapable of doing anything with money but spend it lavishly.

I took a table near the door that led to the first-class private cabins, not too close to any of the windows that lined the two outer walls of the observation deck. I had a deck of cards in my pocket and soon became absorbed in solitaire. I was vaguely aware of my fellow passengers. The occasional staff member circulated discreetly through the room, popping in and out of doors like some automaton on a clock, never too far away from a request for assistance. A woman in a green dress needed a stamp for a postcard. A man in a brown sack suit and striped trousers requested the London *Times*. A pair of older women was consulting Baedeker's *Egypt*. Three men in tailcoats had a large map spread between them on a table, marching salt shakers and pocket watches across the map while arguing in Italian. A young woman sitting near an open window was knitting a baby's jacket from fluffy yellow wool. Two men in expensive silk vests and frock coats were each engrossed in his own reading.

"Black seven on red eight," advised a voice to my side. I jumped.

"William! I didn't see you." I also hadn't seen the black seven. I moved the card, flipped the card underneath, and came up with my ace of diamonds. Good card.

"May I get you anything?" he asked politely.

Seeing that I had just finished my lunch within the half-hour, I wasn't really needing anything. "I'm fine. What's for dinner?"

"Cold capon and ham," he said. "Caviar and foie gras, if you care for it."

I'd rather eat fishpickles. "It sounds like the menu for a fancy picnic," I said.

"No flames are allowed on board," William replied simply. "It's a safety issue. We confiscate everyone's matches and pipes and things before takeoff. The hydrogen, you know. But that also means no hot water for washing up, and no hot food or hot drink."

I'd sort of noticed it on the shorter trips, but now that he mentioned it, it made sense.

"So, do you know how many people are continuing all the way to Constantinople?" I asked William, nodding my head at the other people traveling first-class.

"You and the Professor are the only ones," said William. "Everyone else will disembark in Athens. Of course, new people will come on board for the next leg of the journey."

William seemed to know all sorts of things. He had stories about Greece, about Rome, and places he'd visited when the airships were grounded due to weather. He talked about how the furniture was wicker and the piano was aluminum and the staff and crew were kept to a minimum to keep the weight of the airship down. He told me how the *Nephele* never really flies in a straight line; it oscillates around its flight path in something called 'curvilinear flight'. He had definite opinions about rigid airships versus semirigid airships versus nonrigid airships, and talked at great length about envelopes and radial rings and drag and the center of gravity. He talked about how he was saving his money and building a little dirigible of his own back home, just big enough for one, to race at fairs and festivals.

I didn't know anything about real airships, but it suddenly occurred to me that a little mechanical airship that could fly around could be quite popular. How to keep it from crashing without a pilot or an elevator? How to not lose it in a tree or in a lake? I needed to find out more about airships from William, and I needed to run the idea past Professor Zoltán for his input once I had my basic ideas sketched out on paper. "Wait right here! I need to get my ideas notebook!"

I left William with my abandoned game of solitaire and nearly tripped over my feet in my haste to get back to the cabin I shared with the Professor. The bolt had been shot home again, but my key was in my pocket. I burst into the room in my quest for the notebook I keep all my inspiration for future projects – and promptly forgot about it.

The curtains still fluttered next to the open window. Professor Zoltán was sprawled untidily on the floor.

....

I'm not really sure how they got there, but the captain and the man in the brown suit, who was a German medical doctor, were both standing in the compartment with me.

"Insensible," said Dr. Schmidt, kneeling next to his patient. "Cold skin. Feeble pulse. Irregular dilation of the pupil. A concussion." He attempted to rouse the Professor by shakes and barking questions in his ear. The Professor was still unconscious, but was pitching around on the floor, muttering unintelligibly in our native Hungarian. He was my brilliant Professor, but I barely recognized him like this.

I didn't have much time before the Professor began to retch. I grabbed the chamber pot from the washstand and tried to ignore the sounds he made while I held it steady. Dr. Schmidt seemed pleased as he helped us.

"He will recover," Dr. Schmidt said, checking Professor Zoltán's pulse and observing his breathing after we had wiped him up and sent the chamber pot off with the steward for cleaning. "I will prepare a mustard poultice to stimulate his blood. We will let him rest and heal, and perhaps he will be able to tell us something of his ordeal."

I helped the Professor undress and pulled down the sheets of the neatly made bed, while the doctor prepared a mustard poultice on a flannel and placed it on the Professor's chest. The captain looked concerned and confused as we three piled into the narrow passageway. The captain locked the cabin door with his own key. This had never happened before. Who would do such a thing? And why on the *Nephele*?

"A thief!" I said, excited and upset and not able to shout like I wanted to shout because the Professor wasn't to be disturbed. "His case is missing! Someone knocked him on the head and stole it! Those birds can't be replaced!"

"The airship lands in an hour," the captain said. "Surely we cannot detain our passengers and interrogate them like criminals and prevent them from leaving until the case is found! They would be shocked! Insulted!"

"Why not?" I asked, still upset. Wasn't the captain in charge? Why didn't he act like it? There was nothing I could do to help the Professor's physical state. Why couldn't I at least help him retrieve his birds? They had to still be on the airship, but once we landed, I knew they would vanish for good.

The doctor shooed me towards the observation deck with an impatient "let-the-grownups-talk" sort of gesture. I wasn't about to be rid of so easily, but I saw William lurking at the end of the passageway. "Come with me," he whispered loudly, and I forced myself to follow him back to the table.

My fellow passengers were still in their places with books and maps and letters and salt shakers, unaware of the drama that had just unfolded nearby. Or was one of them pretending and waiting to make an escape with those priceless clockwork birds once we landed in Athens...?

"We need to be detectives," William said quietly. "You need to calm down and think. We only have an hour to solve the mystery."

That made me settle down and focus. "All right."

"Now, let's draw a map," said William. He grabbed some notepaper and a fountain pen from a writing desk and sketched out a rough oval, the shape of the gondola. "Now, at this end of the gondola, we have seven private sleeping cabins and a workstation for supplies." He drew a few lines. Four compartments on the left, four on the right, with a hallway between them. "There's the door to the passage. On this side of the door, you have the first-class observation deck." He drew more lines. "And then over here, you have the kitchen, which separates the first-class observation deck from the third-class observation deck."

I looked at the map. "There's no way for the third-class passengers to get to the first-class part of the ship without being really obvious and walking right through the kitchen," I said.

"That's right. Now, this little square…" William drew a square next to the door which led from the first-class observation deck to the passageway for the first-class cabins. "…is your table, where we've been sitting and talking. No one could access the first-class cabins without passing right by us. And no one could leave the first-class cabins without passing by us as well."

"You mean the thief walked right past me?" I asked.

"Twice, probably," said William. "So think back. How long have you been sitting here, and who passed by you?"

I sat and thought. "I remember when I left the Professor, alone and healthy, I told him we would land in two hours. And after we found the Professor, the captain said that we land in an hour. So I've been sitting at this table for about an hour."

"Good!" said William. "So, what did you see during that hour?"

"I was playing cards at first," I said miserably. "People were moving around… talking… asking for help… things like that. I don't remember."

"Well, all of the crew and staff have been working with us for at least a year," said William. "They're not in the habit of randomly robbing passengers. It's bad for business. But why your Professor's automatons? I know he's the greatest automaton engineer in Europe," he added hastily, "but there are a lot of wealthy, influential people on this trip. Why not steal the Countess of Caldwell's jewel case…" (he flicked his pen to indicate the woman in a green dress) "…or the secret papers of Alario the Pasta King?" (indicating one of the men arguing over salt shakers.)

"How do you know who they are?" I asked him, impressed.

"I always read the passenger manifest," William replied simply. "Shouldn't I know who I serve?"

I sat back and racked my brains. "The Countess was writing letters to people. I don't remember her ever getting up from the writing desk. She asked for a stamp, and the steward gave her one."

William was writing a list of names next to his map. He put an X next to the Countess of Caldwell.

"The Pasta King was with his two friends. I only saw them arguing over a map. They had a bunch of salt shakers they were using for markers, so I'm sure they got them from somewhere, but I never actually saw them go anywhere," I said.

William put tidy little X's next to "Alario (Pasta King)", "Niro (Olive Oil King)", and "Tomassi (Tomato King)". I grinned, wondering if they had been using their map to plot world domination through spaghetti, but then I got serious again.

"Those two grandmas who were reading a guidebook. It was an Egyptian guidebook, which is weird, because we're not going to Egypt. We're going to Greece and Turkey."

"Ah, that would be the two Americans, Mrs. Wilson and Mrs. Marsh, on pilgrimage to the Holy Land. But first, one week in Florence, two weeks in Venice, two weeks in Rome. On to Athens to see the Acropolis. Later on to Egypt to see the pyramids."

"Who tells you this stuff?" I asked.

"People like to talk about their travel plans. Just like you told me how you were traveling, in the most expensive way in the world, to deliver automata to a presumably fabulously wealthy client at a palace in Constantinople."

I stared at him. Had I accidentally blabbed the Professor's secrets? Had William snuck into the compartment, knocked the Professor on the head, stolen his case, hid it somewhere safe, and then kept me company to prevent his crime from being discovered long enough to land in Athens and pass the goods on to an accomplice?

William didn't see my suspicion. He was already bent back over our paper, writing more names. "The woman with the knitting is Miss Easton. She's the Countess' traveling companion. Did she ever move?"

"They ate together earlier, but I didn't realize they were actually traveling together. She sat in that chair the whole time, and the Countess was over at the writing desk. The only weird thing was that the Countess asked the steward for stamps directly. She didn't tell Miss Easton to put down her knitting and get the steward to get her a stamp. But since they were so far apart, she probably wouldn't yell across the room. It would have been easier to ask whichever of them was closer," I said. I tried to remember which side William had appeared from when he had joined me. The door side or the window side? It had been the door side, right? He had remained standing for our whole conversation – it wouldn't have been proper for a waiter to sit down at a passenger's table – but he had moved over to the window side of my table so as not to block the door to the cabins. Hadn't he?

"You've met Herr Doktor Schmidt," he said. "What was he doing while you were playing cards?"

"He asked for a newspaper. And then he read it," I said. "He asked for a London newspaper, which I thought was interesting since he had a German accent, and we were traveling in Italy and Greece. Wouldn't he want local news or home news?" I hadn't seen which way William had approached me. Had he come through the door then turned to tell me how to play my cards, or had he approached the door, but got distracted by my game before he reached it?

"And that leaves Mr. Rokos and Mr. Terzi," said William, looking at the two men in silk vests and frock coats who were still engrossed in their respective books. "They're very famous architects."

"They haven't moved at all." Would William hit me on the head too if he knew I suspected him? My palms were hot and sweaty, and I clenched my fists under the table to keep them from shaking.

"This is hard," frowned William, looking at the paper. "What about your movements? Did you notice any clues?"

I shook my head. "After lunch, I visited the Professor, but not for long. He was sitting on the bed and working on the inner mechanisms of a commission. A clockwork lotus. He suggested that I work on my hedgehog after we departed Athens. I left pretty quickly at that. I played cards for a while. You joined me sometime during my game. I didn't keep track of how many hands I played. I won a few; I lost a lot. We talked for a while. I went to go get my notebook. I found him."

"Was the door open?" asked William.

"No, the door was shut," I said. "I remember, because it was locked, and I had to stop long enough to get my key."

"Did you lock the door behind you on your way out before?"

"No, I was busy thinking about that hedgehog. I didn't even think about locking the door behind me."

"So he locked himself in. And yet somehow, someone got in, banged him on the head, stole the case, and disappeared without you seeing him."

"The window was open," I suggested.

William stared at me. "You seriously think someone crawled along the outside of the gondola? We're a mile over the Gulf of Corinth. There's no railing or ladder or platform. Can you think of anyone being that insane?"

For ordinary jeweled birds, no. For jeweled birds that could listen to a secret conversation and transmit a signal to a hidden receiver... yes. But I had endangered enough of the Professor's secrets. If William had taken the clockwork birds, it was for their gold and their jewels, not because he knew their true value.

"And it's not like you can take someone by surprise like that," said William. "I mean, if someone from outside tried to climb through that open window over there, you honestly think that every person in this room wouldn't know about it before he got his leg over the sill?"

"How could someone hit him on the head, I wonder? He was sitting on the bed when I left him. When the Professor starts working, he doesn't stop to eat, he doesn't stop to sleep, he doesn't stop to go to the bathroom... he has no sense of time. He'd work forever if he could. Dr. Schmidt said he was struck from behind. But how could someone strike him from behind if he was on the bed? That doesn't make sense either. He was anxious for the safety of his little birds. He wouldn't open the door to a stranger. He wouldn't even open the door for me."

I wondered if William would tell me how he did it. But he

looked just as baffled as I felt.

I edged away from my friend. "I'm going to go back to the cabin."

"I'll come with you. Maybe there are clues," said William, setting down his pen and standing up.

Did William want to make sure he hadn't done something dumb like drop his calling card on the floor? "Aren't you at work?" I asked him. "Won't your boss get mad at you?"

"I work in the kitchen. I serve the meals and tidy things up in between. This is my free time." He looked a little hurt. "You don't want to be detectives together?"

What I wanted to say was, "I'm scared of you." But of course I couldn't. Instead, I said, "You said the staff and the crew were innocent. How much crew does the *Nephele* actually have?"

"The chef and his assistant prepare the food. I serve first class. Ahmed serves third class. The first-class steward tidies the compartments in the morning, serves drinks at night, and makes sure everyone has what they need throughout the day. There's a third-class steward as well."

"You said the crew worked on twelve-hour shifts. What about the staff?"

"The airship can't fly by itself," said William. "But fortunately, the passengers understand that if they want foie gras at three in the morning, they need to wait. You can ring the steward for an emergency that you can't handle on your own, but otherwise, we have usual working hours between six in the morning and nine at night."

I did the math in my head. A fifteen-hour working day!

"The captain has a master key. I saw him use it. Does anyone else have the master key to the compartments?" I asked.

"Of course. Like with a hotel. You don't want someone accidentally locking themselves out of their compartment," said William. "And we have to get in to change the sheets, make the bed, empty the slops. The steward has a set, and the captain has a set."

"Could someone steal the steward's keys?" I asked. "Or does he loan his keys out?"

"He'd get fired if he did," said William.

I opened the cabin door. Professor Zoltán snored gently on the berth and muttered in Hungarian. I gingerly sat on the edge of the bed so as not to disturb him.

"When I left him, he was sitting like this," I said. "He had the lap desk on his lap, and the loupe over his eye."

"The lap desk is in the corner," said William. It was neatly set out of the way, as tidy as though he had just set it aside to stretch and take a quick break when an invisible hand had raised itself to attack...

"Oh, there's the loupe," I said. "It's under the washstand. I wonder if it fell off when he fell?" I picked up the delicate optic. The wires were a little bent, but the lenses were intact. It could be repaired.

Dr. Schmidt appeared in the open doorway. I jumped and tried not to yell. I was really on edge. He looked surprised. "I've come to change the poultice and check on Professor Zoltán," he said. He sat down where I had been sitting before I got up to pick up the loupe, and began checking the Professor's vital signs. I watched him.

Tick. Tick. Tick. My head felt like there was something I was supposed to be seeing, something I ought to remember. I felt like a stuck cog that just couldn't quite get past a jam.

And then I saw it. And this time, I didn't try to stop my yell. "Get the captain! Quick! Before it's too late!" I hollered at Dr. Schmidt.

....

Professor Zoltán's head was bandaged up. His mind, normally racing along ten different thoughts at once, was sluggish and quiet, and the calm disturbed him. I knew it would be a while before he felt himself again, but I also knew he was grateful to have just traded a bit of his mental sharpness in exchange for, say, his life.

"So how did you know it was the steward?" he asked. "I still have no memory of anything."

"I had thought it was William at first," I explained. "But it didn't fit. You were so focused on your work, nothing could have interrupted you. Except for room service. The bed was messy when I left you, and has been ever since we left Rome, but when I came back, the bed was made. The steward must have come; you must have set your lap desk in the corner, where it wouldn't get knocked over or trod upon; and he went about his work. Either you let him in, or he let himself in. Normally, a servant wouldn't do his work where he could be seen, but you never left the cabin, not even to eat. He needed the case to disappear before we reached Athens so it would be presumed that it was gone by the time we made it to Constantinople. He was getting desperate. No one pays attention to a servant who's working; I bet it was easy for him to cosh you, grab the case, hide it in the service compartment linens, lock the door behind him so that no one would notice, get on with his duties on the observation deck, and leave the rest to time."

Professor Zoltán looked sad. "The captain tells me our friend the steward is being detained and will be thoroughly interrogated, but I would not be surprised to hear he had been bribed by a powerful enemy of our client. I would not be surprised to hear that an accident befalls him before we find out, either."

It gave my stomach an unpleasant feeling to think that the steward wasn't alone and there might still be danger. The manufacture of items intended for espionage was obviously lucrative, but gold was worthless if you weren't alive to spend it.

"I hope they don't try anything else," I said. "I think I'll stay with you in the cabin. Just for the extra protection."

"Ahh, excellent. My head hurts, but I find myself rather hungry. I take that to be a good sign. Do you think they might have a jar of rollmops somewhere? I'm having an odd craving for them."

"Fishpickles? I don't think so. But they have amazing sandwiches."

The Sugimori Sisters and the Interplanetary Concept Clash

Brigid Collins

Brigid Collins is an author living in Michigan with her husband, Nick, and their cat, Brooke. She writes mainly works of fantasy and science fiction. She has written and published two novels, with her third due to be published this fall. Two of her short stories will be appearing in Fiction River *late in 2014, and she has achieved Honorable Mention in the Writers of the Future Contest. She also enjoys music, video games, and copious quantities of stuffed animals. Brigid Collins has a blog at www. backwrites.wordpress.com and can be contacted through that site, as well as through her twitter account, @purellian.*

Ellen Sugimori fought to keep the heat of shame from showing on her face. If her mom had *tried* to embarrass her in front of the entire sixth-grade class, she couldn't have done a more effective job. Since the move from Lansing, Ellen was a new student this year. She didn't need her mom adding to her status of *weird.*

Ellen watched her mom take her tiny, shuffling steps out of the classroom and braced herself for the slithering snickers she knew her classmates had been holding back throughout the presentation.

Ellen should have said no two weeks ago when her history teacher had asked her to invite her mom to do a presentation on the Japanese tea ceremony for the class.

"But my mom doesn't speak English," Ellen had protested, keeping her voice low so the other students wouldn't hear.

"You can translate for her. Your classmates will be impressed that you speak Japanese as well as English."

Ellen knew they wouldn't. Worse, they would know that her mom wasn't like theirs; she wasn't a normal American mom who made peanut butter and jelly sandwiches for her lunch or drove her to soccer practice after school. They would know that her mom was stupid and weird.

And none of the other kids would be impressed with her mom's choice of clothes.

Why, oh, *why* had her mom come to school in a *kimono*?

As the other kids chattered, Ellen picked up the tea cups and leftover matcha powder. Ellen took the cups to the sink in the back of the classroom to wash them before shoving them into her backpack.

Her mouth was dry from the translating and from standing by the chalkboard for so long, where the air was full of the tasteless white dust. But she didn't ask to go get a drink.

Ellen didn't dare look at any of the other kids for the rest of the day. She couldn't bear to see their teasing faces, so she kept her eyes forward and sat on her hands so she wouldn't accidentally raise them to answer questions.

Instead, Ellen spent the whole class stewing over the culture project she had to do for Japanese school next week. She had to go every Saturday to study her Japanese heritage and language, as if she didn't get enough of that at home. She still hadn't decided what to do for the project since everything she thought of sounded boring and irrelevant. They didn't live in Japan, after all. They lived in Detroit.

People in Detroit didn't do things like the tea ceremony or flower arranging.

When the final bell rang, Ellen pushed her chair back so fast it screeched against the floor. Grabbing up her backpack and swinging it over her shoulder, Ellen dashed out the door ahead of everyone else.

The tea cups clinked against each other as she fast-walked out of the building. Ellen heard them even over the screams and laughs of other students pouring out into the freedom of the afternoon.

Outside, she slowed down and took a deep breath. Summer vacation was almost here, and Ellen thought the neighborhood smelled *green*. Like leaves and sunshine.

She kicked at pebbles on the sidewalk as she walked to her house three blocks away. The fact that they lived so close to school made her nervous, just thinking about how easy it would be for one of her friends to find out what her family was really like.

Ellen snorted. Not so much of an issue anymore, was it?

And her mom called her Eriko! How many times did she have to tell her she wanted to be called Ellen? The name was much more elegant and grown-up. Eriko sounded like a little kid's name.

Not to mention her friends couldn't pronounce it very well.

"Mom's lived in America for thirteen years," Ellen mumbled. "Why hasn't she learned to speak English yet? It's not hard."

Nobody was around to answer her, so Ellen just slouched the rest of the way home.

She reached their driveway at house number 544 and walked up it, careful not to step on any cracks. No weeds poked up from them, thanks to her dad's meticulous yard work every weekend. Their potted flowers added splashes of red and pink to the front walk and porch, all done in a traditional Japanese fashion.

Little Sister has been scribbling on the driveway again, she noticed. Addition and subtraction problems covered the cracked concrete, and dotted lines connected circles like a path on a treasure map.

As if the thought were a magic conjuration, Risako appeared from the back yard. "What took you so long?"

Ellen rolled her eyes. "You first-graders get out an hour earlier than the sixth-graders do."

"Oh, right. Well, do you want to come to Saturn with me?"

"Saturn?"

"I just finished my spaceship!"

Ellen pictured the cardboard and plastic monstrosity that had taken up the corner of the back yard for the past week. "Oh.

Okay, I guess I can play with you for a little while."

The longer she could delay going inside and seeing her mom, the better.

Ellen followed Little Sister around the house, her backpack clinking with every step.

She had to admit, Little Sister's construction was impressive. Any six-year-old could throw slabs of cardboard together and claim it was a spaceship, but Little Sister's creation actually looked like a space-worthy vessel.

Paper towel tubes were bunched together with rubber bands and glued to the sides to be thrusters. The front was a pointed nose cone. Properly curved cardboard fins jutted out of the top and sides. The garden hose curled around from place to place. She even had the clear plastic lid from their toy box as the windshield.

"You sit in the co-pilot's seat, Ellen," Little Sister directed, lifting the toy box lid and clambering into the other side.

Ellen held up the lid and swung her legs into the seat. She put her backpack at her feet.

Inside, it smelled like cut paper and crayons. Little Sister had drawn a control panel at the front with buttons labeled in both English and Japanese. The seats were just big, black rectangles on the floor and back wall of the cockpit.

"Okay, I'm ready for lift-off," Ellen said.

"It'll take a minute," Little Sister said, poking at some of the drawn buttons. "It runs on green energy, so it needs to collect enough green from the grass first."

"Green energy?" Ellen asked.

"We're learning about it in school this week. Mrs. Carter says green energy is better for the planet, so I made my spaceship run on it."

Ellen's lips quirked up, but she didn't say anything. Why couldn't their spaceship be powered by the color green?

"Okay, we're ready," Little Sister said. "Hold on tight."

"Okay." Ellen leaned forward to put her hands on the control panel.

The thrusters fired up, and Ellen flew backward against her black crayon seat as the ship zoomed into the air.

"Ahh! What's going on?!"

Little Sister looked over at her. "We're going to Saturn, dummy. I told you to hold on."

"It's pretend! What did you *do*?" How could Little Sister just pilot her cardboard spaceship like it flew through the air every day?

Little Sister didn't answer her question, too focused on propelling them through the turbulence of the atmosphere.

Higher and higher they flew, and Ellen held her breath. Her ears popped.

Weren't airplanes pressurized so people's heads wouldn't explode or something? She didn't want her head to explode, and she definitely didn't want to get Little Sister's brains splattered all over her school clothes. Mom would throw a fit.

The cardboard and plastic rattled all around them as air buffeted the ship. Ellen scrabbled her fingers around the cockpit, searching for something to hold onto. They flew faster and faster, up and up, and the rushing wind grew louder and louder.

The shaking stopped. They smoothed out and shot away from planet Earth and into the inky, star-speckled darkness of space.

Ellen twisted in her seat, trying to look back towards home, but she couldn't manage it.

"I should have put a window in the back," Little Sister admitted.

Ellen settled back in her seat, letting out a shaky breath. "How long until we reach Saturn?"

Little Sister poked at some of the crayon squares and squinted at the big one in the middle. Ellen realized that it was supposed to be a display screen, but nothing appeared on it.

It was just a square drawn on cardboard, after all.

"Probably only twenty minutes," Little Sister said with a shrug. "Green energy is very efficient."

"Watch out!" Ellen screamed.

The Moon loomed before them through the plastic toy box

lid, so bright it was blinding.

They were headed for a collision!

Little Sister wrestled with the controls. The spaceship turned to the right, but the Moon still got closer and closer.

"We need more speed!" Ellen shouted. "Full power on the thrusters!"

She jabbed at the square labeled THRUSTERS スラスタ, and the ship lurched. They pulled away to the right, just skimming a few feet above the surface of the Moon.

Ellen watched the craters whizz by, trying not to think about how close they'd just come to becoming a crater themselves.

"That was too close, Little Sister," Ellen said, slumping back in her seat. "You have to be a responsible driver."

Little Sister giggled. "You sound like mom."

"I do not."

"Do, too."

"Mom doesn't know the word 'responsible,' and she sounds stupid when she tries to say 'drive.' *Doraibuuuuu*." Ellen extended the last syllable, trying to make Little Sister laugh.

Little Sister did laugh. "Yeah, but she says the same things in Japanese. Be responsible, do your homework, study Kanji! I wish we didn't have to go to Japanese School on Saturdays."

Ellen sighed. "Me, too." Normal American kids didn't have to go to Japanese School.

It wasn't that she didn't *like* her Japanese heritage. Anime was cool, and she had a whole collection of manga. Some of the video games were fun, when she could convince dad to buy them for her. But the tea ceremony was boring, and calligraphy and Kanji sucked. She worried about her culture project again.

She sighed once more, then sniffed.

"I smell burning paper," she said.

"Oh, no," Little Sister moaned. She poked at the buttons and squinted at the blank display. "The brush with the Moon damaged the fuel tank. We're running on fumes!"

"Green has fumes?" Ellen asked.

But there was no time to question it. The sputtering, jerking motion of the ship shook the left thruster loose, and it sent them spinning.

Little Sister and Ellen grappled with the controls to pull themselves into a straight path. When they reached a semi-steady trajectory, a bright plane of rusty red filled their view.

"Mars!" Little Sister squealed.

"We're gonna crash!"

They hurtled through the atmosphere of the red planet. Sweat rolled down Ellen's face and back as their entry heated up the cockpit. The smell of burning paper surrounded her, and she squinched her eyes closed and pressed her lips together to keep from screaming.

A hard jolt and a loud ripple of crumpling cardboard signified their arrival.

....

For having crash-landed on Mars, the spaceship didn't look too bad. The nose was stuck in the red dirt and crunched up, and one thruster dangled by a thin strip of masking tape, but otherwise, it looked as flight-worthy as it ever had.

Little Sister tugged on the back to pull it out of the dirt. The garden hose flopped amongst the rocks, and Little Sister groaned.

"The fuel tank's been completely drained," she said. "I can fix the hole, but we need to find more green stuff to get home."

Ellen glanced around. "But we're on Mars. There's no green here."

Little Sister frowned at the back of the ship, rubbing her chin the way dad did when he was trying to solve a problem.

"I could make an adaptor," she mumbled. "Something to let the ship run on red. But I would need some construction paper and red and green building bricks."

Ellen's heart sank and rolled around in her tummy. "I don't think we'll find any of those here."

"Then we've got to look for them."

Ellen wrapped her arms around herself and followed Little Sister away from the ship. She glanced back at it, trying to imagine how any of this could have happened.

A reddish-brown smudge streaked across the horizon to their left, and Ellen worried about Mars's famous dust storms. She didn't want to get caught in one. The dust rose in puffs around her feet, and the wind dragged it across the ground. It pushed at Ellen's back with its dry chill, urging her to catch up with Little Sister.

Far ahead of her, Little Sister stopped and pointed down. "A rover! Ellen, look."

Ellen came up beside her at the edge of a short drop. They were on top of a plateau. At the bottom, just as Little Sister said, a Mars rover sat motionless.

She thought it looked like a big bird with a long neck and six legs. Maybe a weird dragon? But not a Japanese dragon, because the solar panels looked like wings.

"Great! Maybe we can contact NASA and get them to get us home," she said. She inched herself over the edge and slid down it in a shower of rocks and red dust.

"Hello?" she said to the silent rover. "Uh, Houston?"

Little Sister came over to the rover, brushing dust from her pants. She peered at the machine, and swept a hand over the flat table of dusty solar panels.

"I think it's sleeping, or broken," she said. "Look, it's stuck in the dirt here."

Ellen looked at the rover's wheels. Dirt had piled up around them, rendering the machine immobile. "Can we dig it out and get it running again?"

Little Sister shrugged. "Let's try."

They both got on their hands and knees, scooping the dirt away from the wheels until some of them were unburied.

Little Sister sat back and wiped her hand over her forehead, smearing red dirt across her face. "I don't know if we can get it out. Let me see if I can get it to turn on."

Little Sister clambered up onto one of the solar panel wings and tapped on the camera.

"Be careful you don't fall off," Ellen said as a strong gust of wind whipped around the plateau.

The landscape was nothing like home. No trees or grass grew, no water flowed. Having lived in a flat part of Michigan all her life, Ellen found all these hills unsettling. The red everywhere made her think the place should be blazing hot, but she shivered every time the wind whistled by. If it was going to be cold, there ought to at least be some snow to play in.

Ellen wanted to go home, where she knew how to interact with her environment.

"Agh, I can't do anything without materials!" Little Sister lamented. She leapt off of the solar panels and landed in the dust with a *flump*. "If I had some more cardboard and some pipe cleaners, I could get it working again."

"Is there anything green on it?" Ellen asked. If they could at least get some fuel for their ship, the rover wouldn't be a total dud.

"Maybe underneath? Or inside. Computer chips are green, right?"

Ellen and Little Sister knelt back in the dirt and wriggled beneath the rover's belly.

Ellen ran her finger over a seam in the body. "Let's get this open."

"Halt!"

Ellen and Little Sister both gasped and jumped. Ellen bumped her head against the rover.

From her spot on the ground, she saw four metallic legs marching through the dust and rocks towards them. Each leg was capped with a flat, round foot, which pivoted to conform to the rocky ground.

The metal legs stopped just by the rover, and a whirr of machinery accompanied the appearance of a pair of binocular-like eyes. The eyes scanned over the two of them on the end of a long, snaky metal cord.

"Come away from the silent watcher, Earthlings."

Ellen and Little Sister hurried to obey. Before them stood a four-legged, two-armed robot. The binocular eyes snapped into place above a square metal speaker.

"Are you a rover?" Ellen asked.

The robot rotated its eyes and speaker around the pole that made up its body. "I am a grave keeper. Why have you come to our resting place, Earthlings?"

"We didn't mean to," said Little Sister. "We were going to Saturn, but we crash-landed here. We're out of fuel. Do you have any green stuff?"

"Grrreeeeen?" the grave keeper repeated, lengthening the word like he didn't understand how to pronounce it.

"Green, like grass or trees or Oscar the Grouch?" Little Sister pressed.

The grave keeper rotated its eyes again. "Are you a new version of the silent watcher? We spoke with it before it died, but it did not understand our concept of 'two.' You have a new concept that I do not understand, this grrreeeeen. My analysis shows that this may be blasphemy, and I should take you in."

"Wait, what?" Ellen said.

The grave keeper did not elaborate but reached out with its two arms faster than Ellen could blink. It picked both of them up and hoisted them over its binocular eyes.

"Hey!" Ellen yelled, kicking her legs and pulling on the arms with her hands. "Put us down."

The grave keeper ignored them and walked away from the rover. Its metal feet crunched over the rocks. "I will take you down to City 542 and show you to the Server. It will judge this grrreeeeen, and you."

....

The grave keeper took them to an underground city made of red and brown buildings. The streetlamps shone orange over the pink stone of the roads, where large robots with thick wheels trundled from place to place.

Other types of robots crawled along the sidewalks or hopped across the street. A few tiny ones even flew through the air with rotating helicopter blades.

All of them spoke to each other in a strange, beeping and clicking language of computer sounds.

"What are they saying?" Little Sister asked as two robots swiveled their eyes to watch them pass.

"You don't know?" asked the grave keeper. "That is embarrassing. Our language is simple. They are preparing for our Festival of Calculations tomorrow. Your arrival interrupts our work."

Ellen glanced up at a long yellow banner stretching between two buildings and tried to make out the words on it.

The grave keeper carried them into a large brown building lit with red light bulbs.

A computer hum vibrated down the long corridor, and Ellen stared at the bundles of cables and pipes running along the walls. The grave keeper's four feet clopped like a horse's hooves on the sheet metal floor plates.

They passed under a large ventilating fan. Ellen peered up into it and thought she could see a tiny speck of brown Martian sky far above her. The *whump-whump* of the blades drowned out any sound of outside, though.

Even with the fan, Ellen was sweating from the heat of the machines. Her school clothes stuck to her skin, and beads of moisture collected on her face. She struggled to wipe at them in her awkward position above the grave keeper's head.

The corridor widened, and they arrived at a large doorway. The grave keeper stepped through it without pausing and walked to the center of the room.

Then it brought its arms down and dropped the two girls onto the floor.

"Server, I found two Earthlings on the surface, desecrating the remains of both our dead and the silent watcher. They speak of a concept called grreeeeen, which I calculate may be blasphemy."

Ellen rubbed at her elbow where she'd bashed it against the floor and stared at her surroundings.

The walls of the room flared with tiny lights. They blinked in patterns she couldn't understand. Cables crisscrossed the walls and the floor. The whole place smelled hot and sterile, without a speck of dust in it.

The computer hum increased, and Ellen slid towards Little Sister. Whatever was going to happen, she wouldn't let it hurt her sister.

"Earthlings, *hmmm*? And a blasphemous concept. The penalty for blasphemy is imprisonment until your circuits rust over."

The deep voice came from every direction at once, and Ellen hunched over Little Sister, feeling like a cornered animal.

Little Sister shifted to sit cross-legged. "We don't have any circuits; we're humans. Does that mean we'll be imprisoned forever?"

"Risako!" Ellen hissed.

The deep voice surrounded them again, and Ellen noticed that a number of speakers were set into the walls to create a stereo effect.

"You will be imprisoned for an appropriate time if you are guilty of blasphemy. Tell us more about this grreeeeen."

Little Sister huffed a tired sigh. "Like I told the grave keeper, green is like grass or trees or Oscar the Grouch. It's the fuel our ship runs on. If I could just borrow some construction paper and some red and green building bricks, I can fix our ship and get us back home. The construction paper can be any color, whatever you have is fine."

"Construction paper and building bricks?" the server asked. "We do not have such building materials. And your request does not answer the question of grreeeeen. If you cannot properly explain it, you will be imprisoned."

Little Sister thumped her fists on the floor. "How can you not know what green is? It's a color just like all the others. Some apples are green, and some grapes."

The server whirred in all the walls.

The grave keeper stepped forward. "My own blasphemy calculations are rising. I do not know any of the things this Earthling mentions. Shall we imprison them for however long it takes their circuits to rust?"

"Computer chips!" Little Sister screamed. "Ellen and I were trying to get at the green chips inside the rover when you found us. Surely you know what computer chips are!"

The server rumbled, and the lights quickened their blinking. The heat rose to a blazing level of discomfort. Ellen heard the fan in the hallway rev up.

"You would disassemble one who has come to its final rest in the resting place of the surface? You must be some sort of virus to perform such foul surgeries. Lock them up!"

A siren sounded through the building, and the tromping of boots on the steel floor reverberated into the server's room. Ellen and Little Sister cowered on the floor while three sentry robots marched in. They each held some sort of silver gun in their three-fingered hands, and the soles of their feet were covered with rubber grips like tires.

"Come with us, do not resist," said the one in the lead. Its voice was monotonous.

It reached out to grasp Little Sister by her shirt.

"Wait!" Ellen cried. "Green is like *matcha*. I forgot I had it in my backpack left over from the tea ceremony. We don't need building bricks or anything to get home."

She looked around the room, unsure where the server's eyes were. "Is that acceptable? We'll go home and never come back to bother you about green stuff again."

The server hummed. "A ceremony we understand. We will have one here tomorrow. But this teeee, I cannot calculate. Is this more blasphemy?"

Ellen stomped her foot and screamed. "How about this? You all come with us back to our ship, where I'll show you the tea ceremony. You'll see what green is, and then we can go home."

If the server suggested that demonstrations were blasphemy, she would do something drastic, like eat her shoes.

After a long moment of whirring and blinking lights, the server delivered its verdict.

"My guards and the grave keeper will go with you to see

this teeee ceremony and grreeeeen. They will then decide what percentage of your words is blasphemy and whether you should be locked up until your circuits rust."

Ellen's whoop of victory stopped in her throat when the guards clamped their three-fingered hands around her arms and marched her and Little Sister back down the corridor.

At least they were headed back to the ship, where they could attempt an escape plan.

Out in the cold, red dust fields again, Ellen and Little Sister trudged before their robot captors. The plateau and the ship lay just before them, blurred by the dusty wind.

They passed by the old rover, and Little Sister sighed.

"It would be so great to get that thing working again."

Ellen shrugged and clambered up the side of the plateau. When she reached the top, she stretched a hand out to Little Sister.

The four robots came up as well, the grave keeper moving faster than the guards with his specialized feet.

"Show us this grreeeeen teeee ceremony, Earthlings," said the lead guard once everyone had reached the top. It waved its silver gun at the wreck of their spaceship.

Ellen bit her lip at the sight of the wreckage. "Do you think you can fix the thruster and the fuel tank?" she asked Little Sister, keeping her voice low.

Little Sister circled the ship and nodded.

"Okay," Ellen said. "I'll get the stuff from my backpack, and you work on that."

She fumbled with the toy box lid and tugged her backpack out from the co-pilot's seat. It scraped against the cardboard side some, but she got it up and slung over her shoulder with a grunt.

The tea cups clinked as she walked back to where the robots waited.

"I'll have to do a short version of the ceremony," Ellen explained as she dug the tea items out. "We don't have a hanging scroll, or any flower arrangements, and my classmates already ate all the sweets you're supposed to serve. But we've got enough matcha powder to make the tea."

The robots craned over her as she arranged the tea bowl, the whisk, and the tea scoop with the container of powder on the flattest part of the ground she could find. Luckily, Ellen had some water left in her bottle she could use to make the tea. She tried to ignore their curious stares, but she couldn't help feeling like every move she made had an impact on her ability to get herself and Little Sister out of this situation and back home.

Finally, Ellen couldn't take their hovering anymore. "You four sit down in front of me while I make the tea."

The four robots looked at one another, then followed her instructions. They sat in a perfect line, the three guards looking like they'd just come off an assembly line they were so identical. The grave keeper held itself a little less stiffly, leaning forward with its binocular eyes pushed out to get a better look.

"When will you show us grreeeeen?" it asked. Ellen thought its voice sounded breathless. Was it excited?

"Right now," Ellen said, lifting the matcha container. She pulled the lid off and tipped it over the tea bowl. She shielded the rim of the bowl from the dusty wind, not wanting to lose any of the precious powder. It would be their rocket fuel, after all.

All four of the robots made a crackling sound in their speakers, and Ellen looked up to see them reel backwards in obvious shock. Then they leaned forwards.

"It exists," said the guard leader. "The Earthlings were not lying about the grreeeeen."

"Our big brother will be pleased!" said one. The third guard nudged it with its elbow and hissed, "the server."

"So we can go home?" Ellen asked, pausing in her preparations.

"Show us the teeee, I want to see it," said the grave keeper. It snaked its binocular eyes over to peer into the tea bowl.

"Stop that," Ellen chastised, slapping the eyes away. "You're getting in the way. I'll show you the tea, so long as you promise that we can go home afterwards."

The grave keeper retracted its eyes, and the guards gave her synchronized nods.

"Once you prove that teeee is real, too, you can go. My report will inform the server of the two concepts, and the information you give us will be added to the database for the whole of robotdom to peruse."

Ellen looked into the tea bowl where the pile of green powder waited to be turned into tea. Her performance of the tea ceremony here would inform all the robots on Mars? A shiver of nerves ran down her spine, and she chewed on her lip.

The idea of the robots missing information, like the scroll and the flowers, made her uncomfortable. If Ellen was going to share a piece of her Earth culture, she wanted to share all of it. She pictured herself demonstrating the whole ceremony to a crowd of enraptured robots, and a surge of pride zinged through her.

And if she could wear a pretty kimono, that would be even better.

"Maybe... we could come back some time to show you the whole thing," she suggested. "We could show you other stuff we do on Earth, too."

"Yeah, like baseball and other colors you don't know about," Little Sister shouted from behind the ship.

The grave keeper nodded, and the guards agreed.

"We can show you some of our ceremonies, too, like the Festival of Calculations or the Energy-Saving Fair," said the grave keeper.

"Those sound like a blast!" Little Sister said.

Smiling, Ellen picked up her water bottle and the whisk and made the tea with a gusto she hadn't felt for the ceremony before.

As the robots beeped and made calculations over her tea, and when the six of them poured their cups of tea into the repaired fuel tank, she understood what her mom must have felt when she shared their culture with the kids at school.

....

"Mom?" Ellen cried as she rushed into the house, leaving Little Sister to go through her landing checklist with the spaceship by herself. "Kaa-san?"

"I'm in the kitchen," mom replied in Japanese. She sounded tired amidst the banging and burbling of dinner preparations. "Did you do your homework? You have Japanese School tomorrow."

"I know," Ellen said. "I was hoping you could help me with my project. I want to learn how to do the tea ceremony really well so I can show my friends after school tomorrow."

Her mom smiled. "Of course I'll help you, Eriko."

Ellen grinned and looked out the window. A yellow banner stretched across their neighbor's back yard, ready for a party.

She couldn't wait to go back to Mars.

Pax

Eric Del Carlo

Eric Del Carlo's short fiction has appeared in Asimov's, Strange Horizons, Shimmer, Michael Moorcock's New Worlds *and many other venues. He has written novels with Robert Asprin, published by Ace Books and DarkStar Books. His latest novel, an emotionally charged urban fantasy titled* The Golden Gate Is Empty, *which he wrote with his father Vic, is forthcoming from White Cat Publications. Eric lives in his native California. Find him on Facebook for comments or questions.*

"You'd flip this" — and I flicked the plastic wall switch upward — "and that would come on. It'd be *light*." I was pointing to the ceiling fixture, which of course hadn't come on.

I'd done this a thousand times before. My pack just looked at me like they always do, not understanding. It's hard to admit sometimes: they will never understand.

We were hitting a row of suburban houses that led down into a cul-de-sac where a fire had taken out everything except for some concrete walls. The pack was excited, and I had to keep them from running around, keep them focused — so I really shouldn't have been distracting them with this same old talk about light switches and electricity and How the World Used to Be.

I walked them through the rest of the house. It smelled musty, which was good. It meant no doors or windows had been open in a long time, and that meant no other pack had hit it before us.

"Love the surbs! Love the surbs!" Timmy said, bouncing on his bare toes. I try to get them to wear shoes, but they outgrow any pair so quick, and anyway they're used to going barefoot.

"Settle down, Timmy. Open up that cabinet behind you. See what's in there."

The pack liked coming down from the hills to these suburban streets. Sometimes it was everything I could do to keep the bolder ones from sneaking off by themselves. I tell them over and over that it's safer in the big isolated house we have up on the peak. With the trees and grass so tall around it, you can't tell it's there. But they are young, and they like adventure. They call this place "the surbs." They make up lots of names for things, even though I try to teach them everything right. I've never told them any cuss words, but they've started to make up their own.

"Wow!" I suddenly heard from the garage. It was Lydia. She'd gone ahead, out of my sight.

I hurried, telling the others to stick with me. I didn't like the excited sound of Lydia's voice. I stopped in the doorway into the garage, and my breath froze in my lungs. Lydia grinned wildly. She was holding — or trying to hold — a shotgun in her thin little arms. The cab door of a pickup truck was open, and she must have taken it off the gun rack.

"Cool!" cried Timmy, peeking around my side.

"Hoddy!" yelped Abda. It was another of their made-up words.

I got to Lydia in what felt like one leap, snatching the big brute weapon out of her grip. She flinched like she thought I was going to smack her, and I sure was tempted to. Instead, I realized this was a "teachable moment," as my mom used to say. I have to think like that with all these young ones.

Raising the gun high over my head, I said loudly and sternly, "What is this?"

The pack went quiet. They all know my mad voice. Lydia sucked in a breath like she was about to cry.

"What is it?" I repeated, voice echoing sharply off the garage walls. The shotgun was heavy, but I kept holding it up.

They looked at the floor. Lydia bit down on a sob.

A clear piping voice said, "It's a gun."

The others shrank back, leaving Elwood alone in the doorway. He wasn't tall, wasn't stronger than the others, but he was smart. I had tried to teach the pack to read, and Elwood was the only one who'd even understood the basics.

"Woody's right," I said. "It's a gun. And what do I say about guns? What does every one of you know about guns? Huh? Lydia, you want to tell them?" I knew I was picking on her when she felt bad, but I had to do it, even if it made me feel bad too.

Lydia put her freckled hands over her face and started really crying. Her curly red hair bounced, and her tiny shoulders shook.

"Do not pick up a gun. Do not touch a gun. Do not even look at a gun." It was Elwood again, reciting like he was in school, like if there were still schools. He looked right at me as he said it. There wasn't any sass on his face, but it still felt as if he was making some sort of challenge to me.

I looked back at him for a few seconds. He didn't blink; just watched me.

I had to get on with it. "That's right," I said, then threw the shotgun into the pickup, slammed the door and ordered everybody out of the garage. We finished loading supplies into our sacks, and I marched the pack right out of "the surbs," back up into the hills where we'd been living for about four months. Next month it would be two years since the Big Sick. I've tried to teach my kids about anniversaries, but they don't really understand calendars and dates. Or maybe they just don't care. To them, a year is made up of seasons, not stupid numbers.

....

We'd gotten a good amount of food cans, and I cooked up pots of soup and stuff. I had to wait until after dark so the smoke going up the chimney wouldn't show. They all wanted to eat it *now*, why isn't it ready *now*? Sometimes they just drive me crazy.

The warm food made them sleepy, which was what I wanted. The house had several rooms and enough beds and other places to sprawl out, and I finally got the whole pack down and sleeping.

I had a bedroom just for me. I deserved it. I read a book by candlelight, then put my head on the pillow and pulled the bed's covers over me.

I fell asleep, but I dreamed about the Big Sick — real bad, specific dreams, about my own family — and I woke up sweating and couldn't get back to sleep.

The first I'd ever heard of the Big Sick must have been on the news, or other people worriedly talking about it. It probably all sounded far away to me. When cases started appearing in our country, even in the big city closest to where we lived, it still wasn't real, not until somebody I knew — sort of — got the disease and died from it.

It happened to a man my dad had gone to school with, who he still saw from time to time at the car dealership where the guy worked. I can still see Dad's glazed eyes as he came into the kitchen and said, "Ernesto...the plague got him." In fact, that very scene had just turned up in my dreams, except Dad had kept on reciting more names after that, some I knew, some I didn't. And while he was talking, the green-black sores started spreading all across his face and arms, and his flesh was falling away in ugly hunks, and he just kept naming names until his jaw fell off, and I'd woken up.

The Big Sick. There were other names for it, complicated scientific ones, but everyone I knew called it the Big Sick. *Sick* because people got sick, obviously. *Big* because it was everywhere, all over the world — but also because it was only the big people who got it. The adults.

I heard a soft knocking at the bedroom door. Relighting the candle, I frowned. I had tried to teach the pack old social skills, even though it was kind of pointless. But I couldn't remember ever telling any of them about knocking on a door.

"Come in," I said. The windows were black. It must be the middle of the night. I suddenly realized there might be trouble, and I started sharply off the bed as the door opened.

Elwood stood looking up at me.

"Woody...why're you up?"

"I heard you cry out, like you were having a nightmare." He had thin dark hair and a fading birth mark on his forehead. His dark brows arched over sharp intelligent eyes. "I want to talk to you about the guns. I think we need to have some and to know how to use them."

It was more than a little dismaying to hear, especially the way he said it, so matter-of-fact. "Guns are dangerous," I said.

"Of course they are. That's the point. We can be dangerous to other packs."

"You're all too small for guns." I felt off-balance, like I was apologizing.

"Some of us could handle pistols."

"We don't need to be dangerous to other packs," I said, my voice getting louder now, angrier.

"Sure we do. If another pack threatens us, we can be stronger than them."

"We don't fight other packs. I've told you that. We just go." Which was how we had ended up here. We had been miles away to the south, living off of what was left in a Walmart, when another pack showed up. "Hey, look at where we're living now. Isn't this a great house?" It was, probably the best place we'd had yet, but I knew I shouldn't be arguing with Elwood. He should just do what I said.

His eyes watched me from under those dark brows. "With guns we could stay where we liked for as long as we liked it. Nobody could make us go." It sounded like a very important point to him.

"Guns ain't hoddy, Woody!" I just about yelled.

"I know guns *aren't* hoddy, Leanne," he said calmly, like he was correcting my grammar or whatever. "They're not toys, just like you say. But they're...tools. And we ought to use what tools there are."

I glared down at him and said, "I'm the alpha. I decide."

"You're the alpha." But again he said it like some kind of challenge.

"Go back to bed," I said, my tone low and lifeless now. I felt like I'd lost an argument somehow. "Go to bed." It was all I could think to say.

Elwood went.

We had found him when there were enough of us to call ourselves a pack. Elwood was like all the other kids — half-starved, scared, crying, hopeless. When they were on their own like that after the Big Sick, you really had no choice but to take them in with you. I hadn't really known Elwood was anything special until I saw him studying a map he'd found. We were on the edge of a city. It was way too dangerous to go in there, so I was leading us away. Elwood had the map unfolded where we'd stopped to rest on the side of a road. I went over and looked, and he pointed and said, "We're here."

I looked up at a sign and saw he was exactly right. "How'd you know that?" I asked. He couldn't read, but somehow he had made sense of the lines on the map.

He shrugged. "Just worked it out."

What was he working out now? I wondered. What was this about guns? He must have had this in mind for a while, and had come to talk to me about it at night when everybody else was asleep.

Did Elwood want to take over the pack from me, become the new alpha?

I lay down in my bed again and tried to sleep, not even caring if the nightmares came back.

....

The pack had chores — bring back water from the river, collect firewood — because it seemed important to give them things to do. They needed "structure." Another of my mom's words. Sometimes I try to do what I think she would have done...but she was never in the position I'm in, taking care of almost twenty kids at once in a world that has changed forever.

But I thought we'd done okay. The pack was still together almost two years after the Big Sick, though we had lost a few and gained some others. I'd done my best, and I intended to keep on doing it.

From the house we had taken over four months ago, we could

reach three different large suburban areas. We always needed supplies, so about once a week I'd lead them down to one of the places to hit the empty houses for canned goods and clothes and anything else we needed. I avoided the stores, remembering that other pack that had moved in on the Walmart. That group had been violent, vandal-like, breaking things for no reason.

Sometimes the young ones got out of hand on these raids of ours, finding a bunch of toys and going crazy. Funny though, only about half my kids will play with toys; the others don't understand the shiny plastic things. They have their own games, a hundred different ways to play tag and hide-and-seek. I don't quite understand their rules, but sometimes I just sit and watch. I like to hear them laugh.

Today I took them down the other side of the hill, toward an area of suburban housing named after Native Americans. But I stopped everyone a quarter of the way there. Smoke was coming up from the streets ahead in three different places.

"It's just fire," complained Carlos, who loved the raids best when we found candy, especially chocolate.

"Yeah," Timmy said. "Fires happen." He gave me a big what-can-you-do? shrug.

Fires do happen. Chemicals ignite, gasoline leaks, lightning strikes. But three separate fires were too many. "We're going back," I ordered. That started up a whole whining and cussing chorus, if "zox" and "mudel" can really be called cuss words. I said, "Shut up and get moving!" Which probably wasn't how Mom would have handled it. But she was dead. Everybody in my family was.

I thought of them as we hiked back up to the peak and the hidden house. But the images of black and green bodies was too awful, so I thought instead about how I had managed to survive. I had stayed at the house, where everyone was dead. I avoided the bodies, which were too heavy for me to move, and I probably couldn't have made myself touch them anyway. I watched TV, seeing all sorts of scary stuff and no regular shows until the power went out for the last time. I ate all the food and walked around in a daze. Finally, I packed a bag and got into the SUV in the garage. It took me about twenty minutes to start the thing, then I gunned it right through the garage door and ran it up onto the lawn across the street and halfway up the porch.

Luckily, I'd put on my seat belt. After that I walked. I couldn't drive. It was stupid to try, since almost every street had a wreck or something else blocking it. I walked, and I ate food out of other people's houses and slept in couches of strange homes.

Then I started finding the kids. They all wanted me to take care of them, and that, somehow, was what I ended up doing. It gave me a reason; it gave me something to think about besides myself. The young ones had it worse than me. So I started my pack.

When we got back to the house, I told everybody to stay inside today. That got me another griping earful, but I promised candy later if they were good. I had learned to keep a secret stash.

Elwood came up to me in his quiet way when the pack was inside. "You're worried about another pack down there, right? Maybe we should keep watch today and tonight, in case they come up here. What do you think, Leanne?"

I blinked. It was a sensible idea, and I should have thought of it. I put two kids at upstairs windows and took Maeve outdoors with me to sit in the tall grass. I would make going outside on guard duty a kind of treat, I figured. Maeve was very serious about the watching. She had tangled black hair that she chewed on while her eyes stayed fixed on the rising hillside below. It was strange to remember a world where electricity flowed, planes flew, phones worked, and people—so many people—were still alive.

I didn't have a watch, of course, but I'd learned to figure the hours by how the sun moved. I told Maeve to go in and to send out Bao. He started to get bored pretty quick, so we sang songs, stuff I remembered from my MP3. You couldn't see the suburban area from here, but the smears of the smoke were still in the sky.

I sent in Bao. Out came Vicky.

After Vicky was Timmy.

I wasn't really that worried about the other pack — if there was one — coming all the way up to this peak. Why would they? Pickings were still pretty good down there. Eventually, though, the food would run out, and we would have to move on somewhere else. Someday, probably far in the future, the pack would have to hunt or grow crops, or maybe do both. I don't know how to do any of that. I hope it's a problem that comes along when I'm old, when someone else becomes the alpha. They are all going to grow up, after all. But they won't be adults like I used to know. They won't even be like me, who still remembers How the World Used to Be.

Timmy swatted at a bee, even though I told him not to, and got stung. He started crying, and I took his hand and pried the dead stinger from between two knuckles on the back of his hand. It was swelling a little, but he'd been stung before and wasn't allergic. If he had been...well, there wasn't much I could do about things like that, which was scary. I miss a lot of the comforts of the old world, but maybe I miss doctors the most — just knowing they existed, that somebody would take care of you if you got sick or injured. Of course, they hadn't been able to do anything to stop the Big Sick....

Dark started to come, and I went in and fixed dinner. I didn't light a fire, so we ate cold stuff. Only Carlos complained. Nobody was watching from the upstairs windows anymore. They'd gotten bored.

I went back out when it was night, taking a jacket. None of the kids came with me; they'd figured out guard duty wasn't any kind of treat. The moon was rising, and the stars were out and bright — brighter than they used to be because there's no pollution anymore. I leaned against a tree and hummed to myself and watched the hillside without really seeing it anymore. Tomorrow we would go raid one of the other two places for fresh supplies.

By the movement of the moon, it was getting to be time to go in and make sure everybody laid down to sleep. I gave it a few more minutes, taking a careful look around now, even walking the perimeter of the whole house.

I heard a branch snap. I thought I heard a voice. Two voices. One saying something to the first one in a sharp whisper, something like "Be quiet!"

I froze. Suddenly, my heart was beating so fast it almost hurt. I was in the overgrown grass, but the moonlight was on me. I bit my lip and made myself move, slowly, carefully, back under one of the trees. The closest entrance into the house was around a corner from me. I could hear the pack inside, laughing and squealing and probably tearing the place apart. But the voices I'd heard came from somewhere out in the night.

If they were this far up, these intruders could see through the screening trees to the house's candle lit windows. They could probably hear the kids playing inside. I didn't know what to do. I could only think to just stand there under the tree cover. A real grown-up would come along and tell me what to do. How to get out of this trouble.

Even two years after the Big Sick, I could still have a thought like that. It kind of disgusted me.

And that was what got me moving.

Crouching, I went to where I knew a broken flower pot was. I picked up a pot shard with a sharp point. Then I started circling, watching the slope. The road that led up here had never been paved. Now it was overgrown and about invisible.

I listened. I heard the jingle of metal, and footsteps. Not bare feet — shoes. I gripped the shard tighter.

Light flickered on the slope. Lights. My heart raced again. All the laughter and horseplay from inside the house stopped.

The light didn't come from torches. It wasn't fire. Those, I realized, were *flashlights*. There were half a dozen of them, all converging toward the house. I was still hidden under the trees. I coiled. Whoever these people were, they were a threat to my kids. They weren't going to have a fun time getting past me, I vowed.

Then I heard a metallic click. It was followed by a high, piping, emotionless voice that said, "All of you — back off, or I'm going to start shooting you."

I turned and saw moonlight gleam on a blue-black hunk of metal held up by Elwood's two bony kid-arms. The pistol wasn't shaking in his hands, though. His dark eyes glinted in the stray glow of the flashlights.

That boy was just full of surprises.

I shifted my stance, crunching dead leaves, and one of the beams flicked my way. I'd given myself away. Elwood, just five steps away, looked at me. I watched as the barrel of the pistol jerked toward me.

"Woody—" I said, or only started to say.

Behind Elwood there came a sudden movement, little arms wheeling, thin legs pumping awkwardly, all accompanied by a shrill shriek. This wild shape collided with Elwood's back and took him out like a football player making a dirty hit. Elwood yelped. There was a huge yellow flash, bigger than anything I ever would have expected, from the gun's barrel. The sound was thunder, one great big clap of it.

The pistol flew down, practically at my feet. I waited for the pain, for the blood. As I blinked, feeling hot and cold at the same time, I realized the bullet hadn't found me. But...

"Is anybody hurt?" I asked. That shot might have gone anywhere, even back into the house. "Everyone? Woody? Is anyone shot?"

I looked at the gun lying at my feet. I stared for a long moment. Then I asked those shadowy figures, "Is anybody out there hurt?"

Another long moment passed before somebody said, "No. The shot must've gone wide." It wasn't a kid's voice, or an adult's. It had to be their alpha.

I said, "Good." But I still held the jagged piece of pottery in my grip.

I looked over at Elwood again. Lydia was kneeling on his back, slapping uselessly at his head, missing every other time. Now she was babbling, "Leanne says *no guns*! Leanne says *no guns*! Leanne says—"

"Lydia. Lydia! That's enough, honey. You can get off him now. It's going to be okay." I had no right to say that last thing; I had no idea if it was going to be okay. I squinted out against the flashlights. "We don't use guns. That shot was a mistake. Do you use guns?"

Another long pause, then the same voice said, "No. Do you start fires?"

"No," I said. I realized he meant the three fires we'd seen earlier. So this pack hadn't started them. "We don't do damage for no reason. We're just trying to stay alive."

I heard the crunch of boots. A figure about my size appeared. With the flashlights behind him, he was just a shadow as he approached. He stopped, and I stepped slowly out from under the trees. By moonlight I could see his blond hair, cut short and sticking out. I hadn't cut my hair all this time.

He said, "We've been using that area, Cowichan Valley, to forage. When the fires started, one of my kids saw a group heading up to this peak. We came to check you out."

I glanced and saw my kids' faces pressed against the house's windows, all scared, some crying, some putting on a brave show. They all had to have seen Elwood pull out that pistol he'd grabbed in secret on one of our raids. He had meant to do good, I told myself. He was sitting up now, brushing leaves off himself.

The alpha and I gazed at each other for a while. My heart had slowed some, and everything didn't have such a shiny edge to it anymore. I drew long breaths.

"How old are you?" he asked.

"Twelve years and three months."

"I'm twelve and five months." He sniffed a little laugh. "I guess that's not much difference, huh?"

"Maybe," I said. "Maybe not. You got flashlights. Shoes." The pack had lowered their beams at a wave from the alpha, and I could see the group more clearly now. They had backpacks too, like a scout troop.

"Yeah," the alpha said. "But no guns. Just like you." He smiled like he was really glad to be smiling, like he'd been waiting to do it.

I smiled back.

4

"Jethro Adar Bitterman."

"Leanne Elizabeth Quincy," I said. Some of my pack don't even know their middle names, and hardly any ever use their last names.

I tossed the pot shard and invited them all into the house. I had picked up the pistol, dumped the bullets into my pocket, and tossed the thing up into a rain gutter. I'd get it down later and get rid of it and give Elwood a talking to. Guns might make us strong in the way he was thinking. But guns also took away a lot of options. You could either shoot somebody or not, threaten somebody or not. Those were limited choices.

And anyway...weren't enough people dead already in this world?

Jethro and I sat in living room, watching the kids start to play together, each side forgetting bit by bit that these were *others*, outsiders. Soon Timmy was making everyone look at his bee sting, and one of Jethro's kids showed off a more serious-looking scar on her knee.

"In all the time since the Big Sick," I said, "we haven't met with another pack like this."

"It's hard to know who to trust," Jethro said. He drank from a canteen, then passed it over to me.

I had a swallow of water. "You ever try to tell them about electricity, airplanes, the Internet?"

He laughed. "Yeah, I've tried. But it doesn't do much good."

I nodded, in a way that felt knowing and a little sad. "They've forgotten. Some were so young when the Sick happened they never really knew the old world."

Jethro let out a long sigh. "Kids today..."

I passed him back his canteen. There was still a serious issue to settle. "So—what are we now? I mean, your pack and my pack. Are we all a...pack?" I was hoping we could join up, be one together. That seemed like a good idea to me.

"Pax," he said.

"Oh...packs." Still two separate groups.

He sensed my confusion. "No. Pax. P-A-X. It's an old Greek word or something. It means peace. We're at peace."

I smiled again. Peace sounded good to me. It might be the start of something bigger.

We sat, content and quiet, and watched the young ones romp around the big room like happy little maniacs.

Of USBs and Fingerprints

Salena Casha

Salena Casha's work has appeared in over thirty publications. She was a finalist for the 2013-2014 Boston Public Library's Children's Writer-in-Residence. Her first three picture books were published by MeeGenius Books. One of them, titled Nuwa and the Great Wall, *was featured in the 2014 PBS Summer Learning Project for kids and won honorable mention in the 2014 Hollywood Halloween Book Festival. When not writing, she can be found editing math books, carving pumpkins and travelling the world. Check out her website at www.salenacasha.com.*

The electrical wiring of Kara54's nerves sizzled as she stood outside the door, the echoes of the doorbell ringing in her ears. *Would they like her? Would she function properly?* She fingered the USB port at her side and tried to tell herself that her manufacturers had made her without a glitch, that she came from a top-of-the-line assembly belt, born from the guts of another machine. Her skin, though artificially grafted, was pure shadow and shade, her wiry hair braided in tight cornrows. They'd even given her blue eyes so she wouldn't scare her new family. Underneath it all though, she was just gears, spools and bits of plasma.

Still, a part of her hoped for some semblance of love, the kind that smelled like chocolate chip cookies and hugs; the type she'd seen in glimpses on a handheld screen her handler let her watch.

The door opened a crack, the dark-almond eyes of a seven-year-old gazing up at her. She looked more like a doll than Kara54 was, with jet-black hair and a flowing blue dress. Her right knee was bright red, and her lip was split. A trickle of blood stained her deeply tanned face. Kara54's handler placed a hand on her shoulder.

"Mommy," the girl called behind her. "It's here."

Kara54 blinked. She looked like a girl, didn't she? She tugged at her hair, wondering what it was that made her look less than human. Kara54 swallowed, the motors inside her body working to mimic the movement.

"Oh fantastic, so glad it's here!" the woman before them said. She looked like a larger version of the child, nearly clone-like, and Kara54 wondered how something so natural could appear so artificial.

"You've come just in time," the mother addressed Kara54's handler. "Lila Jo had quite the spill this morning, a traumatic fall down a flight of stairs. She needs to store the memory and forget it. Don't want her being afraid of heights in the future, do we?"

The handler shifted uncomfortably behind her, and Kara54 wanted to turn and wrap her arms around the handler's waist. At the plant, the handler took pity on Kara54, placing electric self-healing Band-Aids over her torn skin and had given her chicken soup-flavored software when virus 29 infected her bunks. She'd spent her entire life off of the assembly line in the handler's care.

"I'll have you sign here and here," Kara54's handler told the mother, gesturing to the form. The handler did not look down to meet Kara54's robotic eyes as her adapted mother signed the adaption papers.

The mother nodded and scribbled on the paper. "Is that all?" she asked, impatiently, wanting to help Lila Jo get rid of the trauma she had suffered.

The handler hesitated on the house's front porch and then crouched down beside Kara54.

"It'll be okay. The Worthys will take care of you, Kara. I promise."

Even though Kara54 loved it when her handler used the human part of her name, there was despair in her words. She detected the lie, small and tight, at the back end of her handler's sentence. She squeezed Kara54 once, hard, released and then turned from her.

For a moment, Kara54 felt the overwhelming, unidentifiable impulse just to run after her handler, sprint down the stairs to her hovercraft and ask her to be her adapted mother. But that wasn't how Kara54's life worked. The handler had no child and no need for a storage robot as Kara54 was often categorized. And Kara54 was not supposed to *feel* anything like attachment, anything that could compel her to chase after her handler.

So why did she?

It took a single, quick-body shiver to shake it off. She didn't have enough time to process or analyze the strange emotional feedback as her adapted mother motioned for her to enter. Strangely, Mrs. Worthy never met her eyes, always seemed to be looking above her head somewhere.

"Come in, come in," Mrs. Worthy said and shut the door with a quick auto click. The place smelled, strangely enough, of dust and pollen even though there weren't any open windows. "Did you come with an instruction manual?" she mused absently.

"No," Kara54 said. "I've been preprogrammed to tell you what you need to know."

"All right," Mrs. Worthy said as she wiped her hands on the pants of her regulation suit and tugged at her ponytail. Mrs. Worthy motioned for Lila Jo to step forward. The girl jutted out her split lip, hands on her hips. Kara54 had never seen anyone look so defiant, so brave.

"What does she need to do?" Mrs. Worthy asked.

Kara54 turned to the girl before her. If Kara54 had been human, she would have been a good five years older than Lila Jo, nearly 12. She'd never felt like a child before, and neither had any of her fellow adaption bots.

"I want you to remember what just happened, your fall down the stairs," she said slowly. She could see Mrs. Worthy's hands tensing at her sides just behind Lila Jo. Kara54 then closed her eyes, the handprint locators on her arm opening to receive the little child's memory.

"Put your hands on my arms," she instructed. "I'll do the rest."

There was a half a beat between when the locators powered up with a low thrum and the moment where they reached out toward Lila Jo to accept her pain. Even though Kara54 made the motion with expertise, she had never had a live test before.

Kara54 was ultimately unprepared for what happened next.

Lila Jo's memories hit her like a wave, sucking her under, filling her lungs and her body. It made Kara54 want to claw for air even though she wasn't suffocating. In excruciating detail, she relived Lila Jo's fall down the flight of stairs, each bump tattooed on the hard drive where a normal human's brain would be. She felt the pain, tasted blood, as she hurtled through Lila Jo's memory.

It could have been years or merely minutes before Kara54 resurfaced in the Worthy's foyer. Mrs. Worthy's hands were clutched around Lila Jo's shoulders, and, somehow, the force of Lila Jo's memories sent Kara54 to her knees. Her body shook, her mainframe rattled as she absorbed the rest of the impact.

"You okay, sweetie?" Mrs. Worthy asked, but her words were directed to Lila Jo, not Kara54. The child wore the strangest expression on her tan face, her eyes meeting Kara54's.

"I was fine. I was always okay, mom," she said, but there was a deep line between her eyebrows as if there was something she couldn't entirely get her head around.

Kara54's body finally processed the shock, and she pulled herself back up to her feet, staggering slightly. She gazed up at the stairs, and her mechanical heart clenched inside her chest. She'd never been afraid of heights or falling before, but now she could barely bring herself to think of climbing the steps.

She bowed her head as Mrs. Worthy hustled Lila Jo into the kitchen for cookies. Her handler had sort of explained what happened to the children Kara54 had been built to help.

"You're a memory repository," her handler had explained. "You'll have the important job of holding the fears and pain of whoever you've been assigned. You protect them from things that could damage them later in life. You help humans attain their potential."

There had been glory in her handler's words, but now, as Kara54 stood alone in the hallway, terrified to lift her foot to the step, she wasn't so sure. She'd never asked what would happen to her own mind in the process. A surge of anger swept over her, unchecked. The handler had probably known the suffering Kara54 would endure but never really explained it to her.

Kara54 wasn't entirely sure how long she stood there in the hall, unable to move forward and unwilling to turn to the door and let herself free. It wasn't until a creak sounded behind her that she realized she wasn't alone.

"Are you the new adaption bot?"

The voice originated from a boy who could have been Lila Jo's twin but closer in age to Kara54. He had the same dark, open eyes. But instead of standing like his sister did, he sat on a metal chair whose legs hovered a few inches off the ground.

"Kara54," she said.

He had a serious face, a wrinkle forming between his brows as he looked her over. "You're living with us now?" he asked.

She nodded, swallowing. He watched her muscles move, fascinated. "We've never had one before," he said. "I thought you'd look different."

More metal than human, he meant, but Kara54 understood. She was a strange combination of gears and skin, with intelligence modeled after her free-thinking creators. She developed like a child and even though her bones and organs were artificial, they were made of a plasma that could grow and collapse just like a human's.

His chair rolled closer to Kara54, who remained rooted in her spot. His legs were strapped to the bottom of his chair, though his fingers and hands could move freely. He stopped inches from her, regarding her curiously.

"Can I?" he reached out and her receptors on her forearm activated, willing to accept whatever pain he offered to her even though the entirety of her body shook.

He recoiled as the jelly and electrodes glinted. "No, not that. Not yet," he said. His voice was quiet. "Can I touch your skin?"

Kara54 looked at him as a mixture of confusion and relief settling across her fibers. Her receptors retracted and he approached once more.

His finger was cool against her arm as he poked the skin on her wrist. Goosebumps traveled up her arms, and he raised his eyebrows.

"You're so human," he said.

He was such an oddity, this boy strapped to the floating chair. Kara54 wasn't sure what to make of him as they stood there, his finger still light on her arm. A door slammed behind them.

"Timothy, you're supposed to be studying," Mrs. Worthy said as she moved between them, her arm held out as if protecting the boy from Kara54. There was a strange expression in her eyes, one that Kara54 wasn't familiar with, but if she had to guess from watching the recordings her handler had shown her for training, it looked a bit like hatred.

Timothy's shoulder hunched forward, his head hanging low but his gaze never left Kara54's eyes.

"I needed to introduce myself," he said finally.

Mrs. Worthy shooed him back into the side room and shut the door behind him. She then turned to Kara54. Mrs. Worthy's shoulders stiffened, her gaze cold, and she tugged on her ponytail. Based on her emotional state readings, she was not entirely happy with Kara54, even though the robot-girl didn't know why.

"I'll show you to your room," Mrs. Worthy said. Thankfully, she didn't move toward the stairs because Kara54 could feel her knees turning to jelly. Instead, they walked straight to the door through which Lila Jo had been first taken.

Aromas of freshly baked cookies and pasta steeped in red sauce invaded Kara54's sensors with a quick shot and crackle. Even though she was a robot, she still had taste receptors in case a child had a bad memory of eating some sort of terrible food, and she could eat even if it did little for her being as a whole.

Mrs. Worthy waved Kara54 impatiently along to what appeared to be a mudroom porch. There was a small closet off to the side, and Mrs. Worthy opened the door.

"This will be your storage area," Mrs. Worthy said.

Kara54 blinked, alarm traveling up her arms. The closet had been hastily brushed and rearranged to fit what appeared to be a small cot and lamp. There was a bedside table made of gnawed wood. The suitcase with Kara54's jumpsuits sat on the floor. This was nothing like the rows of bunks in the adaption center, nor was it like the room her handler had constructed for her. And the way the Mrs. Worthy said *storage area* made Kara54 feel less than human even though she'd been modeled in their image.

Mrs. Worthy looked uncomfortable and picked at dry skin on her arm. "We just, we didn't know what to expect with your arrival. I hope this will do for now. We'll figure out something soon. I'll call you for supper," Mrs. Worthy said, waiting until Kara54 took her seat on the lumpy bed.

Kara54 wrapped her arms around herself as Mrs. Worthy shut the door and left her in the sickly glow of the lamp.

What has my life come to, she wondered there in the almost darkness. This was meant to be her family now, the people who murmured and shuffled just outside her door. In a way, Mrs. Worthy was like the stepmother from that tale about Cinderella. But maybe, as she gazed at the door, it wouldn't turn out that way. Many people heard about adaption bots and never even thought they could be human. Kara54 looked down at her dark skin, tracing the self-healing pores. Though part machine, didn't she count as someone?

....

As Kara54 dozed, nightmares of endless staircases filled her dreams, and she fell down what felt like a hundred. Being the storage membrane for Lila Jo was going to be far more difficult than she originally thought. She awoke, sweating, to the call of Mrs. Worthy.

The circular table had been set with a place for Kara54. Timothy and Lila Jo had already taken their seats, and Mrs. Worthy had arranged the table so that Kara54's seat was directly between Mr. Worthy and Lila Jo.

Mr. Worthy looked up from his newspaper, his eyes narrowing in on Kara54. He was a tallish, thin man with pale skin and jet-black hair.

"How do you do?" he said stiffly, rolling one of his shoulders back. He wore a standard working suit with silver reflectors on the collar and down the sleeves. He probably worked on software of some kind by the way he hunched over his meal, Kara54 thought.

"I'm all right," Kara54 said, no more than a whisper.

He grunted, and Mrs. Worthy cut in. "She helped Lila Jo this morning right when she came in, didn't she, dear? Poor child took a tumble down the stairs, and Kara54 was there just in time."

Kara54 noticed the shift from 'it' to 'she.' Timothy sat, strapped to his chair, his eyes absorbing the scene before him with a thoughtful intensity that Kara54 found slightly startling.

Lila Jo shrugged. Strange looking noodles in an orange-red soup, probably from a decompressor bag, sat on her plate. She moved them around with her fork before looking up. "I don't remember much about it."

"See?" Mrs. Worthy said, turning to Mr. Worthy. "Isn't that wonderful?"

He grunted and half-shrugged. Kara54 analyzed the makeup of his nervous system, saw a strange spike in his agitation levels. Did he not like her? They'd adapted her just for this reason, hadn't they? She couldn't help but stare at him as everyone began to eat. After that, no one really spoke during the remainder of dinner.

Kara54 chewed each strand mechanically, catching Lila Jo or Timothy looking at her every few seconds. The family all looked so strangely similar to one another it gave Kara54 a weird floppy feeling in her stomach. She looked nothing like any of them, being a few shades darker with her strange blue eyes. She swallowed. The food tasted of nearly nothing but, maybe, if she acted like them, they'd think she was more like them and would decide to keep her.

The family spoke about odds and ends like Timothy studying for some random test that would determine whether he should study math or reading more and Lila Jo's automatically erupting volcano she'd designed herself. Mrs. and Mr. Worthy talked about things Kara54 couldn't entirely understand and, since they spoke mostly to one another, Kara54 figured she wasn't *supposed* to understand.

As Mr. Worthy cleared the dishes, Lila Jo jumped from her seat and grabbed hold of her mother's arm. "Can Kara54 sleep in my room tonight?"

The atmosphere in the room went cold. Kara54 could see the mother's thin lips pressing together tightly.

"Fine," Mr. Worthy said, without hesitation. "That's fine."

"Harold," Mrs. Worthy hissed but he shook his head.

"Let her do what she wants. You said yourself that her current room isn't fitting for a child like her."

Lila Jo smiled triumphantly and grasped Kara54's hand. Up and up, she tugged Kara54 to the next floor. Kara54 was sure that her heart was going to stop beating at she mounted each stair. Lila Jo's pain played over and over again across her nerves, flashes of each step wrecking her vision. Dizziness nearly overcame her but suddenly, they crested the top of the stairs and made for Lila Jo's room.

"You all right?" Lila Jo asked, eyebrows furrowed. "You look a bit pale."

Kara54 ignored the nausea in her stomach and shook her head. The girl kept a hand firmly around Kara54's wrist and pulled her through a bedroom door. Kara54 inhaled sharply, the sight receptors on her irises enlarging.

Electrodes of some form filled the walls with rotating hallucinatory colors: cotton candy pinks and robin's egg blues. Her bed was a circular contraption dotted with purple pillows and lavender sheets. Lila Jo didn't have dolls like the girls in TV shows Kara54 had seen. Instead, she had piles of electric blocks, fused together to make hovercrafts and spaceships in miniature. The volcano they'd spoken about at dinner sat in the corner of a bright violet desk, lava overflowing from the top in an electric projection.

"Play with me," Lila Jo commanded. And so, Kara54 settled beside her on the synthetic fibers of Lila Jo's multicolored carpet. Playing with Lila Jo felt like work at an assembly line. Kara54 handed Lila Jo tools as she called for them and watched, fascinated, as the child worked.

"What are you making?" Kara54 asked. She wasn't sure if she was allowed to ask questions, but Lila Jo seemed to have brought her into the secret club that her room embodied.

"Block melder," Lila Jo ordered, hand out, not making eye contact with Kara54. Kara54 passed the small tube to her and watched as the plastic tip lit up. It heated the blocks, melding the model together.

"I'm making SpaceHub 31," Lila Jo said simply.

"Why?" Kara54 asked. Lila Jo had called this play, but it looked like work or training.

"Because I'm going to be a space pioneer when I grow up, and in order to get to the place where they let you up into the sky, you have to create your own ship."

Lila Jo turned her dark gaze on Kara54, the light fleeing the tip of her block melder. "I wasn't afraid back there, you know," Lila Jo said.

"With the stairs?" Kara54 asked. The memories she'd absorbed from Lila Jo itched under her layer of skin, settled in her joints. The fear Kara54 had taken from Lila Jo felt real enough. But how would Lila Jo even remember the fear at all if Kara54 had truly absorbed all her feelings?

"Maybe I was afraid while it was happening. I can't remember that part. It just feels blank, like a movie without sound," Lila Jo said as if reading her mind. "It's not like I haven't fallen before. They're just worried it'll stop me from doing this." Lila Jo waved at the half-complete rocket before them. "Mom worries a lot."

"You can say that again." A voice issued from the doorway, and both Lila Jo and Kara54 looked up. Timothy hovered just within the doorframe, his chair inches off the ground.

"No one invited you," Lila Jo said, cutting her eyes in his direction.

Timothy ignored her and entered, coming to rest just beside the model. "Are you really making another one?"

Instead of answering, Lila Jo just glared at him and kept working. Kara54 watched him as he watched his sister. He acted older than the rest of them. And then there was the peculiarity of his legs.

Timothy caught Kara54 staring. If she had had embarrassment receptors, she would have blushed. But Kara54 was just made of skin and metal, of synthetic plasma, nothing more. She had a database instead of a brain, like a human-shaped computer. Where her heart would have sat was a hard drive that stored preprogrammed emotions. Fear and, a part of Kara54 decided, a little love.

"It's okay," Timothy said. "Everyone looks."

Lila Jo looked up sharply. "Stop being dramatic," she said.

But Kara54 couldn't stop looking at him, now that he'd noticed her. "What happened?" she asked.

"Legs never worked," he replied. "Got twisted up during birth or something. I'll never be able to walk."

Timothy said the words casually, but Kara54 couldn't imagine just sitting somewhere, strapped to a chair for the rest of time.

"I didn't mean to stare," Kara54 stuttered, looking down and taking the outstretched block melder from Lila Jo's hand.

Timothy shrugged. "No one means to, but they do anyway."

"Oh shut up. You *love* the attention," Lila Jo drawled. A small smile lit up Timothy's face.

Kara54 envied them: their closeness, their ability to joke about something that no one else could truly understand. Being adapted meant being an outsider. It meant taking all of your family's fears and internalizing them, recycling them like used paper and moving on. It didn't mean *sharing* but merely *removing and deleting* something that prevented them from doing something or attaining their potential.

Even though Timothy didn't seem to have much interest in Lila Jo's model building, he moved his chair next to Kara54 and set it down on the floor. Together, they moved in almost silence, Lila Jo barking out orders and Timothy passing Kara54 the tools before Lila

Jo could even ask for them. It was like a strangely choreographed dance. And, for some reason, they'd made space for her.

The model was barely a foot high and made of ugly gray blocks, but it was essentially complete. Lila Jo headed off to wash her hands when Timothy turned to Kara54.

"I need to ask you a question. It'll be strange, but I want to ask it anyway, okay?" he said.

His dark eyes were intense, so serious, like an old man was staring out of them at her. Kara54 swallowed hard and nodded.

"What was it like?" he asked. "Falling down a flight of stairs without *really* falling down them?"

Kara54 bit her lip. She wasn't supposed to tell them how it felt. That was the whole point of them adapting her. They weren't supposed to know what it felt like to suffer such intense fear created in a singular moment. But he seemed genuinely curious and the words spilled out.

"Like the earth was going to swallow me. I felt all the bumps she felt."

"Are you afraid of stairs now?" Timothy asked.

Kara54 nodded tightly as that electric shock of fear slammed up her arms at the word.

He touched his finger to his lips, lost in thought. "But doesn't it go somewhere?" he asked.

"The fear?"

"Yeah."

She shook her head. "I'm a storage unit. I hold on to it, file it. It becomes part of my hard drive."

"Fascinating," Timothy murmured.

Kara54 didn't know why he found it so interesting, why she'd even said anything at all. She just wanted to run back downstairs, away from his intense gaze, and closet herself away in the storage unit. But she couldn't will herself to go near the stairs. If she did, she was certain she would fall.

"So," Timothy said slowly, "it becomes a part of you."

Kara54 never really thought of it that way. "Yeah," she replied.

"I guess you're right. It's like I lived it."

"Are you afraid of the stairs now?" Timothy asked.

Kara54 flinched. She didn't even need to answer, but she did anyway. "I didn't used to be," she whispered.

They sat there on Lila Jo's rug, waiting for the girl to return. The Worthys were all so strange, with their dark eyes and whispered words. It looked like Timothy was going to say something again, but the door creaked open. Lila Jo's face peeked in, her cheeks glowing pink.

"Mom says time for bed," she said, looking pointedly at Timothy. With a shrug, Timothy pressed a button on the arm of his chair. The seat levitated off the ground, and he glided toward the door. As he made to leave, Lila Jo flounced into bed.

"Night, Tim," Lila Jo called from her seat on the bed.

"Night, Lila Jo," he replied with a turn of his head. His eyes settled on Kara54, and he gave her a sad sort of smile. "Night, Kara."

Kara. No numbers. Just a single name. She couldn't open her mouth to reply in time and he was gone. She moved through the room as if in a dream as Lila Jo pulled out an extra cot and patted the cushioned mattress.

The lights flickered off and as she lay there with Lila Jo right beside her, she wondered if this was what it meant to be home.

....

The days that followed were excruciating. Every time Mrs. Worthy sensed something that could give Lila Jo any sort of fear, she had Kara54 take it on. It was technically Kara54's job, but that didn't mean she liked to do it. Even Lila Jo rolled her eyes after her mother had yelled at her for eating dessert packages too soon before dinner.

"Mom," Lila Jo said. "It's fine. I'm not afraid of you."

Which only brought on another lecture to Lila Jo about listening to instructions, followed by Mrs. Worthy instructing Kara54 to open her receptors and receive Lila Jo's memories of being yelled at. It only caused Kara54 to feel Lila Jo's anger and fragmented bits of fear toward Mrs. Worthy.

She understood that Mrs. Worthy was just worried about Lila Jo, but she was too protective to the point that Lila Jo only wanted to do more reckless things. It was all too much and it all made Kara54's database hurt.

Then, one night, as she climbed the stairs to Lila Jo's room, she heard Mrs. and Mr. Worthy arguing in their bedroom.

"We can't use adaptions for more than one person," Mr. Worthy said. "You know the rules, Carissa, and we don't know what effects that sort of breach could have."

"I just want to protect our children. Make sure they can be everything that they want to be." Normally, Mrs. Worthy's voice was cold and controlled, like the machine that Kara54 had been born in, but today it cracked. Kara54 paused, frozen on the stair, gripped by both her fear of falling and by the conversation that for once, seemed to center around her.

"He's fine, Lila Jo's fine. Kara is just a girl, a young one at that. I don't think you should keep giving her more memories. It might overload her."

A pause. "But that's her purpose."

"No," Mr. Worthy said flatly. "Researchers aren't entirely sure what *her* purpose is. She's a living, breathing thing. Yes, she has parts of a machine and yes, she can help calm our fears. But she has human parts too. And we don't even know what types of effects that living without fear has on our children."

Their voices lowered as they continued to speak and Kara54's mechanical and plasma heart pounded, anxiety levels rising.

In a way, Mr. Worthy was right, wasn't he? She hadn't told him about the nightmares she had, about how climbing stairs gave her perpetual anxiety. Humans had the ability to live past their fears but Kara54 re-experienced them every day. Maybe she was broken. Maybe there was a wiring error in her system that put these fears on a loop of some sort. She crested the top of the stairs.

Lila Jo's door was closed, and Kara54 hesitated in front of the threshold. Lila Jo was probably asleep and, given her parents' conversation, Kara54 didn't want to wake her. Timothy's door, though, was ajar, letting a soft golden light seeping through.

Kara54 swallowed hard. At least Lila Jo was never afraid of her brother. She stepped up to the door and pushed it open.

Timothy's chair had its back to her against the far wall, his hands typing away at a display. A video game of some sort that flickered and whipped across his screen. The chair thrummed and vibrated, mimicking movements.

"Hi," Kara54 said timidly. She closed the door behind her, and the game paused.

Timothy's chair turned and he stared at her, startled out of the gaming daze.

"Hi Kara," he said quietly. His dark eyes softened in the less-than-harsh light. "You okay?"

Kara had never wondered what Timothy would have been afraid of. But he was human, wasn't he? He was afraid of things. And his mom was worried, that much was clear. Parts of her, the parts logged in her database, feared the woman's anger and her power in the house. She hated being afraid; it made her feel like a coward. She pressed her back against the door and sank to the floor. The rug was soft beneath her legs, the bristles brushing against her bare skin.

"Are you afraid of anything?" Kara asked.

"Lots of things," he said. His voice was steady and measured.

Kara nodded and swallowed. "What sorts of things?" she asked. "Spiders? Stairs? Your mom?"

"I'm afraid," he said slowly, "of people."

People? Such a strange, general fear. Kara nodded and wiped her hands on her jumpsuit's shorts. "Why?" she asked.

"Sometimes people aren't nice. Sometimes they make fun of you." It explained why he was home all the time, why he never went to school like his sister did during the day. Why he was never visiting at a friend's house. The more time Kara spent with the Worthys, the more afraid she became of people too.

"Is it hard?" Timothy asked. "Doing what you do."

He talked about it like it was a job, not all of Kara's life. She nodded tightly. "Yeah. I never used to be afraid of stairs or spiders. Or your mom. But I am now, and even though I know exactly why Lila Jo was afraid of those things, I don't understand why I am."

He nodded and clasped his hands on his lap. "It's okay," he said. "Sometimes we are made in ways that we don't understand." He looked at his legs. She looked down at her hand where, just beneath the surface, her metal bones creaked.

Kara wasn't sure how long she sat there for, in Timothy's room. The door was cool against her back.

"I think we can help each other," Timothy said. She felt the receptors on her arms opening, waiting to receive all his deepest darkest fears, but he waved it away. "I'll help you get over Lila Jo's fears if you help me get over mine."

It was a strange proposition but not so strange that Kara would have refused immediately. She tapped her finger to her lips, knowing that when she closed her eyes that night she'd be submerged in endless flights of stairs and spiders larger than herself and Mrs. Worthy's looming face. Sleep no longer provided her with any comfort.

She nodded and Timothy moved closer to her. "I want to try something," he said, "but you have to trust me, okay?"

Kara nodded and stood so that they were at eye level.

"Open your receptors, okay?" he said. The little absorptions on her arms popped open. "I'm going to give you a memory. Let me know what you think."

His fingers pressed into her skin and the scene before her eyes faded. She was in the Worthy's house but downstairs, and it was summer. The sun drifted in and settled on the flight of stairs. Instead of feeling a jolt of anxiety, a strange sense of triumph overcame her. In the memory, in Timothy's mind, she took a deep breath and raced up the steps. Her heart pounded, her legs ached as she reached the top. And she felt a strange surge of happiness.

The scene faded, and she was back in Timothy's room.

"Was that your memory?" she asked. "How did you climb the stairs?"

"It's that video game I play. It simulates what walking feels like," he said. He stared at her carefully, curiously and waited. "Let's go downstairs."

Normally, just the word would have sent her muscles tightening but this time, she felt nothing.

The fear was gone.

"It worked," Kara whispered. "It really worked."

Timothy smiled triumphantly. Kara recalled the way she could take a painful memory from Lila Jo and leave her without fear. Maybe she could put a healing memory into Timothy's mind too.

"Your turn," Kara whispered.

He hesitated for half a second and then offered his fingers to her. Kara chose a specific memory of the time she'd spent living with her handler. The way she'd hugged Kara and welcomed her into the pre-adaptation home. The way they'd watched old movies on a screen until they felt sick. The way her handler had said that no matter her differences, she deserved to be treated like a person. And so did Timothy.

She watched Timothy as he closed his eyes. His eyelids were dark, his skin glowing in the half-light. She felt his heartbeat slow and the tension in his shoulders fade. When he surfaced, he smiled.

"That helped," Timothy whispered. "Thank you."

The pair looked exhausted but they stayed up the rest of the night, swapping memories, as the morning light approached, Timothy sat up a little straighter.

"I think we should tell my parents what we've found out."

The dawn shifted in shades of gray outside the window. Kara raced down the steps, barely thinking of their danger, knowing they'd found a way out. She halted on the threshold as Timothy caught up.

Mr. and Mrs. Worthy looked up from where they sat at the table and even though Kara felt a slight catch in her stomach at the woman's gaze, she kept standing tall.

"Kara's figured something out," Timothy said. His face was

ablaze with light and happiness. "We can't make her hang onto our fear, so we don't have to deal with it. We can't do this anymore to her. She's a part of our family."

The words slammed into Kara's gut. A family. Not an adaptation. Not Kara54. Just Kara.

Mrs. Worthy frowned. "What do you mean?" she asked.

And this time, Kara met her gaze. She ran a hand over her cornrows and took a deep breath.

"Focusing on happy memories helps us defeat fear," Kara said. "Fear's the bad guy. But we can help each other to keep it away. To learn from it."

Kara thought of the sunlight streaming in, of a fantasy in her head of all of them sitting together at the table, smiling. While none of them were replicas of the other or had the same skin shade or fears or bodies, they could really learn from each other.

"Let me show you," she said and offered her hands.

One by one, Mr. and Mrs. Worthy took them.

Chit Win

Deborah Walker

Deborah Walker grew up in the most English town in the country, but she soon high-tailed it down to London, where she now lives with her partner, Chris, and her two young children. Find Deborah in the British Museum trawling the past for future inspiration or on her blog: deborahwalkersbibliography.blogspot. com. Her stories have appeared in Nature's Futures, Cosmos, Daily Science Fiction *and* The Year's Best SF 18.

It's not the size of the dog in the fight, it's the size of the fight in the dog. ~ Mark Twain (1835-1910)

Ma was taking an awfully long time to read the letter. "Who's the letter from, Ma?" asked Samuel, peering over her shoulder at the entangled-ansible screen. Samuel would have liked an ansible for himself, but Pa said he'd have to start doing odd jobs around the farm to pay for it, and Sam hadn't quite gotten around to doing that, yet.

Ma instantly minimised the screen. "It's from Pasha."

"Aunty Pasha? Can I read it?" asked Sam. He'd always liked Aunty Pasha.

"It's private," said Ma.

"Well, what does she say?"

Ma sighed. "If you must know, she says she's sorry that she persuaded us to come here."

"She does?" Samuel asked. "Why?" This world was great. Sam looked out of the metal-glass window at the sun, low and red in the sky. He could see the township's metal houses glinting in the distance. There was space to breathe on this world.

"You like it here, don't you, Samuel?"

"Well, yes, sure, it's much better than Earth, isn't it? I mean Pa's happy. He's got his job, and we've got a nice place here; you can look after us, and everything. Who wouldn't like this world?"

"Yes."

"Tell me, Ma, tell me what's wrong." He patted her shoulder.

"It's not what I expected. The Gravillers here, they're not like Aunty Pasha or any of our friends on Earth. Pasha was just sympathetic, I think she's embarrassed."

"Do you miss your job, Ma?"

"It's not just that, Sam. This whole set-up is so old-fashioned. The colonists are more traditional than the people on Earth, or on Gravillton, for that matter."

"But it's better than Earth isn't it, Ma? We'll get by."

"Yes, I suppose. We don't have much choice. We spent all our savings getting here." Ma snapped the ansible shut. "Where's your sister?"

"Dunno."

"Well, go and look for her."

"Okay," Samuel said. "And, Ma, I'm sorry."

"That's alright, honey. Like you said, we'll get by. It's just not what I expected." She sighed again. "Now, go and play."

....

Samuel saw Veronica sitting in the dirt by the vegetable patch. He really ought to do some weeding if he was going to get his own ansible. Although his friends back on Earth would be too old to want to talk to him. Maybe he could hook up with some girl. Some Earth girls would probably be interested in talking to someone off-world.

"Samuel, look what I've got," shouted Veronica, breaking into Samuel's interesting line of speculation.

Samuel's heart beat fast in his chest. She'd gone and done it. He'd only asked her to catch one an hour ago. All thoughts of Earth girls forgotten, Samuel ran over. He crouched beside Veronica, peering at the small creature nestled in her arms. Disappointment slammed into him. "It doesn't look very impressive."

"Not it, Samuel, she. All the veoles are girls, you know that." Veronica stroked her small hands over the creature. "I think she's lovely. Hey! Don't grab her!"

"I wasn't," Samuel said. "I just wanted to roll her over to check out her claws."

"Well, don't," Veronica said. "You've frightened her." She picked up the veole and began to make crooning noises to it. The veole's nose twitched in response, and it made some chattering noises.

"Look, Samuel. She's talking to me. Ain't she just darling?"

"Be quiet, Veronica. Someone's coming over."

Samuel squinted into the hazy light until he recognised Berick, the leader of the Graviller boys. Berick walked with his usual confident strut. His wrinkled, moist skin glistened in the dying red light of the afternoon sun. Gravillers were Humanoid, or Humans were Gravilloid. It depended on your perspective. *Berick's okay,* Samuel thought. *He's friendly enough.*

The Gravillers just did things a little differently from the people back home. Samuel looked at his five-year-old sister who was still babbling nonsense to the veole. "Berick's coming over. Don't show me up."

Veronica put down the veole, which scuttled between her legs. "Okay."

The only other kids on this planet were Berick and his gang. If Samuel was going to have any type of fun here, he needed to fit in.

She could be a good kid — sometimes, Samuel thought.

"Hey, what you doing?" Berick asked.

"Not much," Samuel replied.

"Looks like you've got yourself a fighting veole." Berick bent down to examine the creature. When Berick's three primary fingers prodded the veole, Samuel was glad to see that Veronica kept quiet.

"Yep," said Samuel, playing it cool.

"Your sister catch it for you?"

"Yep, seems they like Human females, too."

Only females could catch the veoles. Samuel had found this out in one frustrating afternoon scouring the swamps behind the house. Veoles were native to this world, unlike Gravillers or Humans. The veoles were on home territory. If they didn't want to be caught, they were able to evade even the most persistent hunter. It was annoying that Veronica had been able to capture one so easily. It only took her an hour. That was females for you; they were different.

"You going to fight her?" Berick asked.

"Are you challenging me?" Samuel replied, surprised.

"Well, that's what they're for, ain't it?"

"I suppose." This was fantastic. As the only Human boy in the colony, Samuel had never dreamed that Berick would challenge him to a veole fight. Berick was top dog, the leader of the kids. Yep, the Gravillers were an okay species, no matter what Ma said. They were fair. They didn't discriminate. "Tomorrow suits me" said Samuel, ignoring Veronica who tugged on his arm.

"Yep, suits me, too" Berick said. "But are you sure that she's up to it? She looks kinda small."

"She'll do fine," Samuel said with a confidence that he didn't feel.

"See ya tomorrow, then, at noon?"

"Yeh, great."

Berick ambled off.

Samuel turned to his sister and whispered, "Did you hear that, Veronica?"

Veronica looked at her brother. Her eyes were wide with accusation, "You're not going to fight with her, are you? She might get hurt."

"That's what they're for. They're fighting veoles."

"But . . . ."

"Look, I'm glad you got her for me, but what did you think I wanted her for?"

"But . . . ."

"Don't worry, Veronica. Veoles fight for fun. They never really get hurt." Samuel grinned. "Pa's going to be so pleased. He wants me to fit in here."

There were tears in Veronica's eyes. "But she's so little and cute." She scooped up the veole and held it against her chest. "I'm going to tell Ma." The veole wriggled until it found a comfortable position. Its ears twitched.

"I'm doing it. It doesn't matter what Ma says. That's the way it goes here." Why didn't Veronica understand how important this was? *Berick* had challenged him.

"I'm going to tell Ma what you just said."

Samuel ignored his sister and scrutinised the veole. It did look awfully puny. "Couldn't you have captured a bigger one?"
"She's lovely." The veole uncurled, revealing a small, pink face. It was about the size of a guinea pig. It regarded Samuel with bright, black eyes. Its claws waved in the air. They looked mighty thin, not like the solid looking blade-like claws that Samuel had admired on Berick's veoles. Samuel wondered if Berick had challenged him just to make a fool of him.

Samuel turned away and stated to walk towards the house. "Some fine fighting veole my sister finds me," he muttered. "I'm going to be a laughing stock."

....

Ma was standing at of the stove, stirring a pot of unsavoury smelling food.

"Not Graviller food again, Ma," Samuel said with a scowl.

"If you helped with the vegetable patch, we might have something else to eat."

"Earth vegetables don't like the soil," Samuel said.

Ma whirled around to face him. Her voice, when it came, was tight and controlled. Had she been crying? "Samuel, you'll just have to get used to it. We've nearly finished all the Earth food we brought with us. Graviller food is fine for Humans. It's nutritious."

"It may be nutritious, but it sure smells bad." Samuel sniffed the air. "Yuk!"

"Just get used to it, alright? There's a lot of things we've got to get used to. The food's the least of our problems."

"But, Ma, can't we just have . . ."

"What's all this? What's all this? Can I smell dinner cooking?" Pa walked in. He was a tall man, dressed in Graviller leathers, which hung off his lean frame. He hitched up his trousers as he came into the kitchen.

"Food's nearly ready," Ma said. She viciously stirred the pot. Ma wasn't a great cook. On Earth, her job as a nano-biochemist had taken up most of her time. In fact, Pa had done most of the cooking back home. But women weren't allowed to work on this Graviller colony. Graviller females took care of their kith and kin. Pa said that they were guests of the Gravillers and ought not to rock the boat. That was the reasonable thing. It was a Co-operation rule to follow the customs of the founding species on a colony. And whether Ma liked it or not, this was a Graviller colony.

He didn't like to think about it much, but Samuel thought it was as if something had withered inside Ma. Something else had taken its place: something hard, and something angry. Some days it was so bad that Samuel and Veronica were too frightened to hardly say a word around the place.

Pa was thriving, though. He was an engineer, and the Gravillers respected his unique alien perspective on technical problems. Pa fit in well here. Samuel meant to fit in, too. Now that he had a fighting veole, he'd be able to take part in the veole fights with the other kids. And *Berick* had challenged him. It was wonderful.

The front door opened. Veronica walked through the hall and climbed the stairs to her room.

"I'm going upstairs to see Veronica. She's caught me a veole." Samuel said.

Pa smiled and nodded, but Ma said, "A veole? What do you want one of those for?"

"For fighting, of course, Berick challenged me."

"You're going to fight those little creatures while you boys all stand around and watch?"

"Sure."

Ma was going to say something else, but Pa put his hand on her shoulder and said, "Let the boy be, Sarah."

Samuel wanted to check on his veole. Funny how only females could catch them. That's about all females were good for. He looked at his Ma stirring the stew, and he bit his lip.

Pa said, "Get yourself upstairs, son. Ma will shout for you when supper's ready."

....

"Whatcha doing?" Samuel asked his sister as he walked into her bedroom.

"Just talking to Chit Win. I think she likes me."

"You've named her?" Samuel looked at his sister incredulously. "That's ridiculous. You know she's fighting tomorrow. She's a fighting animal, and you've given her a pet name?"

Veronica didn't seem worried. "The name just came to me. Popped right into my head. I think she's cute, don't you think?"

Cute was not a word that Samuel would have applied to Chit Win. Bedraggled was more like it. She was a skinny rat with strange bags of thin grey skin flapping around her back. She was four-legged, each limb ending in a cluster of sheathed claws. In Chit Win's case, probably ineffective claws. She didn't look like much of a fighter. But, what the hey? At least his sister had got something for him. Samuel shuddered to think what would have happened to him if he hadn't got a sister. He would never have been able to catch one of the veoles. It wasn't quite fair: all the Graviller kids had at least a dozen sisters, all running around getting veoles for them.

". . . never wanted to come here in the first place," the voice of Ma rattled upstairs.

"It's better here than on Earth. There was no space there. And no work for me. Anything is better than that." Pa's voice joined Ma's. Veronica and Samuel sat in silence listening to their parents' argument.

"What about me? What about the children?"

"They'll be fine. They speak good lingo now. They're fitting in fine. We'll build a new life here as a family."

"What about Veronica? What about her life?"

Pa's voice became quiet. They had to strain to hear him, "There are no Human colony worlds, Sarah, and there won't be for another fifty years. You know that. We got to make the best we can of it. Gravillers are okay."

"Normal Gravillers are okay. But not these. I don't know if I can stand it here, Ryan."

"I couldn't take it on Earth anymore, Sarah. I had nothing but the welfare for ten years. We've got to find a way to fit in here."

"We haven't got much choice, have we?"

"I don't like it when they fight," Veronica said.

"Don't worry, Veronica." Samuel put his arms around her shoulders. Pa had explained some things to him; it was different here on this world. Men were expected to be strong here, to shoulder the burdens. That's what Pa had done when he'd taken the difficult decision to bring the family to a Graviller colony world. Samuel kissed his sister's forehead, "It'll be all right. Ma just needs to get used to a few things."

....

Ma and Pa were quiet at supper and very polite to each other. Samuel had been thinking about how he could help the family, like Pa had said. "I'll be fighting in town with my veole at noon, tomorrow. Maybe you'd like to come along, Ma. You could meet some of the Graviller ladies."

"Why, that's a fine idea," said Pa. "What do you reckon, Sarah?"

"I don't suppose there's any harm in it. Better to make the best of a bad job," Ma said.

Samuel noticed that Ma had hardly eaten any of her food.

Pa was happy. "That's exactly what I've been saying, Sarah. We *can* fit in here. We've just got to adjust a little. We've got to fit in with their ways. It's only common courtesy."

"I guess you're right, Ryan."

Ma looked worn out, beat down. Samuel had never thought of

her as old until they came here.

....

The next morning, the family walked to the town square. Samuel thought his mother looked a little better.

Berick was waiting at the fighting arena, a makeshift ring surrounded with a small stone wall. Seemed like word had gotten out about Samuel and Berick's match because there was quite a crowd gathered. Maybe a quarter of the colony's five hundred inhabitants had turned out.

"Pa, I'm nervous."

Pa gripped Samuel's shoulder. "Don't worry. These are good people. They just set store on gambling a little more than we did on Earth."

Indeed. Samuel could see many of the adult male Gravillers engaged in frantic negotiations. He wondered what the odds were on him winning. He glanced over to Chit Win, who appeared to be napping in Veronica's arms. Pretty long odds.

"There's some women over there, Sarah. Why don't you go chat with them?" Pa nodded over to a group of Graviller females,

"I suppose I could try," Ma said. "Are you coming too, Veronica?"

"No, Ma. I want to stay with Chit Win."

Samuel raised his eyes to the sky, "Berick hasn't got his sisters with him. Go on, go with Ma."

Veronica reluctantly passed over Chit Win, who stirred slightly before nestling into Samuel's arms.

"Looks like you're fitting in well with these new ways, Samuel," Ma said. "Come on, Veronica. Let's leave the menfolk to their business."

Veronica said, "Just make sure to stop the fight before she gets hurt."

Ma and Veronica made their way to the Graviller females who were preparing snacks for their families. The unpleasant, pungent smell of Graviller food filled the air.

Pa wandered off to talk to a group of Gravillers he knew. Samuel wondered if he would make a bet.

Samuel walked over to the fighting ring. He tried to look confident, as Chit Win had fallen back to sleep in his arms. He nodded to Berick and looked enviously at the sleek fighting veole Berick placed in the ring. That veole was born to fight.

"That's not a very big veole. I don't think that she'll put up much of a fight," Berick said.

"It's not the size of the dog in the fight, it's the size of the fight in the dog," said Samuel, waking Chit Win and placing her in the ring.

"Eh?"

"It's an old Earth saying."

"Well, let's see what you've got."

Masher Slycher, the self-appointed master of ceremonies, made his way over to the ring. He took a long look at Chit Win, before uttering his harsh Graviller laugh, "Good luck, Human boy." Masher took an ivory whistle out of his pocket and sounded the start of the fight.

Pa and the Graviller males rushed over. It was noon. The fight began. Chit Win looked very small against the magnificent creature that Berick had selected.

The Gravillers shouted encouragements in their own language, forsaking Co-operation lingo in their excitement.

"Fight, Chit Win, fight," Samuel shouted.

Instead of fighting, both of the creatures chattered to each other. Berick's veole unsheathed her claws, but withdrew them after listening to Chit Win's urgent chitterings.

"Looks like veoles caught by Humans like to talk, not fight," Masher said. This comment gained a few sniggers from the crowd.

"Come on, Chit Win," Samuel said. This was embarrassing.

Chit Win ran around the ring as if looking for something. The other veole curled up into a ball.

"What are they doing?" Samuel asked.

"Beats me. Usually they love to fight. They love a good scrap," Berick said.

The Graviller adults looked on. There was muttering. This

wasn't what they'd come to see. This wasn't what they'd bet good credit on. The females came over and stood at the back of the crowd.

Chit Win ran round and round the fighting arena, screeching in her chittering voice.

Berick looked disgusted. He leant over the wall to prod his sleeping veole. "This is what happens when you let Humans join in, is it?"

"I'm sorry," Samuel said. His cheeks were stained red with embarrassment.

Veronica pushed through the crowds, but she couldn't quite get to front of the ring. "Is Chit Win okay? She hasn't been hurt, has she?"

"What's it doing now?" asked one of the Gravillers.

At the sound of Veronica's voice, Chit Win stopped running and raised herself up onto her back legs. Chit Win placed her front paws on the arena wall. She turned her head towards Veronica, and Samuel could swear that he saw a smile on that little rodent face. The two sacs on Chit Win's back began to inflate. Everyone watched in silence, as Chit Win inflated at an unreasonable rate, growing bigger even than Berick's veole, who was still sleeping by the wall of the arena.

"What on Earth?" asked Pa.

Chit Win said, "Veronica." It spoke. It actually spoke. The sound came through an opening Chit Win's inflated air-sacs, but it was clear Co-operation lingo, understood by all.

The market place fell silent as they all watched Chit Win.

"Chit Win will not fight. Chit Win will talk to Veronica."

"Veronica, come here, my love," Pa shouted.

Veronica squeezed through to the front of the crowd and leant over to peer into the arena.

"Ah!" Chit Win's face seemed to light up.

That was definitely a smile, Samuel thought.

"Veronica. Chit Win understands Veronica."

All at once, everyone began to speak.

"Why is it talking?"

"It understands Co-operation lingo."

"Seems like it's formed a bond with the Human female."

"All this time, and they could talk?"

"You know what this means don't you?" Ma's voice was clear and cut through the males' chatter. "It looks like there are three sentient species on this planet. Co-operation law means there's going to be some changes around here. Native species customs take precedence."

Chit Win finally managed to scale the wall of the arena as she bounced over to Veronica, "Chit Win understands Veronica."

"What's it all mean, Pa?" Samuel asked.

"The veoles are all female aren't they?" Masher asked. "I don't know if their customs would suit us."

"Co-operation law is Co-operation law," said Ma. Not even Masher could argue with her on that point. Every species adhered to Co-operation law, otherwise there would be anarchy in the colonies.

"Sure is going to be a lot of changes around here," It was a female Graviller's voice from the back of the crowd.

"Pa, how come we never knew they were sentient?" Samuel asked.

"Looks like they were just waiting for the right mind to come along," Pa said. "I can't believe it. My little girl has made first contact with an alien species. That's the way it is in the colonies. This world is wide open for exploration." Pa looked over to the back of the crowd where the Graviller girls were petting their bothers' fighting veoles. "These little critters have got some kind of connection with the females."

"Wonder what kind of society they've got going?" Berick said.

"Reckon there's going to be a few changes, for sure," Samuel said. He looked at his Ma. She was smiling, and Samuel was, too.

The Best Cheesecake in the Universe

Cory Cone

For my nieces, Madalynn and Sophia.

Cory Cone lives, works and writes in Baltimore, MD. He studied painting at the Maryland Institute College of Art, where he met and married his wife. He now works full time at the college and writes strange fiction in the evenings. His website is www. corycone.com, and you can follow him on Twitter, @corycone

Madalynn leaned her bicycle against the porch steps and gently lifted the plastic container from the bike basket. There was an entire cheesecake inside, and she inspected it thoroughly to be certain it hadn't been damaged on the ride over to Nana's house—Nana's *old* house; technically, it belonged to Madalynn now. She felt the weight of the silver key in her pocket and still couldn't believe that she had a real house of her very own, and she was only twelve!

Madalynn walked up the porch stairs, placed the cheesecake on Nana's rocker and plucked the key from her pocket. A breeze swept through and swayed the rocker back and forth.

Sliding the key into the lock, Madalynn feared that it wouldn't turn. What if this was all a misunderstanding, and the note had been written a long time ago, and Nana had actually changed her mind? The key refused to turn. She looked over her shoulder, praying her father wouldn't come barreling up the dirt driveway and demand to know what she was doing at her great-grandmother's house, alone, and with a cheesecake. She twisted the key harder, but still it wouldn't go.

The sun would soon set, an hour of light remained at best. She needed to get the cheesecake into the fridge and the table set up before she ran out of time. She'd get inside, even if it meant breaking a window and climbing in.

Madalynn shoved her palm painfully against the back of the key and it slid a bit further into the lock. Breath held, eyes closed, she tried once more. The key turned, and the door unlocked with a loud click. Hoisting the cake back into her hands, Madalynn stepped into her house.

....

Nana had died when she was ninety-four, but boasted that she never looked a day over ninety-two. She attributed her longevity to three things: waking with a smile, a glass of chocolate milk three times a week, and always having something to look forward to. Nana loved visitors and even kept a small calendar, so she would not lose track of when she'd be having them. They all came, Nana said, because of her universally renowned cheesecake.

On most of Madalynn's visits, Nana would allow her a slice.

"Only one," Nana would say. "I have to save the rest for my guests." According to Nana, those guests traveled far and wide for the privilege.

Once, when Madalynn was munching away, eyes rolled back in her head because it was always so very tasty, she asked if she could stay and meet the guests. Her father didn't believe that his grandmother ever had guests besides the family. He always warned Madalynn to take everything her great-grandmother said with a grain of especially fine salt. "They must be very fancy if they can make such long trips to visit you," he said once.

Her Nana said, "They are fancy! The fanciest of folks I have ever met. Each one comes once a year, every year, just for a piece of this cheesecake. Some of them have coffee too, but my coffee pales in comparison to the sort they get on their travels. My cheesecake though, they say, is by far the best."

"So, may I meet them?"

"No," said Nana. Madalynn was hurt because she didn't think it was such an unreasonable request. Surely Nana would love to introduce these world travelers to her best and favorite great-granddaughter. "Don't look so sad, Maddy. I've promised them all that I will never tell a soul that they come, though they've spread the word themselves, as my calendar can attest. Still, it must remain secret."

"But you've told *me*!"

"I have, haven't I." She grinned slyly and leaned in close to Madalynn's ear. "One day, you see, I will finally have to leave this earth. Shocking, I know! Believe me, I'd stay another thousand years if I could. But it's true, I haven't got all that much left in me." The thought of Nana dying made the cheesecake taste bittersweet in Madalynn's mouth. "But when that day comes, I'd like *you* to prepare my cake for the guests."

"Me? Really?"

"I think you'd like them, and they you. It has to wait until then though, and you might be sad on that day, but I hope you'll be excited too."

And Madalynn smiled because she really was, though she wondered if they would like her as much as they all seemed to like Nana.

....

Madalynn scoured the kitchen, opening cupboard after cupboard until she found the white cake stand that Nana always served her cheesecake on. She set it on the table and cautiously lifted the cheesecake from the plastic container and transferred it onto the stand. Then, balancing the cake stand as if she were crossing a tightrope, she walked to the refrigerator and set the cake inside.

A photograph of her and Nana greeted her when she closed the door. It was stuck to the refrigerator with an apple-shaped magnet. Nana was smiling in her rocker on the porch, Madalynn grinning ear to ear at her side.

Between the exciting secrecy and the preparations for the visitors, Madalynn had allowed herself little time to grieve. In that moment, seeing the photo and how happy they were together, she realized that Nana had been so much more than just a great-grandmother. She was a friend, a companion, and one of the few people who she never thought she could live without. She wept softly for a brief moment, and then snatched the small calendar from her back pocket to see how many visitors would be there tonight.

The notes for that day mentioned two groups, the first arriving an hour after sunset. Madalynn set the calendar down and scanned the room for candles to begin decorating.

She could cry later. There was work to do.

....

After Nana's funeral, Madalynn went straight to her room to be alone and planned on crying all evening. Her body and mind wrapped themselves into a strange, uncomfortable tapestry of emotions that was completely alien to her. The weight of the loss was in many ways as confusing as it was tragic. But when she entered her room, Madalynn found an envelope had been placed on her pillow. Her name was handwritten in the middle in Nana's recognizable script. It contained a note, a small, pocket-sized calendar, and a key.

Dearest Madalynn,

I know that you are sad, and that is perfectly normal. I am sad too. I'll miss you deeply.

Be sad as long as you'd like, or at least until the first marked date on the calendar I've given you. That is when the first visitor shall arrive after I've gone, and you must be sure to have the cheesecake ready! You're young and probably haven't thought about what may happen to my house when I am gone, but I thought about it a lot. My guests know no other house, and there is simply not enough time for new arrangements. In order to prevent the house from being sold or going to one of your older, reclusive cousins, I have bequeathed it to you. Bequeathed means given. It's yours.

My grandson—sorry, I mean your father—probably won't tell you about this gift until you're much older so pretend you don't know. You'll have to sneak over, but I'm sure that won't be difficult. You're a crafty young woman.

The guests will be expecting you.

The recipe is below. Share it with no one.

"Nana's Cheesecake:"

-Go to the Super Fresh in Primrose and pick one out.

Heartbroken? Don't be. I happened to have one at home when they first stopped by, and I fibbed a little. Never had the heart to change my story.

Our little secret, dear.

Love always, Nana

....

Before long, Madalynn had set the dining room table with several tall red candles and enough place settings to seat six. She had no idea how many people would be stopping by per group, but if there were more than six they'd have to deal with standing. Each setting consisted of a small desert plate, a fleshly cleaned fork, and a coffee cup. A French press sat waiting to be plunged in the kitchen. She also placed a small knife for slicing on the table.

The dining room glowed in the candlelight, and Madalynn was very proud. She hoped desperately that she would live up the visitors' expectations.

Moonlight mixed with candlelight in the room, and a wind moaned just outside the windows.

She couldn't keep still and spent the next half hour checking and rechecking the cake, to make sure it looked okay, and blowing out and relighting the candles so that they wouldn't burn too low before they arrived.

Then, when she thought that perhaps her father was right, and that Nana was making up stories, there came a timid knock at the front door.

Madalynn froze. Her first thought was not that visitors had arrived, but that her father had discovered where she was. She contemplated hiding beneath the table to avoid discovery, but realized if it *was* her father, he would have stormed into the house by then. He surely had a key of his own.

The knocking came again, softly, as if whoever was out there was terrified that someone might actually open the door. Madalynn also heard the creak of the rocker swaying back and forth.

A dark, elongated shadow hovered beyond the window by the door, obscured by the curtains. Whoever stood just beyond the door was trying to see inside. Its shape was skewed and made Madalynn feel dizzy just looking at it. It looked as if the person had to bend over just to look through the window.

Madalynn reconsidered hiding after all.

Again, the knock sounded at the door. Muffled voices spoke.

Madalynn swallowed and stepped slowly through the dining room. She placed her hand on the doorknob but did not turn it.

"Who is it?" she called out, her heart racing.

The squeaking of the chair stopped.

"Oh, she sounds adorable!" said a woman.

"She's actually there?" asked a man. "I was so worried it'd be empty."

Madalynn wiped sweat from her brow and tried to peer through the window to see them, but they were too close to the door now for her to get a good glimpse.

"What brings you to these parts?" Madalynn said, feeling foolish as the words slipped from her lips.

"A delicacy worth traveling for," said the woman.

"And company," said the man.

Madalynn opened the door.

There stood in the threshold the tallest creature she had ever seen. The woman's chest towered far above the door. Motherly comfort radiated from her. A thin blue outfit was wrapped tightly around her entire body, the surface smooth and glimmering in the starlight. It ended at the neck, where the woman's moss-green neck sprouted out of the outfit like a plant stem. Her head was large and oblong, and enormous jet black eyes sat like slate in her face. Her lips were full and red, and were the only feature that looked even remotely human.

Horror gripped Madalynn by the throat, choking her. A scream threatened at her mouth. But the woman leaned down and placed her long gloved fingers gently onto her shoulder, and Madalynn calmed to her touch.

"Gosh, so sorry!" the woman said. Her voice was soothing and slightly raspy with age. It reminded Madalynn of Nana. "Sometimes we forget to warn people. *Surprise!* I'm Agatha, and you must be Maddy."

Madalynn found the will to speak. "Yes, ma'am."

"George!" Agatha said to the other tall creature, lounging in the rocker. He rose to his feet and stood equally as tall as she. "Say hello to the child before we frighten her to death. Where will your cake be then, huh?"

"My dear," said George, and a wave of warmth ran through Madalynn's body. His voice was like the lowest, softest note echoing from a piano. "It is an absolute pleasure. We have heard so very much about you, haven't we, Agatha?"

"Yes," said Agatha. "Nothing but good things, I might add." The two strangers stood shoulder to shoulder on the porch, staring expectantly at Madalynn. "Might we come in?"

Madalynn's face went red with embarrassment. "Oh my gosh, of course!" she said and stepped aside.

Agatha and George bent low and stepped into the house. Madalynn gazed in astonishment at what their absence on the porch revealed. A tiny ship, speckled in blinking lights, sat perched in the yard, smoke hissing from beneath. It was unlike any craft she'd ever seen, but reminded her in many ways of small car, like the one her father took her to school in—if it could fly. She closed the door, excitement filling her to the brim.

The guests had already sat themselves at the table. They were so tall that they had to lean over it, their round, green heads nearly touching above the candles. Their anticipating smiles flickered in the candlelight.

Madalynn retrieved the cheesecake from the refrigerator and carefully brought it to the table. Would they know it was store bought? What if they suspected something was wrong, would they be angry with her? Would they ever come back?

"Please," said Agatha, "do us the honors." She held out her plate.

Madalynn took the knife from the table and sliced two ample triangles of cheesecake. Sweat brimmed on her face. They were going to hate it. They would take one bite and declare it the worst they'd ever had, and then steal her away in their craft to wherever they had come from. What awful, tortuous things would they do to her if they were not pleased with the cake?

She balanced first one slice over to Agatha's plate and another to George's.

They licked their lips enthusiastically and then set the plates tenderly onto the table. They did not begin to eat, but to Madalynn's surprise, each wiped thick tears from their black eyes.

"We are so very sorry for your loss," said Agatha, her words choked with grief.

"She was a dear, sweet friend to us," said George.

Madalynn swiped away tears of her own. "She was a dear friend to me as well," she said.

"She loved you very much." Agatha ran a long finger along Madalynn's cheek. "Talked nonstop about you when we visited. Always told us that when she died, you'd be here to greet us and then, only then, would we know the taste of the best cheesecake in the universe."

Madalynn held her breath. She thought maybe it would be wise to tell them that she had not made it. It was from the store and it might not be as good as Nana's and please forgive her if it's terrible. The guests each picked up their forks, and Madalynn held her tongue.

They carved away the tip of their slices of cake, lifted them teasingly to their lips, and then chomped down. They chewed, and Madalynn's chest ached for air as she watched them for any reactions.

They both moaned in unison, swallowed, and leaned as far

back in their chairs as their tall figures allowed.

Madalynn breathed in a long and thankful breath.

"I didn't think it could be done," said George.

"It seemed impossible!" said Agatha. "But she was right. This cake, right here, that has just passed into my belly, is the best cheesecake in the universe."

"Bar none!"

And Madalynn smiled and clapped with joy. So she had to fib a little, but it was worth it to make these two travelers so happy. She rushed to the kitchen and retrieved the French press and poured them both steaming cups of coffee.

"Oh, perfect!" said George, sipping slowly. "Hits the spot."

Madalynn, her face aching with cheer, said, "I'm so very glad you've come, and that you enjoy the cheesecake."

"It's a highlight of our travels, dear. Wouldn't miss it for the world," said Agatha.

"Where are you two from?"

"Ah," said George, reaching into a hidden pocket in his shimmering blue outfit.

"He loves using this thing," Agatha said, eyeing him sweetly from across the table. Madalynn knew that they must be madly in love.

George produced a small, golden orb and balanced it in his palm for Madalynn to see. It was beautiful, perfectly round, and produced a small humming sound. Before her eyes, it broke apart into a million tinier spheres and they burst about the room, hovering in midair. "This," said George, pointing a tiny blue sphere near Madalynn's face, "is Earth. And that," he pointed across the room to a pulsing orange sphere that was hovering near the door, "is Caliphon."

"That's our planet," said Agatha.

In an instant, the spheres regrouped into the orb in George's hand and he replaced it into his pocket.

"How long does it take you to travel here?"

"Well, it feels like an eternity with this woman!" George said, laughing and banging his hand on the table.

"Oh stop," chuckled Agatha. "Not as long as you'd imagine."

A new knock sounded at the door.

"Please excuse me," said Madalynn to her guests. "It appears someone else has arrived."

"I wonder if it's Trinity," said George.

"You'd just love it if she were visiting today, wouldn't you!"

George winked, and Agatha let loose a hearty laugh.

Madalynn left them to their cheesecake, and walked to the door.

How Nana had kept this so tight a secret, Madalynn would have to learn herself. As badly as she wished to tell the world about her magnificent visitors, she knew that the novelty of it would be tarnished if she spoke of it to a single soul. These were her Nana's visitors, and now they were hers. And so what if it was a store bought cheesecake. She realized that it wasn't so much about the cake, as it was about the company, the journey, and the chance to make new and exciting friends. As her hand wrapped once again around the handle of the door, Madalynn knew that from this day forth, she would always have something to look forward to.

"Who is it?" she called out, and swung open the door.

A Smelly Problem

Angela Penrose

Angela Penrose lives in Seattle with her husband, five computers, and some unknown number of books, which occupy most of the house. She writes in several genres, but F&SF is her first love. She likes writing for anthologies for the variety, and the challenge of writing to a theme. This is her second anthology appearance, with three more scheduled for 2015. You can find her at angelapenrosewriter.blogspot.com

Every kid wants to develop a cool talent – that's just a given, right? The kids at Cody Markham's high school weren't any different, and he'd seen some pretty cool talents. Donna could make a flame jet out of her index finger, although only the left one. Octavio could teleport, which was awesome, even if he had to be able to see the place he was teleporting to. Sammy could make his clothes change instantly to any outfit he could imagine.

So when Cody accidentally discovered he could make people smell different smells, he was pretty disappointed. What good was that? It was pretty stupid, and he hadn't told anyone. He'd almost rather have people think he was a neuter without any talent at all than tell anyone he was the psychic scratch-n-sniff guy who was doomed to be called "Stinky" for the rest of his life.

Right then, he had other things to think about, though. The tardy bell rang and Cody slumped in his seat, weighed down by visions of failing the midterm and trying to explain the screw-up to his parents. And in chemistry. He needed that if he was going to get into med school. If he screwed up in high school, he would have to take some stupid remedial class in college, and that would put him behind forever. He'd end up flipping burgers all his life just because he'd been too busy raiding with his Warcraft guild to actually study. It was stupid and he knew it, but there wasn't anything he could do about it right then. He was going to fail because he sucked.

An awful smell jolted him out of his spiraling panic. He leaned forward in his seat, fanning one hand in front of his face. "Turn that thing *off!*" he hissed at Tonya, who sat at the table behind him. She was messing around with the gas nozzle again, and the sour smell of the gas the Bunsen burners used made Cody want to leave the room even more than he already did.

Someone told Tonya you could get high off the gas, and she was stupid enough to believe it. She nudged it on whenever she thought she could get away with it. It was frying her brain a little at a time – not that she had much to start with.

Tonya mouthed a cuss word at him, but turned the nozzle off. That gave him an idea.

Mr. Hong was up taking roll and would hand out the exams as soon as he was done. But what if there was some kind of emergency?

Cody got out his pencil and calculator so it would look like he was ready for the test. Then he focused his power on Mr. Hong and sent him the smell of gas.

Sure enough, that got his attention. He got up and walked right over to Tonya's bench, scowled down at her and made sure the handle to the gas nozzle was all the way off. It was. Mr. Hong sniffed a few more times and probably thought he smelled some of the leftover gas from when she had been messing around. Cody shut off his power and let Mr. Hong just smell what was really there. After a few more seconds, Mr. Hong went back to his desk.

"Put away your books and notes," he said.

Cody gave him another shot of gas smell.

Mr. Hong's head jerked up, and he sniffed again.

He dropped the stack of exams onto his desk and asked, "Does anyone else smell gas?" Because of Tonya, a bunch of people said yes, including Cody.

Octavio said, "It's just Tonya screwing around again."

"Shut up, jerkwad!" Tonya yelled.

"This smells fresh," Mr. Hong said. "If there's a leak, then it's dangerous. Does anyone else who's not near Tonya's bench smell gas?"

Cody sent the smell to a couple of other people in the front right corner of the room near one of the wall sinks.

Mr. Hong prowled around the corner, sniffing like a bloodhound. Cody made sure he smelled something. Eventually, the teacher stood up and walked to the phone on the wall to report a gas leak in his classroom. Five minutes later they were all outside, clustered in a group near the baseball diamond. The rest of the kids who'd been in the science building were streaming out to join them. A little bit later, kids and teachers evacuated from the rest of the school.

Hah, no exam today! And it was a Friday – Cody swore to himself that he'd study like mad all weekend and get a good grade on the stupid test.

....

By Monday he was muttering "six-point-oh-two-times-ten-to-the-twenty-third" practically in his sleep. He was pretty sure he could figure out the mass of any compound and break it down into percent composition, with a calculator and enough scratch paper. Maybe his stupid talent was good for something after all.

When he got to chemistry, there was a substitute. Ms. Dennison explained that Mr. Hong was on a leave of absence but refused to say why. Maybe she didn't know. She handed out the exams, and that was the end of it.

She seemed like an okay teacher – even let Joey borrow her calculator when the dummy said he had forgotten his – but Mr. Hong was a great guy. Cody was worried something had happened.

Lunch was right after chemistry, and Cody asked around to see if anyone knew anything. By the time the bell rang, he'd heard from a kid whose mom was on the school board that Mr. Hong had been put on leave because the gas company had come out and gone over the room and all the rooms around it, but hadn't found any leak.

It had cost the school money and disrupted classes for the rest of the day. The students had been kept herded together in bunches outside, doing nothing except be bored and antsy until after one-forty. Some kids had snuck away, though, and Brad Menzies had been caught trying to shoplift a pair of pricey basketball shoes during what would've been school hours. They were blaming everything on Mr. Hong for calling in a false alarm.

It wasn't his fault, Cody thought. *What if there had really been a gas leak?* Teachers were supposed to report that stuff, so he'd just done what the rules said.

It had to be the vice principal. Mr. Johnson had always had it in for Mr. Hong. He said he was a maverick and disruptive to the school routine because Mr. Hong didn't always teach straight out of the book. He gave the class cool labs to do, and they'd watched a movie about Marie Curie that made Cody really glad he had modern equipment and stuff. After the magnesium lab, instead of putting all the little strips of magnesium away to use again next year, Mr. Hong had piled them up on top of a wire stand, turned off the lights, and set it all on fire with a Bunsen burner. The whole thing had flared up white-hot. Cody had the image of that huge, hot flame of burning magnesium floating in front of his eyes for almost half an hour after.

That was "wasting school resources," though. When Mr. Hong had paid out of his pocket to replace all the burned magnesium, then it was "making a disruptive spectacle in the classroom." Right, because it was a bad thing that all the kids were talking about it for the rest of the day. How many other teachers got kids talking around campus about what they did in class?

Mr. Johnson was a jerkwad, though, and wanted Mr. Hong out. Cody thought half of it was because Mr. Hong's talent was to know whether someone he was talking to understood him, which wasn't exactly exciting but a good talent for a teacher to have.

All Mr. Johnson could do was make dogs run away by glaring at them, which was probably some kind of telepathy, but it only worked with dogs. It was seriously useless unless you got caught sneaking around in a junkyard or something.

Cody figured Mr. Johnson was probably jealous of Mr. Hong having a talent that was perfect for teaching, and just generally for being a popular teacher, while Johnson had something really pathetic and none of the kids liked him at all. So the fake gas leak had given him a chance to try to get rid of Mr. Hong.

The obvious thing to do was confess. Cody didn't want to do that. Aside from getting in trouble, he'd have to tell about his talent. Then he'd have to walk around with a bag over his head for the next two and a half years.

There had to be something else he could do to fix it.

....

The next day they had Ms. Dennison in chem again. That gave Cody an idea. A couple of times during class, he made her smell gas. She looked around and sniffed, but Cody never kept it up for more than five seconds or so. She didn't say anything at first.

After the fifth time, though, while the class was working on problems out of the book, she got up and went out the door.

Ms. Dennison was only gone for a minute. She came back with Ms. Anza, the physiology teacher. Ms. Anza was a short, gray-haired woman who didn't take crap from anyone. Her tests were so tough, Cody knew kids who'd gotten negative scores. He wasn't looking forward to having Ms. Anza next year, but right then he was happy to see her. If anyone had the nerve to get in Johnson's face after everything that'd happened, it was Ms. Anza. He made sure she smelled gas too.

She sniffed around a few times, scowled, and said something to Ms. Dennison. Ms. Anza marched out looking grim, and Cody kicked back, trying hard not to grin. He got back to working on the problems, sure Ms. Anza would go chew Johnson's ear off and prove Mr. Hong wasn't a nut.

....

The next day, Ms. Dennison was still there. The word around campus was that Mr. Hong was still in trouble and probably wouldn't be coming back.

Cody figured out that part of the problem was people only smelled gas in the classroom sometimes. Only during the class he was in, actually, and he really didn't want anyone making that connection.

He'd have to do something to make people smell gas when he wasn't there. All he could think of was making it leak gas for real. Then anyone would smell it any time, and a real gas leak would show up on the detector when the gas company came. They'd fix it, and everything would be okay. Mr. Hong would come back.

At the end of class, Cody dropped his calculator down by the side of his bench before he headed out with everyone else going to lunch. He ducked into a bathroom and combed his hair for five minutes. He wanted to make sure he didn't drop any hairs over by where the gas lines were, because investigators would be able to nail him if he did, just like in the cop shows. When he was done, he took a couple of deep breaths and went around to the door that led into the heart of the building where the science office was.

Students weren't supposed to go through there unless a teacher was with them. The office was between the outside door and everywhere else, so you couldn't sneak past without being seen.

If you looked like you belonged, though, you could walk right through; anyone who saw a student just heading on in, not trying to sneak or anything, assumed they were meeting a teacher in their office.

Cody walked past the department secretary who was on the phone. She didn't even look up. He headed left down the hall and kept going, then slipped into the chem classroom and shut the door. The windows by the main door were tinted so you could see out, but you could only see in if you put your face right up to the glass with your hands cupped around it. No one would probably come in until the end of lunch. Cody expected to be done way before that.

In fact, he'd better be done way before that. Ms. Brown, the principal, was great at catching kids pulling stuff, but only if she got to the crime scene right away. That was her talent at work: she could see one hour back in time, any place she was standing. Cody's plan was to get the gas leak going right away, leaving at least fifty minutes or so of the lunch hour. He was betting that it would take longer than twenty minutes for people to figure out what was going on and think of calling Ms. Brown. He might get in trouble, but he might not. It was a gamble, and it was worth it to get Mr. Hong back.

Cody had watched the guy hooking up the gas line when his parents bought a new stove, so he knew what they looked like. Just to make sure, he opened the cupboard under the sink at the end of his bench. There was a water pipe and next to it was a narrow copper pipe leading up toward the gas nozzle. Score.

Once he was sure he knew what the gas lines looked like, he went to the bigger sink in the corner, and opened up the cupboard door. There was no gas nozzle on the counter, but there was a copper line coming through the wall between the chem class and the inner hallway. From there it split to all the benches.

The metal pipes were pretty thin. Cody pulled his sweatshirt sleeve down over his hand then reached in and grabbed the pipe right above the valve. He jerked it back and forth, first just a little, then more. It only took a minute of messing with it before he could smell gas.

It was only a little, but that was enough.

He got his calculator and headed back out the way he'd come. He was ready to wave the calculator at the secretary if she questioned him, but when he came back through the office area, she was standing at the microwave with her back to him. Cody was pretty sure nobody saw him.

....

It was about fifteen minutes into Algebra Two when an announcement came over the speaker ordering everyone to evacuate. The math building was right next to the science building. While the students shuffled along, griping and laughing and generally taking forever to get away from a building that was about to blow up for all they knew, Cody spotted Ms. Brown heading across the quad toward the science building. She had long legs and was walking fast, but she wasn't running. Cody glanced at his watch and kept an eye on her. There had been at least fifty minutes left of lunch, plus five minutes after the bell rang before classes started, then fifteen minutes into class – that was an hour and ten minutes, so she was too late and he was clear.

Cody saw the gas company truck when it pulled into the parking lot. That was it; they'd find the leak, fix it, and it would all be over. Cody was so relieved that the mess was finally cleaned up, he sat down on the grass and worked on an English paper that wasn't even due until Monday.

....

The relief lasted until the next afternoon when Cody got a note in his last class telling him to report to Ms. Brown's office right after school.

Cody panicked. He had to be busted, and they were gonna expel him for... oh, man, he'd caused a gas leak! In a classroom. Deliberately. He hadn't thought about it before, not all the way through. It had just been the easiest answer to the problem. It hadn't really hit him that anything could happen. People could've been hurt.

If someone had walked up with a cigarette, which some teachers did, and if they were late from lunch, sometimes they'd take the last couple of drags right outside the door. There could have been a huge explosion.

No way, calm down, you can't possibly be busted, he thought, trying to get the voice in his head to stop squeaking and hyperventilating. *Ms. Brown didn't get there in time to get an image. You didn't leave any fingerprints or anything, so there's no way they know it was you. It's gotta be for something else, so don't panic, or she'll know something's up just from that.*

After school, Cody wandered out to his locker like he always did, dumping books he wouldn't need and stuffing books he had to have for homework into his backpack. Then he headed toward the main office. He gave his name to the secretary, and ten seconds later he was sitting on a hard plastic seat right in front of Ms. Brown's desk. He'd figured he'd probably have to wait at least a few minutes before she was ready to see him, but it seemed she had been waiting for him. That was bad.

Ms. Brown stared at him for half a minute or so, studying him like she was trying to figure out whether to step on him or just swat him with a rolled-up newspaper.

"Cody Markham," Ms. Brown said. "Tell me what you were thinking yesterday at lunch, so I can figure out whether I should call a psychiatrist or the cops?"

Cody's heart blew up to fill his whole chest, then stopped. He couldn't breathe, couldn't speak. The only part of him working was his sweat glands, and they were on overdrive.

He managed to say, "I didn't do anything," without choking on spit or squeaking.

"I saw you."

"You couldn't have!" A thought popped up and Cody added, "Because I didn't do anything." He was busted.

She ignored his protests. "Why, Cody? You're a good kid. You've never been in trouble, never even had detention. If it was just a stupid prank, I'm definitely calling the cops and I'll tell them to test you for drugs, because this isn't something you'd do in your right mind. You do know the building could've exploded, right?"

"Yes! I mean, no! I mean….Cody closed his eyes and leaned back in his chair so his face pointed at the ceiling. *That's it*, he thought. *I'm an idiot, she's gonna expel me and I'll probably go to jail. My dad's gonna have a heart attack and ground me till I'm thirty. If I'm not still in jail.*

"Why?" she repeated. "I can't figure out what would make you do something so incredibly stupid. Explain it to me."

"I just… I wanted Mr. Hong to come back." Cody sat back up and looked straight at her, wanting her to get it. "He's a great teacher, and it's not his fault Johnson's got it in for him and grabbed on this dumb excuse to go after him. It's not his fault, and I wanted to fix it."

"How do you know it wasn't his fault?"

"Because I smelled gas too, so did a bunch of other kids. So did Ms. Dennison yesterday morning, and Ms. Anza. I was watching them, and I could tell they smelled something. It wasn't just Mr. Hong imagining stuff."

"Yes, and it's strange that no one smelled anything before or after fourth period – the class you're in."

"Maybe nobody asked them, or maybe they didn't notice."

Ms. Brown raised both eyebrows in what was an obviously fake surprise. "Really? How likely is it that anyone would not notice a gas leak? The stuff stinks for a reason."

"I don't know. I wasn't there."

"Exactly. You weren't there." She glanced down at an open file on her desk, then back up at him. "You don't have a registered talent, do you Cody? That's unusual for someone your age."

He put on a defensive expression and a slightly aggressive tone and said, "I could still get something. Some kids don't get anything till they're nineteen or even twenty. I have time."

"Unless you already have a talent and just haven't told anyone."

"That would be stupid. Why would I want everyone snarking at me about being neutered if I had a talent?"

"That's a very good question. The only answer I can think of is that you have a talent that would get you even more grief than not having one at all."

"That'd suck," Cody said in a flat voice.

"I imagine it must. It's still not an excuse for almost blowing up a building, though."

"I didn't!"

"I saw you, Cody. I'm really interested to hear why one of my better students would go suddenly crazy and pull a stupid stunt like this. If you're just going to keep denying it, though, that's fine; I was only curious. I wanted to know why this happened, in case there was something I could do to prevent it in the future. If not, then I'll just call the police and let them handle it from here."

She picked up the phone and started dialing a number.

"Wait." He closed his eyes and slumped back in his chair. "All right, hang on."

"So? I'm waiting, Cody, but not for very long."

"It's just... it's dumb."

"That's a given. I still want the specifics."

Cody looked away, with his eyes unfocused because all he could see was every dumb thing he'd done since this mess started. He said, "We had a midterm on Friday in Mr. Hong's class. I didn't study, and I was afraid I'd fail." He told about how Tonya was always sniffing the gas from the burners, and how that'd given him an idea. He was practically whispering when he told about what he'd done and how he'd done it, because it was still the stupidest, most useless talent anyone ever had anywhere. When he told Ms. Brown, he knew it was going to get out. That actually made him cringe more than the threat of being punished for busting the gas pipe.

"I just wanted more time, you know? I know it was dumb, but I was desperate, and it seemed like a good idea right then. But I couldn't let Mr. Hong get fired because of me, so I had to fix it. Just making people smell gas in my period wasn't enough, they still didn't do anything. It had to be real so everyone would think Mr. Hong had been right all along. I didn't think about someone sneaking in with a cigarette or something until way later, and it was too late." He sat up, looked at Ms. Brown again and added, "And I know you didn't get there until more than an hour after. You couldn't have seen me."

Ms. Brown sighed and rubbed her face with one hand, like she was tired. She finally said, "I don't suppose it ever occurs to you kids to get your schoolwork out of the way before you go screw around?"

The answer to that one was obvious, so Cody didn't say anything.

He was wondering about something, though. She had gotten over to Mr. Hong's room too late to see anything with her talent. But she'd said she saw him, more than once. Ms. Brown wasn't the kind to right-out lie, even to a kid, just to set a cheap trap. Mr. Johnson, sure, but not Ms. Brown.

What if she had seen him?

"You can see more than an hour back." His tone was accusing, and he was kind of ticked off. That was cheating!

"I didn't need to see more than an hour back," she said, perfectly calm. "I just had to make you think I did."

"But then how'd you know to pull it on me? You didn't try it on every kid in school just hoping to get someone to jump."

"You were seen going through the office."

Cody snorted. "By who? The secretary was on the phone and didn't twitch when I walked in, and she had her back to me and didn't twitch when I left. There wasn't anyone else."

They stared at each other, neither saying anything. Cody knew it was all down to how serious Ms. Brown thought it was, and whether she was willing to have her secret spilled.

She finally sighed and glared at him. "All right, this is what we're going to do. You had a momentary attack of idiocy, motivated by your desire to fix a problem you caused a teacher. You went about it completely wrong. You are never, ever going to do anything like this again. If you so much as get a detention for tardiness between now and the day you graduate, I'll expel your butt. You are going to go talk to Ms. Lalande in the science prep room and volunteer to help her for an hour every day after school – cooking agar, stocking lab kits, whatever she needs. You can do that until you graduate, too."

Cody opened his mouth to protest, just out of reflex, until she added, "I know you want to get into med school. Experience working in the prep room can't hurt. It's not all washing glassware; you got good grades in chemistry last semester, so Mr. Hong will probably be willing to tell Ms. Lalande that you know a mole isn't just an animal that digs up gardens. Prove yourself, and she'll probably give you some more interesting things to do."

Huh. That didn't sound too bad. Better than jail, right? "Okay." He nodded.

"Good. I won't tell Mr. Hong or Ms. Lalande why you're there; they can assume you've become suddenly industrious and eager for additional experience."

Cody nodded again. That was good. He'd hate to have Mr. Hong knowing what an idiot he'd been. He felt his shoulders hunching up a little just at the thought.

"And one final side deal," she added. "You don't tell anyone about your theory that I can see more than an hour into the past, and I won't give anyone any reason to start calling you Stinky. Deal?"

Cody nodded again, a lot more vigorously that time. "Deal. Definitely a deal."

"I'm serious, Cody. No one else knows except a couple of faculty members. If even a hint starts spreading about it, I'll know it came from you and all our deals are off."

"Yes, Ma'am."

"Good. You can go, then. And I'll expect to hear that Ms. Lalande has a new assistant by the end of tomorrow."

Cody repeated, "Yes, Ma'am."

He walked to the science building prep room to see if he could catch Ms. Lalande before she left for the day. Having Mr. Hong back would be awesome. And Cody wasn't in jail. That was awesome squared. And nobody, except Ms. Brown, knew about his stinky talent – awesome cubed.

The Care and Feeding of Your Pet Robot

Phoebe North

Phoebe North lives in upstate New York with her husband, her daughter, and her cat. She is the author of Starglass *and* Starbreak, *a science fiction duology from Simon & Schuster Books for Young Readers. Find her online at www.phoebenorth.com.*

Taki woke up when the light came in all orangey through the shutters. Her room was hot and wet. Condensation collected on the peeveesee sheets Ma had used to patch the ceiling. Once, before Ma had done that but after the storms wrecked the roof, dust rained in like falling stars. Now the yellow plastic bowed, pregnant with the weight of sand. The afternoon's heat was on, and Taki had overslept. That was her first clue that her implant was malfunctioning.

Taki ambled up from her cot, her legs bare and sweaty under her shorts, and aimed a swift kick at Ellay Tu. Toe contacted metal. Wheels wheeled back. But it took a moment before the voice chirruped in her mind.

(This, of course, was clue #2.)

<C'mon, worthless,> she chided the bot. <You forgot to get me up.>

Ellay Tu's gears groaned. On other mornings, Taki liked to think the robot yawned like a kitten might, but only in the cool and early mornings when Taki herself was in a better mood. Now, not nearly. Not even when she felt the buzz of her robot's voice.

<Up, up!> was all that Ellay Tu said at first.

Taki gave her head a shake and headed for the kitchen. She ignored the whirl of wheels behind her, the sing-song voice of the machine that trailed behind.

<Up up up and good morrow!>

Taki frowned, scratched herself. She didn't see what was so good about it. Ma was at the sink rinsing off the dishes. She didn't seem to think it was much good either.

"Up so late?" Ma asked, speaking over her slender shoulder to her daughter. There was annoyance in Ma's voice, a thin sort of urgency. "You have a match today."

"My implant's on the fritz," Taki said. She gave Ellay Tu a glance. The bot had fallen silent. This was clue #3. Usually, it wouldn't give her a moment's peace during meals. Taki reached inside the icebox, fished a can of juice out of the lukewarm water. Ellay Tu offered Taki a can opener, but she ignored it, popping the top off against the edge of the counter instead. "I'll need to visit the tinker."

"Again?" Ma was elbow-deep in the water recycled from last week's shower, but she stopped, running a damp wrist over her brow. "You know we can't afford it."

"Ma—!" Taki began. Ellay Tu proffered a handkerchief, preparing itself, Taki guessed, for a tantrum. But Taki was thirteen now, too old for hysterics. She shot Ellay Tu a vicious glare.

"Really, Taki," Ma went on. Ma was good at ignoring the drama between her daughter and the robot. But then, she'd had plenty of practice over the last five years. "It's not that I don't appreciate the credits you two bring in. In fact, we'd be starved without them."

Ma let out a high, weird laugh. Taki fought the urge to roll her eyes. That wasn't the half of it, after all. Ma made some scratch doing the neighbors' mending, but not nearly enough. She left school young, she often said, when she was pregnant with Taki. Never wanted to be anything more than a mother. Back then, she could afford the luxury of it. But now. . .

Still, Ma went on. "I just bought you that new pair of boots. And the modulator you spent all summer whining for."

"I *needed* the modulator," Taki said. "Or else Ellay's specs would have kept me out of the arena."

"We can't afford it. You'll have to find it at the scrap yard," Ma said, just like that, like she'd decided. She turned back toward the sink, facing Taki with her back. Taki felt her hands ball into fists, felt the words she knew she should never say.

"We can owe them."

Ma didn't even bother looking at her daughter. She shook her head real sad.

"Oh, Taki—"

Taki pushed her weight past the table. Her hip hit the top, rattling the dishes. The squeal of Ellay Tu's wheels followed her from the kitchen.

"I know, I know!" she shouted down the hall. Her lip curled as she mimicked her mother's voice. "Better to be poor than to owe anybody nothing."

"Anything," Ma replied. Taki slammed the front door shut, imprisoning her mother's voice behind it.

"Whatever!"

....

After the two of them wriggled in through a hole in the clapboard fencing, Ellay Tu stood watch. Not well, though. The worthless thing just waited for a minute when a pair of mongrels snarled up to them.

"You good-for-nothing bot," Taki called, looking down from the pile of garbage she'd half-scaled. "*Do* something."

Finally the bot got rolling, its wheels working back and forth, its grabbers sparking. The scrap yard mutts bowed, jumped back. Taki squinted, trying to urge the bot to close its grabbers. But Ellay Tu just couldn't catch them, no matter how hard Taki tried to will it so.

<Get 'em, Ellay. Sic. Sic 'em!>

The bot swiveled its sensors back toward Taki. She could

almost swear its viewer narrowed, like the machine was trying hard to understand. An artifact of the malfunction – it shouldn't have been this hard. Ellay Tu finally charged forward, snapped the pincers shut. The big dog's ear was caught within the robot's grip. The dog yelped, twisted, broke free. It wasn't until the three of them scampered back behind one of the towers of old tires that Taki at long last set to work.

She scrambled up over the rusted frame of an ancient automobile. Her robot began to follow before hitting a hubcap, then wheeling back.

<Really, you should know better,> Taki thought, giving her head a shake. Ellay Tu just drove forward again, hitting the hubcap square. If it hadn't been so halfway to funny, Taki would have thought it pitiful. She climbed higher, beating back a smile. Then she plunged her gloved hands into the tangle of old cables, wriggled her fingers around, and started yanking stuff out.

A teevee tube. An old kazoo. A handheld generator that she thought she might be able to sell until she saw the circuitry was fried. She tossed it to the side. That's when she spotted it, sticking out of the heating element of an ancient toaster.

A mobo. Old. Ess-eye-ess by the looksee. The board was cracked, but the chips looked good. And the teepeeyou especially, which was what Taki needed. She bit down against the fingers of her glove and pulled it off, then ran the edge of her dirty nail along the chip's seam. This would be her third processor in as many years. And secondhand, to boot. She wondered whose head it had once been lodged in. Worse, she wondered what Da would have said.

Would have been ashamed, most likely.

She'd gotten into botting on account of him. She'd been six, older than most, but it took that long to convince him to let her give it a whack. He'd wanted a boy, you see, to bot with him. You always saw them down at the arena, men and sons together. But not daughters.

Sure, there were *girls*. But they were always older, sometimes women, even. They squatted on the edge of the pit, their eyes clouded as they urged their robots forward. But they never talked, and def not to a rangy brat like Taki. So she'd felt special when her Da finally let her sit beside him during his matches; better, even, when he let her walk right in and fetch his bot when it was over.

He'd had an Ellay Wun. Shiny red with a green display. Ma had long ago sold it for scrap. But before that, when her Da finally took her down to the tinker to buy her bot, there'd been no wondering. Ellay Tu had always been the bot for her.

Da held her hand through the first operation. She couldn't *feel* anything, of course. They numbed the skin, and then, when they went in deep, there was no feeling. She'd been scared, sure. Six. Just a kid. When you're little it's *weird* to have someone muck about your head. But Da had got her through it.

Thinking about it, Taki reached up and touched her hairline. It had been four months since she'd last been yanked open. Her black hair had finally grown long enough to mask the panel. And of course, there was no telling that the thing would even *work*.

<What a waste it is,> she thought, as she finally tore out the teepeeyou. She hadn't meant to speak it to her bot. Hadn't even realized she had, until she heard the whistle wander up from the ground.

Ellay Tu looked at her. Da would have scolded her to hear it. "They're just machines," is what he always said, when she'd put on a pout over one of his bot's damages. And Da was smart. He knew this stuff. Back in the day, it had been what the company paid him for, after all. But right now? *Her* robot looked downright mopey.

"Yeah, I mean you," Taki shouted, as she shoved the chip into her pocket.

....

"Tell her not to move," Wallace said, as he leaned in close with the scalpel.

As usual, he spoke to his apprentice, Bronner, and not to Taki. It had been like that for a while now. When Taki was a little one, the old man was all crinkly-eyed smiles and warm bear hugs. But since last year, when she turned thirteen, he'd drawn away. He touched her careful now, like he was scared he'd break her. Even had his pren shave her head for him.

"Don't move," Bronner said, and he flashed a view of his crooked teeth at her. It's not like she had much choice. She was already strapped in tight to the table. Worse, she couldn't feel a thing above her ears. Even her eyes were stuck forward, fixed to Bronner's ugly mug. She could hear Ellay Tu wheeling around with one of the spares, an old Are Seven they'd rebuilt from scratch. But she couldn't cast her gaze over to see if her bot was winning.

"Every time I bring the scalpel over," Wallace said, dropping it on the tray with a clatter, "she flinches back."

Bronner was looking over his broad shoulder at something Taki couldn't see. "It's because her bot's upset."

Wallace let out a grumble.

"Sorry," Bronner said. His pale skin pinkened as he turned back. "Her bot is . . . agitated?"

"Better, but not much," Wallace said. He pushed up from his wheelie chair then went over to the rusty sink to give his hands a wash. Taki didn't know why. It's not like he'd even *done* anything. "You finish her up. I don't have time to deal with some wriggling charity case."

Bronner leaned over in his seat to watch Wallace go. Then he went to the sink himself.

"Guess he's a busy man," he said to Taki, real mild as the old pipes rang and clanked. He was near seventeen, tall, well-muscled and with a dark mop of curls. His easy manner meant the other botters hardly gave him any time, but down at the arena, on those rare moments when he showed his face, he always won. To Taki, that made him worth hearing, mostly.

"And you're not?"

Bronner shrugged. "It's either help you out or muck the toilets again. Not that Wallace cares either way. He's been drunk out of his head since dawn cracked." He stared down toward the hallway for a moment then gave his head a shake, as if to rattle out some thought he couldn't bear thinking. At last he planted himself in the tinker's chair.

But as he readied his tools, there was a great squeal of wheels, the crunch of metal. Bronner looked down at the floor, lifting his eyebrows in bemusement.

"Your bot. She just took out the Are Seven."

"It," Taki said fast, "It's not a her. It's an it." She paused. "If anything, Ellay Tu *would* be a boy. But it's an it."

Bronner picked up the scalpel. "Okay, but you gotta quiet *it* down."

"What am I supposed to do?" she protested. Wasn't her job to make sure her Ellay behaved.

"It knows you're getting all worked up. It's worried for you."

"Is not! It's just a machine. Doesn't even know what's going on."

"A high end brand like an Ellay? Sure it does. Why do you think you keep burning out your thought processor? That hunk of metal probably dreams with you."

Taki screwed up her face. She'd never heard that before. Da never said a word about it. The idea felt . . . invasive. It made her feel naked and wrong. Her cheeks and ears began to warm.

"You're wrong! My Da said..."

But Bronner wasn't listening. Instead, he chose this moment to dive in, using his scalpel to slice open her head. She couldn't feel him cutting – just a distant pull, like someone gave your braid a tug. Of course, it had been years since her hair had been long enough for braids. And now it was down to nothing again – the clippings left on Bronner's workbench.

Across the room, Ellay Tu let out a frantic whoop. Taki could definitely feel *something* now, another tug, a spreading warmth.

"Chip?" Bronner asked, offering his open hand. Taki fished it from her pocket. The pren held it up to the light for both of them. It was a little smudged from her fingerprints. But Bronner still gave a nod.

"Good," he said. "Nice find." With that, he snapped it into place. There was a moment when her whole mind went a sort of piss-gold. Then the chip booted up, and Taki heard Ellay Tu give a whistle.

No, that's not right. It spoke again, right into her head.

<You're back! You're back you're back, oh back, oh wondrous return!>

Taki rolled her eyes. All that processing power wasted on such piddling thoughts.

....

When he got her all sewn up, Bronner made her wait awhile in the workshop. It didn't make much sense to her. When Wallace fixed her, he always shoved her right out the door. But it was almost sort of nice to sit on the bench in the corner, a blanket clutched over her shoulders, surrounded by the broke-down pieces of other peoples' bots.

"You have a match today?" Bronner asked. He'd hefted his Are Seven up unto his workbench and was going at it with a Phillips head.

"Yup," Taki said, while in her head her robot crowed: <A match! A match! A wondrous match! I will take down all comers. Crush them in my fists!>

Ellay Tu gave his pincers a squeeze. Taki squinted.

"Does yours ever talk like that?" Taki asked. Bronner looked over, frowning.

"Like what?"

Taki blushed deeply. She'd forgotten he couldn't hear, too. That was a beginner's mistake. "All poetic-like."

"Nah," Bronner said, shrugging his shoulders. "But Ellay's are known for that. It's a gentleman's bot, you know. My main unit's an Effzy Tenner. You know what they're like."

"No," Taki said. She always tried to avoid letting other botters know that Ellay Tu had been her one, and only, model. But Bronner seemed a decent enough sort. She didn't think he'd let the others know she was such a nubie. "What're they like?"

Bronner squinted down at the Are Seven. "It's always all rah rah war and blood and guts and stuff with them."

"I guess that would make sense," Taki said. "On account of the war and all."

"Exactly."

With that, he set the Are Seven back down on the floor. It rolled forward a couple inches, its grippers out. Ellay Tu gave a frightened whistle, then hid beneath the legs of Taki's chair.

<That brute! I won't be inconvenienced by its bullying antics anymore!>

"Oh, you wimp," Taki said. Then blushed. She'd done it again, spoke like Bronner could hear it. But Bronner didn't seem to mind. He just let out a belly laugh.

"Maybe he's saving his strength for his match today."

"*It*," Taki said, and she heard an echo of Da's voice in her voice. "*It*s match."

"Sure," Bronner said, shrugging, "That, too."

....

<A good day for a match!> Ellay Tu crowed as it rolled itself over the yellow dirt and gravel. <A fine moon in a bully bully sky!>

The robot was right, of course. Though the desert sky was interminable and blue, a white moon was lit up bright against the horizon. The day was hot. The arena was guaranteed to be hotter. But for some reason, her brainless bot was convinced this moon was a good portent. That's what it said, over and over again.

<Gods blessed moon!> it gushed. <Wonderful day of victory. And my Taki's chip all fixed!>

<You're so weird,> Taki said, without humor as she held the steel door open for her robot, then walked into the arena.

It took a moment for her eyes to work. At first, everything was splotches of light against black. But then the arena's old topography came into view: the snack stand, stinking of grease and ketchup and lousy with teenage boys; the parts store, where richer botters could just *buy* whatever new cranks or cogs they needed. Beyond were the pits, a big concrete space split by concrete dividers. The shouts of dozens of men echoed beneath the high ceiling, underscored by the sound of metal crumpling, of rusted wheels turning, of victory.

Taki felt her pulse speed up. She licked her lips, rushing toward the registration desk.

"Name?" The middle-aged man behind the counter was so dirty that his skin looked gray. They'd been through this before loads of times. But it never, ever changed.

"Taki Nakamura."

"Bot model?"

"Ellay Tu Wun Wun Six Dash Bee."

There was a clacking of keys. The man's terminal was hooked up to a portable generator, and it gave a great whirl after he entered the data. A cloud of dust blossomed on the seepeeyou, then settled again. The man reached across the counter and handed Taki a placard.

"Board's to your left," he said, with a jerk of his thumb – as if she didn't already know.

Taki swaggered over, the thin rectangle of plastic clutched against her palm. There was one slot open, near the bottom, for a fight that started ten minutes on. She slid her name into place, grinning at the square, neat letters, the lines of black against white.

Then her eyes drifted up, sweeping over other names. They were familiar. She didn't have to work to sound out the syllables. Until her eye caught on one, near the top. A new name. Taki took the letters in, her tongue curling as she sounded it out in her mind.

An-gel-eek. Angelique. A girl's name. A new girl's name. She felt a flash of emotion, hot and weird, looked over her shoulder as if she expected to find this girl – this Angelique, whoever that was – standing there.

But the only one there was her robot. He watched her, his viewer tilted, and gave a curious whistle.

"What are you looking at?" she groused, and stalked off for her first match of the day.

....

The first match was what Ellay Tu called a *glory*. You know, a real knock-down drag-out. But her robot bobbed and weaved and moved exactly where Taki wanted it. When it worked like this, botting was a joy – her bot an extension of her own body, but better. When she went to fetch Ellay Tu from the pit and shake the hand of the sullen teenager she'd beaten, Taki took a mental note to thank Bronner. He'd done good work. And for free, too. That counted for something.

But her opponent scowled as he squeezed her palm in his. "I can't believe I lost to *two* girls today," he said, before hefting his bot in one hand and huffing off. Taki stood there, blinking.

Angelique. It had to be.

Her name was like a curse. It hung over Taki all afternoon. She heard men muttering it on the sidelines – heard them talking about her bot and its stats. An Ecksay Tenner. Brand new. Those were true battle bots, covered with hard black plastic that gleamed even under the arena's dim lights. Taki watched as her dinky little Ellay, all dented copper and turning green at the edges from the years it'd gone unpolished, clanked forward at its opponent.

It was their third fight, and things were starting to go downhill. Ellay Tu hesitated once before weaving, and the grippers of a smooth new Ellay Leven managed to fix themselves onto its viewer. There was the sound of crumpling metal. When she urged it to wheel away, the bot's response came back anguished.

<I am trying, Taki! I do my best.> But it just hobbled back and forth, caught within the Ellay Leven's grip until the match bell sounded.

Taki didn't bother with a handshake. In fact, she left Ellay Tu there, alone in the dusty pit, and ducked into the washroom.

There was no separate room for girls. Just the long, fetid trough and the men standing over it. Once Da had stood guard for her at the mouth of the doorless stalls. But no such luck now. She'd learned which stall was safest – not the last, which was always overflowing with waste, but the one beside it. And she'd learned to squat quick, too, pulling her trousers down just enough to do her business but not share it with the outside world.

But there was no privacy. Even as she peed, Ellay Tu's thoughts intruded.

<It was a noble battle, Taki. I did try my best. Did you see how

large and new it was?>

She pushed the bot's thoughts away as she bent at the waist over the dingy sink. As usual, she avoided looking at herself in the cracked mirror. What was the use? She was nothing to see.

<That's not true! You are a lovely lass!>

Her gaze flickered, fell on her own bald form. She could see the shape of the implant beneath her sallow, sand-pale skin. Black stitches worked a crooked line over her scalp. Her eyes were sunken – cheeks were sunken, too. She could see the sinews in her neck.

A man jostled her as he passed. He didn't seem to register her as a girl. They never did. She might have well as been invisible, and no wonder.

<Taki? Eagerly I await our next match, for which the bell tolls soon.>

She gave a sigh, wiped her hands against her trousers, and trudged back out to the arena.

....

At last the time came to face the music. Angelique. She squatted at the far end of the pit, shining her bot with a clean white cloth. She was just a little older than Taki – fourteen, or fifteen, maybe – but the curves of her body marked her as a different sort of creature entirely. Her teeshirt, too new for all this dust, hugged the swell of her hips and chest. Black curls were knotted back at the nape of her neck. Taki couldn't even make out the shape of the girl's implant beneath her hairline but sure enough, her robot stopped and started when she did. It was like the girl had been born to bot.

Her robot was top of the line, the casement as glossy black as Taki had figured, and seamless. The line of its viewer seemed near invisible until it swiveled around and looked right at her.

Taki looked away.

She led Ellay Tu to the center of the pit. Angelique didn't even bother accompanying *her* bot out. Instead, she sent the robot over alone. It moved over the dust on silent wheels, and then settled in, staring at Ellay Tu.

But Ellay was unperturbed.

<Easy peasy!> it announced. That was a phrase it used lots. She was never entirely sure what it meant, other than that her bot was pleased. It rolled to and fro on creaking wheels. <The Ecksay series has blind spots as large as the Atlantic.>

<The what?> Taki asked, and she swung her leg over the concrete divider. Ellay Tu began to spout a definition on its viewscreen, but it was so far away by then that she couldn't see the words at all. Taki cast her gaze at the ceiling girders.

The match bell rang.

Taki squatted low, her fingertips barely touching the dusty ground beneath. If she squinted, she could almost see the world through her robot's viewer. Her bot was right, of course. Beneath its hard carapace, the Ecksay was full of hot spots. The machinery was weak, then, its reflexes probably slow. So long as Ellay Tu kept it within sight, victory would be easy.

The Ecksay took the first lunge. It moved silently, but left plenty of time for Ellay to dodge back. At her command, Ellay swung its grabbers wide. They struck the plastic casement once, twice. Ellay Tu sensed a crack. Across the pit, Taki heard it too.

The Ecksay sputtered back. This was Ellay Tu's chance – time to move in for the kill. Taki urged the viewer left, then right, chasing a dark shadow of movement in the periphery of his vision. That's when Taki saw it. Angelique, kneeling on the far side of the pit, laughing up at a tall, familiar figure.

Bronner. He was handing her a soda. An ugly smile split his wide face in two.

The girl tucked a loose curl behind her ear. She wasn't even watching the match. Instead, her eyes were on the tinker's pren.

And his eyes were on *her*. On Angelique. As he flirted and flashed his teeth at her. It was as if Taki were transparent compared to Angelique, as if Taki were less real. Bronner saw Angelique, and Taki did too.

But what she didn't see was the Ecksay heading straight for

Ellay Tu.

Taki heard a hard *k-thunk*. She swiveled her head only to find that it was Ellay Tu. The grabber, once extended proudly, was now bent back toward the ceiling – an unnatural angle. Ellay's viewer spun round and round, but, though Taki urged it left, it didn't see the Ecksay closing in. It gripped Ellay, pushed. The old bot's wheels gave a squeak of protest.

<Oh no,> was all it thought.

....

For the longest time, Taki didn't move. She stayed crouched against the dust-strewn ground, two fingers pressed to dirt, even after Angelique approached to offer Taki her hand. Taki noted with some muffled pleasure how odd her features were – close-set eyes, thick lips and nose just a touch too near together – but only grunted back. And when she saw Bronner hovering behind, she waved him off. She couldn't bear to look him in the eye, much less *speak* to him.

<Taki? Taki?>

She went to fetch her winnings. She stared down at the credit slip as if she could will the words to change. Seven credits. Not enough to cover Ellay's damages, much less give the change to Ma. She stuffed it down into her trouser pocket.

She stalked across the arena, past the squatting men and squabbling bots. She was halfway to the pit when she felt it happen – something deep inside her that had once been slippery as oil was now congealing, growing sticky-hot and hard. She walked faster, and faster still, until she reached the concrete divider and launched both her long legs over in one swift movement.

<Taki?>

Ellay's mopey viewer gaped up at her, widening in curiosity. She didn't care. She aimed a swift kick at it, then another, and a third. Her boots dented the metal, left a space that seemed big enough for her to curl up into, or almost. She kicked again, this time hard enough to topple the bot onto its side.

When it was finally over, she fell back, panting, set her hands on her knees and hung her head. The color that was now stretched from one corner of her mind to the other wasn't the pale yellow of a reboot, but crimson red. Still, it pulsed back with every heartbeat that sounded in her ears. Her anger faded.

She went over to her robot. Its wheels were spinning in the empty air. At first, Ellay Tu didn't answer her. Its rusted body was dented now. Pitiful. But when she set it upright, its viewer narrowed, taking her in.

Tentatively, it wheeled forward, then back again, gave its viewer a timid spin.

<Taki, I am ever so sorry for my failure. Ever so.> The voice was high and nervous in her mind. Taki felt an ache squeeze her chest.

Her robot saw her, even when no one else did. He thought her worthy, thought her good, even at her worst. When she reached out and patted his dented casing a spring popped off the broken grabber. She slid it back into place.

<That's okay,> she said firmly. And she knew it would be. They were much alike, Ellay Tu and Taki. Dented. Rusted. Off-kilter.

But at least they were together.

She gave his casing one final pat, and then turned and left the arena. He waited a moment, scanning the darkness. Then he found her. No matter how fast she walked, or how far, he would always follow.

The Wreck of the Airship Octavia

Amy Griswold

Amy Griswold has written two gaslamp fantasy/mystery novels with Melissa Scott, Death by Silver *and* A Death at the Dionysus Club *(Lethe Press) and has short stories forthcoming in several anthologies. She also writes* Stargate Atlantis *tie-in novels for Fandemonium Books. She lives in North Carolina with her partner and daughter and works as an educational testing content specialist. Find her online at amygriswold. livejournal.com or follow her on Twitter at @amygris*

"Get down from there, you tomfool," I snapped at Della as she balanced on the airship's railing, stretching on her toes to crane her neck over the side. Her skirts were flying up like she was about to set sail, and I didn't want to watch her go overboard.

"I want to see better," she said, clinging to the rail one-handed as she turned to frown at me. "I won't let go."

"If the wind comes up, it won't matter if you let go. You'll be over the side and gone." I clipped my own safety harness to the railing and then to her dress's sash, ignoring the way she stiffened and pulled away from my grimy hands.

"I'm not afraid of heights," she said, but she did climb down before she unfastened the harness. I wiped my hands on my trousers, thinking there was no reason to be afraid of a little dirt. I wasn't afraid of heights either, but I had a healthy respect for the length of the drop to the green prairie racing by far below us.

"Then maybe you won't mind blowing away, but I'll be in

trouble for letting you," I said. "My ma said I was to keep you out of trouble."

My mother was the captain of the *Octavia*, which had the distinction of being the fastest passenger airship running between Boston and San Francisco. I have worked on the ship since I could toddle around clipped to the rail to keep me from tumbling off. Most trips I spent happily up to the elbows in grease in the engine room. I could fix a slipped gear or a stuck valve as well as any engineer, and I wasn't afraid of the steam.

This trip, I'd been saddled with Miss Della Oglethorpe, our passenger's daughter, on the grounds that being both girls and the same age, I would keep her entertained. She may have been eleven by the calendar, but it seemed to me she had all the common sense of a child of three. That didn't seem to register with my mother. Neither did the fact that the only girls I knew were other airship rats, children of captains whose playrooms were a mile in the air.

Her father, Mr. Archibald Oglethorpe, was someone important with the railroads, going out to San Francisco to work on the new line being built from west to east. Della wore dresses that seemed to be made out of nothing but lace and had a bot as a governess to teach her sums and manners, a luxury I hoped my ma didn't get any ideas about me needing. But the bot was turned off and packed away in the hold. Della's father was apparently far too important to keep an eye on his daughter for himself, which left me as her grudging host.

"There's nothing to do," Della said.

"You've got books, haven't you?" I'd heard the stokers complaining about having to help lug them aboard.

"I've read them," she said. "And I've been charting our course using a sextant, but it hasn't changed for hours." I saw what I assumed to be the sextant in its box lying by her feet, perfectly placed if the deck tipped to go flying and brain some poor chump who didn't expect the air to be full of heavy brass objects.

"Pick that up and stow it away," I said. "We've got proper instruments on the bridge, anyways. No one uses sextants anymore."

"I expect you've got all kinds of books aboard somewhere," she began, like a wheedling kid hoping for penny candy.

"Oh, who has time for books?" I said. We didn't have any aboard except manuals on engineering and navigation, and I'd looked into those enough times to conclude I'd rather learn how the engine works by taking parts of it apart myself. "Now go on below. Can't you see there's a storm coming up?"

The clouds were lowering black on the horizon. Della clung to the rail in apparent fascination. "Can't we stay and watch a minute?"

I was supposed to entertain her, I reasoned. All right, if letting her see what happened when the wind picked up scared her enough to keep her below decks in the future, I wouldn't be sorry for it. I was just doing what she wanted.

"At least clip onto the rail," I said, digging a spare harness out of one of the deck lockers and tossing it to her.

She barely caught it and held it like it was slimy. It might have been a bit dirty, but there were more things to do aboard the *Octavia* than scrub every bit of harness until it shone.

"Put your arms through and then wrap it round your middle," I told her. I ended up having to put it on her, although I wasn't sure how to fasten some of it with her wearing skirts instead of trousers. It would do well enough until someone told us to get away from the rail, I figured.

The storm came up fast, and rain began spitting at us. Thunder cracked, the dark cloud brightening with flashes of lightning, and I waited for Della to turn tail and flee. Instead, she seemed entranced, although she let out an exclamation of dismay when a gust of wind threw rain in her face, soaking her dress and hair.

I wanted to ask her if she'd expected rain wouldn't be wet when the world abruptly went white. There was a noise like stone crashing on stone that seemed to come from inside my head. Then it was dark, and my head was ringing, and for some reason, everything smelled like smoke.

Even muddled as I was, I realized we'd been struck by lightning. The deck was aflame. If the gas bag above was aflame as well, there wasn't any hope for *Octavia*. I looked up but couldn't see anything through the smoke and leaping flames.

The heat was beating against my face, and sparks were sizzling against my shirt sleeves. I scrambled back against the rail and realized something was hanging over it. I still felt stupid and stunned, and it took me a minute to realize that it was a person. Della was dangling from the straps of her harness, her arms caught in it and twisted above her head. She opened her mouth as if shrieking, but I couldn't hear her over the screaming of the wind and the ringing in my ears.

I started to pull her up then looked back. The fire was racing across the deck, fast enough that I guessed the lightning bolt had hit an oil tank or punctured one of the reserves of lifting gas. Pulling her up would be pulling her into the flames.

I dropped down over the side instead, my own harness keeping me hanging upright. I looked down, craning my neck. I'd hoped one of the escape balloons was stowed below us. It was more or less below Della and somewhat less below me.

Before I could think better of it, I worked my way along the rail to Della. She clung to me with the kind of grip that pulls swimmers underwater.

I reached up and unhooked her harness from the rail. For a moment her weight pulled me down, and I was afraid I wouldn't be able to reach mine. We swung dizzyingly, and my fingernails scrabbled at leather. Then they closed on the clasp, I unfastened it, and we fell.

We tumbled into the basket of the balloon. I fell on something hard that I wasn't expecting and said a bunch of words my ma liked to believe I didn't know. I shoved the hard thing out of the way and clipped my harness to the balloon's frame, hoping Della had enough sense to do the same.

I turned the crank to start filling the balloon with gas from the pipe that led into the airship's structure, hoping that sparks weren't raining down from above and that the pipe itself wasn't hot enough to set the gas afire. And that the fire wasn't spreading across the deck to the canopy, and that my ma wasn't trapped behind a wall of flame.

There wasn't anything I could do about any of that, I told myself grimly. I kept turning the crank, yanking it around until my arm ached.

Finally, the balloon seemed full. Sparks showered down and caught in Della's skirts. She beat at them with her hands as I reached for the release catch. One more yank, and we were drifting free, whipped away from the airship by the gusting wind.

Neither of us moved for a while. I knew I ought to steer, but my hands were shaking too hard to grip the ropes, which made me furious. Only silly passengers were afraid, I told myself, but it didn't make the shaking stop.

"I can't see the *Octavia*," Della said after a while. She shook my shoulder when I didn't answer. "Peggy, I can't see the ship."

When I looked, I couldn't either. "They'll come back for us," I said.

"If they can."

"If they can't, they'll land," I said. "And then they'll come back for us." If one of the gas bags was punctured, and they couldn't make San Francisco, they'd land somewhere near the rail line. They could take the railroad to San Francisco, and take another airship back to look for us. That was what they'd do.

I ignored the gnawing little voice that said there wasn't much food or water in the balloon's little equipment locker. I certainly didn't listen to the voice that said the *Octavia* might be going up like a firework with all hands aboard. I tugged at the ropes, trying to get some control over the balloon in the battering wind.

"I've got to get us down," I said.

"Can't you go after the *Octavia*?"

"This is a balloon, not an airship," I said. "It goes where the wind goes! Don't you even know that?"

She made a noise, and I realized some of the wetness on her face was tears rather than rain. "I thought you might know of some way."

"Well, there isn't one," I said. "All I can do is steer a little and try to put us down somewhere level."

We came down in a field of grass. The storm was passing off, the sky a lighter gray with only a spatter of rain. I clambered over the side of the balloon as soon as it slowed to a scuttering pace across the ground.

"Hand the locker out to me," I said.

"What?" Della said, clinging to the sides of the balloon as it went on scuttering.

"We can't anchor the balloon," I said, clinging to its outside. "So we're going to have to jump. So hand me … the … locker." My feet were skating across the ground, and it occurred to me that we probably should have just thrown the locker out when we were still a few yards above the ground. The balloon skipped and came down hard. A pain jarred up through my right ankle.

Della struggled with it. "It's too heavy!"

"It's still clipped in, look –" I leaned precariously over the side, pointing, and Della clawed at the clasp, finally opening it. The locker came free, and Della heaved it over the side and tossed another box out after it. She followed by tumbling out of the basket herself and lay in a heap in the grass while the balloon skated away, rolling and tumbling and then catching the wind again, seeming to shrink as it retreated across the featureless plain.

I started to haul Della to her feet, and yelled as I put my weight on my right leg. I sat down abruptly myself.

"Is it broken?" she said, sitting up and looking at my ankle.

"How should I know?" It hurt like the dickens. When I tugged my boot off, it hurt so much I saw stars.

"Can you move your toes?"

I moved my toes obediently. "More or less."

"Then it's probably not broken," she said, but I wasn't sure how much she knew about it.

We sat there for a long time, both of us just glad to be on solid ground.

"They're not coming back for us right away, are they?" Della asked.

"They may not even know we're missing," I said. "We're supposed to be below."

Della opened her mouth, like she was going to say something about the chances of the *Octavia* not having burned up to cinders and then shut it again. "So we're going to have to stay here for a while," she said.

"There's food and water in the locker," I said.

I switched the locker on, and it extended its legs. It was a sort of brainless bot, being able to walk along if you led it like a dog but not see or think for itself. It was stored with its clockwork wound up, but every few hours it would have to be wound up again.

Investigation proved we had food for maybe a week, if we called a few bites of jerky and ship's biscuit a meal, but only one large bottle of water.

"Water's heavy," I said in defense of whoever had packed the locker.

"They'll probably find us before we run out of water," Della said.

I kept my mouth shut. I'd seen the high plains as we passed over them a hundred times, and there were green rivers, but also miles and miles of empty grass between them. If we started walking, we might find a creek or a river or nothing.

I had no idea where we were. Somewhere in Wyoming, I figured, but I wasn't even sure of that. I'd been paying attention to Della, not to the landmarks below or the readings of the instruments on the bridge. We might be a few miles from a railroad town or a Pawnee village, or many miles away from anyone at all.

"They probably will," I said.

When it got dark, we lay down in the grass and tried to sleep. Della said she wasn't sure she could sleep without a bed, and I wasn't sure I could sleep without the movement of the airship under me. Neither of us wanted to think about the idea of wolves. There was a firelighter in the storage locker, but we didn't have anything to burn but grass.

"What happened to your father?" Della asked after a while.

"I'm sleeping," I said, but after a while I gave up pretending to sleep and sat up. "He died when I was little," I said. "But he left us the *Octavia*. So we get by all right." I tried not to think about the fact that if Ma and the *Octavia* were both gone, I'd be lucky to grow up in some charity orphanage.

"My mother died when I was little," Della said. "But at least I don't have to work."

I rolled over onto my elbows. "If I didn't work I don't know what I'd do."

"Read. Learn things. Play music."

"I can whistle," I said, and demonstrated, whistling a hornpipe. She smiled a little. Her face was smudged with soot, and her hair was coming down out of its coiled braid. Mine was cut boy-short. I shook my head again, wondering what the weight of braids would feel like.

"I can sing," she said. She looked at me sideways like I was going to laugh at her, but it was too quiet with only the noise of insects and the wind through the grass. I was used to the whirr of engines.

"So sing," I said.

She sang "Silver Threads Among the Gold," and "My Grandfather's Bot," and newer songs I'd never heard. When she finished she lay back in the grass, gazing at the full moon hanging high above the plain. "I'd like to go there someday."

"You can't really take an airship to the moon," I said. "You couldn't breathe."

"They'll figure out a way," Della said. "Like the way they seal up the big steam trains so that the smoke doesn't blow inside."

"You'd have to have tanks of air," I said.

"Some of the big trains carry air tanks now."

"I didn't know that," I admitted. I haven't heard much about the new fast trains they're building, except that my ma worries that they'll make fewer people want to travel by airship. It doesn't worry me. I can't imagine wanting to be cooped up in a train when you could fly.

"So we could do it."

"Well, not us. Somebody."

"Why not us? I want to go." She looked at the moon like she could see something there that was invisible to me. Maybe having a rich father meant she wasn't used to thinking there were things she couldn't do. But when I thought about it, I wasn't sure why it couldn't be us to go to the moon. They'd need engineers who knew something about flying, after all.

We didn't fall asleep until the sky was lightening. The sun was climbing toward the middle of the sky when I woke up, and my throat felt parched. My ankle was so swollen I couldn't get my foot back into my boot. Della tore strips from her petticoat without protest, and I wrapped it up tight, which made it possible to yank my boot on, although tears came to my eyes. We passed the water bottle back and forth a few times, and when we'd both drunk, it felt alarmingly light.

"I think we're going to have to walk," Della said.

I hauled myself up, trying to put as little weight on my right foot as possible. "Which way?" I asked.

"We have to wait until mid-day," Della said.

I sat down heavily on the locker, which made a whir of protest and folded up on its feet. I had nursed some hope that I was light enough for it to walk with me sitting on it, but clearly I wasn't. "And what, may I ask, happens then?"

Della opened the other box to reveal the brass gleam of her sextant. "I can take sightings to figure out our latitude." She withdrew a battered navigational manual and a lead pencil from the sextant's case. "And then we'll know whether we're north or south of the railroad and how far away it is."

"What if we're a hundred miles from the railroad?"

"I don't think we can be," Della said calmly. "We were following the railroad's path before the storm came up. I could see it from the deck. If we're close enough to walk, we just have to make sure we're walking the right way. And then we can follow the tracks until a train comes, or we reach a station."

"What if we're not close enough to walk?"

"Will you be quiet? You're distracting me," she said, and raised her sextant to the sky.

I wanted to ask who she thought she was, telling me what to do, but I didn't really have any idea what to do myself. It seemed to me it couldn't hurt to let her try. She scribbled notes with her pencil and sat back down to do calculations.

"Well?" I said when I couldn't stand it any more.

"I'm checking my sums," she said without looking up. When Della finally raised her head, she was smiling. "We're twenty miles north of the railroad," she said. "Only twenty miles!"

It seemed like a long way to walk to me. I could climb all day, but there wasn't very far to walk aboard an airship. Twenty miles was more trips round the Octavia's deck than I could imagine ever wanting to make.

"We could be there by sunset if we hurry," Della said. "Come on!"

We weren't there by sunset, needless to say. I couldn't walk fast on my throbbing ankle, and I was pretty sure I couldn't have walked as fast as Della at the best of times. Apparently, on surveying trips with her father, she thought nothing of hikes that seemed punishing to me. I trudged along steering the locker on its leash, and occasionally resting my hurt foot on it while I caught my breath.

"Shouldn't we be able to see the railroad from here?" I asked when we camped that evening.

"There's nothing to see but the rail line," Della said. "And the grass hides that until you get close."

"But if there's no station, and we haven't seen a train coming yet …"

"There's one at least every week," Della said. "So it can't be many more days." There were only a few sips of warm water left in the bottle. We waited as long as we could stand it before we drank them.

The next day was worse, with no water and the knowledge that we had no water pushing us to move faster. By the time I could see the long line of the tracks in the distance, my ankle hurt like it was touching a hot iron with every step. I made myself quicken my steps, promising myself that when we reached the rail line I could collapse.

We did, and I did, sitting down heavily in the dirt next to the tracks. "I can't go any further," I said, and I meant it.

"There's probably a station inside of a hundred miles," Della said.

"A hundred miles might as well be the moon."

"For me, too," she said in a small voice. She sat down next to me, her hair straggling down her back and plastered to her forehead with sweat.

I buried my face in my knees, wishing as hard as I could that when I lifted my head, the *Octavia* would be hanging in the air above me, unburned and perfect, with my ma letting down a hanging basket to take us both aboard. I raised my chin and saw only the hot chalky sky.

"Peggy," Della said after a while. Her voice was hoarse, but there was a sudden interest in her tone. "The locker can walk for half a day when it's wound up."

"It might make ten miles before it wound down," I said. "If it even kept going in the right direction."

"But that's using all its energy to walk," she said. "How far do you think it could go if it ran along the rails?"

I looked at the locker, and looked at its legs. They had smooth wheels in them as part of the gearing of the knees, and I could just about see how they might come apart and go back together to hold the wheels on the track and the locker upright. But making the legs pump in the right direction to make it move …

"I don't know if I can do it," I said.

"You said you didn't mind working," Della said, and that was really the thing that made up my mind, because I decided I'd rather be trying to build a rail car out of a walking bot than thinking about how thirsty I was and what would happen if we didn't find water.

"I don't," I said, taking out the little tool kit in the locker. I started taking the legs of the locker apart.

By the time I had it built, I had a sick stomach from working in the heat with nothing to drink. Della did most of the work of winding up the locker. I took a turn when she couldn't crank the handle anymore.

She'd written a note, like we were shipwrecked mariners. *We are south down the rail line without any water and not much food. We are survivors from the Octavia. Adele Oglethorpe and Margaret (Peggy) Duchesne.*

I held my breath as I switched the locker on. It shuddered for a moment, and its legs started pumping. The wheels that rested on the track started turning. It started moving, slowly at first then picking up speed, whirring along even faster than I'd hoped it would go. It swiftly rattled its way down the track to the north, and we watched it until it was out of sight.

I closed my eyes and tried to sleep, but I couldn't sleep. Della sang for a while, her voice raspy, and then stopped when she got too hoarse for me to hear the words. We sat and waited, until it seemed like all the world was grass and the rail line, stretching forever empty in both directions out of sight.

I opened my eyes when I heard Della humming a song. I realized she wasn't humming; the rails were singing to themselves. "Della," I said. I shook her shoulder when she didn't answer. It took a long time for her to stir, but when she did, she sat up, her eyes going wide.

"There's a train coming," she croaked.

She scrambled up and hauled me up. I had to lean on her arm to stay on my feet. At first we couldn't see anything. Then a speck in the distance grew to an ant, a toy train, and then a real blessed train thundering towards us trailing smoke. Just as I was afraid it couldn't see us, it began slowing, its whistle sounding loud and low.

A woman jumped down before the train came to a stop and came running towards us. It was my ma, still in her captain's uniform. When she reached me and swept me up in her arms, her wool jacket smelled of smoke. I started gulping and couldn't stop. Her strong hands smoothed my hair.

"Here's water," a railway porter said. He handed me a cup, and I gulped some down then managed to loosen my grip on the cup so the porter could hand it to Della. Della leaned on her father's arm. It seemed to me that there were tears in his eyes behind his spectacles, although maybe it was the smoke.

"Did the *Octavia* burn?" I asked, the words scraping my throat.

"We got her down and put the fire out. I expect we can salvage her," Ma said briskly, although I knew those kinds of repairs didn't come cheap. Her arm was tight around my shoulders, like she was afraid I'd blow away in the wind.

"Please let me cover your repairs," Mr. Oglethorpe said. "I expect my engineers can get you back in the air without too much delay."

"That's very kind of you," my ma said in a tone that suggested she thought he had sunstroke. I expect I was staring just the same myself. Most passengers wouldn't take kindly to nearly having an airship burn around their ears.

"It's the least I can do in return for what your daughter did," he said, resting his hand gratefully on Della's shoulder.

I opened my mouth to explain that we wouldn't have found the rail line without Della, but my throat was too sore. Instead, I just shrugged to let Della know that I would tell the whole story once talking didn't make me cough. And that's what I did.

By the time we pulled into the nearest station the stars were coming out and the moon was lifting over the horizon.

"We'll go someday," Della said, turning her face up to the moon. Although the moon still seemed awfully far away, I figured she was more than likely right.

Robot Sister Number Phi

Marilag Angway

Marilag Angway started her foray into science fiction and fantasy sometime in the early '90s by reading books written by females for females. She had no idea that these books were far and few at the time and feels lucky to have had the opportunity to be inspired by female authors to think big and never stop imagining. When she isn't scribbling her mind away, she's lending what brainpower she has left to a good cause: the molding of preschool minds. Gotta start them young, right? You can find Marilag's bookish and writing and randomy ramblings at storyandsomnomancy.wordpress.com.

There was nothing angelic in Angel's screams. In fact, there was nothing angelic about an irate Angel at all, with her big, buggy red eyes and her dog-like snarl and her wild, curly hair. Shai could not understand why her parents even named her older sister after something that was so peaceful and serene and every bit as un-Angel as can be.

She doubted very much that angels threw shoes or retractable forks at their younger siblings. Angel sure did.

Shai ran out of her older sister's room. The door *pffed* shut, followed by the thud of a small red shoe. At least Shai thought it was a red shoe that Angel threw at her. Angel loved the color red.

Once the door closed, the screaming stopped. It probably went on for a little longer on the other side, but that was the beauty of doors and walls. They muffled the sounds coming from inside the room. With a big sigh, Shai walked back towards her room and came face to face with the meta-sitter, its skin glossy brass and glass head sparking with blue electricity. "Disturbance. Is there a problem—" it took a moment to scan the girl, then, "—Shai?"

"Nothing," Shai said.

"Detected screaming in Bedroom Four," the meta-sitter continued, "Have you been rummaging again?"

Shai heaved her shoulders, remembered that the meta-sitter was not good with body language, then said, "No." Shai placed her hands at her back, holding onto the silver and gold bracelets she'd taken from Angel's jewelry box. When the meta-sitter said nothing else, Shai pointed her chin out, pouted, and said, "She was just mad I went into her room again."

"You should learn not to disturb your older sister," the meta-sitter said. It whirred, clicked, and rolled toward Angel's door. "Go back to your room," it said to Shai, who was only too happy to leave the hallway.

Once her own door closed, Shai giggled. She jingled the bracelets and knew her project would be complete soon. All she had needed was the jewelry.

....

Shai's Bedroom Five was at the other end of the hall and looked nothing like Bedroom Four. Angel had taken some pains to organize her things into shelves and closets and cupboards. All of her shoes had been on one side of the room, and her bags and jewelries were covered in thin, plastic bags and stacked on metal shelves that protruded from the walls beside her four-poster bed. Angel's clothes hung inside a closet with a numeric pad, and all she had to do to access them was to touch the screen next to the closet with the right clothes selected. Angel wasn't very attentive, but she paid much attention to her clothes. Anything that looked remotely strange in her closet sometimes caused tantrums, ones Shai could not understand.

Shai kept her room in disarray, which bothered Angel so much that she'd refused to go in ever. There were clothes on the cushioned mattress, which was inside a butterfly tent since Shai did not desire a typical bed, on the carpet floor, on the couch, on the small chairs that circled a tea table. Shai owned one pair of outside shoes, which she wore inside as well, and one pair of really nice shoes that was not wrapped up in plastic and stacked on a shelf. All of Shai's metal shelves contained books and papers and notebooks, some old and frayed and battered, some smelling of newness that could only come from the newly bought and newly published.

She did not own any jewelry.

"You will get your first bracelet on your twelfth birthday," Mama had said one day after Shai questioned her. Shai was only ten. That made things worse, because Angel had turned twelve that week.

"Why twelve?" Shai had asked. "Why not ten?"

"Because you're irresponsible," Angel had said, puffing her chest and smiling with a knowing smile. Angel did a lot of things that sounded impressive, but Shai was not fooled. "Responsibleness happens when you're *my* age."

"Responsibility," Mama corrected and nodded. "Patience is the first step to responsibility."

Shai hated it when they treated her like a kid. She was smart, she read a lot, and she knew that the girls in her books did not wait for responsibility to arrive in gift-wrapped packages like Angel did. Some eleven-year-old girls were learning to become roboticists and mechanics and scientists who ended up building rockets and floating buildings and robots that looked kind of like humans but were not. Genius Girls, her mother had called them. Girls who tested so high on The Assessment that the government had taken interest in their education. Not every girl was a Genius Girl. Angel wasn't, but that didn't seem to stop her from believing that she knew more than Shai.

The Assessment declared that Shai was not a Genius Girl either, so she had not been sent to the special academies at the center of the nation, even though she had started reading at three and knew her mathematics at six. She was not very good with tests, and The Assessment was a collection of different tests to make one long test that took hours and sometimes days to complete. Shai never finished The Assessment; she fell asleep on top of the mathematics problems after she'd doodled all over the back.

Papa had been more amused than disappointed. When he received the results, he put up Shai's mathematics page on one of his large corkboards like a certificate. "Cheer up, starshine," Papa said when Shai felt all kinds of miserable. "Your assessor is a fool. If he'd been paying attention to your doodles instead, he'd have seen your brilliant ode to – are those penguins? Yes, I thought so – Sierpinski's triangle. It's a work of art, truly, my star."

Papa hadn't cared that his daughters were not Genius Girls.

"Everyone has different interests," Papa said, "All that book learning in the academies have nothing on practical application and passion. And you, my girl, have the Passion with a capital P." And so he taught his youngest daughter about electricals and mechanicals and roboticals. And he often called Shai his "Star Who Shines."

Shai's father built robots that were used all over town, and sometimes he would allow Shai an opportunity to place a part and set the wires. Once he had even let her help design a robot's personality code. But she had never built a robot on her own or without her father's supervision. In normal circumstances, Shai would never have attempted it.

Until Angel found out one day what Shai was doing while Angel went to school. Shai was being unladylike, Angel said. Ladies did not smell of oil and metal and heat. They did not have tattered skirts and matted hair and greasy skin and calloused hands. They did not follow their fathers around with wrenches and screwdrivers and a pocketful of gears and bolts.

"I don't *want* to be a lady," Shai said. She stuck her tongue out. "Ladies are estupidas."

"I am *not* stupid!" Angel shrieked. The argument escalated from there.

"Stop it, you two," Mama said, splitting the girls up on separate sides. "You're hermanas. Act with a bit more decorum, will you?"

Sisters were overrated, Shai thought. And that was when she decided she'd build herself a better model.

....

Only Father knew about Shai's little laboratory, because he had been the one who helped her build it. It was inside her room just behind the large bookshelf that was twice as wide as Shai and three times as tall.

She pulled at her bookshelf and moved it a few feet away from the wall. She stuck her hand out and patted the wall until she came across a button. She pushed the button and a door slid open, making the same *pffed* sound as Angel's bedroom door. Past the door, lights brightened, and the large screen at the front powered on. In a woman's voice, it said, "Greetings, Mistress Shai. How can I be of service?"

The girl held up her prize, the silver and gold bracelets, and she placed it on the center table. "Bring up Robot Sister, please. I would like to finish her."

"Certainly, Mistress Shai. One moment." The screen, which had shown an image of a bald, blue talking face, went black, whirred for a moment, and came back to life. The bald face returned, smiling. "Detecting several versions of Robot Sister. Which option would you like?"

"The latest one." Shai had been working so long on the robot that she could not remember what version she had stopped at.

"Bringing up latest model, version nine point two," the voice said. "Initial assessment: personality and power drives installed, mechanical limbs functioning at ninety point one, zero, two percent efficiency, and eye-hand coordination calibrated to provided parameters. Debug recommended. Debug now?"

"No," Shai said. She examined her work of art – for it was a work of art, indeed.

Robot Sister was a head taller than Shai and made out of many different scraps and parts from Papa's private office. The robot's entire plating was made of bronze, which was much darker and shinier than Shai's mestizo skin. The arms were mismatched and stiff, one side a long broom handle (shortened so it passed the hip a bit), the other a piece of curved wood from an old rocking horse, which curved just above the hip. The legs were both metal and came from a discarded three-legged stool, which was no longer three-legged.

The eyes had been tricky, for Shai could not find a pair that mimicked the ever-changing hazel that she and Angel had, so she settled for the glass eyes on a life-sized doll that she had received from her Tia Kassandra. Shai never liked the doll anyway, it was dressed all in pink frills. The frills and the pink made the doll look too creepy, so she extracted the eyes and put the doll away at the back of her closet.

The robot's body was dressed comfortably in one of Angel's hand-me-down Sunday dresses, which were normally too long for Shai to fit. The hem of the skirt reached down to the ankles, and complimented the nice shoes that Shai almost never wore.

Shai fastened the bracelets around Robot Sister's head. Once done, she arranged the circles so it looked like hair ringlets that hung a little above the robot's cheekbones. The robot was complete.

"Debug now," Shai said.

"Debugging," the computer said. "Full debugging E-T-A: twenty minutes."

She would show Angel that she didn't need her as an older sister. Having a robot one would be much more fun and much more helpful. The computer ticked down the time in low whispers. The only sign of life coming from the robot was the beeping of its computerized torso.

Shai smiled, sat on a cushy bean bag and waited.

....

Angel's first word had been "quinceañera." At least, that's what Shai's mother told her friends over and over again. Most kids tended to start their speaking journey with "mama" or "papa" or some other word that described parents. Or food. Shai's first word had been a normal request to be fed, "pudding" or "pie" or some such, no one really remembered. To the immediate family, it hadn't been as humorous or as complicated as "quinceañera."

Robot Sister's first word had not been a word at all. Instead, it uttered a string of numbers that was unfamiliar to Shai. "One point six one eight zero three three nine eight…"

The numbers continued, making Shai dizzy. She could not remember it all, and she did not think Robot Sister would stop anytime soon. "This sounds like an extremely long number," Shai said in the middle of the robot's counting.

The robot slowed its count. "…eight…three…four…that it is."

"What is it?"

"It is a ratio of extreme importance for a body like this one," Robot Sister moved its torso, almost like it was going to spin, but stopping as it twisted a little to the left. "Though this one is made of asymmetric parts, this one is of divine proportion."

Shai stared. "But why the numbers?"

"The numbers make life," Robot Sister said.

"Doesn't biology make life?"

"All life is biology, all biology is physiology, all physiology is chemistry, all chemistry is physics, all physics is math," Robot Sister said in a soothing rhythm, almost like a song. "Quote, unquote. Marquardt. Numbers are the essence of human life."

Shai nodded. She decided that even though she only understood some of what Robot Sister said, it was better than to not understand at all. Already Robot Sister's intelligence far surpassed Angel's, and Shai was fine with this.

She pulled at Robot Sister's skirt and said, "Can we go out now?"

"This one can do as you please," Robot Sister said. "For you brought this one to life. What did you have in mind?"

. . . .

The park was at the end of the town near the café and children's playground and the long bridge-slash-elevator that took people up towards the floating city. It was far too long of a walk for Shai, but only three stops away if she took the speedbus. With Robot Sister following close behind, Shai boarded the bus and gave the automated driver – a computer screen with a friendly, orange bald face – two tokens, one for Robot Sister and one for herself.

Because bus drivers were no longer people, it was easier to get on a bus and not be turned away as long as there were tokens available. Mama had spoken of days long ago when bus drivers used to be people, and sometimes that meant bad news.

"Some of them frowned for so long that their unhappiness was plastered on their faces," Mama said. "Mi madre always kept me close and away from the unhappy drivers. Nobody wants to see them in a bad mood at the start of the morning. It spoils the entire day."

Shai did not know if that was the reason why bus drivers were now automated. Papa told her this reasoning did not account for too many "variables."

"Don't accept one explanation as the absolute truth," Papa said, winking. "Sometimes there's more to things than the one perspective you know."

All Shai knew, as she sat on that bus with Robot Sister standing next to her, was that while the automated driver was cheery enough, there were actual people on the bus that were bound to spoil anybody's mood with their long, frowning stares and their miserable expressions.

One old woman even went so far as to point at Shai and then at Robot Sister. "And where are you taking *that*, young lady?" the woman croaked, her finger wagging disapprovingly between Shai and Robot Sister.

Shai straightened on her seat. She would have ignored the lady or would have answered impolitely, but she was taught better manners than that. One always respected one's elders, Mama used to say, especially when out in public. The elders had been around since before the Age of Mechanicals. They demanded respect, even when some of them grumbled about the "sorry youth of today." Shai always heard bad things about the "youth of today," but never about the "youth of yesterday." Weren't they one and the same?

Robot Sister whirred, looked at Shai and awaited a response.

"The park, grandma," Shai said as politely as she could. Then, proudly, she said, "I just finished Robot Sister today."

The old woman snorted. "Nothing new about that. My grandson's been building robots since that Genius Academy dragged him out to City Centra." She snorted again. "That's not a particularly good robot to lug around. It's all scrap and uselessness. What good is it?"

Shai deflated and could not find a proper response.

So it was Robot Sister who said, "Good is unquantifiable. The purpose of this one is companionability, which this one is serving currently. Logically, this one believes that is the essence of usefulness."

The bus halted at a side street, and the automated driver's voice boomed all over the bus. "We are now in Hypatia Lane. Repeat, Hypatia Lane. Next stop, Curie Cross."

The old woman stared, frowned, then hobbled to the exit. "Your robot's as silly as you, girl." Once she was off, the bus continued to move.

Shai's cheeks were warm and red, and she had grown angry by what the woman had said. She had been on the verge of an Angel-like tantrum, but the anger didn't bubble forth because next to her, Robot Sister continued to speak in a pleasant voice.

"The park is located between Evergreen View and Euclid Hills," Robot Sister recited. "It is filled with flora and fauna, all of which hold proportions of most agreeable states. There is even a pond filled with ducks and swans and geese, although during the winter, the pond freezes over and the birds have flown to warmer climes."

And so Shai relaxed as Robot Sister droned on. And she looked out the window, ignoring the other stares and frowning faces.

....

Angel was at the park.

She did not see Shai until one of her friends pointed her out. At first, Shai stood there, hoping that maybe Angel would just ignore her like she did most days whenever they saw each other at school or at family parties. Angel had many friends, and so she was always busy with them. Busy enough to want to ignore Shai, who had almost no friends. Shai's friends had been accepted to Genius Academy, and she had not.

Robot Sister clicked and whirred. Shai thought maybe Robot Sister was reciting the numbers again, only this time it was doing so in silence. She took Robot Sister's curved hand and began to pull it away from Angel and her friends, to another part of the park.

"Did you make that?" Angel asked.

Shai stopped and turned around and said, "I did." It was a proud sort of moment for Shai.

Angel's friends laughed, but Angel did not. She frowned like she always did, like her favorite red bow had been dyed purple and green, and it was not supposed to be amusing, because the bow should be *red*. Like roses and cherries and stop signs. Shai thought she would say, "That's unladylike of you," but Angel did not say such a thing. Instead, Angel said, "Papa helped you?"

Shai shook her head. Papa had been extremely busy lately. He would not have been able to help her, even if Shai had asked.

Robot Sister placed her mismatched hands on its metal hips, and it pursed its metal lips to say, "It is not ladylike to stare." The voice had been almost identical to Angel.

The way the robot mimicked Angel seemed to surprise her friends. One of them, a boy named Thomas, laughed. "Angel, she sounds better than you! Where did your sister get all these parts? It's like she rummaged from the garbage or something!"

Angel's friends laughed again. Shai refused to look at them and continued to pull Robot Sister away.

"Are those my bracelets?" Angel breathed. It would have been a whisper, but she repeated it louder, and everybody heard the disappointment in her voice, Shai included.

Robot Sister's broom-limb moved up, as if to touch the bracelets that had made up its hair. This time, Angel's friends booed her, with Thomas calling Shai a "thief" and a "sneak" and more words that would have made her cry, if not for Robot Sister's whirring and clicking and spouting of times tables and ratios that ended irrationally.

Shai clenched her fists and glared and stomped away. She did not like her sister's friends, and at that moment, she did not like her sister at all. Robot Sister followed from behind, its rubber-soled feet crunching on the grass softly and in rhythm.

If Shai had been paying attention to the continued laughter behind her, she would have seen Angel's thoughtful, disapproving face. And she would have seen that Angel was no longer looking at Shai and her robot, but at Thomas, who had laughed and ridiculed, and at her best friend Reeja, who had called Shai a thief and a sneak and a silly bum.

Most of all, Shai did not see the look that Thomas gave Robot Sister, because if she had, she would have told the robot to run.

....

The magnet playground was one of Shai's favorite places. It was set up into four different courts, two for four players, and two for two players. She and Robot Sister had gone into one of the small courts, and Shai took gloves out of a box next to the court entrance. She wiggled her fingers inside the glove, and thought about whether Robot Sister needed gloves as well.

The robot had already entered the court, and Shai saw that Robot Sister was already zinging magnets away from it with its polarizing metal body. So Shai followed.

Playing Magnits was like playing table tennis without the bouncing; using the metal gloves, one person would push a magnet away and send it to the other person at the end of the court. If the other person failed to stop the magnet from flying off past the court table, or if the magnet touched the ground on the other player's side, the person who pushed the magnet gets a point. Likewise, the other person gains a point if the first person doesn't push the magnet with enough force, leaving the magnet on the first person's side. And this happened back and forth until a person's points went to ten.

Shai often played the game with Papa. Her father was a master Magnits player, and he liked teaching Shai a thing or two about mathematicals and mechanicals as he pushed magnets toward his daughter. He used his own reshape-able magnet – a clever invention he patented when he was only twenty-eight – at Shai, and Shai would have to identify the shape before sending the magnet back to her father.

"Octagon," she would say, and the magnet would *zing* back to Papa, who nodded and reshaped the magnet again.

Trapezoid, oval, diamond, dodecahedron, pentagonal trapezohedron. The shapes became harder and harder after every correct guess, and there were so many -hedrons that even Shai's exemplary memory could not remember them all.

Robot Sister did not ask about shapes, though. Instead, it *zinged* Greek letters toward her. Shai was not very good with the letters, and the first game ended quickly, Robot Sister racking up ten points within minutes. The second time, Shai recognized alpha, beta, gamma, delta, and made points that way. The third time, zeta, eta, theta. She began to rhyme them together. Mu and nu. Pi, chi, psi, xi.

Shai had just been on the verge of winning her first game against Robot Sister, but had lost the match point when someone spoke up on the court sideline.

"I like your robot, Sneak," Thomas said, sneering the word "sneak" like Angel would sneer the word 'slug.' "Give it to me."

Shai let the magnet *zing* past her. *Phi*, she thought. Robot Sister walked to Shai's side of the court, aware that the game had been over. "This one detects a disturbance, Mistress Shai."

But they could not leave, because Thomas and his friends had blocked the entrance. There were two boys and Thomas, and two girls, one of which Shai recognized as Reeja. Angel was not in sight.

"You deaf, Sneak?" Thomas said, louder this time. "I want your robot."

"No." She stood her ground. She heard her mother's voice, and how she often told her daughters to never let el abusador win.

"These people are estupidos and know nada about the greater world. They are not like tu padre, who is always kind to anyone he meets. There is only one way to deal with un abusador," Mama said, rolling her R's and speeding over the S's. Shai had known the anger in that tone, because her mother always went quickly from English to Spanish and back whenever she was irritated with something. "And that is to face him and fight."

It was harder to do when Thomas had friends who would help him. Shai only had Robot Sister.

Robot Sister moved, pushing Thomas with its mismatched hands until he yelped and gave way. "Come now, Mistress Shai, this one believes it is time to go home."

Shai decided to run past Thomas, who grabbed her wrist and twisted. She cried out.

Robot Sister pried Thomas' hands out of the way, and this time it was he who yelped. The boys and girls scattered away from the robot, and Shai was free to move. She hurried out of the magnet court and off toward the playground exit.

After a few seconds of running, she stopped and turned. Robot Sister was no longer following her.

The two boys with Thomas had grabbed both of Robot Sister's limbs and pulled. The arms fell to the ground, landing with a loud *clunk clunk*. Robot Sister tried to move, but the girls had pushed the robot back to Thomas, who punched and kicked its legs.

Shai stood there a moment, shocked and numbed and all sorts of miserable. Then she ran back, her small body tipping forward like a bull charging at a torero after seeing red. She hit one of the girls – Reeja, she thought – and the two of them flew toward the ground, Shai on top and scrambling up.

The other girl pulled at her hair and Reeja recovered quickly enough to give Shai a pinch. Shai yelled and bit Reeja's arm, then tried to yank her hair out of the other girl's grasp.

Beside her, she heard a loud *clank*, and saw that Robot Sister had lost its legs. The torso seemed strange on the ground, and there was no escape after that. Robot Sister whirred and emitted alarms that cried like screaming cats, but nobody was headed to the magnet playground to check on them. Shai would not be able to save the robot she spent so many days and weeks to build.

When Thomas and the two boys rounded back to Shai, she knew she had lost. And while she still fought, it was only a matter of time before Thomas would start punching her. She fought back the tears, but her eyes blurred anyway. She cried for Robot Sister, whose only response now was to go back to reciting numbers.

"One...point...six...one...eight..." The counting was slow and broken. Within seconds, it died down. Robot Sister ceased to function.

She did not see the punch or feel Thomas' fist on her stomach. But she knew it had happened because her body moved back while her arms remained where they were, held by the two boys who'd come to help the girls with Shai. She was numb, and she closed her mind to the pain.

The next punch did not come. The cruel hands around her loosened, and Shai broke away, pushing one of the boys down in her attempt to escape. Nearby, Thomas had fallen, and so had Reeja.

Angel stood there, her hands curled up into fists, her ribbons in disarray, and her red shoes scuffed with dirt and dust. Her face was almost as red as her shoes. She was yelling, but not at Shai.

"Don't you *dare* harm *my sister* again," Angel said, kicking Thomas, who doubled over on the floor. She glared at the other two boys, who backed away. If Shai had not known any better, she thought she had seen fear in their eyes. Fear at the way Angel stood there, fierce and regal, even when she did not appear at all ladylike. "Or I *will* kick you where it *really hurts*."

There is only one way to deal with un abusador. And that is to face him and fight. Angel had listened to Mama that day, too.

Thomas whimpered and sniffed. Reeja, who'd landed on the ground with her rump, backed away. "Angel, we were just—"

"Go," Angel said, her hand grabbing Shai's wrist. When she said no more, the boys and girls ran, leaving only Thomas, who ached too much to get up.

Angel took a deep breath and prepared to kick the boy again. She stopped when Shai pulled her away. Then, with one quick stride, Shai knelt beside Thomas, and slapped him once on the face. She stood up, satisfied.

Thomas hobbled out of the magnet playground soon after.

Angel and Shai stood for a long time to watch him go.

....

It was Angel who moved first. She picked up one of the fallen robot arms, then the other, and touched the bracelets on Robot Sister's head gently. She looked at Shai with a frown. "I'm still mad at you for taking them," she said. Then she knelt by Robot Sister and began to put the arm back together.

"Why are you doing that?" Shai asked, confused. In fact, she was confused at why her sister saved her at all. And when did Angel learn how to put robots back together?

"It's a good robot," Angel said. One of the arms held, and she moved to work on the other. "Papa would be proud."

Suddenly, more tears threatened to spring from Shai's eyes.

"What's her name?" Angel asked, distracting Shai before she could let the tears fall.

Shai paused. Suddenly, Robot Sister seemed to be too strange of a name. The robot was not like her sister at all. No one was.

"Phi," Shai finally said, remembering the last Greek letter that the robot had sent toward her during their game of Magnits.

Angel nodded once and continued to work on attaching the other arm. When there were no more words between them, Shai searched for the two robot legs that rolled away. She returned, and Angel nodded again. The two worked in silence to bring Phi back to life.

There was nothing angelic about Angel as she stood on the magnet playground, her dress ruined, her curly hair all over her face, her eyes red and blazing and bug-round. Angel's skin would be mottled and bruised later, though she did not seem to feel as many aches and pains as Shai did.

No, Angel was not angelic in any sense of the word.

But at that instant, Shai did not mind this at all.

The Cliff

Vanessa MacLellan

A champion of NaNoWriMo, Vanessa MacLellan is an avid reader of anything with pizazz. Words have been her companions since she was ten, forcing atrocious adverbs upon her mother. Her fantasy novel, Three Great Lies, *has been accepted by Hadley Rille Books and is scheduled for release in the summer of 2015. She's had three short stories published by online magazines. When not in the office or writing, she bird watches and hikes. Vanessa can be found at vanmaclellan.com*

Again, today, we climb the cliff. Little Fritz gets the farthest. His slim, worm-like fingers dig into the tiny cracks that line the canyon's gray stone face like the bars of the guards' gate. Myrtle barely clears the talus fanning out at the base of the ribbed basalt cliffside, her fingers more like unyielding iron. I sit near the full loading cart, watching, knowing I won't make it up the cliff. An adult almost, my gangly body doesn't even fit into the smaller mineshafts anymore. I watch the young ones though, and cluck like a cuckoo bird when I hear the guards' horses pounding our way.

The clomp of hooves reverberates off the high surrounding walls, and I make the call, pulling my right cheek back and clicking my tongue. Then I roll it to make a three-beat squirrelly noise, one that, as little ones new to the pit, caused us to giggle when Ashid and Linton tried to teach us.

It doesn't hold the laughter anymore.

Myrtle ceases her senseless scramble, and Jilly, Bert and Hair Lip

Chip surf down the gray stone until they skate across the soft delta of dust at the bottom. Little Fritz dangles by one arm, and I run over in the hopes I can catch his tiny, frail body if he falls, but he drops from one handhold to the next, a little monkey in boy's skin.

And then the guard rounds the protruding jut of basalt.

"Hey, you scabs. You working over here?"

The guard stares down at us from the back of his roan horse. I wonder if he knows about our escape attempts. The sun glares behind his head, so I have to squint up at him. Most of the younger ones won't look him in the face, but I have to. I'm the oldest.

"We are working."

Behind me, Chem coughs, the liquid sound of phlegm and gunk gurgling in his lungs.

The guard gestures at the mine carts lined up on the track, nearly filled with rocks splashed with bright blues and greens, sometimes stained with orangey blooms, different in texture and dazzling in the sun.

"Three more carts and you can come in for the night." He pulls his horse's head around and trots off. We watch him ride away. Seven cars are full. Thirteen sit empty. Though the colorful rocks are hard to find, three more isn't unthinkable.

Jilly grabs onto my shirt, weaving her fingers into the holes of the fabric. "Dani, I don't want to go back down there. You said we'd be done today. You said." Her big brown eyes hack at my compassion more than her words.

I close my eyes, think. Take in a breath. The inside of my nose tickles with crusted dust.

"Jilly, Little Fritz, Shasta, you three stay out here. No climbing! Sort the rocks and ready the carts for the guards. Timmy Tim, help them out. The rest of us, three more carts."

Hair Lip Chip gathers up the torches, lights one by scraping a metal strip against a stone. The ends are wrapped up with cloth, tacky and reeking of something sharp and unnatural. Like pee, but stronger, harsher. Our torches flare up as we touch them to the flame, and give off black smoke.

Into the mine we descend, tools dragging against the ground. Chem coughs and spits.

....

I did see a cuckoo once. I think that's what it was. A long-tailed shadow that crossed the open mouth of our canyon with high walls. We don't see much sky down here. Our window above reaches from the narrow tip of the pit where the mine shaft sinks into the earth and widens out near the far end where the hut and guards' gate are. On that farther end, a trail winds up and out of the pit, a level pathway carved into the hard stone that surefooted horses can traverse. They carry supplies, water and food down to us and take away the rocks the guards find so needful.

They are just rocks. You can't eat rocks.

That was the day I saw Ashid for the last time. Three guards charged up on horseback, a roan, a silver, and a chestnut with white socks, and demanded the full twenty mine cars. I was young then, Jilly's age, or maybe Shasta's.

"And none of that crap you've been pulling up. Better ore. Solid copper. We know the vein's down there. Send the smallest in to find it."

I remember how my body tensed. Twenty carts. They never demanded twenty carts before. A labor I couldn't even comprehend.

It trapped my mind in a loop of worry. Could we get the twenty carts? Would it be of the bright greens and blues like they wanted, or even better, the orange? I worried about getting the carts out, always heavier when filled with more of the metal. About dehydration. I hoped I could carry my own weight, not let anyone down.

I didn't worry about Ashid. She was older than all of us. Smart, quick on her feet. She told night stories with cuckoos and lions and fields of golden grasses in them. She'd almost reached the lip of the pit once, so the tale went. I hadn't been around long enough to know that the older ones went away.

After we'd filled the twenty carts, each of us worn down to our heart and soul, the guards hooked the carts up to a horse train and took them through the gate and up the cliffside trail. Ashid was told to go with them. I didn't know I should have been worried. I didn't know I should have said good-bye.

It was past sundown when she followed the guard on the silver horse. And then, slicing the cobalt sky, a cuckoo flew, calling out our warning sign.

....

The sun has yet to rise when I climb out of the hut, holding the door with my fingertips until it snaps closed on rusty springs. Nobody else is awake as I face the east, waiting for the sky to lighten and show me that things can change.

Last night I had a dream, an odd vision of trees, tall and blocking out the blue sky. Maybe a lost memory, from before the pit. Their leaves were as big as hands. Bigger. And they danced and sang and gave off smells. The guards sometimes talk about hunting in forests, surrounded by trees. One spoke about birds that ran on the ground and animals like horses with horns that bounded over logs and stones. I know there is more out there than flies and spiders and those little brown lizards. I close my eyes to the purpling sky, wishing I could still be asleep. In my dreams, my life has more meaning.

"…going to close the mine down soon…"

The words slip down from the canyon wall trail, sinking through the still, empty air.

"…not worth the effort…"

My ears strain to catch more of the words.

"…glad to be done with…"

I crawl closer to the guard shack at the metal gate and fencing that separates our pit from the passage out. Descending along the switchback are two swaying lights.

"The Commander said to work 'em till the end o' the week. Close the place down after that. Moving the kids to Chertwood. The oldest is to be reassigned. The girl, the long haired one."

"That's your business." The men go quiet; their horses reach the canyon floor, the clopping of their hooves like the heartbeats of stone giants. The lanterns swing under their steady gait. "You restationed yet?"

"Yep, the Midland pit. You?"

"Back home." The man chuckles as my heart threatens to give away my location. "Done with this desert."

I turn and run quietly back to my hut, to the children, to the only family I have ever known.

....

It rains only a few times a year. The sky above turns gray and just opens up, dumping buckets on us. It transforms the entire canyon into a red mud pit, the clay slurry dressing up the gray basalt. The little ones love it, splashing around, getting dirt and grime in every crevice. They'll never be clean again, I think, but smile as they enjoy the water over their skin, slippery with the mud. I remember when I used to splash and play, throwing handfuls of wet clay at the others. A day of celebration, because we can't go down in the mines. The tunnels funnel the water away, sometimes flooding them. As a little one it was fun, until I realized no work meant half rations. Luckily, this time I'd caught the scent of rain on the wind and kept some bread and apples from yesterday to give the youngest four. They would not have empty bellies tonight.

We're day three into the week. I've not told anyone the secret I earned in the dark, but they sense something's changed. The guards demand more and more carts, and I fear the dreaded twenty will conclude our time here. And I wonder where Chertwood is, and where will they take me.

I stand there, in the water, clothing soaked, water washing away the tears on my face, cooling my aching eyes. I'm not sure why I'm crying, it's just that I feel shredded inside.

....

Though we've enough work to fill the entire day, I insist we take a break as usual. The children bolt their food and within minutes, Little Fritz is dangling from a rock ledge. He's taken a different crevice that juts into the western edge of the sky-high cliff like a tongue stuck out in mockery. The offshoot is typically in shadow, and right now the hot light of the day's peak is slipping away.

Myrtle and Bert and Chem all stand at the bottom, giggling and watching him. I bite into a cracker, praying.

"Go for it, Little Fritz!"

I hold my breath, heart pressed against my sternum as he swings forward and backward, a pendulum on a pivot, and then he lets go. My heart stops. My breath catches. His little hand, reaching, reaching, misses the outcrop he's aiming for.

"No!" I race forward, cracker tossed to the ground.

Little Fritz scrambles for another rock, red and jagged, and cries out as he loses his grip, palm grinding against the stones. Fingers clawing at the stone, he catches hold of a spur.

"Fritz!"

He looks down along the rock wall, finds a hollow for his foot, gains a better handhold, looks at his hand, wipes it against his bare side. I catch a smear of red. Then he grins down at us, all teeth and gums. "I'm okay."

My heart beats again.

Later that night, after sixteen carts, Little Fritz relaxes in my arms. I used the same burlap for our feet to wrap around his hand, having washed the blood clean with a little bit of each person's water ration. His expression is content as I tell the story Ashid told me when I was little.

"…and she set her feet one at a time. She'd been at it for days, the sun rising and falling four times. Her tummy rumbled, for she hadn't brought enough food, and her fingers bled from the biting rock. Below her the guards watched, because they were all too big and couldn't chase her up the wall. They yelled at her and told her to come down. Told her to find the copper. To crawl down the mine. Do you know what Helen said?"

The little ones sitting around me, in unison, say, "I'm going to fly away, fly away free!" Even Richard joins in, his shifting voice cracking as he carries the 'free' longer than anyone else.

"She stuck out her tongue—" Jilly pokes hers out, causing the others to giggle, "—and focused on the cliff wall. The cracks. A lizard poked his head out of one, letting Helen know that crack was deep. Following the hints from her friends she made it to the top. The guards yelled as she went over the edge, out of the pit. 'Get down here!' they said. And what happened to her up there, once she was out of the pit?"

Little Fritz grins, his tongue poking out from the hole where his two front teeth should be. "She turned into a cuckoo."

"A bright yellow cuckoo!" Shasta adds.

"And then what?" Myrtle asks the children.

Again, in unison, they say, "She flew away free!"

Storytime ends and the little ones are set upon their nests. Except for Little Fritz. I hold him still. With them asleep, I can't ignore the glances from the older ones, but I can pretend. Little Fritz hasn't earned the worry that's darkened Myrtle's face, or Bert's. I want to protect that face so strongly. I squeeze his small, sleeping body, and he whimpers in protest. I brush back his thick black hair.

"Dani?"

Myrtle offers me a bowl. It's steaming and smells of meat and celery. I nod in thanks but can't let Little Fritz's body go; he might wake up. She sets the bowl down and nods at me, only questioning with her eyes. She's getting older now. She understands.

The youngest of our tribe sniffs in his sleep and I pet his hair again, soothing out the little line that carves its way between his eyebrows. Keep your peace, little one. I'm watching over you.

I wonder what my face looks like when I'm asleep, dreaming of greener lands.

....

I clutch the little ones close to my chest. I think today is the day. One week. I count the day of rain. We gather together as the sun warms the sky, ready to go to the mine and do our work.

A guard walks up; his horse is beyond the gate. He hands over a canvas sack of foodstuffs: potato, carrot, some flesh wrapped up in paper. "Twenty carts today." It's less food than a normal day's ration. "Better get on it." Something heavy reflects in his eyes, especially when he looks at me. A quick dash away from my own, hiding a kind of shame undetected from any of the guards before.

"Come on, kids," I say and usher them all to eat some porridge prepared from yesterday's supplies and ready ourselves for a grueling day.

"Twenty carts?" Timmy Tim asks. Though still a child—his linen shirt hanging past his wrists—he's old enough to recognize the enormity of such a task.

I nod, not allowing myself to speak, afraid of what words might sprout from my mouth.

We march to the mine and I tell stories of Ashid and Linton, and stories of forests and goats and deer and rabbits: mythical creatures.

Myrtle gives in. "What's wrong?"

I stare at her, catch her gaze, don't let it go for a second. Then I smile, my cheeks bunch up, my lips curl. "Today is the day Little Fritz makes it out."

Everyone cheers. Especially loud is Little Fritz.

"And we're all going to help him. We'll fill the carts, then after the guards check us at half day, we'll quit the mine and let Little Fritz climb!"

Myrtle, Chem and Richard don't know what to say to my sassiness, but I am the oldest.

Only seven carts are full when the guard on the roan performs his accounting. Even with the day of rain, the week has exhausted us. The rocks don't have much color to them and the guard grumbles about the quality before he rides away.

I gather my children around me. "Come here, Little Fritz." I burlap his knees and hands, paying special attention to the red swollen scrape. I offer him a little bag of the finest dust and tie it around his waist, and another with a ration of food.

And then I set him free.

The laughter of the children rolls down the canyon. I want to tell them to quiet down, the guards might hear, but it probably doesn't matter, and the children know this. Little Fritz takes the western tongue again, secluded and cast in shadow. Like one of the striped brown lizards, he shimmies up the wall, higher and higher, his fingers probing for cracks only his impish body can use. He dips his fingers into the pouch and finds a passage invisible to our eyes. From a nose of rock, he jumps up, snatching a lump that looks like a shadow and hauls himself up. He's tiny up there, and we cheer him on. "Go, Little Fritz!" My voice rises up with the others.

In no time, he reaches the spot of his fall. One glance for us, a grin, and he launches himself. Suspended in air, he seems to fly, like a cuckoo. I can't look away. He's reaching, floating, soaring... He catches a knob, swings, pulls himself up. Collectively, we release our breath. He's ten feet from the top. Five. His little toes dig into the wall, smooth like glass from this distance. Three. Two. His hand reaches up, over. His feet dangle in midair, and then, with a wiggle, he's gone.

We are silent.

A gust funnels down through the pit, picking up dust and grit. I shut my eyes and only listen. The wind and horses hooves. And in the distance, a cuckoo cries.

Where You Belong

Jeannie Warner

Jeannie Warner spent her formative years in Southern California and Colorado and is not afraid to abandon the most luxurious environs for a chance to travel anywhere. She has a useless degree in musicology, a checkered career in computer security, and aspirations of world domination. Her writing credits include blogs of random musings, thriller novel manuscripts, stories in Tightbeam *online magazine, KnightWatch Press'* Rom Zom Com *anthology, the* Mad Scientist's Journal, *several police statements, and a collection of snarky notes to a former upstairs neighbor. She lives in the San Francisco Bay area near several of her best friends whom she refers to as "minions."*

The cargo game was going on in the hold when we found her, a waifish blonde with blue eyes that took up half her face. Bongo dragged her out from behind the cartons that marked one side out for our playing field. He held her up dangling in the air by the wrist as he yelled for me. "Hey! Lookie here, Dodge!"

We all stared, players of a now-abandoned game gathered around. I could tell right off she was a stowaway and clearly not born in space. We don't often see anyone our age that's planet-born like she was with her upright skeleton grown straight and true with a decent daily protein ration, not to mention the unusual hair and eyes. I'd have guessed her at six years old due to her size, but the way her temper flashed at being found and gaped at I doubled the guess to nearer my own age.

"Hey! Put me down!"

"Ain't that interesting. Did you order us a newbie back at launch, Bongo?"

"No sirree, Dodge. No newbies." Bongo grinned. "I just pumped the fuel."

"Me neither. Any one of the rest of you lot offer a little girl a lift somewhere?" My gaze swept over our crew, who shook their heads as one.

"Reckon she's a stowaway, then." I adjusted my cap firmly over my forehead, folded my arms, and stared as the girl dangled. "Put her down. You know what we do with stowaways, little girl?"

Her voice was soft with an accent when she spoke. "You put them to work. I asked at station."

That rocked me back on my heels a little. There was a small rustle of nudges and whispers among the players arrayed behind me. "Heh. If they're useful. You don't look useful. You look like a dirt-licker. Ain't got no useful bends at all."

Her eyes widened as she looked over the various deformities of the rest of us. Save for me, the crew was all space-born mutts, and I'd been out here since I was a tyke so my bones didn't finish growing straight. Tiny and Mouse were both under four feet, Tiny because his legs were spindly, useless things and Mouse because his legs were missing below the knees. Paris doesn't have a straight line in his body. Out here the food is crappy, the gravity is low, and accidents twist the body; not a lot of standard builds. That's what dirt-lickers call themselves, standard. There is no standard here in space; you grow however you grow. Everyone adapts to their job, and no one gets wasted.

The girl lifted her chin. "Don't matter. I'm here and willing to work. Word on the station was that if a kid works hard, then they can have a good enough life in one of the FAGNs."

"Station brats tell you that?" I spit to one side.

She nodded stubbornly. "Yeah. Said it was safe enough, and if you work, you eat." Her gaze skittered around the players again, pausing on Mattie who had settled in just at my other elbow. The girl stared, but Mattie is immune to it. Mattie's fifteen, but station-born. She'll never grow beyond her four feet, but her stunted, bowed legs and over-developed shoulders mark her as a solid worker in space salvage terms.

See, you don't need legs without gravity. You just need strong arms and a healthy respect for the laws of motion and mass. Mattie's twisted body can move tons efficiently, for all that she'd be almost crippled in the full-gee on a planet. We can't go 'home' to a planet, us FAGN kids. We've adapted. Me? I aim to be a captain one day.

"Reckon so. You know anything at all about salvage ops?" I asked.

She shook her head. "No. But I know ships. On my home world, they build liners. Galaxy-class. My mom's flat was close to the shipyards, and sometimes I helped bring tools and things."

Bongo whistled. "Galaxy-class liners. They're spendy. What do they move, a thousand people?" Bongo had never seen a thousand people in one place before.

"More'n that. Ten thousand," the girl asserted before sighing. "Don't matter. Just I know how ships go together, so I know how they ought to come apart for scraps. I shipped for a few months, too. I can work."

From overhead on the catwalk, Captain Bill's voice boomed out. "What's all this now? Who's that?" We all looked up to see him leaning over the railing, pointing at the stranger.

The girl's shoulders flinched at his tone and volume, and I found myself swelling a little, protectively. "Uh, this here's… what's your name then?"

"Olivia."

Typical dirt-licker name. I amended it. "This here's Ollie, Cap. We signed her on at the last station to try a run with us."

Bill is a big man. His hair and eyes are black, his skin dusky and covered in scars from drinking and fighting. He made a point of clanging down the catwalk to make an entrance, the steel sounding with each tread. He's a big man in any case, but when he's angry, he can fill the whole stair. "Oh we did, did we? Who authorized that without my permission?"

In for a penny, I thought. I stole another deep breath and stood up as straight as I could. "That'd be me, Bill."

The blow was about what I'd expected. Bill's fist slammed into my cheek and sent me back about five feet. It was sudden, impersonal, and emotionless. That's why he's a good captain. It's not personal, and he's always consistent. "I don't have time to coddle a newbie. We have work to do. Contracts to fill. And there's no extra rations." He looked the girl up and down, from dirty feet to unbrushed hair that feathered down around her face. His voice lowered to something merely growly. "You'll share your rations since she's your problem, Dodge. Do the paperwork." And with that he turned and headed back up the steps again toward the bridge.

I let out a breath that I didn't realize I'd been holding. The rest of the crew cheered weakly and went back to the game, stealing looks back. Ollie came over to help me up, but I shrugged off her hands. "I'm fine. It wasn't as bad as it coulda been."

Her fingers lightly touched the red mark on my cheek then fell away. "I was worried he'd kill you. They say that the captain is life and death on these federal ships. They say it isn't safe."

"Then you seem like an idiot for shipping out on one," I pointed out. We call FAGN the *Frustrating Agents of General Negligence* but it's really a federal program for managing orphans—poorly. As long as no one sees abused orphans on vid, the news streams don't get a story. No one wants to see us. We are the embarrassing remnants behind the laws about space mining and exploration and leftover children. "Federal guidelines say we all get equal treatment, equal food, one room each, and access to online skim-training. So you're throwing us off a little, but this run's supposed to be short. Bill's all about keeping clean on the books."

"I don't want him to report I'm here!" Ollie said.

"You do something illegal? Look, if you're going to be here I gotta know." It seemed unlikely the girl would be wanted for violent crime, but given the light fingers on our crew, I didn't equate youth with innocence.

She hesitated. I gave her a look right back, and she relented. "Momma was a cruise line entertainer on New Svenska." We both knew being a lounge entertainer didn't have a good reputation, but she didn't say anything more, and I'm not a jerk. "She was careful, but I came along anyway. My daddy was mad since I wasn't "pure. Apparently, he wanted to inherit things before he has kids, so they have to give him the family money. Momma passed me off to a crèche for a few years, but people asked questions cause of my looks." The girl tugged on her blond hair, a rarity among the muddled genetics of star travel. New Svenska was very famous for being big on racial purity. The ruling class might be inbred, but they were sure pretty on the skim-vids.

"But you get kicked out of the crèche at twelve," I pointed out.

"Yeah. Mama got us a berth on a liner, and we shipped out with her as a singer doing the tourist run. I worked in housekeeping."

The ache in my face dulled to a mild throbbing as she talked, and I gestured her to follow me. "Keep talking."

I couldn't see her shrug, but I felt it at my back. "Daddy found out we were on a New Svenska liner and put out a fire order. He could do that because his family owned the cruise line. When we hit the first nonautomated station, mama and I were turned off ship. She got sick and died there."

No one who ends up on this ship has a happy story. If you don't blub about it, you can do just fine. "Well, we do salvage here," I informed her. "Decent profits. You got any hours logged in a v-suit?"

"Just the usual drills." She meant the monthly drills on any ship or space station. You have to make sure everyone knows how to get into a vacuum suit right quick in the event of a hull compromise. Space is deadly.

I nodded. "That's more than some dirt-lickers." We reached my cabin, and I gestured inside. "You'll sleep in here for now, since you're my problem. But since you ain't got any stuff to stow, let's go on down to find you a suit. We're on our way to a job."

She peered inside. The walls were plain fiberglass with banded reinforcements and a single light panel overhead. A slab of a bed cantilevered from the wall holds my snarl of thermal blankets with some trinkets and bits around on the floor that I've salvaged for myself.

I don't think the notion of sharing a bed bothered her. I hear they all sleep together in a crèche, like puppies. We often did out here, too. Space is cold, and heating is expensive on long runs, so Bill kept the place chilly to cut costs.

We continued to a storage room where we keep suits. There's a lot of variety in a v-suit, and Mouse was a deft hand with a needle and sealant for making the varieties we needed to suit up the various crew that came our way. Ollie was small and still straight, so she fit a spare standard model that we hadn't cannibalized for parts and fabric yet. We tested the oxygen, safety harnesses, and radio then fetched it back to my berth. Our berth, at least for this run.

The overhead speaker crackled, and Bill's voice came on. "Target acquired. Suit up, children. You know the drill. Dodge, take the newbie and keep her with you."

I kept an eye on Ollie as she suited up, but true to her claim she seemed to know her way around a v-suit okay. I traded my antique LA baseball cap for a helmet. We checked each other's seals from the outside, and headed down to the main hatch together where the rest of the crew had abandoned the ball game to suit up. Our equipment was loaded up into the staging bay, and the iris to the main cargo hold telescoped shut. Through the speaker in my helmet, I heard the hiss of air being pumped out of the bay. "Everyone raise your hand if you can hear me," Bill's voice crackled through my ears. We all raised our hands.

We waited a moment, feeling the shudder of small maneuvers as Bill lined us up with the salvage target. Then our feet came off the deck as he cut the rest of the gravity, and we floated in place as the outer hull door opened. Beyond was infinite black with distant stars. Just in front of all that nothing was our target: a smallish transport ship floating dead in space. It was a new model by the look of it, not like our usual long-outdated salvage runs. I wondered what had happened to make them abandon it. But it's cheaper to make ships than fix them these days, with the materials they use and how quick things go obsolete. No one builds to last any more.

One at a time, we jumped over to the derelict, a slow and controlled push that took us over to the other ship's hull. I jumped beside Ollie and watched to make sure she attached her magnetic tether to the ship's hull properly.

Long-armed Paris was already sticking the corrosive tape around the unlocking mechanism when Ollie leaned over and touched her helmet to mine. The inter-suit connection turned on. "Why doesn't he use the external release trigger? It's a T-94X."

"The what? Is that a new upgrade on this model?"

"It's got a new feature to improve the response times for search and rescue," Ollie's voice suggested pride in the knowledge. "Any ships manufactured since last year have them. This is a new model, fresh off the blocks." Her gloved hand stroked the plated exterior. "Should I show you?"

"Hell yes," I said, then turned on my general radio for a moment. "Paris, we have another way in. Save the tape." I nodded to Ollie.

She released her magnet, and with great care went hand-over-hand toward a panel some three meters from the main door. She pressed and rocked the small panel there in some pattern too quick for me to catch. Then her small gloved hand snaked inside a hole that opened up, all the way up to the elbow. A moment later there was a silent wave of pressure as the main hatch popped out three inches.

"What's going on over there?" Bill demanded, testy at the silence.

"We're in, captain. Ollie found a short cut."

"Did she, now? Good. Carry on."

"Mattie, take Ollie here with you and do the bridge, and I'll meet you there," I ordered. "Tiny, take Bongo and Mouse and sweep the bay for cargo. Paris, the usual."

Inside the derelict hold, the residual ambient light from the solar cells was dim. Our helmet lamps painted wide spots of light as we all looked around at the various boxes and wiring there. "I say, that was lucky," Paris's voice came over the headset. He'd paused just inside the door to lock it in the open position. "I think someone booby-trapped it."

I floated over to take a look. I couldn't make heads or tails of the mechanism but there were definitely small lumps of something held around the lock by tape with wires. "That's new," I agreed. "Think that means they planned to come back for it?"

"I reckon," Paris started carefully undoing the wires. "I'll take it with us. Never know when a little plastique will come in handy."

I broadcasted, "Watch your step, all. Someone clearly planned to come back here. There could be more traps." The group scattered through the ship in search of anything not nailed down. And if they could get the screws off quickly, that didn't count as nailed down.

There's not many places to hide things in a small transport ship, so it didn't take us long to strip it pretty clean. The ship was comprised of one main crew cabin with bunks, two additional passenger cabins, engine room, mess, medical, bridge. I did medical, then passed Mattie just exiting the bridge and found Ollie still there. She was stripping data chips and spare sim-wave parts into a pillow case that came complete with the pillow still intact. Inside her helmet, she lifted her narrow chin as if daring me to say something about the bit of luxury, but I didn't. Clearly, the girls peeked in the cabins first.

I pulled spare electronics as well for a bit, keeping an eye on Ollie although she knew her way around a screwdriver. "Keep on, then. Meet me back at the hold entrance when that's full."

I headed next to the mess hall to grab up spare food packaging. Mattie was already there, pushing sacks of water twice as big as she was back toward the cargo bay. Even in nearly normal G, she can handle a lot of weight, but in zero-G she could push tons without effort. I felt a faint clanging of the hull as Bill attached the siphons outside on the refueling pipes. Waste not, want not, as he always says. With the rest of the fuel and power sucked out, the ship went dark save for the lights on our helmets.

We all met back at the door. Due to sheer mass, Mattie jumped over first with the water supply. Bongo, Tiny and Mouse had large cartons and went next, once Mattie was on the other side and ready to catch. That's how we transferred large objects between ships, a careful game of catch that we practice in the bay at home. It sure moved cargo faster than the way the manuals advised.

I could see Ollie wanted to jump with her pillow by the way she held it protectively, but I stopped her. We didn't do it that way. "Throw it." Mattie stood on the other side, ready to catch. Ollie did a slow push of the pillow off between the ships just as Bill's voice snapped out a little harsh on the general feed. "Ware the fuel line!" The long hose, still streaming stolen fuel that emerged frozen as bits of tiny rock and gasses, snaked around in between the ships and hit the pillowcase, sending it off toward the black.

I don't know if Ollie said anything in her suit, but she pushed off hard to go and intercept it. I swore – she jumped more enthusiastically than she should have, and caught the pillow just fine. Problem was, the two of them went tumbling off end over end toward nothing. It was a newbie move, and I was careless that I hadn't seen it coming.

I grabbed my own anchor, thumbed on the magnet, and slammed it on the hull of the salvage. Then I jumped hard after Ollie. I needed the momentum to overtake her before my line ran out. I heard Bongo over the loudspeaker. "We got drifters, cap! Ollie and Dodge!"

Bill's voice went hard over the speaker, but I wasn't really listening. "Give me a spin directional?"

I only had one real shot at this – most ships are not designed for tiny little adjustments to catch people floating in space. Bill's good, but people are too small and space is mighty big. I saw Ollie up ahead, her whole body wrapped fetal-style around the pillow case. I turned on the broadcast so she could hear me. "Ollie! Straighten your legs!" My heart was in my mouth as I spread my arms as wide as I could to try and catch her. Now it was all about distance.

She heard me, and although stretching out her legs didn't slow her spin in zero-G it gave me something bigger to aim for to try and catch. The distance closed as I felt the cable playing out from my waist in a long snake behind me. With every inch, my safety was assured while hers was in doubt. But I had jumped even harder than she had. My hand caught her foot just as there was a jerk at my belt. I held on for all I was worth, adding a two-handed grip.

We hung there for just a moment in the black. Touching, I could hear her deep, gulping breaths and feel the shaking of her shoulders even through the suit. Hand over hand, I pulled her even with me. "Hey. Hey, I got you."

I could see her head nod behind the faceplate and the tears running down her face. We floated there with her ridiculous stuffed pillow between our bodies. "I'm so sorry. I panicked," she whispered.

"I know." I freaked out once when I was a kid myself. Bill was the one who pulled me back safe. "It's okay. It happens to everyone once."

She nodded, her panic easing. One of her hands let go of her death grip on the pillow and held my arm. "I won't. I swear. Please don't dump me at a station again."

"We're alive. That's all that counts. When you survive, you get to keep playing the game. You're home." I felt the tugging on my cable as the others reached it to start hauling us back in to safety.

Olivia's eyes met mine. "I'm gonna survive."

"You bet you are."

They pulled us back to the decompression bay, and we finished the op. Bill resealed our hull and engaged the grav. Everyone made a point of pointing and laughing at Ollie, who tripped into an undignified heap, but the laughter wasn't mean. It was more relieved that no one died.

Bill's voice over the speakers was commanding. "Dodge. Bring the flotsam up to the bridge. Now." His voice silenced the laughter, subduing the general unloading and stowage of the new cargo. I gently pried the pillow case out of Ollie's hands and passed it to Mattie. "She'll dump the goods and leave the pillow for you in our cabin. We gotta go."

We climbed the catwalk up toward the door of the bridge where we paused. I looked back at Ollie's pale face then patted her shoulder. "It'll be okay." She nodded back, and we went in.

The cockpit of our ship is pretty small, and Bill filled it like a white dwarf just before it goes supernova on you. The view screens showed the abandoned ship drifting back in our wake on one screen, with nothing but stars on the other. Bill punched a couple more buttons, and I felt the thrum of the main drive kick in. Then he turned to look at the two of us, silent.

Ollie shrunk a little behind me at first, then straightened her shoulders and even stuck out her chin a little. Bill's voice was mild when he spoke, catching me by surprise. "All in then, Dodge?"

"Yessir. Ship shape and stowed proper."

He nodded once, beetled gaze flickering over to Ollie. "So you know some tricks, do you? Not entirely worthless, although you could have cost us some good components with your idiocy. Follow orders. Do what you're told. That's how you survive, always doing what you're told by them what know better. Got it?"

Ollie nodded meekly.

Bill seemed satisfied, and leaned back in his chair with his arms folding behind his neck. "What was that you were telling Dodge earlier? You know the same tricks about the new liner models? They all got a simple way in like that?" Ah, of course he was listening to the intercom. It's his ship.

The girl hesitated. "I...don't know about the New Dubrovnik line. But New Svenska does. Not on the main gangway, of course. Just on the back near the supply bay doors, where catering and laundry service goes. I've been in and out of them a lot on refill runs." She mimed the placement with her hands, small and deft. Bill's eyes never left them.

"Good enough," he pronounced. "Go on, get some rest." She

turned to flee out the door.

I would have followed, but Bill's meaty paw landed on my shoulder. "Talk to Mouse and Paris," he said quietly. "See if they think they can get through the inside locks on a galaxy-class."

I scratched my head. "I don't follow?"

"I been thinking since I first heard her say it," Bill said. "You know, we do okay at salvage. But if we had a way into a galaxy-class liner, quiet-like, we could take our pick of passenger goods without them ever being the wiser."

I couldn't contain my look of shock. "Rob a live ship, Bill? Are you crazy?"

Bill grabbed my face with his hand, palm over my mouth while he hit a button to shut the door out. His voice rumbled more quietly, "No I ain't. I aim to retire. One really good job with a decent haul and I could settle down somewhere quiet-like. Find a station and live decent, with all the protein I want. Maybe even fresh food now and again, and more than one change of clothes."

I felt dazed. "I thought you liked the way we live here. We're a family, you said."

Bill shrugged and let go. "You and I both know it's been a long while since we've gotten anything from the Fed for supplies. We've been supporting ourselves for years. And I won't leave right away. But I'm thinking you're qualified to run the whole op soon enough, if I teach you some things. You'll be citizen age next year. You want this ship?" I did, with every fiber of my acquisitive heart. Words were cheap, so I just nodded. He seemed satisfied. "Okay. Chat up Tiny and Paris. We got some planning to do."

The next few sleep-cycles were filled with schematics and planning. Bill arranged some sort of information swap for the data we pulled off the derelict ship, and got us a full set of liner details with maps on the inside.

"This would do it, Cap," Paris traced a line. "This goes into every expensive cabin, all in a row. We do these two lines, stern and aft, and then pop out quick again. It's a great steal. But how we gonna get in and out of all those doors? Won't they see us?"

Bill looked smug. "You leave that to me. I've got it figured out. We'll make one stop first."

The next day, he took us in to a refill station along the rim of an ice ring frequented by the cruise liners. Most of us stayed on board while Bill, Bongo and Mattie hauled our salvaged cargo out to sale. They came back with the usual provisions and some wrapped bundles that turned out to be cruise liner uniforms. Mattie flat out told us where to go when we asked her to fix them, so it was us boys that sat around cross-legged, needles and thread working to alter them to fit our bodies. Ollie helped. She'd done laundry before, as she reminded me.

The one item that didn't get altered much was a bit of frippery, a dirt-licker girlie dress for Ollie. "Here's the plan, see," Bill laid it out for all of us as Ollie tried on the frock. "We float up to the ship and let ourselves in when she stops for water at the rings. Ollie gets us through the servant's door with her safety latch trick. I'll go first in case there's trouble. You follow, we change into uniforms, and march on in proud as you please."

He patted Ollie's head, and she looked startled. "Ollie here will be a misplaced passenger. I'm just doing my duty to find her family so she can be delivered to the right cabin. Can you cry on command, girl?"

Ollie blinked. "I'm not sure."

Bill's hand tightened a little on the girl's head. "Oh, we'll find some tears for you if need be. So there it is. Paris will get us through locked doors, and Olivia will get us through the rest. If we do it at one of the mealtimes, the cabins should be fairly clear on board. Steal them blind, and get off ship fast with a better haul than the usual scrap. Jewelry, mini-comps, furs – just think of the luxury goods! I know just the guy to fence them, too."

I didn't have any doubt Bill could deal with trouble or security. I've seen him in a fight.

"I've never stolen anything," Ollie whispered at last, looking less than happy.

"And you won't this time," Bill said mildly enough. "You just get us on that ship and look adorable and lost, and we'll be out of there before the meal shift is over. Then back home, we cut loose, and let the liner just drift away from us. We float dark, we won't even blip on their scans until we hit quarter-orbit away."

It was two weeks later I actually saw a galaxy-class liner right in front of me on the screens. It looked like a whole floating white planet of luxury and pleasure, and I burned a little with envy. Then, just because I felt bad about it, I patted the console of our ship. "It's okay, baby. I still love you better." She'd be mine one day soon; my heart was given already.

The liner was perched above the ice rings, clearly harvesting while the tourists snapped photographs of the striped planet below. Our ship drifted into place with only little pneumatic releases. We all listened in on the liner's broadcast announcements until we knew their sleep cycles and dining arrangements.

Ollie led the way, her slender hand slipping in to undo the latch that released the small hatch. Inside the liner when we had air again, we de-suited and tossed on the uniforms of the staff to head deeper into the liner. Bill led the way, and Paris opened each electronic lock with his usual wizardry. Ollie drifted with us, looking more like she belonged in this place than any of us with her perfect frame and proportions.

Five staterooms we hit fast as you please, and Bill's bag was bulging nicely when we hit the one on the end. Paris got the door open, and Bill and I had just walked in. I called out my usual, "Room service!" announcement, which so far had gone unanswered.

This time, a quavering voice was raised in reply. "I ordered nothing."

We froze as a wheeled hover chair turned in place. A white-haired man connected to many tubes sat in the chair, his monitors beeping. Tufty white brows raised over sharp eyes for all his frail form and voice, that blue gaze seeming to pierce our hand-stitched uniforms to see how we didn't fit them properly. "You're not supposed to be here. Who are you?"

Bill stepped forward with violent intent, but Ollie unexpectedly pushed her way to the front. "Grandpa!" She rushed over to take the old man's hand where it rested on the arm of his chair. "I was lost and I…Oh! I'm sorry. You're not my grandpa." She batted her lashes in the routine we'd worked out.

They looked a bit alike, I had to admit. Blue eyes, both of them. White hair and blond, pale skin that doesn't see sunlight unfiltered.

The old man's hand turned over and caught at her wrist before she could pull back away. "You look familiar, girl. Where have I seen you before?" He dragged Ollie closer, peering through his glasses to see her face. The other hand punched at buttons on his chair. Bill looked uneasy at that, but no alarms started that we could see, no lights beeping.

"Dunno, sir," Ollie whispered gamely, keeping to the charade. "I've never seen you." She looked at her hand as he turned it over, presenting her wrist to his chair and holding it there for a moment before she jerked away.

The old man let her go, pushing his spectacles up his nose slightly as Bill moved to collect her. A green light flashed on the chair and the man looked downright shocked. "You're a match? Dear lord, you're a relation. I have an heir."

That surprised all of us, even Bill. He was quickest to speak up. "Wait. You're related to this here girl? Ollie?"

I stared around the suite, my jaw dropping slightly as I considered for the first time the wealth involved in such a place, such a room on such a liner. This guy was calling our Ollie his heir?

Ollie was pale, backing toward the door way. "No sir, I ain't nobody, no how."

"Olivia, stop and listen to the nice man," I urged, moving to cut off her escape. She looked furious that I used the old name for her. I grabbed her shoulders and leaned to whisper close. "Think! He clearly wants you here. You know, people don't use words like heir without meaning to keep you in a good way."

She stared at me for a long moment before turning to deliberately look around the cabin. And it was worth the look, with every comfort imaginable. There were pillows and blankets on a soft-looking bed, with art on the walls and everything. Beyond a doorway, there was a room with a bathtub that looked like it would contain actual water. I could see naked longing in her face, and I thought, *That's it. She's gone.*

Then Ollie took a deep breath, her chin lifting in a stubborn way. "It's not Olivia. It's Ollie." I was stunned.

The old man in the hover chair floated behind us. "What? Girl, if you're a relation…I thought I was alone. Not one of my children survived. My brother's son is heir to us both, and somehow you have his blood. If something happened between you and your father, I want you to know I don't care. I'm your uncle, and I'm plenty rich." His thin lips curved into a patronizing smile. "I will protect you, and you will want for nothing."

"Is there some kinda reward?" Bill asked, but was ignored.

Ollie looked at the man in the chair for a long moment, her gaze older than her years. "Your machine is wrong. It's impossible, and I will not be mocked." We were all shocked quiet at that, three of us staring as she turned and held a hand out to me. "Come on, Dodge. I remember the way back home, now."

I took her hand because I had to. There was iron in her tone, and the sort of determination in her face that I saw in my own when I looked in a mirror and thought about being a captain one day. "Yes, ma'am."

Behind us the old man started to call something out, but then there was a thump and he went quiet. Bill passed us, stuffing something shiny into his pockets. "Come on, quick."

He led us out and away back down into the hold. We didn't need to discuss it further. Our burglary was done, and dice were cast in a way I could not have predicted. I'm not sure I could have turned down a life of luxury and wealth, so I asked Ollie about it as we were fast changing back in to v-suits.

"My mom was always her own person," Ollie said. "They rejected us, her and me. That world pushed us away. Yeah, maybe I want stuff. But then I'd have to learn to be someone else, and I don't know if I'd be any good at it."

Paris and the others were already out of the airlock on their way back to our ship. Bill smirked and shook his head. "You're crazy, girl. But we got a place for your kind of stupid. Come on, then. Let's go home before the alarms start."

Finally she smiled. "Yeah. Home."

One by one, the last three jumped back to our freighter, disengaged, and drifted off into the frozen rings of the planet below. The liner was left behind us, shining like the biggest block of ice you ever saw.

Repeat After Me

Alvaro Zinos-Amaro

Alvaro Zinos-Amaro is co-author, with Robert Silverberg, of When the Blue Shift Comes. *Alvaro's short fiction and Rhysling-nominated poetry have appeared in* Analog, Nature, Galaxy's Edge, Apex, BuzzyMag, The Journal of Unlikely Entomology, *and other venues. Alvaro has also published reviews, essays and interviews in* The Los Angeles Review of Books, Clarkesworld, Strange Horizons *and elsewhere, and currently edits the roundtable blog for* Locus *magazine.*

The idea of getting Niv to experience the play seemed to spring wholly formed in Mina's mind. She was sure her younger brother would like it. She didn't stop to consider the obstacles – or the dangers.

It happened on a Saturday morning after breakfast. The family lingered at the kitchen table, discussing the day's plans. As always, these plans had been provided by the Randomizer. While Mina helped Niv into his flexsuit, their parents discussed the play they would be watching that night.

Suit securely fastened and activated, Niv began his crawling exercises on the living room floor. Mina looked at him, wishing she could do more to help. He avoided her eyes, as he did with most people. Their parents watched a brief holo-preview of the play. As the play shimmered in the air, Mina saw a secret glow in Niv's eyes. That was the moment Mina decided. "I want to come to the theater with you tonight," she said.

Mina's father, Kouros, gave her a look. "You do?"

Mina nodded. "Yes."

The servos in Niv's suit had warmed up and were buzzing more loudly now. He finished his crawling exercises and began his arm-folding ones.

Kouros' eyes met those of Goli, Mina's mother. "You've never expressed any interest in the theater before, sweetie," Goli said. "Why now?"

"I'm ten now," Mina said with defiance. "I'm allowed to have new interests."

"Of course." Goli smiled, ending the preview and rising from the table. "But I'm afraid tonight's play is only meant for grownups. And Niv would miss you. You guys have a play date tonight."

Mina scrunched her face. Her mother didn't have a clue. Mina cared about theater as much as she did Tenebian dung beetles. *Less*, come to think of it. But she had glimpsed Niv's interest in the play. And since Niv was too young for theater, Mina decided to bring the play home to him. That meant Mina had to be in the audience so she could secretly record it. She was positive Niv wouldn't mind missing out on a play date with her if he knew the payoff, but now was not the time to explain. "I want to go," Mina insisted. "*Please*."

"Not tonight, dear," Kouros said. He stood up and sipped coffee. Mina and Niv got up too. The kitchen bots moved in, cleared the table and did the dishes. Everyone sauntered to the living room. "But I will enter it into the Randomizer for you."

"It won't be the same play some other day!" Mina complained. During tonight's performance, the bot actors would perform intense acrobatics: hopping, jumping, swinging, spinning, even somersaults. Those were exactly the things Mina was sure had sparked Niv's curiosity. Next week's play could be anything at all, like two bots discussing the weather over tea.

"Of course it won't be the same play," Goli said. "That's the whole point, Mina. Every performance is different, a one-time event. You know the Founders' belief that variety –"

"Yeah, yeah, I know," Mina grumbled, cutting off her mom. Mina raised her voice to an unpleasant pitch. "'Variety is the spice of life'," she mocked.

"Hey." Goli crouched down beside her. "It's a very important idea, Mina, and I need you to take it seriously. It's the reason we're no longer on Earth."

Mina rolled her eyes. She knew all about it and didn't wish to be lectured. Bots had become cheap, efficient and intelligent – so much so that they could design themselves. The bots could keep the world running. The humans split into two groups: the Doers, who wanted them turned off because they felt that work made life meaningful, and the Thinkers, who wanted to be free from labor so that they could focus on other things. The Thinkers left Earth and founded the colony of Malakbel on Tau Ceti's closest planet. Mina's parents were second-generation Thinkers, and that made Mina a Thinker. But some days Mina wondered whether she might not be more Doer. Speaking about that usually got her in trouble, so Mina kept those thoughts to herself.

"I don't mind variety," she said, crossing her arms. "But I don't see why things have to be different *all the time*."

Every aspect of life on Malakbel was "spiced up" with variety: for months at a time, Mina wouldn't receive instruction by the same bot tutor twice. She couldn't wear the same clothes, and her alarm-clock woke her up at a slightly different time every day, and so on. It had been fun for a while, mostly when she was too young to really understand how things worked. Now Mina was fed up with it. And then there was Niv. There was something wrong with him, but none of the adults was sure what. The bot doctors prescribed physical therapy as a way of strengthening his "undeveloped lower brain," a phrase that had stuck with Mina, but which she didn't understand. How many brains did one have, anyway?

Kouros cleared his throat. That usually wasn't a good sign. "Mina, what did you have for breakfast yesterday?"

Mina sensed a trap and considered before replying. "Buttered croissant."

"And what did you have today?"

Mina's father could have easily got that information from one of the kitchen bots. It was their responsibility to prepare the food for the household and ensure that no two consecutive meals were ever the same. But Kouros was making a point by *interrogating* her. Still, she refused to be intimated.

"Peaches and toast," she said. Mina didn't mention the half croissant she saved from yesterday.

"Hmmm. CC78 reports he found croissant flakes in your study room this morning."

"I – I – didn't eat all of it in the kitchen yesterday, that's why. I was too full, so I saved a piece for after my first study period yesterday morning."

"Then why didn't HH52 find the flakes last night when he cleaned the room?"

"I don't know," Mina said. "Maybe he needs to be replaced. He didn't get all the hair out of my purple brush yesterday, either. Lousy bot."

Kouros didn't seem quite satisfied with Mina's explanation, but he dropped the affair.

Meanwhile, Niv had finished his exercises and had turned on a three-dim animation. It would be an exaggeration to say that he was watching it. His eyes peered off into the distance, as though he were looking right *through* it, instead of *at* it.

Goli tapped on a panel. "There," she said. "I've instructed the Randomizer to add a child-friendly play to our plans sometime next week."

Mina glanced at Niv, who didn't react at the news. She forced herself to look pleased. "Thanks mom," she said. But Mina was already thinking of excuses to get out of it. Tonight's performance was the only one she cared about.

....

Each day the Randomizer produced a schedule of activities. Sometimes they were group activities for the whole family, like going to Manat beach, or hiking in the Dushara Mountains, or reading the same book at the same time and discussing it. Not all activities lasted just one day: some were trips to faraway places. During those times, the Randomizer made an exception to the daily pattern, providing several days' worth of plans at once. Those were Mina's second favorite days. Her favorites were the "wildcard" days, in which the schedule was deliberately left blank, and everyone could do as they pleased.

Many activities were individual, or included only bots as partners. Tutoring for Mina or Niv, tennis for their dad, painting or yoga for their mom. The family had fed the Randomizer thousands of things that everyone wanted to do. It drew on that list for its daily decisions, adding in thousands of its own recommended activities, always ensuring variation and balance. New activities, like Mina's request to attend the theater, could be input at any time.

This Saturday was no exception. According to the schedule, before Mina's parents attended the theater in the evening, Mina was supposed to go hang gliding, and Niv was supposed to use bots to design the next version of his flexsuit.

But Mina didn't *feel* like hang gliding today, no matter how optimal the Randomizer said the air currents were. She had started reading a book yesterday and wanted to see how the story ended. She knew the Randomizer would include the book in her schedule sometime in the next few days. She felt her whole being sag at that thought. That felt like an eternity away.

"What's the matter, sweetie?" Goli asked. She was getting ready to go horseback riding. Horses on Malakbel had been genetically engineered for such speed that special repulsion suits were needed, which activated only in case of an accidental fall. Mina remembered riding along with her mom once. She had fallen off and bounced right up from the ground, not getting a scratch. It kind of took the excitement away, Mina thought.

"I'm sick and tired of the Randomizer bossing me around," she told her mother. "I want to read. Or go horseback riding with you. *Not* hang gliding."

Her little outburst attracted attention. Niv came out of the design room and hovered ten feet away. Dad marched down the stairs, wearing a bathing suit. "What's this?" he asked Goli.

"Let me handle it," Goli replied.

Dad shrugged and shuffled out to the pool. Moments later, they heard a splash. The Randomizer had assigned him a hundred laps in various strokes and at various speeds.

Goli lowered her voice so Niv couldn't hear them. "Mina, sweetie, have you started noticing any changes in your body?"

Mina frowned. "What kinds of changes?"

"The puberty signs. You know, the ones we talked about."

"Oh," she said. "No."

"You seem to be moody lately, that's why I ask."

"I'm moody because I hate that things are always the same."

"But they're *never* the same!" her mom said, and laughed.

The sound made Mina grit her teeth. "You know what I mean, Mom! Getting our schedule from the Randomizer – we do that *every* morning! The Randomizer is not the boss of me!"

Niv silently stepped a few feet closer. He wasn't staring directly at his sister or Mom, but it was clear he was intrigued by their exchange.

"But Mina, the Randomizer doesn't tell us what to do; it just remembers what *we* want to do and arranges things in a more stimulating way than we could arrange for ourselves."

"I want to decide *when* I do something. Why is that so hard to understand?"

Goli took a deep breath. "Do you remember Saldom's theorem of self-determination?" she asked.

Mina pouted. Of course she did. It had been drilled into her since she was five. Which meant, as of last week, she'd been told about it for *half* her full life. But Mina wasn't about to make things easy on her mom. "No," she said.

"Then let me refresh your memory. It states that human beings are not the best selectors of activities that maximize their happiness, because they're skewed toward short-term rewards over long-term growth. Bots are the best selectors, because they're objective. The Randomizer gives us balance and looks out for our long-term happiness."

"Whatever. I *hate* the stupid thing."

"I know your tutors have walked you through the proof. Are you saying the theorem is wrong?"

"I can't follow the math," Mina said. That was not exactly true. Mina was exceptionally good at math, but she never chose to pay attention during those lessons. "It *could* be wrong. It could be a trick on the part of the bots. How would I know?"

"You don't think *I'm* lying to you, do you, Mina?"

Mina sighed. "No," Mina said in her most surly voice.

"Then believe me when I tell you the theorem is right. It's in our best interests to keep using the Randomizer. It will make us happier than doing whatever we want to *when* we want to. Okay?"

Mina shrugged.

"Hang gliding is terribly exciting," Mina's mom said. "I loved it years ago. You'll be in the sights of the hang gliding escort bots at all times, of course, so no need to be scared."

Mina turned away, towards Niv, who was retreating back to the design room. Her mom resumed preparing for her horse ride. "I'm not scared," Mina mumbled, and then gestured to Niv when she was sure that her mom wasn't looking. She scrambled to her room. Mina wasn't scared because she had no intention of complying. The bots would try to report her disobedience to her parents, but she had a plan for that.

Niv appeared a few moments later. His face had its usual blank expression on it. His long, gangly arms dangled awkwardly at his sides.

"Come inside," Mina said, in a hushed voice.

He hesitated. She knew he understood the consequences. He should be working on the new flexsuit. Not doing so would mean a reprimand. Worse, if the suit wasn't ready when he needed it, it might set back his physical therapy, though maybe he wasn't thinking that far ahead. After several more seconds Niv stepped forward.

Mina closed the door and clapped twice. All the bots in her room, regardless of size or function, swarmed towards her position.

"At your service," they said in perfect unison. Their not-quite-human voice was smoothly modulated.

"Teach us about recording devices," Mina commanded.

"Recording devices for which sense – sight, hearing, taste, smell, or touch?"

Mina considered. "Sight. Three-dim holo. And hearing. And it needs to not only record, but transmit too. In real time."

The bots proceeded to teach them, illustrating with holo-projections. They even assembled themselves into a facsimile of one of the devices Mina asked about. Mina played with it for a while, and the bots made sure it responded just like the real device would have.

"See, Niv," Mina said, "this is what I was going to use to record the play for you at the theater."

His face lit up.

"You'd like to see it, wouldn't you?" Mina teased.

His head bobbed up and down, as if in slow motion.

"But mom and dad won't let me go with them. Bots, is it possible to make a smaller version of this device?"

"It is," the bots said in their calm monotone.

"How much smaller?"

"By using laser-based optical tweezers, we can preserve basic functionality down to the micron level. Energy requirements and resolution limits become prohibitive at sub-micron scales."

Now it was Mina's face that brightened. "Micron level? That's great! Can you make one that size that can be activated remotely?"

"Remote functionality would require an increase in size," the bots said, "to the millimeter scale."

"That's fine! How long would it take you to make a millimeter-sized recorder that can be used remotely and that sends out data in real time?"

"The following materials would be required." The bots produced a list. "Once these have been provided, it will take an estimated five hours to assemble the device."

"How long until my parents leave for the theater tonight?"

"Five hours and forty-five minutes."

Mina faced her brother. He slinked back towards the wall. "Niv," she said, "I need your help. I need you to get me this stuff in the next forty-five minutes. And make it so that the bots don't tell Mom and Dad what we've been up to."

Niv was uniquely adept at bypassing their home security systems and reprogramming bots, and Mina was counting on his help. Last time he'd done something like this, also at Mina's insistence, they had both been grounded for a week. It had meant one week of not doing whatever the Randomizer said, so they hadn't minded. This time, Mina reasoned, none of the materials the bots had asked for were really dangerous; they required adult clearance simply because they were delicate.

"I..." Niv began. He didn't look at her. "Maybe... I don't think this is a good idea."

"Don't be silly," Mina scoffed. "You want to see that play, right? I know *I* do!" She dialed up her enthusiasm, making it as infectious as possible. "It'll be so great! C'mon, aren't you curious about what the adults won't let us watch?"

His voice was meek. "They... they're just trying to protect us."

"We don't need their protection! Not if it means a life of slavery to the Randomizer! Don't you want to be free?"

Niv straightened up a little. "I... I don't like... the Randomizer."

"I know you don't. Who would?" It was the same way she'd convinced him last time. "So help me get these things, and we'll get a recording of the play. We can watch it whenever we want. It'll be our secret. No one has to know."

Niv was quiet for a long time. Mina didn't push any harder. Instead, she got closer to Niv and caressed his forehead and hair. "Poor boy," she said, in what she imagined would be a maternal way. "You need some freedom. Some fun."

She stood there, stroking his hair, until at last he softened. "O-okay," he whispered.

"You're the best, brother," Mina said, and meant it.

....

"Have a great time," Mina said with her hands behind her back.

"Thanks, sweetie." Her mom's expression was somewhere between bemused and quizzical. "How was your hang gliding?"

"So much fun. The Randomizer was right after all. Floating up in the sky was… incredible."

"I'm glad," Goli said while putting on her coat.

Kouros slipped into his jacket and patted Mina on the back. "Make sure your brother is well looked after. We have all the bots in child care mode, so you'll be safe in case of any emergency. And don't wait up for us."

"Okay Dad," Mina said. "I'll be responsible."

As her parents approached the door Mina's hands, still behind her back, fidgeted. She had to fight to keep her voice from giving away her excitement. "Can I get a hug?" she asked.

"Awww," Goli said, looking at her daughter.

"We're going to be late," Kouros said, and stepped outside.

Goli lowered herself to Mina's height. During the embrace, Mina leaned in and kissed her on the cheek. At the exact moment when Goli closed her eyes, Mina's hands released the millimetric recorder on the front of Goli's coat. Self-adhering, and the same shade of brown as the coat fabric, it was nearly invisible even from up close. Unless her mom ran her hand over it, Mina thought, there was no way she'd realize it was there. Even then she'd probably just mistake it for a fleck of dirt.

"Gotta go now." Goli unwrapped her arms, rose and smiled. "Love you."

....

They nestled on the floor of Niv's room, piling on blankets and cushions. They dimmed the lights, imagining they were part of the theater's audience. Mina, again with Niv's help, locked all the house bots outside the room, not wanting to be monitored or disturbed.

"It's about to start," Mina observed in hushed tones.

Niv's eyes shifted to the right and to the left of the images floating in the air. Every few seconds his eyes rested a moment before continuing their roving.

The transmitter was working perfectly. It was self-orienting, adjusting for optimal position, like a normal camera. Its tiny lens also adjusted for changing light levels. The images that streamed before Mina and Niv were of startling clarity, completely detailed and all enveloping.

Their parents sat down about ten minutes ago, and the last of the attendees were finding their seats now.

Then the theater house lights lowered, illuminating only the stage.

Everyone went quiet.

"I..." Niv started.

"Shhh," Mina said and held her finger up to her mouth.

Niv lowered his head.

She placed her hand under his chin and pointed his face back towards the display.

The sleek, shiny black bots with their sleek, shiny black arms and legs and their impressive struts and pistons came out on the stage. They had been specially designed for gravity-defying acrobatics. The audience applauded at the mere sight of them.

Mina clapped too. Niv copied her, pressing his hands together.

The performance began. Mina couldn't help but smile. Peripherally, she noticed Niv was not only watching, but seemed utterly entranced.

....

That night Mina dreamed that her brother could fly.

Or maybe she dreamed that she herself could fly. In the morning, it was hard to remember.

....

Life returned to normal after that Saturday—with one exception. The Randomizer still ruled Mina and Niv's lives. But when their parents weren't around, which was a lot of the time, they re-watched the recording of that glorious display of bot coordination and aerial prowess. Mina enjoyed it, despite her initial disinterest.

But after the fifth viewing, she started to become bored. The thrill the first time was not knowing how things would turn out – which stunts would be performed, in what order, whether even bots could pull off such seemingly impossible feats. Without the suspense, she thought it was kind of lame.

Niv didn't seem to have that problem. In fact, he appeared to become *more* fascinated, not less, with each viewing. Soon Niv was the one actively urging Mina to join him and watch the recording yet again. She went along with it a few more days, just to please him. But then she realized Niv didn't really need her. When he watched the performance, the rest of the universe seemed to disappear for him. So the next time he asked she politely declined. He didn't seem to mind at all. Good, Mina thought. She didn't want to feel like she was abandoning him.

Soon after, Niv's behavior started to change.

One night, after dinner, when the family left the dining area and the bots moved in to clear the dishes, Niv turned around and joined the bots. This confused the bots, who interpreted his presence as a command to retreat. But as soon he stepped back and they came forward again, he again started trying to help them clean up. Again they retreated. Niv started crying. More like howling, really. Mina hadn't heard him make a noise like that since he'd been a toddler. What was the matter with him?

Goli responded immediately to the tantrum, hugging Niv, asking him what was wrong, caressing his forehead and hair in that way he found so soothing. He calmed down for a moment.

Then Niv pointed to the bots, who had now cleared away all the dishes, and started crying again. It took ten minutes for him to settle down.

After Mina pretended to go to bed, she inched to the top of the stairs and overheard her parents talking. Her mom had given Niv something called "me-la-tonin" to calm him down. Which probably explained why he'd started yawning a few minutes later. "Just to help him get a good night's sleep," Mom said. Mina didn't like the sound of it. That night her dreams were formless and troubling.

The next morning she knew that there was still something wrong with Niv. During breakfast, he sat next to one of the bots, instead of on the chair that had been assigned to him by the Randozimer. Amazingly, Mom and Dad didn't make a fuss.

Later, Niv refused to do his exercises for the day, and Mom and Dad let him get away with that too. *Maybe I should start throwing more tantrums*, Mina thought. Then she reminded herself that Niv really was a special case, and her worries for his wellbeing returned.

Sometime in the afternoon, as Mina was being tutored on basic genetics by JJ39, she heard her mom yelling. Her mom's voice was muffled, as though it were coming from outside.

"No!" her mom was saying. "Niv! Stand back! Don't do it!"

Mina raced out of her room, down the stairs, and followed the sound outside their home's main entrance, where Goli and Kouros stared, pale-faced, at the roof.

Niv was standing on the edge, waving his arms as though they were wings. He had a goofy grin on his face, and he seemed completely oblivious to his parent's cries or to how close he was to a twenty-foot drop.

"I've told the bots to get up there and bring him down safely, but they don't seem to be responding," Kouros muttered.

Of course not, Mina thought. Not if Niv didn't want them to.

"Let's activate code yellow," Goli said.

"But..." Kouros began.

He was silenced by Goli's eyes. "None of that will matter," she said. "We need to save our son."

Mina had heard stories about code yellow. It was an emergency signal that would draw a special taskforce to your location to help with whatever the problem was. After the emergency was resolved, there would be an investigation into what had caused the crisis. If the cause was found to be parental negligence, children might temporarily be separated from their families. Or parents from their children. All the findings would be fed into the Master Randomizer, which might determine there was a better match out there. Mina shuddered at the thought.

Goli was about to enter the code yellow command into her wrist band when the unthinkable happened.

Niv jumped.

Instead of falling to sure doom, Niv soared through the air, completed two somersaults, spun three hundred and sixty degrees, and landed perfectly on his feet.

Then he bowed.

It took Mina' stunned brain a few instants to recognize the move. It was from the theater piece. She was sure of it. Something one of the bots had done and had drawn much applause from the audience.

Mom and Dad ran over to him, crying with joy, and Mina joined them. It was only when they hugged Niv that they realized there was something odd about Niv's clothes. They seemed to be hiding something, something inflexible and artificial.

"What's this?" Goli asked, and they peeled back his sleeves, and unbuttoned his shirt.

"Looks like a new flexsuit," Kouros said.

He was right. Now Mina could see the suit's servo-pads and layers. Instead of putting it over his clothes, as he usually did, Niv had dressed himself over it. And the suit was different, too. It must be the one he had been working on. It was stronger and made of more connected parts. Obviously, it had given him the ability to perform the amazing jump. *It's like an exoskeleton*, Mina thought.

Then she understood.

"Look at the colors of his clothes, Mom."

Goli did, but didn't see anything unusual. "Just plain black," she said. "What about it?"

"Don't you see?" Mina said. Tears filled her eyes. It was all her fault. If she hadn't – if she hadn't – "He's dressed in black, and he has his new flexsuit under his clothes. He's pretending that it's part of his body! *He's pretending that he's one of the bots from the play!*"

Her parents' eyes bored down on her.

Before she could start her confession, Niv said, "She's right. I want to be more like the bots."

All eyes, including Mina's, now turned on him. Despite the astonishing jump he'd performed moments ago, his voice sounded confident and calm.

More surprising than that, he made eye contact with each of them, and then smiled.

....

Mina was grounded for the following week, spending most of the time in her room. She missed her tutor bots, her friends, and even Mom and Dad. Fortunately, once in a while, Niv would sneak in a surprise visit, cheering her up.

He wasn't like the old Niv, distant and unreadable. Ever since the jump he'd continued to change. He was becoming more expressive, articulate, and in general better at interacting with Mina and, she guessed, everyone else. And his obsession with bots – his wish to behave like them, his pretending that he *was* one – continued unabated as well. Mina didn't mind it. She thought it was weird, sure, that Niv would want to spend hours sitting inanimate in one location, or performing boring, repetitive tasks over and over. But it was his choice, and whenever he told her what he was up to, he seemed to be happy.

Apparently, the same couldn't be said of their parents. One day, Niv marched into Mina's room, severe worry lines etched into his forehead.

"That's it!" he said. "They're so freaked out that they've scheduled me for a psych eval. Yesterday I was out in the back garden, walking back and forth with the bot who was mowing the lawn, and Dad just stood there the whole time, studying me like I was some kind of insect. I'm sure that's when he decided."

"Uh... how long did you walk along with the bot?"

Niv narrowed his eyes. "Not that long. Maybe an hour or two. And I wasn't *just* walking with it. I was making the same noise and movements it was making."

O-kay, thought Nina, that's *normal*. But she didn't say anything.

"That's not the point," Niv complained, waving his hands in the air. "Didn't you hear me? They've scheduled me for a psych eval!"

"I'm sorry," Mina said. A psych eval would go into Niv's permanent medical records, and it meant a yearly check-up for the next ten years. Also, Mina had heard the test could hurt. In some cases, it could even make you pass out. She said, "Is there any way to get you out of it?" Her mind started racing, coming up with plans.

"No." Niv sighed. "But thanks for the thought."

"If you need me, I'll be right here," Mina said.

The next morning a white-haired psych engineer and his team of diagnostic bots arrived and subjected Niv to a battery of questions and tests. Mina knew because she had placed her millimetric recorder in Niv's study, where the testing was underway, and she used it spy in on the proceedings from her room.

Mina could tell that the psych engineer was confused by what he discovered. Several times he paused to repeat a question or rescan his readings. He had a befuddled look on his face. Finally, when he announced that the tests were done several hours later, a family meeting was called. Mina was given permission, after some pleading, to join in.

"It's quite remarkable," the psych engineer said. "My tests show that Niv's desire to emulate bot behavior really doesn't have anything to do with the bots themselves, and everything to do with repetition and predictability."

"Repetition and predictability?" asked Kouros.

"To use a metaphor, Niv's brain perceives his life as an ever-changing sea of unpredictability. It has been looking for a safe place, a refuge island that will provide stability amid the turmoil, regularity and order among the changes. The bot theater piece so engrossed him that he's imprinted on that, in a manner of speaking. Bots always perform the same tasks. Their world, unlike ours, is boring – orderly and predictable. They're not subject to the variations that Randomizers assign us. That's why Niv wants to be more like them. And the game of pretend is what's allowed him to come out of his shell and begin to integrate his emotions and thoughts into a single sense of self. His lower brain development is amazing."

Mom said, "So what's the treatment? He can't continue to pretend he's a bot the rest of his life."

"The cure may be simple indeed. I recommend that Niv no longer be subject to the Randomizer. In fact, you should create a set schedule for him that repeats every single day. Eventually you can wean him off of it, but for now it will provide the sense of structure that his brain needs in order to let go of the bot fantasies. How does that sound, Niv?"

Mina could barely contain her joy at the news. Niv's eyes widened with enthusiasm. "When can I start?"

Mom and Dad looked at one another. "We'll do that," Mom said. "Thank you for your help."

The engineer prepared to leave, but Mina stood in his way. "I have another question," she said. "Could the Randomizer have been the *cause* of Niv's condition in the first place? And what about other kids like him?"

The engineer's face turned cherry red. "Ah, yes, well," he said. "Those are, um, excellent questions. More research is called for, of course. But, based on what I've seen so far, there is a chance that you're right, young lady."

"I knew it! I knew it!" Mina cried out. "We'll all be happier without the Randomizer!"

"It would be premature for everyone to abandon it completely," the engineer chided. "But perhaps your parents may want to... relax its enforcement somewhat, as they see fit, of course. Think of it as a lot more wildcard days."

Then he and his bots left.

Mina gave Niv a quick kiss on the cheek and bolted up the stairs.

Niv knocked on her door a moment later. "Why the rush?" he asked.

"I'm going to take another look at Saldom's theorem of self-determination," Mina said. "Maybe I can figure out what's wrong with it." She thought about Niv's skills with programming bots, the way his mind craved order and logic. He was two years younger, and she was much better at math, but it was worth a shot. "Wanna help?" she asked.

"I'd love to," he said, sitting down beside her.

Jigsaw

Douglas Smith

Douglas Smith is an award-winning Canadian author whose work has appeared in thirty countries and twenty-five languages. His fiction includes the urban fantasy novel, The Wolf at the End of the World, *and the collections* Chimerascope, Impossibilia, *and* La Danse des Esprits. *His nonfiction guide for writers,* Playing the Short Game: How to Market & Sell Short Fiction, *has just been released. Douglas is a three-time winner of Canada's Aurora Award, and has been a finalist for the John W. Campbell Award, CBC's Bookies Award, Canada's juried Sunburst Award, and France's juried Prix Masterton and Prix Bob Morane. His website is www.smithwriter.com and he tweets at twitter.com/smithwritr.*

Still in shock, Cassie Morant slumped in the cockpit of the empty hopper, staring at the two viewplates before her.

In one, the planet Griphus, a blue, green and brown marble wrapped in belts of cloud, grew smaller. Except for the shape of its land masses, it could have been Earth.

But it wasn't. Griphus was an alien world, light-years from Sol System.

A world where nineteen of her shipmates were going to die.

And one of them was Davey.

On the other viewplate, the segmented, tubular hull of the orbiting Earth wormship, the *Johannes Kepler*, grew larger. Cassie tapped a command, and the ship's vector appeared, confirming her fears.

The ship's orbit was still decaying. She opened a comm-link.

"Hopper Two to the *Kepler*," she said. "Requesting docking clearance."

Silence. Then a male voice crackled over the speaker, echoing cold and metallic in the empty shuttle. "Acknowledged, Hopper Two. You are clear to dock, Segment Beta Four, Port Nine."

Cassie didn't recognize the voice, but that wasn't surprising. The *Kepler* held the population of a small city, and Cassie was something of a loner. But she had no trouble identifying the gruff rumble she heard next.

"Pilot of hopper, identify yourself. This is Captain Theodor."

Cassie took a breath. "Sir, this is Dr. Cassandra Morant, team geologist."

Pause. "Where's team leader Stockard?" Theodor asked.

Davey. "Sir, the rest of the surface team was captured by the indigenous tribe inhabiting the extraction site. The team is..." Cassie stopped, her throat constricting.

"Morant?"

She swallowed. "They're to be executed at sunrise."

Another pause.

"Did you get the berkelium?" Theodor finally asked.

Cassie fought her anger. Theodor wasn't being heartless. The team below was secondary to the thousands on the ship.

"Just a core sample, sir," she said. "But it confirms that the deposit's there."

Theodor swore. "Dr. Morant, our orbit decays in under twenty hours. Report immediately after docking to brief the command team." Theodor cut the link.

Cassie stared at the huge wormship, suddenly hating it, hating its strangeness. Humans would never build something like that.

Consisting of hundreds of torus rings strung along a central axis like donuts on a stick, the ship resembled a giant metallic worm. A dozen rings near the middle were slowly rotating, providing the few inhabited sections with an artificial gravity. The thousands of humans on the ship barely filled a fraction of it.

"This wasn't meant for us," she whispered. "We shouldn't be here."

Humans had just begun to explore their solar system when Max Bremer and his crew had found the wormships, three of them, outside the orbit of Pluto.

Abandoned? Lost? Or left to be found?

Found by the ever curious, barely-out-of-the-trees man-apes of Earth. Found with charted wormholes in Sol System. Found with still-only-partly translated, we-think-this-button-does-this libraries and databases, and we-can't-fix-it-so-it-better-never-break technology. Incredibly ancient, yet perfectly functioning Wormer technology.

Wormers. The inevitable name given to Earth's unknown alien benefactors.

Five years later, humanity was here, exploring the stars, riding like toddlers on the shoulders of the Wormers.

But Cassie no longer wanted to be here. She wished she were back on Earth, safely cocooned in her apartment with Vivaldi playing, lost in one of her jigsaw puzzles.

She shifted uncomfortably in the hopper seat. Like every Wormer chair, like the ship itself, it almost fit a human. But not quite.

It was like forcing a piece to fit in a jigsaw – it was always a cheat, and in the end, the picture was wrong. Humans didn't belong here. They had forced themselves into a place in the universe where they didn't fit. They had cheated—and they'd been caught.

And now they were being punished.

They faced a puzzle that threatened the entire ship. She'd had a chance to solve it on the planet.

And she'd failed.

Cassie hugged herself, trying to think. She was good at puzzles, but this one had a piece missing. She thought back over events since they'd arrived through the wormhole four days ago. The answer had to be there...

....

Four days ago, Cassie had sat in her quarters on the *Kepler*, hunched over a jigsaw puzzle covering her desk. The desk, like anything Wormer, favored unbroken flowing contours, the seat sweeping up to chair back wrapping around to desk surface. Viewplates on the curved walls showed telescopic shots of Griphus. The walls and ceiling glowed softly.

Lieutenant David Stockard, Davey to Cassie, lay on her bunk watching her.

"Don't you get tired of jigsaws?" he asked.

She shrugged. "They relax me. It's my form of meditation. Besides, I'm doing my homework."

Davey rolled off the bunk. She watched him walk over, wondering again what had brought them together. If she could call what they had being "together" – sometimes friendship, sometimes romance, sometimes not talking to each other.

They seemed a case study in "opposites attract." She was a scientist, and Davey was military. She was dark, short and slim, while he was fair, tall and broad. She preferred spending her time quietly, reading, listening to classical music and doing jigsaw puzzles. Davey always had to be active.

But the biggest difference lay in their attitudes to the Wormers. Davey fervently believed that the alien ships were meant to be found by humans, that the Universe wanted them to explore the stars.

To Cassie, the Universe wasn't telling them everything it knew. She felt that they didn't understand Wormer technology enough to be risking thousands of lives.

He looked at the puzzle. "Homework?"

"I printed a Mercator projection of topographic scans of Griphus onto plas-per, and the computer cut it into a jigsaw."

The puzzle showed the planet's two major continents, which Dr. Xu, head geologist and Cassie's supervisor, had dubbed Manus and Pugnus. Hand and fist. The western continent, Pugnus, resembled a clenched fist and forearm, punching across an ocean at Manus, which resembled an open hand, fingers and thumb curled ready to catch the fist. Colored dots, each numbered, speckled the map.

"What are the dots?" Davey asked.

"Our shopping list. Deposits of rare minerals. That is, if you believe Wormer archives and Wormer scanners."

"Cassie, let's not start," Davey said.

"Davey, these ships are at least ten thousand years old."

"With self-healing nanotech-" Davey replied.

"That we don't understand."

"Cassie..." Davey sighed.

She glared, then folded her arms. "Fine."

Davey checked the time on his per-comm unit. "Speaking of homework, Trask wants surface team rescue procedures by oh-eight-hundred. Gotta go." He kissed Cassie and left.

Cassie bit back a comment that this was a scientific, not a military, expedition. The likely need for Trask's "procedures" was low in her opinion.

She would soon change her mind.

An hour later, Cassie was walking along the busy outer corridor of the ring segment assigned to the science team. Suddenly, the ship shuddered, throwing Cassie and others against one curving wall.

The ship lurched again, and the light from the glowing walls blinked out. People screamed. Cassie stumbled and fell. And kept falling, waiting for the impact against the floor that never came, until she realized what had happened.

The ring had stopped rotating. They'd lost artificial gravity."

She floated in darkness for maybe thirty minutes, bumping into others, surrounded by whispers, shouts, and sobbing. Suddenly, the lights flicked back on. Cassie felt gravity returning like an invisible hand tugging at her guts, followed by a sudden heaviness in her limbs. Hitting the floor, she rolled then rose on shaky legs. People stood dazed, looking like scattered pieces in a jigsaw that before had been a coherent picture of normality.

What had happened?

The intercom broke through the rising babble of conversations. "The following personnel report immediately to port six, segment beta four for surface team detail." Twenty names followed. One was Davey's.

One was hers. What was going on?

An hour later, her questions still unanswered, she and nineteen others sat in a hopper as it left the *Kepler*. Hoppers were smaller Wormer craft used for ship-to-surface trips and exploration. With a tubular hull, a spherical cockpit at the head, and six jointed legs allowing them to rest level on any terrain, they resembled grasshoppers.

The team faced each other in two rows of seats in the main cabin. Cassie only knew two others besides Davey. Manfred Mubuto, balding, dark and round, was their xeno-anthropologist. Liz Branson, with features as sharp as her sarcasm, was their linguist. Four were marines. But the rest, over half the team, were mining techs. Why?

Davey addressed them. She'd never seen him so serious.

"The *Kepler's* power loss resulted from the primary fuel cell being purged. Engineering is working to swap cells, but that requires translating untested Wormer procedures. We may need to replenish the cell, which means extracting berkelium from Griphus for processing."

That was why she was on the team, Cassie realized. Berkelium, a rare trans-uranium element, was the favored Wormer energy source. It had never been found on Earth, only manufactured. Her analysis of Griphus had shown possible deposits.

"Like every planet found via the wormholes," Davey said, "Griphus is incredibly Earthlike: atmosphere, gravity, humanoid populations-"

"We purged a fuel cell?" Liz interrupted. "Who screwed up?"

Davey reddened. "That's not relevant-"

"Operator error, I hear," Manfred said. "A tech misread Wormer symbols on a panel, punched an incorrect sequence-"

Liz swore. "I knew it! We're like kids trying to fly Daddy's flitter."

Cassie started to agree, but Davey cut them off.

"We've no time for rumors," he snapped, looking at Cassie, Liz, and Manfred. "Our orbit decays in three days. I remind you that this team's under my command – including science personnel."

Manfred nodded. Liz glared but said nothing.

Davey tapped the computer pad on his seat. A holo of Griphus appeared. "Dr. Morant, please locate the berkelium."

Cassie almost laughed at being called "Dr. Morant" by Davey, but then she caught his look. She tapped some keys, and two red dots blinked onto the holo, one in the ocean midway between Pugnus and Manus, and another offshore of Manus. The second site was circled.

"Wormer sensors show two sites. I've circled my recommendation," Cassie said.

"Why not the other site?" a mining tech asked.

A network of lines appeared, making the planet's surface look like a huge jigsaw puzzle.

"As on Earth," Cassie said, "the lithosphere or planetary crust of Griphus is broken into tectonic plates, irregular sections ranging from maybe fifteen kilometers thick under oceans to a hundred under continents. This shows the plate pattern on Griphus.

"Plates float on the denser, semimolten asthenosphere, the upper part of the mantle. At 'transform' boundaries, they slide along each other, as in the San Andreas Fault on Earth. At 'convergent' boundaries, they collide, forming mountains such as the Himalayas."

A line splitting the ocean between Pugnus and Manus glowed yellow. The line also ran through the other berkelium site.

"But at 'divergent' boundaries," Cassie continued, "such as this mid-oceanic trench, magma pushes up from the mantle, creating new crust, forcing the plates apart. The other site is deep in the trench, below our sub's crush depth."

Davey nodded. "So we hit the site offshore of Manus. Any indigenous population along that coast?"

"Yes," Manfred said. "From orbital pictures, they appear tribal, agrarian, definitely preindustrial. Some large stone structures and primitive metallurgy."

"Then defending ourselves shouldn't be a problem." Davey

patted the stinger on his belt. The Wormer weapon was nonlethal, temporarily disrupting voluntary muscular control.

"Could we try talking before we shoot them?" Liz said.

Davey just smiled. "Which brings us to communication, Dr. Branson."

Liz sighed. "Wormer translator units need a critical mass of vocabulary, syntax, and context samples to learn a language. Given the time we have, I doubt they'll help much."

"With any luck, we won't need them," Davey said. "We'll locate the deposit, send in the mining submersible, and be out before they know we're there."

Looking around her, Cassie guessed that no one felt lucky.

The hopper landed on the coast near the offshore deposit. The team wore light body suits and breathing masks to prevent ingesting anything alien to human immune systems.

Cassie stepped onto a broad beach of gray sand lapped by an ocean too green for Earth, under a sky a touch too blue. The beach ran up to a forest of trees whose black trunks rose twenty meters into the air. Long silver leaves studded each trunk, glinting like sword blades in the sun. She heard a high keening that might have been birds or wind in the strange trees.

Southwards, the beach ran into the distance. But to the north, it ended at a cliff rising up to a low mesa. Cassie walked over to Davey, who was overseeing the marines unloading the submersible and drilling equipment.

"Cool, eh?" he said, looking around them.

She pointed at the mesa. "That's cooler to a rock nut."

He looked up the beach. "Okay. But keep your per-comm on."

Cassie nodded and set out. The cliff was an hour's walk. Cassie didn't mind, enjoying the exercise and strange surroundings. She took pictures of the rock strata and climbed to get samples at different levels. Then she walked back.

They captured Cassie just as she was wondering why the hopper seemed deserted. The natives appeared so quickly and silently, they seemed to rise from the sand. Cassie counted about forty of them, all remarkably humanlike, but taller, with larger eyes, longer noses, and greenish skin. All were male, bare chested, wearing skirts woven from sword-blade tree leaves, and leather sandals.

They led Cassie to stand before two women. One was dressed as the men were, but with a headdress of a coppery metal. The other was older and wore a cape of cloth and feathers. Her head was bare, her hair long and white. Beside them, pale but unharmed, stood Liz Branson, flanked by two warriors.

The older woman spoke to Liz in a sing-song melodic language. Cassie saw that the linguist wore a translator earplug. Liz sat down, motioning Cassie to do the same. The male warriors sat circling them. The two native women remained standing.

Cassie realized she was trembling. "What happened?"

Liz grimaced. "We've stepped in it big time. The Chadorans, our captors, believe a sacred object called 'the third one' lies underwater here. Only a priestess may enter these waters. When our techs launched the sub, the natives ambushed us from the trees with blowguns. They grabbed the techs when they surfaced."

"Where's Davey?" Cassie asked, then added, "...and everyone?"

"Taken somewhere. They seemed okay."

"Why not you, too?"

"The tribe's matriarchal," Liz said. "The old woman is Cha-kay, their chief. The younger one, Pre-nah, is their priestess. Because I'm female and knew their language, Cha-kay assumed I was our leader. But I said you were."

"You what?" Cassie cried.

"Cassie, we need someone they'll respect," Liz said, her face grim. "That means a female who didn't defile the site. That means you."

"Liz, I'm not – wait, how can you talk to them?"

Liz frowned. "It's weird. The translator produced understandable versions within minutes, pulling from Wormer archives of other worlds. That implies all those languages share the same roots. The Wormers may have seeded all these worlds."

Cassie didn't care. "What can I do?"

"Convince Cha-kay to let us go."

"How?" Cassie asked.

"She wants to show you something. It's some sort of test."

"And if I fail?"

Liz handed Cassie the translator. "Then they'll kill us."

Cassie swallowed. "I won't let that happen."

They led Cassie to a long boat with a curving prow powered by a dozen rowers. Cha-kay rode in a chair near the stern, Cassie at her feet. Pre-nah and six warriors stood beside them.

They traveled up a winding river through dense jungle. Conversation was sparse, but sufficient to convince Cassie that the translator unit worked. After three hours, they landed at a clearing. Cassie climbed out, happy to move and stretch. She blinked.

Blue cubes, ranging from one to ten meters high, filled the clearing. They were hewn from stone and painted. The party walked past the cubes to a path that switch-backed up a low mountain. They began to climb.

Cassie groaned but said nothing, since the aged Cha-kay didn't seem bothered by the climb. As they went, Cassie noticed smaller cubes beside the path.

Night had fallen when they reached the top and stepped onto a tabletop of rock about eighty meters across. Cassie gasped.

A huge cube, at least fifty meters on each side, nearly filled the plateau. It was blue. It was glowing.

And it was hovering a meter off the ground.

Cha-kay led Cassie to it, and Cassie received another shock. On its smooth sides, Cassie saw familiar symbols.

The artifact, whatever its purpose, was Wormer.

Cha-kay prostrated herself, telling Cassie to do the same. As Cassie did so, she peeked underneath the cube. A column of pulsating blue light shone from a crevice to touch the base of the artifact at its center. Reaching down to her belt, Cassie activated her scanner. She'd check the readings later.

Rising, Cha-kay indicated a large diagram on the artifact. In it, a cube, a sphere, and a tetrahedron formed points of an equilateral triangle.

"It is a map. We are here," Cha-kay said, pointing to the cube. "The gods left three artifacts, but hid one. The third will appear when the gods return and lay their hands on the other two." Then, pointing to the outline of a hand on the artifact, Cha-kay looked at Cassie.

"Touch," she said.

With a sudden chill, Cassie understood. The Chadorans believed that the humans were the Wormers, finally returning.

This was the test on which the lives of her shipmates, of the entire ship, depended.

Reaching out a trembling hand, Cassie felt resistance from some invisible barrier and a warm tingling, then her hand slipped through onto the outline on the artifact.

Nothing happened.

Murmurs grew behind her. Feeling sick, Cassie looked at Cha-kay. To her surprise, the old woman smiled.

"Perhaps," Cha-kay said, "it rises even now."

Cassie understood. Cha-kay hoped to find that the third artifact had emerged from the sea when they returned to the beach. Cassie didn't share her hope.

They spent the night there. Pretending to sleep, Cassie checked her scanner readings. They confirmed her suspicions. The column of light showed berkelium emissions. The artifact was connected to a deposit as an energy source.

The next day, a similar journey brought them to the second artifact, located on another flat mountain peak. The only difference was the artifact itself, a glowing red tetrahedron at least fifty meters high. Cassie again saw a column of light underneath and detected berkelium. She touched the artifact, again with no apparent effect, and the party began the trip back.

Cha-kay seemed to have grown genuinely fond of Cassie. She told Cassie how her people found the artifacts generations ago, eventually realizing that the drawing was a map. They learned to measure distances and angles, and determined that the third artifact lay in the coastal waters. Priestesses had dived there for centuries but found nothing. Still they believed.

Cassie did some calculations and found the Chadoran estimate remarkably accurate. Still, she wondered why the Wormers would locate two artifacts in identical settings on mountain plateaus, yet place the third underwater. Perhaps the third location had subsided over the years. But her scans showed no sunken mountains off the coast.

Cassie enjoyed Cha-kay's company, but as they neared the coast, her fear grew. Cha-kay fell silent as well. As the boat reached the beach, they stood at the railing, clasping each other's hand, scanning the waters for the third artifact.

Nothing.

Cries arose among the warriors. Pre-nah approached Cha-kay. "The strangers are false gods," the priestess said. "They must die."

Cha-kay stared across the ocean. Finally, she nodded. Cassie's legs grew weak as two warriors moved toward her.

Cha-kay raised her hand. "No. This one goes free. She did not defile the sacred place."

Pre-nah didn't look pleased, but she bowed her head.

They landed, and Cha-kay walked with Cassie to the hopper.

"When?" Cassie asked, her voice breaking.

"At sunrise, child," Cha-kay said. "I am sorry."

Cassie boarded the hopper. She engaged the auto-launch, then slumped in her seat as the planet and her hopes grew smaller.

....

After docking, Cassie went immediately to the briefing room as Captain Theodor had ordered. She quickly took a seat in one of a dozen Wormer chairs around a holo display unit. Dr. Xu gave her a worried smile. Commander Trask glared.

Theodor cleared his throat, a rumble that brought everyone's gaze to his stocky form.

"I'll be brief. Our orbit collapses in nineteen hours. Attempts to swap fuel cells were unsuccessful. The team sent to extract the berkelium has been captured and faces execution. Only Dr.

Morant escaped."

Everyone looked at Cassie. All she could think of was how she'd failed.

Theodor continued. "Dr. Morant will summarize events on the planet. Then I need ideas."

Cassie told her story, then answered questions, mostly dealing with the artifacts. Will Epps, their expert on Wormer texts and writing, after analyzing her scans, agreed that the artifacts were Wormer.

The team began reviewing and discarding proposals. Finally, Theodor made his decision. A platoon of marines would drop outside the Chadoran city. Three squads would act as a diversion, drawing warriors from the city, while one squad slipped in for a search and rescue. One hour later, a hopper would drop two mining subs at the berkelium site.

"Sir, the priestess dives there daily," Cassie said. "When they see our subs, they'll kill the team."

"That's why I'm giving the rescue squads an hour head start," Theodor replied. "It's not much, but our priority is to replenish our fuel before our orbit decays. I can't delay the berkelium extraction any longer."

Cassie slumped in her seat. Davey, Liz, the others. They were all going to die.

Trask stood. "If Dr. Morant could provide a topographical display of the area, I'll outline the attack plan."

Cassie tapped some keys, and the planetary view of Griphus appeared, including the jigsaw pattern of tectonic plates.

A jigsaw puzzle. Why couldn't this be that simple?

"Zoom in to the landing site," Trask said.

Freezing the rotation over Pugnus and Manus, Cassie started to zoom in, then stopped, staring at the display.

No. It was too wild. But maybe...

She began tapping furiously, and calculations streamed across the holo.

"What the hell's going on?" Trask asked.

Theodor frowned. "Dr. Morant?"

Cassie looked at her results. Incredible. It fit. It all fit. But the time span...

"Dr. Morant!" Theodor barked.

Cassie's head jerked up. Everyone was staring. Her idea was wild, but it fit. And she liked things that fit.

"Captain," Cassie said, "what if we proved to the Chadorans that the deposit site is *not* sacred?"

Theodor frowned. "Discredit their religion? I don't —"

"No," Cassie said. "I mean, prove that it isn't sacred because..." She stopped. What if she was wrong? But it was Davey and the team's only chance.

"...because the third artifact isn't there," she finished.

Trask snorted. "Then why will they kill to protect the site?"

"Because they *think* it's there, based entirely on the diagrams on the artifacts."

"And you think those diagrams are wrong?" Theodor asked, but his voice held none of Trask's derision.

"I think they were correct once," she said. "But not any more."

"So where's the artifact?" Theodor asked.

Cassie's hand trembled as she tapped more keys. Two green lights appeared inland on the western coast of Manus followed by a red light just off the same coast, forming the triangular pattern diagrammed on the artifacts.

"The two green lights are the known artifacts. The red light is both the supposed underwater location of the third and our targeted berkelium site."

She swallowed.

"And this, I believe, is the actual location of the third artifact." She tapped a final key. A third green light appeared.

Everyone started talking at once. Theodor silenced them with a wave of his hand. He stared at the display.

On the eastern coast of Pugnus, on a separate continent and an entire ocean away from the underwater site, blinked the third green light.

Theodor turned to Cassie. "Explain."

"It involves tectonic plate theory-" she began.

"I know the theory. What's the relevance?"

Cassie tapped a key. The midoceanic trench between Pugnus and Manus glowed yellow.

"That trench is a divergent boundary," Cassie said, "where new crust is being formed, pushing Manus and Pugnus further apart every year. But that also means that sometime in the past, they looked like this." The plates began to shift. The two large continents moved closer until the fist of Pugnus slipped into the open hand of Manus like a piece in a puzzle. Someone gasped, as the third green light on Pugnus aligned itself over the red light offshore of Manus.

Theodor nodded. "You're saying the Wormers originally placed the three artifacts as the diagrams show, but the missing one moved relative to the other two as the continents separated."

Xu shook his head. "Cassie..."

Cassie sighed. "I know. The time frame is...difficult to believe."

"How old are the artifacts if your theory is true?" Theodor asked.

Xu answered. "At least as old as the core sample from the deposit site, which formed as the trench started to spread. Cassie, what was the isotopic clock dating on the sample?"

Cassie hesitated. "Its age was thirty, uh..." She swallowed. "...million years."

The eruption of exclamations made Cassie want to slink from the room. Theodor again waved for silence.

In desperation, Cassie turned to Will Epps. "We know that these ships are at least ten thousand years old. But couldn't they be much older?"

Several people squirmed. Their situation was bad enough without being reminded that they were relying on alien technology at least a hundred centuries old.

Will shrugged. "There's so much self-healing nano-tech, we can't estimate their age accurately."

"So any Wormer technology could be much older as well,

right?" Cassie asked.

"But thirty million years..." Xu shook his head, as did others. Cassie was losing them.

She turned to Theodor.

"Captain, it all fits. It explains why the Chadorans have never found the artifact. Why our sub didn't see it. Why Wormers placed two artifacts on mountains, but supposedly put the third underwater. They didn't. They put it on land too."

"Can't we scan for the artifact?" Trask said.

"The other two don't show on scanners," Epps said. "They're shielded somehow."

"So the third artifact *could* be where the Chadorans say it is," Trask replied.

Cassie sat back, feeling defeated. Then something struck her.

"Both artifacts I saw are located over berkelium deposits, yet neither site appears on the mineral scans. The artifacts shield the berkelium too."

"So?" Theodor said.

"We detected berkelium at the underwater site. That means nothing's shielding it. The third artifact isn't there."

Trask started to protest, but Theodor raised a hand. "I agree with Dr. Morant. It fits." He stood up. "Cassie, I'll give you the same lead time. Take a hopper down now."

Cassie was already sprinting for the door.

....

On a mountain plateau, across an ocean from where they had first landed on Griphus, Cassie and Davey stood, arms around each other's waist.

"So you saved me, the team, the entire ship," Davey said, "and made one of the most important discoveries in history. Not a bad day."

Cassie grinned. "Actually, the toughest part was convincing Cha-kay to fly in the hopper. Now she wants a world tour."

Beside them, happiness lighting her face, Cha-kay gazed at a huge glowing yellow sphere hovering above the ground.

The third artifact.

With one difference. A beam of energy shone from the sphere into the sky. The beam had begun the moment Cassie had touched the sphere.

Cassie's per-comm beeped. It was Theodor. "Dr. Morant, all three artifacts now appear on scanners, all beaming to the same point in space –"

"A new wormhole," Cassie interrupted.

Pause. "How'd you know?" Theodor asked.

Cassie grinned. "I'm good at puzzles, sir."

"Hmm. Anyway, Earth's sending a second wormship. We'll all have the option of returning home or exploring the wormhole. Once again, good work, Morant." Theodor signed off.

"You didn't mention your theory," Davey said.

"That the wormhole leads to the Wormers' home world? Just a hunch."

"Explain it to me then."

Cassie nodded at the sphere. "I think the artifacts were a puzzle – and the wormhole the prize."

"For us or the Chadorans?"

"For us. Another bread crumb in the trail the Wormers left us." She shrugged and laughed. "It just fits."

Davey nodded. "So what about you? Back to Earth or through the wormhole?"

"Wormhole," she said.

He raised an eyebrow. "Okay, that surprised me."

Cassie grinned. "Hey, if the Wormers liked puzzles, they couldn't have been that bad." She stared at the artifact. "Besides, we solved their puzzle, saved ourselves, became heroes to the Chadorans..." Her eyes followed the beam up towards the heavens.

"Maybe we fit out here after all," she said softly.

When Mama Went to Dumfries

Wendy Lambert

Wendy Lambert writes fantasy and science fiction and is a graduate of the 2013 Odyssey Writing Workshop. Her stories appear in Necrology Shorts *and in the prose and poetry collection,* In the Shimmering. *She works as a school librarian and lives in Utah with her husband, children, and a menagerie of pets. Too often, she reminisces of past trips and daydreams of future adventures to far away places hoping to get lost in museums or ancient ruins.*

Crabby old Constable Duncan came during supper to arrest papa. Papa had ordered Kenna to stop poking at the last chunk of tattie in her stew and eat it. And it was as she'd feared. As soon as Kenna had swallowed that tattie, Papa had sent her straight up to bed. It wasn't fair that Rory got to stay up. At thirteen, Rory was just three years older and a mere head taller than she. But when Papa threatened to give her a skelping, Kenna had scurried up the worn ladder, blackened by scores of dirty handprints.

This past fortnight, she'd flung herself across the tattered and patched quilt and rolled the length and width of the bed as if she were a prized swine wallowing in a cool bath of mud. A swine without all its pen mates. Mama had taken her sisters along with baby brother to visit Auntie in Dumfries. No elbows to disturb her blissful sleep. Yet, Kenna could not be expected to sleep when words pricklier than a hill of thistle were being swapped below.

"I'm not saying I wished for him to go, but Finlay was a bum.

He was always wandering away leaving my sheep to fend for themselves. Did ya check the Black Bull?" Papa asked.

"Do ya think I'd have come an hour's horse ride if Finlay was to be found in a pub?"

"Maybe he's at St. Andrews Kirk, repenting of his ways?"

"Do na be acting this way, Nevin. Ya know why I'm suspicious."

"Guthrie's death was an accident. My name was cleared."

"There's still a cloud of doubt in the minds of the villagers –"

"It was an accident . . . I got a new machine –"

"Ya refused to respond to the birds I sent. And now ye're not answering straight. It makes ya seem guilty. Finlay's missus already thinks ya've done him in – that your sheep are grazing over his grave."

"My papa dinna do anything!" Rory yelled.

Papa waved Rory to silence and stroked his moustaches the way he did when the gears were working in his head. "I've lost three sheep these past few days to a wolf or something. Perhaps it ate Finlay too."

"Wolves haven't been seen in these parts for more than a decade."

"Well, something's getting them. Quite unnaturally, too. Flesh and innards are picked clean. All that's left is a pile of wool and cracked bone."

"So that's why the herd's within a stone's throw of your house. Ya should've asked for help hunting the beast."

Papa scoffed. "The other farmers thought I was off my head and would na help. It'll surely come hunting again tonight. Old Rufus is guarding them–"

"Ye're dodging the issue. I've come about Finlay. His missus says he'd been herding yer sheep at the top of the hill. She'd brought him a basket of supper. Found the sheep and his crook, but no Finlay. That was four days ago."

"He deserted his post, leaving my sheep to be eaten. If anything, I should be bringing charges against him. I've six mouths to feed. Each sheep gone is food out of their mouths. I'm still paying for my new dipping and shearing machine too."

"No one's going to have sympathy for ya when Finlay's gone missing . . . especially when five men heard yer threatening words not more than a month back."

"I'd sent him to Moffat to fetch supplies. Hours later, I found him emptying my purse at the Black Bull. It was my money, ya see? I dinna mean no harm. Hired him back, dinna I?"

"Finlay's missus says ya lured him back to kill him."

Papa jumped out of his chair, sending it crashing to the floor. His face matched the color of his moustaches and thin hair. "He apologized and paid me back. Finlay was a worthless blootered, it's true, but I dinna kill him!" Constable Duncan's glare burned hot enough to send the kettle whistling. Papa set his chair right, but not before looking up at her. "Kenna . . . to bed."

Kenna dashed to the wardrobe, threw off her dress, and shimmied into her nightgown. She gave no thought to braiding her mass of tangled strawberry-colored locks. Just because she could, Kenna settled square in the middle of the bed and spread her arms and legs wide under the cover of the quilts. The drifting sounds of heated conversation and the bleat of sheep filled her head. No matter how tight she squeezed her eyes, sleep would not come.

Rising to her knees, Kenna felt the wall above the bed for the lump of cork and tugged at it. As she always did, she smelled the fruitiness of it before clenching it in her palm and peering out the cork-sized hole in the wall. Constable Duncan had argued with Papa so long, the sun had sunk completely behind the hills. The constable's horse whinnied as it stood tethered to the post just outside the front garden.

The day's rain choked the hills with a thick fog. A short distance beyond the front garden, the sheep stood, huddled together beside the barn, circled by Rufus. Kenna couldn't see the sheep, but the yellow glow of Rufus's eyes lit the fog, making his progress round the sheep easy to track. The squeak and metallic thump of Rufus's paws could be heard between the shouts. He'd need a good oiling in the morning.

"He dinna do anything. Ya can't take him!" Rory shouted.

Kenna poked the cork back into its hole and scrambled to the top of the ladder. She flattened herself against the floor and peered between the top rungs. Papa's hands were in front of him, shackled. "Is this really necessary? I said I'd come peacefully."

"Can't take any chances. If Finlay turns up or I do na find his body by sunset tomorrow, I'll let ya go." Constable Duncan gripped Papa's coat and spread it round his shoulders. He reached for the door.

"Ya take care of Kenna," Papa said to Rory. "Send a bird to your Mama," Papa said. "Do ya understand me, boy?"

Rory nodded.

Rufus's bark split the night. The chorus of sheep cries joined the din of barking. Something had come for the sheep.

"My sheep," Papa said. "Let me go."

"Ya stay put. I'll see what's out there." Constable Duncan pulled his electro-gun from his holster and slammed the door behind him.

Kenna near slid down the ladder. Rory had Papa's shotgun in hand and took a step behind him.

"Stay here, Kenna." Papa raised his bound wrists and pointed a finger at her. Rory followed after Papa.

Kenna pressed her face up against the window. Papa and Rory raced through the garden of cabbages, turnips and tatties, carrots, and vines laden with peapods, and disappeared into the mists.

Rufus barked and growled. Bursts of light rippled through the fog, illuminating nothing. Constable Duncan's voice and strange high-pitched wails echoed about. The horse tied to the post whinnied and stamped its feet nervously. The sheep bleated. The shotgun cracked again, and again, and again. Then silence.

Kenna's breath fogged the glass. She wiped it away with her sleeve. Where were they? She opened the door and watched the swirling fog.

"Papa?"

When he didn't answer, she tore into the night. There they stood, at the edge of the sheep pen, just staring as if struck. "Papa?" She ran to Papa and wiggled her way between his shackled wrists. Papa lifted her up and she curled her head into the crook of his neck.

Papa carried her to the house. He clung to Kenna for many minutes, pacing back and forth upon the creaking floorboards. Then, at last, set her down.

"When I tell ya to stay put, ya stay . . . do ya understand?" His angry words clashed with his eyes as wide as the full moon and cheeks as pale as wool.

"Aye, Papa." Kenna scurried to the table and cleared away the plates. She set them into the basin and lifted the kettle of hot water hanging over the neglected fire and poured its contents into the basin. Kenna rushed to the fire and tossed two logs onto the flames. Not even Rory chided her when she near smothered the last of the flame.

"What was that?" Rory asked. "It took four shots to bring it down . . . it . . . it ate him."

"Constable Duncan?" Kenna fingered a plate in the basin. "What ate him?"

Rory shrugged. "Do na know. Stood on two legs and was taller than a man. It tossed balls like . . . like lightning. Its skin was black and shiny and it's . . . mouth . . . ." He shivered and rubbed his arms. "Its mouth opened wide like a snake. It ate Constable Duncan, and then there was a grinding sound – like one of those songbirds makes with its gullet of rocks."

"Was it a gorilla?"

Rory laughed. "No. They live in jungles or zoos or somewhere. Do na eat sheep and do na eat constables. Or at least I do na think so. . . . It took a bite of Rufus too."

"Is he okay?"

Rory shook his head.

Kenna's eyes flooded with tears.

Papa picked up the lamp and opened the door. He shook like leaves quaking in the autumn winds. Kenna had never seen such fear take hold of Papa, and it turned her own curiosity cold. Though she stood near the fire, a shiver raced up her spine.

"Rory, come with me," Papa said. "Kenna, ya stay put."

Papa held the lantern and Rory gripped the gun. They disappeared into the night. Upon the mantel, Mama's clock ticked, marking each agonizing second. Footsteps at last thudded against the hard earthen path to the house.

The chain linking Papa's handcuffs dangled free, the cuffs still clamped around his wrists like too-tight bracelets. Papa held the lamp in one hand and in the other, a bulging burlap sack knotted closed at the top. Kenna flung the door open, staring at the sack Papa set beside the granite step.

"What's in the bag?" Kenna asked.

"Never ya mind . . . to bed with ya both."

Kenna followed Rory up the ladder, glancing back to see Papa retrieve a bottle from the back of Mama's cupboard. His hands shook as he gripped the bottle and gulped down the amber liquid.

"What's in the bag?" Kenna whispered to Rory.

"Ya do na wanna know." Rory stretched out his suspenders, rolling them from his shoulders and disappearing behind a ragged blanket drawn across a rope and held by clothes pins.

"But I do wanna know."

Rory's boots thumped to the floor.

"Rory."

He threw back the blanket, standing before her in his nightshirt. His eyes were wild in the half-light. "It'll just scare ya."

"I'm already scared," she whispered.

Rory gave a thoughtful nod. "It's what's left of Constable Duncan."

Kenna gasped and covered her mouth.

"Bones, all broken and stripped of flesh. And bits of clothes and boots . . . even his coat buttons."

"What's Papa going to do now?"

"I do na know."

Kenna crept from her bed to peer at Papa. He sat at the table, one hand propping his head up, the other held the bottle. He raised it to his lips, drinking courage.

....

The sheep bleated and chickens squawked at not getting their breakfast at dawn. Even the cow bellowed, protesting the fullness of her udder. Kenna opened her eyes. Waves of morning light leaked from the two windows below, filling the loft with dim light.

Kenna bolted upright. Rory was gone. She scrambled down the ladder. Papa's bottle and chair were empty. She threw the door open. The sack and horse were gone too.

Slipping her feet into mud-spattered boots, Kenna ran past the cabbages and carrots and vines laden with peapods, slowing as she approached the farmyard. A gelatinous sheen of yellow-green puddled over the ground. Kenna knelt, catching her reflection in its surface. She reached out a finger.

"Do na be touching that!" Rory said.

Kenna jerked her finger away and looked up at Rory holding a feed bucket. She scooted away from the puddle.

"It's the creature," Rory said. "It turned to liquid when I shot it dead."

"Why'd it eat our sheep and Constable Duncan?"

"I suppose it was hungry."

"Where's Papa?"

Rory shoved the feed bucket towards her. "Ya ask too many questions. Go feed the chickens. Papa will be back soon."

"Where'd he go?"

"Had to take Constable Duncan's remains to town, dinna he? Now ya get to feeding the chickens or I'll skelp ya till ya can't sit on yer bum for a week."

"Ya ain't Papa or Mama. Ya can't touch me."

Rory smacked her. Kenna recoiled, dropping the feed bucket and holding her stinging cheek and fighting back tears.

"I'm in charge while Papa is gone. He told us to feed the animals and then lock ourselves inside . . ." Rory paused and glanced over his shoulder and then back at Kenna. "This morning we found another set of footprints and another sheep's bones."

Kenna bit her lip and knelt beside the spilled feed, scooping it back into the bucket, refusing to look at him. She marched across the yard, squeezing between sheep, only pausing at Rufus. She swept her fingers across the smooth bronze of his face.

"Oh, Rufus."

His midsection exposed, the gears and pistons mangled, riddled with teeth marks. She kissed the nose of her dog and hurried towards the chickens before Rory could take another swipe at her.

....

Rufus littered the table. Rory pounded a twisted gear flat causing the whole table to bounce. Kenna held the lamp close so Rory could inspect the gear. He reached in and clicked the gear into place.

Rory tapped the mechanism inside. It swung back and forth, back and forth. Cogs turned. Kenna exhaled and chewed at her fingernails. Rory fixed another crudely pounded piece of metal over the ragged hole of the belly. Rufus's eyes flickered then blazed yellow.

"Help me lift him," Rory said.

Kenna circled her arms around the chest and head of the clockwork dog. Together they lifted and set Rufus on the floor. A paw twitched. Then the others. The dog's mouth worked, and he whimpered.

Kenna knelt beside Rufus, patting his head. "It's okay, boy. Rory fixed ya up good." Rufus rolled over and with a thump and grate, sat up. "Good boy, Rufus. Good boy." Kenna wrapped her arms around the dog and kissed him soundly. The dog wagged his tail.

Tap. Tap. Tap. Something rapped on the door. Rufus turned with a growl, knocking a chair to the floor with his tail. Rory held a finger to his lips and tip-toed to the window craning his head to see who or what was at the door. His face flooded with relief. He unlatched the lock and opened the door. The flutter of wings rustled and squeaked as the copper messenger pigeon flew round the kitchen, spiraling down to the table. It landed with a click of its tiny claws on the table and folded its wings. It hopped to the edge of the table and cooed till Rory picked it up.

He pressed the button, and a compartment opened releasing a

small scroll of paper.

"What's it say?" Kenna grabbed for it.

Rory swatted her hands away. "Give me a minute." He angled it towards the light. "It's to Mama." His hands fell to his sides, his face grew ashen.

"What's it say?"

"Papa's been arrested. They think he killed Finlay and Constable Duncan. Deputy Clacher's taking him to Glasgow on the first train in the morning . . . to wait trial for murder."

"Papa dinna murder anybody."

"They do na know that, do they? They was already suspecting him 'cause of Guthrie and Finlay, and he shows up with a bag of Constable Duncan's bones."

"I know what to do," Kenna said.

"What?" Rory asked.

"We need to catch one of those creatures to prove Papa didn't do it."

....

The wide footprints disappeared near the ravine. At its edge where the earth sloped into a sea of moss-covered trees and boulders, lumps of grass and heather cradled bones and fur of small animals. Kenna knew the eaten animals by the color of their fur entwined in crushed bones: the gray of a squirrel, the black and white of a raccoon, and the red of a fox.

She stared long and hard at the largest pile. These were not the bones of squirrels, foxes, raccoons, nor even sheep. These bones were human. From the bits of cloth and hat and hair and pipe, it was Finlay.

"We should take him to town," Kenna said.

"No, they'd think Papa killed him too."

Taking hold of tree limbs and boulders, they descended to the narrow ravine floor. Kenna kept within inches of Rory, fingering his shirt to keep steady and brave. He didn't even yell at her when she bumped into him when he came to a sudden stop. She recoiled and rubbed her nose. Rory gasped. Kenna stole a peek around him.

"Crivens," she whispered. A shiny metal tube like an airship cabin with wings of metal stuck out of the churned earth. A swath of broken trees a couple hundred feet long cut up the ravine where the strange ship had plummeted to the ground. One of the ship's wings tilted towards the sky, near severed from it. "How'd an airship get here? There's no balloon."

"It is na like any airship I've e'er seen."

Kenna looked up at the sky almost expecting to see another strange airship fall from the sky. When nothing fell, she settled onto a spongy lump of moss.

Rory looked her up and down. "What ya doing?"

"Waiting. Expect they're like wolves, only coming out of their den to feed at night. We'll get it to chase us, just like we planned."

....

The blackness glowed with faint blue light. A door at the end of the ship opened. Kenna sucked in a breath and gripped Rory's arm. Two forms lumbered from the doorway spouting shrill squeaks and clicks. They'd eaten their sheep – she was sure.

The creatures walked around the ship fiddling about in the holes with their fingered claws. Their skin gleamed black and their arms were long, just as Rory had said. She imagined their wide mouths opening like snakes and devouring her sheep and Constable Duncan and Finlay. Imagined them grinding up their prey in their gullets and spitting out the bits they didn't fancy.

A long time passed before one of the creatures went back inside the ship, leaving the one. Rory gave a nod and chucked a stone at the creature. The rock skidded across the wing and dropped beside the creature. It bent and plucked the stone from the ground. It turned slowly towards the trees and brush. It popped the stone into its mouth, swallowed it, and turned its attentions back to ship.

Rory threw another stone striking the creature in the back of the head. It jerked around.

"Run," Rory whispered. The creature took a couple steps towards them. "Baaaah, Baaaah, Baaaah," Rory made his best sheep sound. "Go." Rory shoved Kenna up the hill. "Now, Kenna."

The creature ran towards them. Kenna and Rory scrambled up the steep slope, grabbing at roots and branches for handholds. Breaking from the trees, they raced across the hillside. Rory was just a step behind. The creature thundered twenty paces behind him. The plan was working! Kenna's heart thumped, her breaths, quick and light.

Her foot caught on a nub of grass, sending her sprawling. Kenna fell hard, her teeth clicked together, her bones jolted with the force of the fall, her palms covered in thistle. She screamed.

Rory grabbed her by the back of her smock and dress, pulling her upright. He wrapped his arm around her back and under her arm, supporting her weight till she found her feet again. Light exploded from behind, hitting the ground beside Rory. Too close. Her stomach soured, and she thought she'd sick up.

"We're almost there," Rory huffed. "We need to move faster. It's gaining."

"I can na."

Rory near lifted her from the ground, dragging her when her feet floundered. "Catch him with the machine . . . ya can do this . . . just like it's a sheep."

"Aye."

They bolted into the sheep corral. Rory headed up the ramp leading to the second story of the barn. The creature paused, raising its head and letting out a shrill cry. Kenna squeezed between the crack of barn doors and pulled them closed.

She slammed her hand against the button on the sheep dipping and shearing machine. With a gurgle and rasp, the machine belched to life, a plume of smoke puffed out of the stack. Gripping the handle, she spun the wheel operating the picking arm. Rory darted into the barn, down the ramp leading to the shearer and dipper. The creature lunged towards him, swiping with its long arms and fingered claws. It tossed another burst of lightning. Rory ducked. The electricity flew past and hit the barn wall, leaving a black mark.

"Kenna!" Rory screamed, running out of ramp.

Kenna moved the gripping arm. Papa had let her practice all summer, even on some actual sheep at shearing time. He'd even let her dip them in the insecticide. But Rory had held the sheep still. Catching a moving target wasn't easy.

The creature went for him again. Rory ducked and scrambled between the guardrails. The creature bent, reaching its long arms in the space between the rails and catching Rory's foot. It worked up Rory's leg, reeling him in like a fish.

Kenna lowered the claw over its head. She yanked the lever down and spun another wheel, clamping the tines tight. The creature, so focused on Rory, noticed too late the vice clamping round its head. The creature flailed, batting at the tines and arm. Kenna turned the wheel counter-clockwise, lifting the creature off its feet. The picking arm flexed under its weight.

Rory grabbed the cricket bat and smacked the creature in the head five times. The creature went limp. Rory lowered the bat, poked it and jumped away.

"Did ya kill it?" Kenna asked.

"I do na think so. Dinna turn to a puddle-o-goo, did it?" He poked it again, just to be sure. "Get the rope."

....

Fog blanketed the valley, hiding town. By the time the sun rose and burned away the fog, the first train to Glasgow would be long gone with Papa.

Kenna insisted that every last inch of rope on the farm be used to restrain the creature. A harnessed Rufus pulled the cocooned creature towards town, tilling the muddy road behind. Rufus trotted along, his wagging tail squeaking, when, for what seemed like the hundredth time, he drifted towards the edge of the road.

"Stand . . . come," Rory said. Rufus flopped to the ground, his tail still wagging. "Dumb dog." Rory kicked him. Kenna punched Rory in the shoulder.

"Do na kick him."

"He's not working right."

"Ye're the one who fixed him." Kenna patted Rufus on the

head. "Rufus," she said with a melodic lilt in her voice. "Come."

Rufus's ears swiveled, and he got to his feet. He crossed back to the middle of the road. The creature, at last awake, struggled. Its cry echoed in the early morning air.

"It'll wake everyone in town." Kenna clamped her hands over her ears.

"Good. They'll know Papa is no murderer."

They chased Rufus down after another jaunt off the road to herd a rabbit before reaching the outskirts of town where the woolen mill's machines sat quiet. It wouldn't be long before steam puffed from its stacks and the looms rattled.

The creature's shrieks brought bleary-eyed faces to windows that turned sour at the sight and sound of them. Rufus trotted into the village green and flopped down.

"Find Papa," Kenna said. Rufus barred his teeth and growled. "Rufus . . . find Papa." Rufus lay in the grass, framing his head with his paws. "Come . . . away to me . . . sit . . . down . . . hold . . ." Kenna tried each command. She knelt beside Rufus and patted his head. He let out a half-hearted growl. "Find Papa," she whispered.

Rory tugged on her shoulder. "It's no use, he's broken. We gotta get to Papa before he's taken."

"It's eating the rope," Kenna said. Some of the creature's teeth poked out from the rope. It struggled something fierce against its restraints. Rufus jumped to his feet and turned on the bound creature. He barked and peered up at Kenna, wagging his tail. "Good boy. Find Papa."

Rufus led them to the jail. Kenna threw open the door, making Deputy Clacher jump as he slurped up his beans and bite of egg.

"What is it?" he asked. The creature let out a long, loud shriek. They all clamped hands over ears. "What in the name of all that is holy have ya got?"

"Please, sir, let my Papa go. This is what's eating the sheep and people." Kenna smiled her best smile.

"I do na know what ya-"

Rufus bolted past Kenna, knocking her down, and through the door, bumping Deputy Clacher back into the kitchen. The creature wailed as it thumped over the threshold and bounced against walls. Rory helped Kenna up and they chased after. Rufus stood on his back paws, the others pressed against the jail cell bars. Papa set down the remains of his breakfast and approached Rufus. "Sit."

Rufus sat.

"Papa," Kenna rushed to her father, squeezing her face between the bars. Papa knelt and touched his forehead to hers. Tears spilt down her cheeks.

"It's okay." He kissed her head and stroked her dirt-stained cheeks.

"Let him go." Rory faced Deputy Clacher. "This is the creature that ate–"

"I can't hardly see what animal ye've got, but, yer Papa already said ya shot the animal to death . . . said it turned to liquid when it died. So, this isn't the same animal is it?"

"No, sir, but it's just like the one that ate Constable Duncan. I promise. We saw it. We found them in the ravine. There's one more of them besides this one. They're living in a tube like an airship with wings and no balloon."

Deputy Clacher squatted beside the creature and touched one of its sharp teeth poking out of the rope. "That's quite a story ye're telling. And maybe it's true, but I've a signed order from the judge to transport your Papa to Glasgow. Killing a constable is a very serious offense."

"Ye're not listening. Papa dinna kill nobody. The creature ate them and then spat the bones and stuff it dinna like back out. That's what it does. It eats squirrels and rabbits and raccoons and our sheep. And it eats people who try and stop it!" Kenna shouted.

A distant shriek sounded from outside. The cocooned creature shrieked back. Screams from villagers followed. A man darted inside, breathless. "There's something . . . animal . . . monster. It ate MacLeod when he poked his head out the door."

"See!" Kenna shouted. "Let my Papa go!"

Deputy Clacher grabbed his electro-gun and rushed out the door and down the street before the echo of her shout faded. The creature let out another earsplitting cry.

"Kenna, Rory, ya've got to go hide. Now–"

Kenna reached her arms through the bars, grabbing for her Papa. "I won't leave ya, Papa."

Papa wrapped his arms around her. "Another creature is coming to get this one and, it's very mad. Ya go with Rory–"

"I'm not leaving."

"Kenna."

"No."

Papa kissed her again on the forehead and peered above her. "Rory." Papa gave a silent nod.

Rory grabbed Kenna round the waist and yanked her from her hold on the bars. The creature drowned her cries. It shrieked till Rory's knees buckled and he dropped Kenna to cover his ears. Its call was answered.

Deputy Clacher zoomed past the window, chased by the creature shooting at him. Lightning flashed from the creature. Clacher dropped to the ground. Then it had him. With its long, sharp fingers, the creature lifted Deputy Clacher up. Its mouth ratcheted open, making space, and then swallowed Deputy Clacher, keys, buttons, and everything down to his boots.

"Lock the door!" Papa shouted. "Hide upstairs."

Kenna looked to her Papa and to Rory. She mustered her courage. "Rufus, go home!" she called. Rufus's ears twisted back and forth. His head cocked to the side. "Home!"

Rufus gave a hearty bark and dashed out the door, the screeching creature dragging behind. The hunting creature, with bulging belly and gurgling and grinding sounds arising from it, lumbered after Rufus. The weight of Deputy Clacher in its belly slowed it down.

"Lock the door and hide! This isn't a game," Papa said.

"We have to fix it. We can't let them eat everyone." Kenna blew Papa a kiss and rushed out the door with Rory.

But Rufus, once free of the jail loped down half a block then ran in circles, chasing his own tail. "Rufus . . . steady," Kenna called. She came as close as she dared, leaving a space between her and the creature. The dog slowed and then sat on his haunches. "Away to me," she called, ordering him towards her. Rufus barked twice and growled at the approaching creature. "Home. Go home."

Rufus wagged his tail and circled round a fountain topped with a bronze statue of a sheep before tearing down the street. Rufus disappeared in the thick fog, the bound creature wailing behind in its tangle of ropes.

The creature in pursuit charged the crowd, snapping its teeth. Its claws tore the air in fury. Kenna and Rory skirted around the men and creature, keeping close to the houses and shops.

The creature stopped and its jaw ratcheted open, regurgitating the leftovers of Deputy Clacher, a slimy mass of broken bones, and buttons, and keys. It wailed once again. Lightning swirled round its hands, and it threw it into the group of men then disappeared into the fog.

Rory and Kenna crept past the fight, keeping close to the shops and houses. They passed by the Black Bull, the clockmaker, the tailor's shops, and reached the outermost edge of town by the woolen mill. Behind them, the fog glowed with sizzling light. Shouts and screams blared. She hoped the creature had fallen, not another person.

Kenna and Rory, safely beyond the fight, took to running. Rory skidded to a stop. A mound of empty rope lay on the road. He cast a wary glance into the fog, and picked up the end of the rope where the creature had broken free of Rufus's harness.

"Rufus!" Kenna yelled.

Rory clamped his hand over her mouth. "Shush. Ya trying to get us eaten?"

A gust of wind scattered the fog, revealing the dark form of the creature, standing and watching them with its cat-like eyes. Its wide mouth spread from ear to ear and when opened revealed rows of small sharp teeth.

Rory grabbed Kenna's hand and yanked so hard it nearly pulled her arm right out of the socket. He led them to the closest building, the woolen mill. Frantic tugs found each door locked.

"There." Kenna pointed to a window above the main office door, cracked open. "Help me up." Rory hoisted her from his hands to his shoulders and she stretched, gripping the edge of the casement. Rory pushed her higher and higher till she shimmied through the window. Keeping one hand firmly on the windowsill, Kenna swung her legs down and stared at the drop below.

"Kenna?" Rory pounded on the door. "Kenna?"

She dropped to the ground and wrenched the door open. Rory tumbled in and she slammed the door and bolted it closed. The creature gave a frustrated squeal. Kenna leaned against the door, exhaling and closing her eyes. "Do ya think he can get in?" The door rattled, the first blow nearly shattering the frame.

"I have an idea," Rory said. Kenna followed Rory through the mill's office and onto the factory floor. In the dark, he felt along the wall. "Help me find the power switch."

She and Rory had come to the factory since they were little to sell their wool. "Here," Kenna said and smacked the button hard. The pumps bringing the water from River Annan hummed to life, filling the boiler. With a whirr of gears and a burst of steam the machines surged into motion. Lights flickered about the two-story high room revealing spinners, weaving machines, and enormous vats of dye. Mounds of wool shifted on conveyor belts feeding the spinners, twisting the wool into yarn and finer threads. From there, the threads fanned out like spider webs to the looms, chugging back and forth, weaving the finest cloth in all of Scotland. And some from their own sheep no less!

"Just like last night." Rory pointed at the arm and gripper above the dye vats used to pull colored fabric from the vats and transfer them to the chutes behind. "We capture him with that."

Kenna grinned. Recapture the creature and save Papa. Kenna raced up the spiral staircase to the control room as the creature came barreling onto the factory floor. Below, Rory dodged behind a loom when the creature squealed and shot lightning at him.

Kenna surveyed the wide control panel fitted with all sorts of levers and dials. It was nothing like Papa's machine. She yanked on the biggest lever. The gripping arm did not move. She twisted a dial and the conveyor belt leading up to the vat slowed down. Spheres of lightening flickered on the floor below. Kenna raced her hands across the panel, pulling, turning, pushing every lever, dial, or button till the arm moved. Grasping the correct lever, she pushed it back, swinging the arm down.

Rory dashed from behind a row of spinners towards the descending gripping arm. "Over here ya big oaf!" The creature squealed and began making another ball. Kenna jerked the lever down. The arm sailed in front of the creature. It ducked to the side and sidled past. Kenna shoved the lever back up, and spun the dial. The gripper lurched up too late. Rory turned to run. The lightning left the creature's hand and exploded on Rory. The charge sizzled all over him, jolting him to the ground.

The creature moved towards him.

"No!" Kenna screamed. "To me!" She raced down the stairs. Its eyes focused on her. "Ya can't eat him!"

She tore her boot off and threw it at the creature. It fell short, but the creature came for her. Round the dye vats she led it, circling again and again till she realized it no longer gave chase. Kenna crept round the tall vat, feeling the warmth of it on her back. She took a step from the vat, looking at the curve ahead of her.

Feet shuffled behind her and she spun around. The creature grabbed for her. Kenna jumped onto the metal stairs leading to the top of the vat. The creature followed. She backed away, inches from running out of stair. The creature cupped its hands together, working the electric light. There was nowhere to go. Kenna crouched, ready to reach for the guardrail. As the creature brought its arm back, Kenna grabbed for the rail, swinging her legs through.

As Kenna dangled from the railing, she peered up, hearing the shrill cry of the creature and boom of paws smacking against the metal stairs. In a blur of bronze legs and yellow eyes and snapping teeth, Rufus leapt at the creature, knocking it and him into the indigo dye.

Kenna swung her legs back onto the stairs and peered over the end into the vat. Bubbles and waves sloshed about the open tank. The bubbles stopped, and the indigo color bloomed with yellow-green goo. The surface grew still.

"Rufus?" Kenna called. Nothing below moved. "Rufus."

Her heart thumped loudly in her ears whilst she made her way back to Rory. Kenna knelt beside him. She shook Rory with both hands. "Rory, oh, Rory." She pressed her ear against his chest and listened for a heartbeat. She drew in a calming breath, but the only thump she heard was the rush of her own blood. "Please be alive, please." She stared at him long and hard, at last seeing the shallow rise and fall of his chest.

Jumping to her feet, Kenna ran out of the mill, down the road past the townsfolk standing and talking in alarmed tones pointing at a yellow-green puddle. She pushed her way through the throng gawking at the bits of Deputy Clacher and grabbed the keys from the pile. Kenna darted between the legs of a man trying to stop her. Ignoring the calls of the villagers, Kenna made for her Papa. Her hands trembled as she stuck the key into the lock.

"Papa . . . Rory's hurt bad," she cried. Papa folded her in his arms and didn't let go of her the entire way he ran to the mill. Papa would make things right. She was sure.

....

"Is that so?" Mama muttered raking the comb through.

"Ouch!" Kenna patted her hands to her head.

"It would na hurt so if ya'd brushed ye're hair."

"Aye, Mama," Kenna said. "And then Lizzie paid me a haypenny to show her the airship with wings but no balloon."

"Did she now."

"Aye, and then I took her sissy and brother ta see, but there were men in fine wool suits with real airships, taking it away. All Papa got from it–"

"Hullo?" Papa called through the door. "I've got someone I

want ya to meet."

"Ouch!" Kenna swatted Mama's hand aside and stood up from the bathtub beside the fire, grabbing at her dress, hung over the blanket pinned up for privacy.

"The water's so dirty, I'll have to empty it for anyone else gets a bath. Ya dinna bathe the whole month I was gone, did ya?"

Kenna didn't answer. She threw open the door. Papa, and Rory with a crooked smile, stood beside the most beautiful dog Kenna had ever seen. The dog's eyes glowed blue in harmony with the silver-colored metal of her body from the strange ship. The sheepdog glistened like a sparkling jewel in the sun. Kenna knelt beside her, circling arms around her neck.

"She's perfect!" The sheepdog's tail wagged. "Her name's Fenella."

A Universe of Talk

Evan Dicken

By day, Evan Dicken battles economic entropy for the Department of Commerce and studies old Japanese maps at Ohio State University. By night, he does neither of these things. His work has most recently appeared in Analog, Shock Totem, *and* Escape Pod, *and he has work forthcoming from publishers such as Daily Science Fiction and Chaosium. He very fondly remembers trips to the used bookstore in his pre-teen years, where, to the occasional chagrin of his parents, he would spend his entire allowance in the fantasy and science fiction section.*

Kaela had never thought aliens would be so *boring*. The K'spoolp looked and smelled like old potatoes; worse, they took *forever* to reply to anything her father and Captain Lee said. When the aliens came aboard the spaceship, Kaela had been so excited she could barely sit still. As the minutes dragged into hours, her enthusiasm melted like ice cream in the summer sun. Now she had to try not to roll her eyes every time the K'spoolp asked another question about the trade agreement. This wasn't what Kaela imagined when she had begged her father to take her on the mission.

"In section three, paragraph two." The biggest K'spoolp waved a pale tentacle at the view screen. "It mentions the transport of eight million tons of chocolate to our homeworld. Will the K'spoolp be required to pay for the containers?"

"Of course not." Kaela's father smiled. Kaela could tell from the way his eyes crinkled at the edges he was getting fed up with the aliens, too.

Kaela wished for the hundredth time that her father had let her bring her chat prism. Although Earth was too far away for Kaela to talk to any of her friends, the prism still had a bunch of books, games, and trideos. She almost groaned out loud when she realized it was Friday: *Glenda Galaxy* would be on today. Kaela's friends would all be over at Carmen Chang's house watching on Carmen's big trideo projector. Kaela had hoped her trip with her father would be like the show, with high-speed intergalactic chases, cool aliens, and laser-sword duels. Well, maybe not *exactly* like the show—Kaela didn't think she'd want to duel any dangerous aliens like the Vex or Mantiks—but pretty much anything had to be better than this.

"Acceptable," the biggest K'spoolp said at last, then turned back to the view screen. "In section four—"

"Friends." Kaela's father spread his hands. "Perhaps we can continue this discussion tomorrow?"

"Acceptable," the biggest K'spoolp said after a few minutes of discussion.

Kaela jumped out of her chair, almost forgetting to do the bow her father had made her practice before the meeting. The K'spoolp plopped down from the benches and wobbled away, talking amongst themselves.

"Well, that was a waste of time," Captain Lee said as soon as the door slid shut. "Trading chocolate for engine parts. We should be asking for weapons. The Vex—"

Kaela's father glared at the Captain.

"What about the Vex?" Kaela asked. She'd heard the peace talks weren't going well, but no one had said anything about fighting.

"Nothing." Her father scratched at his beard, something he always did when he was nervous.

"But—"

"It's late. You must be starving, Kaela," her father said in that sweet, sticky voice adults use when they're trying to get kids to shut up.

Captain Lee smoothed the creases from her uniform. "I'll have dinner sent to your cabin."

Kaela made a sour face. She *was* hungry, but that didn't change how unfair it was that they were keeping something from her. One way or another, Kaela was going to find out what was really going on.

·····························

"You did a good job today." Her father hugged her when they were back in their cabin. "I'm proud of you, Mikaela."

Kaela pulled away. "I hate it when you call me that."

He looked at the floor then at his desk. "I know the K'spoolp are...difficult. Real diplomacy isn't like on Gail Galaxy—"

"*Glenda* Galaxy," Kaela said. He was right, though. Glenda Galaxy wouldn't have wasted time with silly diplomats, she would've just drawn her sword and said, "Take me to your leader."

Kaela flopped down in one of the chairs bolted to the floor. Her father's desk was a mess, stacks of paper threatening to cover the knickknacks he always brought with him. All that junk, and Kaela hadn't even been allowed to bring her chat prism. Why couldn't he just keep his stuff on the computer like a regular person?

She picked up a fat wooden doll without arms and legs and felt something rattle inside.

"Your mom gave me that." Kaela's father stepped up beside her. "Twist the top."

Kaela did, and the upper part of the doll came off to reveal another smaller doll inside.

"They're Russian nesting dolls."

"How many are there?" Kaela popped the top off the smaller doll to find an even smaller one, and another, and another.

"A whole family." Her father gave a sad smile. "Do you ever miss your mom?"

Kaela set the dolls down. He wasn't going to distract her that easily. "I want to know about the Vex. Why is the Captain worried?"

"Captain Lee is a military officer. It's her job to worry."

"Nice try." Kaela knew her father well enough to recognize when he was avoiding a question. "I thought we were in peace talks with the Vex?"

"We talk with the Vex, but we never get anywhere." He picked up the dolls, slowly slipping them back inside each other. "Real diplomacy requires more than talk. You need to understand the other person."

"I don't get it." Kaela ran her hand through her hair, which was curly like her father's but not as dark.

"You have to be able to see things from their perspective." Her father pursed his lips. "Like the K'spoolp. They focus on little details because everything in their society is neat and predictable. They get up at the same time, do the same things every day, and everyone sticks to a schedule."

"That sounds boring."

"For us, maybe, but the K'spoolp like it." He set the doll down. "It's easy to judge others when you don't take the time understand them."

Kaela almost snorted. It was just like her father to talk about understanding aliens while ignoring his own daughter.

"What about the Vex?" Kaela asked.

"It's complicated."

"*Tell* me," she said angrily. "I'm going to find out eventually."

He sighed. "You're right. It's the peace talks. Everything is falling apart. There might be another war. That's why I brought you out here. Earth may not be safe."

Kaela swallowed. "I—"

The room shook, scattering papers all over the floor. A siren blared outside their door and the lights flickered.

The ship was under attack!

. . . .

Her father activated the desk projector. "Captain, what's going on? Is it the Vex?"

Captain Lee's image appeared over the desk. "A Mantik ship just appeared right next to us."

Kaela frowned. She didn't know much about the Mantiks, but no one really did. The Mantiks' technology was so advanced that not even the Vex bothered them. They flitted around the galaxy like hummingbirds, traveling light years in the blink of an eye. Glenda Galaxy once found a baby Mantik in a crashed ship. When she took the baby home the aliens gave her a laser sword that could cut through anything, but Kaela was pretty sure that was all made up.

"What are they doing here?" Captain Lee asked.

Kaela's father scratched at his beard.

"Ambassador, why are the Mantiks here?" the Captain asked.

"I invited them," Kaela's father said in the smallest voice she'd ever heard him use.

"You *what?*" Captain Lee shouted.

"I didn't think they'd actually come," he said, then turned to Kaela. "I need to speak with Captain Lee. In private."

Kaela crossed her arms. First the Vex, now this. She was through being left out.

"Mikaela."

Kaela didn't budge.

"We don't have time for this," Captain Lee said.

Kaela's father shot her an exasperated look, then pressed a button on the screen. Captain Lee's image shifted to the bedroom projector. He walked inside, waving the door shut behind him with an irritated flick of his hand.

Kaela padded over to the door, but couldn't hear anything. Her father must have switched on the noise dampeners. She went back to the desk projector, but the security lock was on. Although she'd figured her father's password out a long time ago, Kaela wasn't sure if she should use it. She swallowed; it wasn't like she was going to get in *worse* trouble, right?

"Ekaterina," Kaela said her mother's name. An image of the three of them appeared. They were on the beach near Cape Town, back before the Vex had bombed it. Kaela had been just a baby, then. Her father was dangling her feet in the ocean, smiling as she kicked at the waves. Kaela's mother stood a little way off, looking out to sea, one hand raised to shield her eyes against the sun, her long, red-brown hair glowing in the afternoon light.

Kaela waved the image away then touched the chat icon, making sure to turn off the video and audio inputs so they wouldn't know she was listening.

"I'll take the diplomatic shuttle," Kaela's father said.

"They could blow you out of the sky, and I couldn't do anything about it," Captain Lee said.

"If we could open diplomatic relations—or better yet—trade with the Mantik, the Vex wouldn't even think about attacking."

Captain Lee looked unconvinced. "This isn't the first time we've tried to talk to them. I won't let you risk—"

"*Won't?*" Kaela's father stiffened. "I command this mission, and I am going to speak with the Mantik."

"Ambassador, I—"

"Get my shuttle ready. That's an order."

Captain Lee's jaw tightened, then she nodded.

The images disappeared, and Kaela had to scramble to switch the projector off before her father came stomping out of the bedroom.

"Dad—"

"Not now."

"I want to—"

"Enough!" He whirled on her, his expression so furious Kaela barely even recognized him. "What I'm doing here is important—to me, to the world, to our *people*. I don't have time to explain."

"You never have time!" Kaela was on her feet, although she didn't remember standing. "It's bad enough you leave me home alone all the time. I thought this would be different, but I'm *here* and you still ignore me."

"Mikae—*Kaela*." The anger left his face. "It's just…the Vex, your mom—I can't let it happen again."

He held out a hand, but Kaela backed away. Tears stung her eyes as she waved the door open and ran out into the hall. Her mom; everything was always about her mom. Kaela was still alive, still needed her father. All he could do was hang onto the past.

Why couldn't he understand?

Something tightened in her chest as she ran down the hall. He didn't really care about her. If he did, he wouldn't be gone all the time. She blinked away the tears, anger rising within her. She'd cried the first time her father left, the first time he missed her birthday, and all the other first times he'd let her down. She wouldn't cry now.

Kaela wasn't going to be left behind again.

The door to her father's shuttle was locked, but it opened with the same password he used on his desk display. Adults were sometimes stupid like that.

Kaela closed and relocked the door and squeezed into one of the equipment lockers. After a little bit, Kaela heard the door open. There was a little rumble as the shuttle left the docking bay. Still not quite believing what she'd just done, Kaela settled down to wait.

She had come to see aliens, after all.

....

The inside of the Mantik ship looked like one of the crystal vases Kaela's aunt Bongani used for lilies from her garden. The walls and ceiling seemed to be made of cut glass and glowed with rainbow light.

Kaela hid in the shadow of the shuttle door. The Mantiks towered over her father like giant praying mantises with four insect legs and two long arms folded close to their chest. Their bodies looked like they were chipped from gemstones. At first Kaela thought the two aliens were statues, but they turned their heads as her father approached, watching him with eyes like polished rubies.

"Greetings." Her father bowed low. "I am—"

"WE CANNOT SPEAK." The aliens' mouths didn't move, but the voice was loud enough to make Kaela flinch. She edged forward to get a better view.

Her father scratched his beard. "Well, may I talk with someone who—"

"YOU CANNOT SPEAK."

"I—"

"RETURN TO YOUR SHIP AND DEPART."

"But, my message—didn't you come to talk?"

"WE CANNOT SPEAK. RETURN TO YOUR SHIP AND DEPART."

"But—"

"RETURN TO YOUR SHIP AND DEPART."

The look on her father's face was the same as whenever he talked about Kaela's mother. He turned and glanced up, straight at Kaela.

Her father opened his mouth, but the aliens were quicker. The Mantiks blurred across the room, breezing by Kaela's father to stand over her. She wanted to run back into the ship but couldn't seem to move.

"Leave her alone!" Her father ran toward the aliens.

"SPEAK," the voice said.

Kaela swallowed, her throat suddenly dry.

"SPEAK."

She tried to think of something, anything, but her mind was spinning. All she could think of was when Glenda Galaxy saved that baby Mantik, except the Mantiks on the show didn't look like *real* Mantiks and Glenda had been so calm, and she always knew what to say, and—

"SPEAK!"

"Take me to your leader." The words just popped out.

Kaela didn't have time to feel stupid. The aliens picked her up, surprisingly gentle despite their size, and carried her back across the room.

"Kaela!" Her father tried to grab her as they sped past, but she was too high up.

The far wall melted into the floor, and the Mantiks carried her down a long, twisting hall. Her father's shouts grew distant then stopped altogether. The aliens brought her to a small room and set her down then stepped back into the hall. Kaela stood, but a wall rose up between them, trapping her.

She beat at the door, yelling, but only succeeded in hurting her hands. Then it hit her—she was trapped. It was the sort of thing that happened to Glenda Galaxy all the time, but that was just a stupid show. In reality, it was cold, lonely, and terrifying.

Glenda Galaxy never would've cried, but Kaela did.

....

There was no warning when the aliens came back. Kaela was curled in the corner of the small room, trying to ignore her rumbling stomach and scratchy throat, then the wall disappeared and four Mantiks were in the room.

"What do you want?" Kaela asked.

The Mantiks said nothing as they carried her back down the hall. Her father and the shuttle were gone. The landing bay was open, but instead of stars and space beyond the doors, there was an alien landscape.

Tall, twisted, trees with thin crystal leaves clinked and rattled in the breeze. There was no grass or undergrowth, only a thick carpet of light blue moss with occasional patches of red rocky earth showing below. Kaela caught a glimpse of mountains in the distance, rising from the forest floor to touch the thin, curling clouds up above. There seemed to be some sort of castle on the nearest mountain, but it was too far away for Kaela to make out any detail. The air was warm, but musty like the old papers on her father's desk.

The forest was quiet but for the soft thumps of the Mantiks' feet on the mossy ground. Kaela tried to twist free, but they only held her tighter.

"Put me down!" she said through gritted teeth.

They stopped and put her down.

The Mantiks stood still, but Kaela didn't like the way they were watching her.

"Go away! Leave me alone!" She rolled onto her stomach and started to push to her feet. By the time she stood, the Mantiks were gone.

The clearing was empty. The surrounding leaves jingled in the breeze like a thousand distant wind chimes. Kaela went to the edge of the clearing to peer back at the way they'd come. There was no sign of the aliens. Even the ship was gone.

When she'd yelled at the Mantiks, she hadn't expected them to actually *listen* to her—after all, no one else did. Kaela tried to swallow, but her throat had gone scratchy as sandpaper.

Kaela looked around—nothing but moss and trees as far as she could see. She tasted a bit of the moss, but it was so bitter she had to spit it out. The trees didn't have any fruit or nuts, only the strange, glassy leaves.

She thought about what Glenda Galaxy would do then decided she didn't care—Glenda Galaxy was stupid. Kaela began to wonder if she hadn't made a big mistake, not just sneaking onto her father's shuttle, but telling the Mantiks to leave. As much as she hated to admit it, the aliens hadn't actually hurt her. The voice on the ship had said they couldn't speak. Maybe they were taking her to someone who could?

"Hello? Is anyone there?" Her questions echoed through the forest. "Come back!"

No one answered. Kaela was alone.

The castle—someone *had* to be there. Maybe if she climbed a tree, she could see it again. Kaela found a big tree with low branches. The bark felt like coiled rope, and the sharp, crystal leaves scratched her hands, but Kaela managed to climb enough to see. The forest stretched all around her, but she saw the castle beyond, the lights in its windows like stars against the darkening sky.

She climbed down, and took a deep breath, trying to stay calm. At least she had a direction, but the castle was so far away.

Just then, she heard a loud splash in the distance. Water.

....

Kaela took a couple steps toward the noise before the snarling started—loud, angry roars and high-pitched whistling. It sounded dangerous, but Kaela was so thirsty she didn't care. She gathered a few rocks from ground then padded across the moss, trying to move as quietly as possible.

The ground sloped toward a large pond. Two creatures stalked around the edge. They looked like a cross between a hyena and a centipede; long and low-bodied with wide, fanged jaws, they scuttled on hundreds of clawed feet. The creatures snarled and snapped at a third, different creature that stood in the middle of the pond.

Unlike the hyenapedes, it only had six legs. Its body was big and round like a boulder. Two enormous arms ended in claws like a crab. Its head was small, with large, dark eyes and a small, oval mouth. It swung a claw at one of the hyenapedes, but the creature dodged back while the other circled around. The boulder crab whistled, but couldn't turn fast enough to fight both hyenapedes.

Kaela made a small noise in the back of her throat. The smart thing to do would be to climb a tree and wait. When the hyenapedes were finished, she could have all the water she wanted. It happened like this all the time on the savannah: hyenas would corner and kill a zebra or cape buffalo—it was just how things were. But Kaela wasn't on the savannah, and she knew she couldn't stand by and watch the boulder crab get eaten.

Her first rock hit the bigger hyenapede on the nose.

"Get out of here!" she shouted, throwing another stone at the creature as she ran toward the pond. The hyenapede twisted to snarl at her, but she kept throwing and shouting. Hyenas back home were cowards and would almost always run away rather than fight. Kaela just hoped hyenapedes were the same.

The hyenapede backed off, growling, then turned to run. Kaela gave a small smile just before something slammed into her back. Although her jacket took the worst of the attack, Kaela could feel the thing's claws scratch across her shoulders. She twisted and kicked, feeling stupid for not keeping the other hyenapede in sight. It pulled back, drool dripping from fangs the color of dry grass, then it was gone.

The boulder crab lifted the hyenapede from the ground with one claw and threw it into the trees with a crash.

Kaela grabbed a rock and came up to her knees, but the remaining hyenapede was already disappearing back into the forest. She dropped her rock, breathing hard. If that wasn't the stupidest thing she had ever done, it was pretty close.

There was a low whistle then a shadow fell over her. Slowly, Kaela turned to face the boulder crab.

It regarded her for a moment, then cocked its head. The move reminded Kaela so much of her neighbor's golden retriever, Milo, that she couldn't help but giggle.

The boulder crab whistled again.

Kaela tried whistling back, but her lips were too dry.

"Eat me if you want, but let me get a drink first." She cupped her hand to scoop up some of the water. It tasted like metal but was cool and clear. Kaela drank until she felt ready to burst.

Her stomach growled.

"I don't suppose you have any food?" She rubbed her stomach and made an eating motion.

The boulder crab moved off a short distance and began digging with its claws. As Kaela watched, it stripped away the bitter moss and red gravel, revealing what looked like a patch of shiny, blue apples. It stooped to suck up a few, then stood, crunching happily.

Kaela picked one up, dusted it off, and took a tentative bite. It tasted like banana—not her favorite flavor, but she wasn't going to complain.

Together, she and the boulder crab finished off the whole patch.

"Thanks. Uh...I don't suppose you have a name?" she asked.

The boulder crab cocked its head, then whistled.

"Whistler." Kaela smiled. "Nice to meet you, I'm Kaela."

Whistler whistled.

....

They spent the night by the pond—Kaela on a bed of soft moss, Whistler half-submerged in the water. Kaela woke and was strangely relieved to find the alien standing over her. They ate more of the ground fruit, then Kaela climbed a tree to see where the castle was.

The big alien followed when Kaela left, moving at a slow but steady pace. The hyenapedes came back twice, once in the early afternoon and once just after nightfall, but with Kaela throwing stones to keep the creatures from getting behind Whistler, the big alien was easily able to scare them away.

Kaela and Whistler walked all the next day and the next, occasionally stopping to dig up more groundfruit or drink from a pond. Each morning Kaela would climb a tree. The castle wasn't getting much closer, but it *was* getting closer.

Kaela found herself talking to Whistler—about home, her dad, everything. The alien never talked back, of course, but it would cock its head and whistle sometimes. It was nice to have someone listen to her, even if it couldn't understand what she was saying.

Once, a big storm swept down from the mountains, tearing the leaves from the trees and spinning them into a whirlwind of sharp glass. Kaela spent hours crouched beneath Whistler's big, rocky body, listening to the leaves shatter and crackle all around. Afterwards, she noticed some cracks in Whistler's shell, and did her best to pack them with moss so they would heal. She didn't know if it would help, but the alien seemed to enjoy the attention.

On the fourth day, they saw some other boulder crabs in the distance. They were chipping at a big piece of stone with their claws. Whistler didn't seem to care, but Kaela stopped to watch for a minute. They opened a big crack in the rock, which split open like an egg to reveal another boulder crab inside. It surprised Kaela to see that the baby boulder crab was the same size as the others. The only way she could tell it apart was that there were no cracks in its shell.

"So, you guys come from rocks?" Kaela asked when she caught up to Whistler. "That's weird."

Whistler stopped, then stood perfectly still.

"It's okay. On Earth, we've got birds and lizards that lay eggs."

Whistler was quiet.

"C'mon, don't be like that. I'm sorry I called you weird. I only—" Just then, Kaela noticed what Whistler was staring at.

They'd reached the mountains.

....

Kaela kept climbing even though her hands hurt. She'd expected there to be some sort of path or stair up to the castle, but all they'd found were rocky cliffs. They'd been climbing for hours, and the castle was still just out of reach. She could see it clearly, though. It looked like something out of a fairy tale, with walls of white stone and tall towers that spiraled like unicorn horns.

Whistler scrambled up beside her, wedging one huge claw into a crack in the stone. The alien didn't have much trouble climbing, although it knocked loose all sorts of rocks and pebbles.

"Just a little rest, then we keep going," Kaela said.

Whistler gave a soft hoot and closed its eyes. It made Kaela smile to see that she wasn't the only one who was exhausted.

A little rest turned into a long one. It was early afternoon before Kaela felt ready to climb again. It was harder going than before—the slope was steeper, and holds were harder to find, especially for Whistler, who had to start chipping holes in the stone just to keep climbing.

Finally, they reached a ledge wide enough for even Whistler to stand. At first, Kaela was grateful, until she saw the cliff. The castle was just above, but between them and it was a sheer face of rock without even the smallest crack or handhold.

Kaela's throat tightened—they'd never be able to climb that, and they were *so* close. She felt the tears coming but squeezed her eyes shut until they went away. Crying wouldn't help anything.

She looked, and noticed that although the ledge got thinner, it continued around the mountain.

"Stay here," she said to Whistler. "I'll look for another way up."

Kaela started to edge around the cliff when the stone trembled under her hands. She looked back to see Whistler chipping at the rock again. This time though, when the alien hit the stone, long cracks ran up the cliff face.

"Whistler, stop!" Kaela yelled.

There was a rumble from overhead, and boulders rained down on the ledge. One of them hit Whistler's shell and the alien stumbled.

Kaela ran over to Whistler, pulling at its claw as rocks fell around them. "C'mon, this way!"

When Whistler stood Kaela could see one of its legs had broken off. She bit her lip and kept pulling. Together, they ran around the ledge only to find a gap where a piece had fallen away from the mountain. There was no time to look for another way.

Kaela took a deep breath then jumped. The breath whooshed from her as she hit the other side. She scrambled up, trying not to look down. Kaela shouted for Whistler to follow her.

The big alien leapt just as a slab of rock slammed down behind. Whistler hit the ground next to Kaela, slipping and scratching with its remaining legs, barely balanced.

Kaela jumped forward and took hold of Whistler's claw, pulling as hard as she could. Her arms felt like they might pop out of her shoulders, but she kept hold. Slowly, Whistler tilted back. They scrambled along the edge, just barely avoiding the falling stones.

Kaela almost shouted for joy as she saw the mouth of a cave up ahead. They stumbled forward to collapse just inside the cave entrance, panting as rocks tumbled down outside.

It seemed to take forever for Kaela's heartbeat to go back to normal. Whistler patted her on the back with one huge claw and gave two soft whistles.

"You're welcome." Kaela's smile slipped as she saw Whistler. In addition to the missing leg, parts of its shell had broken away entirely. There was no blood, but Kaela could see what looked like crystal underneath the wounds, which probably wasn't good.

"Can you walk?" She pushed herself up.

Whistler stood, if a bit unsteadily.

Kaela grimaced. The cave looked like it went back and up into the mountain. Kaela hoped it led up to the castle, and whoever was inside could help them.

....

As they limped deeper into the cave, rock gave way to smooth, glassy walls that glowed like the inside of the Mantik ship. The floor sloped upward, and Kaela almost cheered when she saw the castle just beyond the cave exit.

She stopped as she noticed about a dozen Mantiks outside the castle. "Maybe we should wait and see—"

Whistler walked right past her, waving its claws and hooting happily.

"Whistler, wait!"

The Mantiks turned. They moved to surround Whistler, then one stepped forward and knocked the big alien to the ground. Kaela barely had time to scream a warning before they were all on Whistler, smashing and tearing at its shell.

"Stop! Go away!" Kaela shouted, but the Mantiks ignored her this time.

She stooped to grab a stone, then ran forward to help her friend. She hit the nearest Mantik. The alien turned, knocked the rock from her hands and scooped her up.

Kaela kicked and punched at the Mantik but couldn't break free. As the alien carried her away, she looked back to see Whistler disappear under a swarm of Mantiks. There was one last whistle, then silence.

Kaela went limp in the Mantik's grasp, feeling like someone had emptied her out.

The alien carried her through the castle, but Kaela couldn't seem to focus. Even when it set her down on a soft pillow, she lay still, too sad and angry to think.

Welcome, Human. The voice echoed in Kaela's thoughts. She felt light and warm, like she was about to fall asleep.

Kaela sat up. The room looked like a greenhouse, with panes of clear crystal suspended in a rocky frame. There were piles of pillows on the floor, and soft drapes hung from the ceiling.

An alien sat across from her. It was smaller than Kaela, with arms and legs as thin as twigs and large eyes that broke the light into rainbows. Its body seemed to be made of frosted glass and looked so delicate Kaela thought it might crack every time the alien moved. In its hand was a globe of blue crystal.

"Did the Mantiks trap you here, too?" she asked.

I am a Mantik. The blue crystal glowed as the Mantik talked. Kaela knew the alien wasn't speaking her language, but the words in her head made sense. *You asked the children to bring you to me.*

"Children?"

Yes. As the alien spoke, images of the Mantiks from the ship filled Kaela's mind, but instead of the scary mantis creatures, she saw them as young explorers. It seemed strange, until she realized she was seeing them from the alien's perspective.

"How?"

The translator. It held up the blue globe, and Kaela realized it was translating more than just the alien's words.

Your child wished for us to speak. An image of Kaela's father appeared in her mind, and she snorted.

"That's my *dad*."

But he is larger than you. Kaela saw images of the big Mantiks cracking open like cocoons and the tiny adult ones crawling out.

"Humans start out small *then* get big."

We have made a terrible mistake.

Kaela could feel the alien's confusion and sorrow but didn't care. She crossed her arms, anger over Whistler breaking through the warm, fuzzy feeling the translator was projecting. The Mantiks had made more than one mistake.

"Your children killed my friend."

Whistler.

"How did you—?"

Like you understand me, I understand you. The alien raised the translator globe. *Your friend is not dead.*

There was a scuffling noise behind Kaela, and she turned to see one of the bigger Mantiks in the doorway. It was shinier than the others, the edges of its shell less worn. It regarded her for a moment then cocked its head.

"Whistler!" She was up and across the room in a heartbeat, hugging the Mantik. After a moment, it hugged her back.

"Why is Whistler so quiet?" Kaela asked.

As babies we listen, as children we watch, only as adults do we speak. We come from the stone, and like the stone we wear away.

Kaela saw images of boulder crabs—baby Mantiks—hatching

from rocks then wandering the woods until they cracked open and became children. They went out to see the universe before returning home to become adults—old and wise, but too fragile to move. Each was hidden within the one before like so many nesting dolls.

You taught Whistler much. Kaela felt the alien's gratitude as well as sadness for all the trouble they'd caused her. *You will be returned to your people, with our apologies and a gift.*

"Gift?"

Your father wished to trade. We cannot do this—your people are not ready yet. But we will allow you to choose one thing to take back with you.

"I want Whistler."

The alien made a soft hissing noise, which Kaela realized was laughter. *The universe is open; Whistler can go anywhere. Although we do not look in on other races unless we're invited.*

Kaela looked up at Whistler. "Will you come visit me?"

Whistler cocked its head then patted Kaela on the shoulder.

Kaela chewed her lip. There was so much to pick from. With the Mantik's weapons, Earth could defeat the Vex. Once, paying the Vex back for her mom would've seemed right to Kaela, but now all she could think about was how many Vex kids might lose *their* mothers to Human bombs. She didn't want anyone, Human *or* Vex, to have to go through that.

With Mantik engines, Human ships could travel anywhere in the blink of an eye. There were so many places to explore, so many other aliens to meet. They might not all be friendly, though, or might be so different that Humans couldn't talk to them. She didn't want any more misunderstandings. All that Kaela had been through had happened because the Mantiks and Humans didn't understand each other.

Kaela smiled. She knew what she wanted.

"The translator."

The Mantik paused, and Kaela knew the translator was explaining her reasons—Earth didn't need more weapons or ships or engines. It needed a way to understand and to be understood.

That is a wise choice, Kaela. Are you sure you aren't an adult?

They both laughed.

The Mantik handed her the globe.

"Thank you." Kaela stood and gave the bow she'd practiced with her father.

Whistler will carry you back to the ship. The journey should be much quicker this time.

"That's something I've been wondering," Kaela said as Whistler picked her up. "If you live here, why do your ships land so far away?"

The Mantik gave a little hissing chuckle. *We don't want to disturb the babies, of course.*

Whistler carried Kaela from the castle and down the mountain. She couldn't help but think of how far she'd come in the past few days. Kaela wondered if her father and Captain Lee would be mad she hadn't picked a laser or an engine. After thinking about it for a bit, she decided it didn't matter.

She held the translator tight and smiled. Whatever happened, she knew they would understand her.

The Rocket Maker
Mike Barretta

Mike Barretta is a retired U.S. naval aviator who currently works for a defense contractor as a pilot. He holds a Master's degree in Strategic Planning and International Negotiation from the Naval Post-Graduate School and a Master's in English from the University of West Florida. His wife, Mary, to whom he has been married to for 23 years, is living proof that he is not such a bad guy once you get to know him. His stories have appeared in Baen's Universe, Redstone, New Scientist, Orson Scott Card's Intergalactic Medicine Show *and various anthologies.*

~ We've chosen to end our anthology with a slightly different story. In the following piece, Mike Barretta reminds us that sometimes the heroes are the people who believe in us and make our adventures possible. - Corie & Sean Weaver

Miguel Cervantes leaned his broom against the chain link fence. He grasped the fence as high as he could reach and stretched his aching back. His left shoulder was higher than his right, his right hip higher than his left. His back described a gentle S-curve that in some circumstances could be considered elegant. Instead, it was a birthright into constant pain. If he had been born in a richer or smarter country, he could have been fixed. In Haduras it was not possible.

He walked back to the broom and swept, wincing with each careful step and sweep. The airport paid him to keep the fence line clean. He collected great drifts of paper food wrappers, cigarette butts, and newspapers. Anything thrown from a car window accumulated along the fence that separated the road from San Paulo International Airport. The airport had two permanent residents, an ancient DC-3, stripped of its engines and a slightly less ancient Boeing 767 that comprised the entire state-run airline.

The sky moved, and the tropical sun vanished behind a thunderhead. A storm front breeze washed over him like hot breath. Miguel mopped his brow with a red bandanna and returned it to his back pocket. He turned his face skyward and caught a few raindrops on his face. It felt good for now, but soon it would turn into a drowning afternoon torrent. A crack of thunder split the sky, and Miguel turned to look so he could decide the best direction to seek shelter.

The clouds brightened from within. Some inner incandescence burned as if the occluded sun was falling to earth. A fiery orange and red glow suffused and spread within the humid hovering mass. The thunder did not stop. It changed into a continuous rolling roar, a guttural fury that shook Miguel's bones. The roar increased in pitch and turned into a pointed shriek. Miguel clapped his hands over his ears.

"Santa María, Madre de Dios, ruega por nosotros pecadores," said Miguel. He dropped to his knees and watched the sky, alert for his grandmother's second coming.

A lance of white fire stabbed from the cloud base and a silver needle descended. He knew what it was. The machine fell like an angel suspended on a pillar of light. Spindly legs extruded from stubby fins as it slowed its descent. The engines roared louder and puddles from the earlier rain shower flashed into steam and roiled away in billowing white clouds. A hot wave of air washed over him and scattered his piles out into the road. He shielded his eyes with his hands, peering between his fingers. The silver ship touched down. Springs compressed with a springy groan as the rocket felt its weight again. The ship settled, its round landing feet splayed and sunken into molten tarmac. Its engine bells trembled with immense powers. Itinerant weeds burst into flame and blew away in gobs of gray smoke. The beautiful ship, the most beautiful thing he had ever seen straddled the blasted and glassy ground. The engines roared over his pounding heart. His eyes captured the magnificent sight of it all. He could smell the acrid tang of hot metal and feel the moist heat prickling his skin. The engine guttered out and the world stood still.

Bacigalupi, the capital city, enjoyed a brief moment of silence after the upset and then started again as if nothing extraordinary had happened. He heard sirens and saw the presidential limousine barreling down the road towards him. Motorcycle riders flanked the big black SUV. He pressed himself against the fence and they roared past. The windows were tinted a deep black so it was impossible to see who was within, but it had to be El Presidente rushing to greet the astronauts or perhaps to take them hostage depending upon his mood. A pickup truck followed, its bed crammed with police officers in shabby sweat-stained uniforms and assault rifles. They hooted like school children and banged on the roof of the truck exhorting the driver to catch up to El Presidente. A beer bottle flew from the truck, missed Miguel, and shattered on the road. They were gone, and he turned back to the rocket.

The rocket ticked and pinged with the music of cooling metals. Miguel knew what he must do. Twisted spine or not, he would fly. It was his destiny and even as garbage from others richer than he swirled around his feet he knew it did not matter. He would ascend the mounting sky on a pillar of fire and gaze upon unfiltered starlight.

He leaned into the broom pressing the straw into the dirty ground to finish sweeping the road.

....

He walked home in a wondrous daze, thinking about the rocket.

"Monstruo! Monstruo!"

He turned and saw three children from the village.

"Monstruo!" they shouted and ran away. They knew he could

never catch them, and even if he did what would he do with them?

As Miguel lay in bed, night drifted in the window and wrapped around him. Raindrops pattered on broad tropical leaves and sang on the rusted tin roof of his home. He rolled over trying to get comfortable, but his twisted spine would not let him. Nightsong colored the dark, and he knew the bird. He had seen it once with his grandfather. It was an omen, a phoenix. The birds were so rare as to be considered nonexistent or even mythical, but he knew they were not. They were not the burst-into-fire kind, but they were equally fabulous. Miguel's memory of the sighting was undulled by time.

The bird sang its song, and he fell asleep to music that rich men would spend fortunes to hear. Miguel dreamed of his own phoenix, sleek and silver, exploding from a nest of fire into the infinite sky.

Without weight he would float free from gravity's pain.

....

Miguel finished sweeping the court's steps. He packed his cleaning supplies and walked to the national library. The library held little interest to El Presidente so it was always short of funds and located in an industrial district. He limped past boxes of books soaking in the humidity. A blast of unexpected cool air wrapped around him as he left the light and entered the relative gloom of the library. Books were stacked here and there, in no particular order, under scattered fly-specked industrial lights. A little old lady with thick glasses approached him.

"Buenos dias," said Miguel.

"Eh," she muttered.

"I am looking for books on rockets."

"Cohetes, cohetes, cojones, eh, come this way." She cackled at her obscenity.

He followed her down twisting turns. The library was a labyrinth, a maze of books donated from other countries and indifferently cared for. She stopped and scratched her whiskered chin

"No, no, this way."

She backtracked a bit and after a few moments touched a cardboard box on an industrial pallet. A hand-lettered sign on the side of the box proclaimed "Espacio."

She left him.

Miguel approached the box and saw it was half filled. Overhead, an industrial light gleamed like a star upon heaps of *Amazing Science* magazines with outrageous covers and pulpy, yellowed paperbacks without covers. He reached inside but could not touch any books. His back would not let him bend over. He dragged over a box to stand on, but still he could not reach. He looked around and saw he was alone. He took out his pocket knife and cut a door into the box. He opened the door, climbed in and sat inside the box labeled "Espacio" and thought it marvelously prescient. Dust motes swirled and spun above his head like galaxies. He sorted and shifted not finding anything pertaining to the construction of rockets, but he read nonetheless lost in the wonder-filled articles. He dug deeper becoming increasingly dismayed and then he found it: *Visions of the Future.* The book had a sticker on it that said "discount" and as he perused through the fantastic pictures within he wondered how something so fabulous could be discounted. Space shuttles plied the stars. Great cities orbited the earth. Men floated free in bubbles of air. Mars beckoned. Were dreams so cheap in the north that they could be discounted?

The book did not tell him how to build a spaceship, it told him why. It was good enough. He took the book to the front counter to check it out. The old lady was gone replaced by an equally old man.

"Bah, you may have it."

"Gracias."

"Useless," offered the old man.

Miguel knew better.

....

A hoard of wood, pipe, sheet metal, angle iron and other miscellanea, taken from structures that his grandfather had disassembled for money, sheltered under scavenged tin roofs.

Nothing was thrown out. Ever. Only the rich could look at something and say it had no value. What Miguel's grandfather had not devoted to plantain and banana he used for storage for his hoard. Everything was useful sooner or later.

"Fools," he remembered his grandfather saying. "They pay me money to take useful things away."

Miguel remembered toddling along after his grandfather. His grandfather always made him walk except when he couldn't. The old man always understood the limits of Miguel's endurance, and then he would pick him up and say, "Mi amor, I will carry you now."

Miguel had gone to school for all of three days. So brutal was the taunting that his grandfather withdrew Miguel and taught him himself. Old and poor did not mean stupid. More often than not, it meant clever and honest.

Miguel's mother died in childbirth. His twisted back would not come from her womb easily, and she had bled before a doctor could get to her. His father tried to love him, but turned to drink and vanished into the city never to be seen again. Miguel's grandmother waved her hands in strange patterns to ward off misfortune and evil when he entered the room. Once, she cursed Miguel openly, and her husband slapped her to the ground. From that day on she only cursed him with her eyes.

Miguel was as loyal as any grandson could be. When his grandmother died, Miguel wept for his grandfather's sake. When his grandfather died, Miguel wept from the depths of his heart. He inherited the small farm and a modest amount of money.

Miguel sat straddling the great beam salvaged from who knows where and began to hew it into the shape he desired. It took him all day to carve and shape the first piece of his rocket, and he was happier than he had been in a long time. As the sun set, Miguel ate a meager dinner of rice and beans. He fell asleep in his chair and dreamed of soaring. His feet slipped from the earth, and he careened across the sky wrapped in silver and trailing fire.

Outside his window a phoenix roosted in the tree communing

with Miguel's dreams. It regarded him solemnly and then began its soft nightsong considerate of the dreaming man.

....

The children came. They lingered at the edge of his property testing their bravery. They watched the rocket's skeleton rise from the ground. They were not rich enough to go to school, and something strange was going on. Typically, they would yell Monstruo! Monstruo! And then run away shrieking and laughing, but today something irresistibly different was happening. They stayed. Miguel gestured, and the littlest one approached cautiously. Two or three others followed. Then more till they surrounded him.

"Que es, Senor?" asked the littlest.

"Es cohete," said Miguel. "And I will fly away to the sky."

"Imposible," offered a child.

"No, it will fly to the moon and farther."

The younger children beamed. The older scoffed. A few left. Of those who stayed, Miguel set them to tasks. When he stopped they did not leave. He retrieved a book his grandfather read to him: *Donde Viven los Monstruos?* His voice was soft and gentle and perfect for reading. When he was done the children pleaded for more, but he sent them home to their own dinners.

It was a good day.

....

He filled his days with hammering and carving and shaping the bones of his rocket. Children came again and he set them to working in the same manner his grandfather had set him to working: with gentle instruction and patient demonstration. When lunch time came in mid-morning, Miguel would light his outdoor stove to cook a stew of vegetables and meat. Sometimes he would make bread or fry a great heaping plate of bananas. He knew that for some of the children it would be all they ate that day. His savings dwindled but what could he do? They were here.

As the days went on and the rocket rose, the number of children multiplied and Miguel found himself teaching them proper Spanish and mathematics, so they could speak and calculate accurately. He did not know as much as he thought he should but what he did know he would share. He taught them English for the same reason his grandfather taught him, because for some odd reason, it was the language of discovery and science and business. When he tired of explaining the same thing over and over he stopped building and taught all of the children at once. His rocket construction slowed, but he found he did not mind so much.

....

Miguel was shaping a strut when a new child appeared. His name was Alonso and he was dark and quick and very clever. Alonso came from the streets of Bacigalupi and had a type of wary feral nature not found in the country children. Alonso was ever ready to defend himself with wicked wit or quick fists. He was not mean to the young or weak. He had a curious patience with them. The children gravitated around Alonso to listen to his stories of the streets. He had a gifted way with words and a natural disposition for leadership. He appointed himself second-in-command and worked with an intensity that the others could only aspire to.

Alonso devoured every book within reach. When he ran out, he found more. One day Alonso came back with a box of school texts. Miguel did not ask where they came from, but he suspected a school had been robbed the night before. Miguel realized that his informal lessons had become formalized. In the cool mornings Miguel would sweep the children together and instruct them. In the afternoons they built the rocket. Curious and suspicious parents appeared and spied on the school. Gifts of food and company and lesser things appeared.

Each evening Alonso left with the other children. None of the others knew where he went. One day Miguel followed. He tracked the boy to an abandoned shack on the edge of a ruined farm. From a distance, Miguel watched Alonso spark a small fire to life, and then alone, without any supper, go to sleep.

....

"Alonso," said Miguel. "You know how to find things. Can you find me someone to help build the rocket full time? Do you know of anyone that can? I do not have any money. All I can do is give room and board."

Alonso considered for a moment and said no, he did not.

"This is too bad. These children they take up so much of my time. After supper, I have to think about how to build this coheta and run this school. It is too much for one man."

Alonso thought for a moment.

"I could," said Alonso. "Maybe."

"It will be very difficult there is much thinking that goes into building a rocket and running a school. I do not know if someone so young is up to the task."

"I am. I can think very hard."

"Bueno," said Miguel. "You will have to."

....

The children were expert scavengers. Whatever they thought was useful for rocket building was brought, and each time Miguel would hold up the perfectly useless object and pronounce it exactly what was needed to make the rocket fly. Somehow, somewhere the object was installed with artful precision to the child's delight. Alonso was an expert scavenger of a different sort. He devoured knowledge with furious intensity. At night, after dinner, Miguel would watch Alonso read texts on geometry and calculus and physics and, in his watching, came to his own cruel understanding of reality. Passion and enthusiasm were not enough. It took armies of experts, legions of engineers, and billions and billions of pesetas to make a rocket fly. He wondered where his initial foolishness came from to think a wooden rocket festooned with car parts and old TV sets would ever leave the earth. Still, it was too late to stop.

A reporter came and did a story about the rocket in the jungle. They filmed planks of mahogany steaming in old steel barrels and then fitted in graceful curves. They filmed children in the school. One day a long black SUV parked in the dirt road at the edge of his property. Police and men with powerful black suits fanned out across his property. The Minister of Education entered the illegal classroom and berated him for running an illegal school. El Presidente entered and walked slowly around the room. He paused at his own portrait.

"Bueno" he roared.

He looked to his minister. "Buy this school desks and books and ..and..a computer."

El Presidente's entourage applauded his generosity.

"Now let me go see the cohete," said El Presidente.

Miguel took El Presidente to the rocket, and the man roared with laughter. El Presidente had seen a real rocket up close. He had gone inside it and no matter how finely crafted and graceful the mahogany rocket was, it would never go into space.

"So you are crazy and ugly, eh?" said El Presidente.

El Presidente's entourage roared with laughter

Miguel looked to the ground.

"Eh, I am just making fun. I will talk to my aviation minister. You must get a permit to fly a rocket."

The entourage laughed again.

"I am making more fun. You should be used to it."

The photographer set up and positioned all the children around El Presidente. Miguel was kept aside as no one wanted to see a picture of a cripple. With the photos taken, El Presidente's staff passed out buttons and stickers and candies and the smallest denomination the country had.

Before they left, El Presidente embraced him and whispered. "You are a dangerous man, senor. Nothing more dangerous than a man with a dream." He looked at the rocket. "Even a foolish dream."

The children chased the SUV down the road, school and rocket forgotten. Alonso stayed.

Miguel sat down on a step. His back ached, and he felt very sad. Alonso sat down next to him.

"I am a terrible old fool. Of course, it can never fly."

Alonso put his arm around him.

"It already has. That is why they are here."

....

Alonso poured through all the books the Minister of Education delivered. At night he used the computer, and within two years he had earned a high school diploma. He then applied and was accepted to a northern university to study astrophysics.

"It is impossible," said Alonso with the conviction that only a frustrated young man can possess. "I cannot go. Even with the scholarships it is too much."

"Nothing is impossible. Look we have built a rocket."

"A rocket. It is a pile of junk. It can never fly. You have made me into a bigger fool." With that he left the house and went to the city.

Miguel stayed up waiting, but Alonso did not come back home. Miguel waited some more, and when the moon had risen to its zenith, he heard the nightsong of a phoenix. Something fluttered in the trees and he went to see. Avian ghosts shifted and moved in the shadows and began their soft singing. He saw the phoenix feather lying on a ground silvered with moonlight. It was worth an incalculable fortune or violent death. He picked it up and wrapped the feather in tissue paper. Tomorrow he would bring it to the hotel where the bird watchers hatched their futile plans.

....

The scientists lounged around the pool. They were startled to see a crippled hunchback approach them.

"I have a phoenix feather," said Miguel.

The scientists laughed.

"Oh boy, mi amigo, if I had a dollar for every phoenix feather that some peasant brought me. Show me," said a skinny sunburned scientist.

"Not here," said Miguel

"Dios mio," said the scientist. "Follow me."

They went through the lobby and up the elevator. The scientists wrapped themselves with towels. Their pasty white skin puckered in the cool hotel air like a plucked chicken's. In their room, they positioned themselves in front of machines that hummed and purred like jungle animals as they warmed and came to life.

"The feather," said a scientist.

Miguel unwrapped the feather and held it out.

A collective gasp escaped the scientists. They were used to dyed peacock feathers or trimmed and snipped feathers of exotic but identified birds that were sold to witless ecotourists. This one, at the very least, was different. If it were a forgery, it was the most exquisite they have ever seen.

Miguel handed it over and the scientist regarded it for a moment, shifting it back and forth in the light to see it beam with an inner radiance. He took a knife and scaled the root of the calamus, the hollow central shaft of the feather. He put the scrapings in the machine and waited.

The machine hummed furiously. Lights flashed with urgency. Across a screen G's and C,'s and T's and A's marched across the screen like ants. Faster and faster, the screen blurred with scrolling alien proteins.

The machine proclaimed the specimen as unidentified and the scientists leaned in to watch. The machine hummed and sequenced and collated. The scientists looked at each other. The letters swirled and spun, aligning themselves, weaving into complex patterns that took form and shape. The unraveled DNA resolved into an image.

An archaeopteryx imperator.

"This is going to bigger than bigfoot," said one scientist.

"This is going to be larger than loch ness," said another.

"The mother of all birds," said the third.

The image, just a simulation, showed a toothed bird even more fabulous than anyone had ever imagined. It was as magnificent as could be for any creature that had been flying uninterrupted for more than 150 million years.

"Where did you get this feather? We have been looking for evidence for years."

"I will tell you, but first, the price," said Miguel.

"The price? What price? This is the scientific discovery of the century, bigger even then those Siberian mammoths."

Miguel retrieved his feather.

"Wait. What do you want?"

Miguel told them, and they conferred.

"I will make a phone call to our sponsor."

The scientist went into the next room and after a few minutes came back out.

"It is agreed."

Miguel handed over the feather.

"You must tell us where you found it."

"When your end of the deal is done. You must not let El Presidente know. You hold death in your hand."

....

Miguel searched for Alonso. He walked the dirty streets of the poorest and most violent section of Bacigalupi. Music dueled in the streets. Whores and criminals threw taunts at him as he limped down the alleyways peering into bars. He found Alonso bellied up to a bar surrounded by young toughs and women in tight cloths and gaudy makeup.

"Alonso," he said.

"Hey, muy feo," said a thin man with a scarred face

"Monstruo," said another. "Mira." He shoved Miguel, and he fell to the beer-splattered floor.

"Alonso," he said again. "I found a way."

Alonso turned and saw Miguel on the floor.

"Basta ya," said Alonso.

Miguel struggled to his feet, and his leg was swept out from under him. A hand extended to pull him up and he took it gratefully. He was halfway up when a violent slap knocked him back to the floor.

Alonso threw a punch and knocked the slapper away. The bar exploded into violence and curses. Miguel watched Alonso fall into a savage pattern that he had suspected but never seen. When it was over Miguel was still on the floor but so where his attackers.

Two men backed away from Alonso and shouted empty threats. With Alonso's help Miguel climbed up off the floor. They left wary of pursuit.

"I found a way," said Miguel.

"I should not have doubted," said Alonso. "Lo siento, perdoname por favor."

....

Alonso was gone. He finished his studies at the university earning degrees in astrophysics and engineering. He visited when he had the time and wrote infrequently, but it had been a year since the last visit and three months since the last letter.

Sometimes the children would show up to play on the rocket but mostly not. El Presidente was gone replaced by another El Presidente who allowed the non-governmental organizations to come back. One of them built a school in the village. Perhaps it was for the best. He was old and tired now, and sometimes in the night his heart raced and woke up anxious and scared.

Miguel sat on his porch, drank a cold beer and watched the sun set. The stars peered down and the nightsong of the phoenix laced the air, but he could not find the bird in the darkening trees. Hundreds of miles away scientists searched, and he felt comforted. He would not repay the bird's generosity with betrayal.

In the pale moonlight, a figure walked up his path. As it came closer he saw that it was Alonso. He was tall and broad shouldered. His hair was cut short.

Miguel stood up. Unsteady. His joints cracked like wet wood in a fire. His bones hurt.

"Alonso mi hijo," said Miguel. His eyes blurred with tears.

They embraced and held onto each other for a long time. They sat on the porch, and Alonso told him about school and studies and showed him a picture of a beautiful young girl, his fiancé. He told him how he was accepted into the latest group of astronauts and that after training he would go into space.

"Marvelous," said Miguel. "I am so proud of you."

"I came back to thank you."

"For what?"

"For building a dream. Look at that." He gestured at the mahogany rocket rising from the jungle foliage. Scudding clouds raced in front of a full moon.

Here in the moonlight with Alonso, Miguel did not feel so foolish. He slapped at a mosquito. "It is late," said Miguel. "And I am an old man. I will see you in the morning Alonso."

Miguel stood up and groaned. He made his way inside.

No, he thought, maybe not so foolish after all.

....

Miguel woke, flushed with a strange heat and confused. He woke Alonso.

"What is the matter? What is wrong?" said Alonso.

"I have to fly the rocket, Alonso. I have to fly."

"Miguel, it is late. Manana por favor."

"Ayuda me, Alonso."

"Okay, okay."

Miguel climbed slowly and stopped frequently to rest and breath. They climbed past the baubles and gizmos and the repurposed Christmas lights and old television sets. As they climbed to the top of the rocket, he flipped switches and turned valves. Lights flashed and blinked, and water surged and sang in the pipes for no other reason than to inspire wonder. He paused to see the paint smeared handprints of children that had helped build the rocket and when they reached the top Alonso helped him into a chair built for his curved back.

"I am ready. Fly the rocket. Turn on the switches! Turn on the switches and tell me what you see. Please, tell me what you feel!" said Miguel.

....

The rocket roared as the engines exploded into life. It trembled. Explosive bolts fired with a percussive resolution and freed from restraint the rocket rose into the night sky, accelerating faster and faster, a whirl storm of foliage lofted by the hot exhaust and boiling steam spun beneath the rocket. They soared through patches of dark cloud, pierced the rising moon and rolled, arcing to the east plowing through the atmosphere.

"Max Q go for throttle up," said Alonso. The engines peaked in intensity burning thousands of gallons per second. A bright blade of curved light filled the cabin as they pushed towards the terminator.

"It's beautiful," said Miguel. "Take me higher."

The pressure eased. The engines cut out and a warm peace suffused his body. The mahogany rocket traversed its silent orbit. Sunrise, brighter than he had ever seen filled the cabin. Miguel looked through windows of his cohete at the ordinary people that spun far below. His fingers fumbled for a moment and unfastened his harness and he floated free tethered only by Alonso's grip on his other hand. His curved spine uncoiled in the glorious weightlessness and for the first time he was without pain.

"I made it," said Miguel in a soft faraway voice.

"Of course you did, papa," said Alonso.

....

Miguel was not heavy. Weightlessness seemed to have added itself to his quality. Alonso carried him down, and he sat at the base of the mahogany rocket cradling the curved old man as if he was a child. It was still dark in the pre-dawn light and a shadow coursed over them. An archaeopteryx imperator spiraled into the clearing and lighted upon a branch draping its plumage almost to the ground. Another followed and then another until the clearing around the rocket was filled with a wild chorus of ancient aviators.

The birds sang and mourned, and when the sun rose over the mountains, they broke and caressed the air with graceful wings honed to perfection by time and desire.

If you enjoyed the 2015 Young Explorer's Adventure Guide, please take a moment to review it where you purchased it!

We're always happy for you to come by the site, let us know what you think, and take a look at the rest of our science fiction and fantasy books.

DreamingRobotPress.com

Or email us at books@dreamingrobotpress.com

Continue reading for a sneak preview of *The Seventh Crow* by Sherry D. Ramsey, available in the summer of 2015.

SEVEN CROWS, A SECRET THAT HAS NEVER BEEN TOLD...

The
Seventh
Crow

SHERRY D. RAMSEY

CHAPTER ONE

Rosinda trudged home with her head down, her backpack weighted with the homework Mr. Andrews had assigned for the night. Skeletal leaves crunched under her feet along the side of the road.

A low croak made her look up, and she saw the crows. They stood scattered in a loose line in the grassy swath beside the road, their glossy black feathers reflecting the late afternoon sun, each just a wingspan away from the next. Every one had its bright black eyes fixed on her. Rosinda stopped.

The words of Aunt Odder's crow-counting rhyme popped into her head. This was one of the many things she had struggled to relearn over the past year. She counted the crows under her breath, chanting the rhyme.

"One crow, sorrow; two crows, joy; three crows, a letter; four crows, a boy," Rosinda said, her eyes resting briefly on each crow as she counted down the line. "Five crows, silver; six crows, gold—" She trailed off, looking around for a seventh crow. The rhyme always seemed to run out after six. Maybe crows didn't like big groups.

Just like me. She turned back to the road.

From a tree just ahead, a black shape dropped like a falling branch. A seventh crow. This one, bigger than the others, swooped on silent feathers to the ground just in front of Rosinda.

"Seven crows, a secret that has never been told," it said in a gravelly voice.

Rosinda froze, the weight of her backpack forgotten. Had that just happened?

Someone's playing a trick. It wouldn't be the first time. She forced her eyes from the crow, looking to both sides and glancing over her shoulder. Someone could have followed her from school, one of the boys, with one of those gadgets you could talk into and play your voice back in all sorts of weird ways. They must have heard her saying the crow rhyme. A chance to tease her. Yes, they must be hiding in the long grass, or behind a tree—

"There's no one else here, if that's what you're thinking," said the crow, hopping closer. "Just you and me. And them," it said, cocking its head toward the other six crows, "but they don't really count, since they won't be joining the conversation." The crow made a sound almost like a chuckle.

Then it's the accident. Rosinda's throat tightened. The head injury had taken away practically all her memories except for the past year, and now she was losing her mind.

The crow seemed to read her expression. It shook its head, black feathers ruffling. "There's nothing wrong with you. This is real, and it's important."

Rosinda swallowed. "What do you want?" she asked. Her voice was a raspy croak, almost like the crow's. The world seemed very tiny, shrunk down to this autumn-splashed stretch of road, herself, and the seventh crow. She hoped she wouldn't faint.

"I have some things to tell you, Rosinda," the crow said.

Rosinda's hands flew up to cover her mouth. The crow knew her name?

"Please try not to be alarmed," the crow said kindly. It cocked its head to the side, studying her. "Do you want to keep walking or sit in the grass over there?"

Rosinda's legs felt wobbly. "I'll sit," she whispered. Almost as if they knew what she'd said, the other six crows hopped off a little distance. Rosinda walked to a nearby tree, sliding her backpack off and hugging it to her chest. She sat on the carpet of multicolored leaves with her back against the rough bark. The crow followed and stood just beyond her feet, regarding her with bright eyes.

"I'm afraid this is not the best news," the crow said. "Your

Aunt Oddeline has been kidnapped."

"What?" Rosinda's heart thudded in her chest. Her Aunt Odder was the only family she had here, with her parents in a hospital in Switzerland for the past year. The year since the accident. "How do you know this?"

"I know because of who I am and where I come from," the crow said. "I think she's safe for now, but you're going to have to trust me. My name is Traveller."

"Who would kidnap Aunt Odder?" Rosinda asked, jumping to her feet. The backpack rolled unheeded in the leaves. "I have to call the police!"

The crow lifted a wing. "That won't do any good. The guards of this land—your police—will have no way to find her."

Rosinda's breath caught in her throat as if she'd been running. "Who kidnapped her?"

The crow shook its head again. "I don't know. I have suspicions, but—no."

"Can you help me find her? There must be something I can do!"

"I don't suppose you know where Prince Sovann is?"

Rosinda shook her head impatiently. "I don't even know who that is."

The crow made a sound like a sigh. "Then you'll have to come with me, Rosinda. You'll have to come home to Ysterad."

For a brief moment something shimmered at the back of Rosinda's brain, the stir of a thought, or a memory, triggered by the name. She struggled to catch it, bring it to the front of her mind, but it was gone as quickly as it had come, leaving her feeling tired and slightly sick. The autumn air pricked her skin, suddenly cold. The hard, hot feeling in her stomach was anger.

"I have to go home," she said.

"Yes," the crow agreed, "we'll need to gather some things."

"No, I mean I'm going home. Alone. Home to my house. Mine and Aunt Odder's. I don't believe any of this. I'm dreaming, or hallucinating, or maybe I have a brain tumor. Maybe this is something else left over from the accident. I don't know and I don't care." Rosinda's breath came hard and fast. She grabbed her backpack and slung it over her shoulder. "Don't follow me," she said, and hurried back to the road. Rosinda felt the crow's gaze on her back but she wouldn't look at him.

She strode along the gravelled shoulder, her thoughts in a jumble. There was no sound behind her, no soft flapping of wings overhead. Maybe the crow had taken her seriously and stayed behind. Rosinda had a flash of misgiving. What if she got home and Aunt Odder wasn't there?

She pushed the thought aside and kept walking, the riot of red, gold, and orange leaves now garish and too bright. No cars passed. She and Aunt Odder lived in a small house on an out-of-the-way road, and it took her half an hour to walk home from school. Rosinda didn't mind. She was a loner by nature. She hadn't made many friends in the year since she and Aunt Odder had come to Cape Breton. Maybe other kids were wary around her because of her memory loss, the way sometimes she couldn't think of the right word for something, but she didn't think that was all of it. She just didn't fit in.

Rosinda rounded the last corner, and the house came into view, a narrow, two-story cottage at the top of a curving gravel driveway. It looked completely normal, and Rosinda let out a breath she'd barely realized she was holding. Everything must be fine. A wisp of grey smoke curled out of the chimney, Aunt Odder's beat-up little hatchback sat in the driveway. The kitchen window framed the silhouette of Filara, Aunt Odder's cat. Rosinda hurried up the driveway.

"Aunt Odder!" she called when she opened the kitchen door. The radio played softly on the counter. Filara jumped down from the windowsill and bounded across the kitchen floor to Rosinda on silent feet, curling around her legs. Rosinda reached down and stroked the animal's silky head absently as she listened for Aunt Odder's welcoming voice.

It didn't come. The house was silent, as if it also held its breath.

Rosinda slung her backpack onto the kitchen table.

"Aunt Odder! Where are you?" she called again. The kettle was still plugged in, the teapot standing beside it with the top open, waiting for hot water. She glanced inside. Two teabags lay on the bottom. Rosinda touched the side of the kettle and felt a bare hint of warmth. It must have boiled a while ago and then shut off.

It wasn't like Aunt Odder to boil water and not make tea.

Rosinda went to the tiny sitting room, her throat and chest tight. The computer hummed quietly on the corner desk near the window. The television was off. Rosinda ran up the stairs two at a time. It took only a glance to see that the two bedrooms and the bathroom were empty.

The house was empty. Aunt Odder wasn't here.

Hot tears blurred Rosinda's vision, but she blinked them back. Before she could decide what to do next, a terrible racket erupted downstairs. Rosinda glanced around, grabbed a heavy, wooden-handled umbrella from beside Aunt Odder's door, and raced back down the stairs. Could this day get any worse?

She plunged through the kitchen door and skidded to a stop. Filara stood in the middle of the table, her patchwork of calico fur standing straight out. She hissed and spat in obvious fury.

The crow perched on the corner of the counter near the radio, wings spread wide as it screeched at the cat.

Whether it was the sudden reappearance of the crow, or the noise of the creatures, or her growing concern for Aunt Odder, Rosinda felt her worry turn to anger.

"Stop it!" she shouted, striding into the kitchen. She banged the umbrella down on the table and scooped Filara up. The cat struggled for a moment, then went quiet in her arms.

The crow immediately folded its wings, ruffling its ebony feathers for a moment until they fell elegantly into place. It made a sound that reminded Rosinda of a man clearing his throat. "Ahem. I apologize, Rosinda," it said in a quiet voice. "The cat startled me when—"

"When you broke into my house?" Rosinda snapped. She didn't want to imagine how the crow had done that.

"Well, yes," the crow admitted. "But you've seen by now I was correct. Your aunt is not here."

"That doesn't mean she's been kidnapped," Rosinda started, but her voice trailed away. What did it mean, after all? Aunt Odder was always here when Rosinda came home from school. If she'd been out in the garden, Rosinda would have seen her. And she hadn't finished making her tea.

Rosinda had to accept that the talking crow was not a hallucination. She felt her anger and her energy drain away. Keeping the cat on her lap, she lowered herself into Aunt Odder's creaky wooden rocker.

"What did you say your name was?" Rosinda asked quietly. Her hands trembled slightly as she stroked Filara's fur for reassurance.

"Traveller," the crow answered. "Do you think we can talk now?"

Rosinda nodded. "I think," she said slowly, "you'd better tell me everything."

Visit DreamingRobotPress.com to find out when *The Seventh Crow* is released, and learn what Traveller tells Rosinda!